RENNO—Young in the number of his summers but old in his wisdom of battle and men's passions, this great Chief of the Seneca is now entrusted with a sacred quest . . . a journey into a dangerous Western land, led by the Manitou's prophecy, and driven by the raging fires in his heart.

BETH—Untamed in spirit, her radiant red hair as wild as her desires, she will come as an omen into the lives of Seneca, Quapaw, and Apache and fall captive to love and a cruel desire.

EL-I-CHI—Skilled in the use of tomahawk, bow, and the white man's rifle, this valiant brother of Renno will discover the cry of a wounded heart for the bloodlust of revenge.

HOLANI—Equal to any brave on horseback or in battle, this lithesome Chickasaw girl faces a woman's most devastating choice with her first taste of love.

FATHER SEBASTIAN—Robed in a habit as black as his heart, the Spanish priest clothes his greed in piety as the lure of the gold leads him toward a treasure he'll kill to possess.

BLACK EAGLE—Born into the ancient culture of the "Free People," he proudly follows the Apache way to ride tall, fight to the death, and drive the white man from the Western lands.

The White Indian Series
Ask your bookseller for the books you have missed

The White Indian Series
Book XIV

APACHE

Donald Clayton Porter

Created by the producers of
Wagons West, Children of the Lion,
Stagecoach, and Saga of the Southwest.

Book Creations, Inc., Canaan, N.Y. • Lyle Kenyon Engel, Founder

BANTAM BOOKS
TORONTO • NEW YORK • LONDON • SYDNEY • AUCKLAND

APACHE

*A Bantam Book / published by arrangement with
Book Creations, Inc.*

Bantam edition / August 1987

*Produced by Book Creations, Inc.
Lyle Kenyon Engel, Founder*

ISBN 0-553-26206-8

Published simultaneously in the United States and Canada

PRINTED IN THE UNITED STATES OF AMERICA

KR   0 9 8 7 6 5 4 3 2 1

This is a work of fiction. While the general outlines of history have been faithfully followed, certain details involving setting, characters, and events may have been simplified.

North America - 1786

.... RENNO'S JOURNEY TO DEVIL'S MTN.
—·—·— RENNO'S RETURN JOURNEY

PACIFIC OCEAN

California

Colorado River

LOUI
(Spain)

APACHE

DEVIL'S MOUNTAIN

Texas

CO MAN CH

MEXICO
(Spain)

Rio Grande

·APA

Mounted Spanish Infantry

©BOOK CREATIONS INC.

QUEBEC

Canada
(Great Britain)

MONTREAL

St. Lawrence River

Maine
(mass.)

SUPERIOR

HURON

ONTARIO

Vt

n.H.

BOSTON

MICHIGAN

ERIE

New York

mass

Ct.

R.I.

DETROIT

Pennsylvania

n.J.

NEW YORK CITY

PHILADELPHIA

SSOURI RIVER

Northwest Territory

OHIO RIVER

x

md

De

States

Virginia

ATLANTIC OCEAN

ana

Kentucky

anses River

QUAPAW

KNOXVILLE

Tennessee

North Carolina

HOT
SPRINGS

d River

South
Carolina

R.

CHARLESTON

RST
NCOUNTER

Georgia

United

MISSISSIPPI R.

NEW ORLEANS

Plains Indian

CORPUS
CHRISTI

GULF OF MEXICO

CHE·

TOELKE '86

Prologue

*T*he moon was full as it rose in the east after the third day of fasting. Renno, son of Ghonkaba, grandson of Ja-gonh, in whose veins flowed the blood of the great white Indian, knew no thirst, felt no hunger. Led to seek counsel with the manitous and the spirits of his ancestors, he welcomed the great burst of light as he chanted his prayers for wisdom and advice.

As time stood still, he saw the most powerful totem of his clan, a great bear, muscular, massive, his white teeth exposed in his open mouth.

"Share your wisdom with me," Renno whispered.

"West," the vision whispered back. The eerie sound seemed to seep from the whispering of the trees, to fade quickly into the darkness.

For a moment Renno feared that he was being told that his time was near, that he would soon join his ancestors in the spirit lands of the West, but the voice gained strength and became a reverberating growl. The bear's fierce visage became the beloved face of Renno's father.

"The way is far. The mountains are dry. Trust the white one and alert yourself for the sign of the cat, for there is a child who will become a great chief at risk. The flame-haired one is the future."

"Do not leave me so puzzled," Renno said respectfully.

"Your son . . ." the voice said, growing more distant.

"What of my son, Father?"

"He will be a great chief, but you will know sorrow."

"Wait, wait!" Renno implored as the great light faded, but the vision was gone.

Many moons would come and go before he would know its full meaning.

Chapter I

The Norman towers at the western end of Beaumont Hall spoke of its age, and the additions that had continued into the time of William and Mary—good, solid construction of Norfolk flint—gave it a look of permanence. The original viscount of Beaumont had chosen the site well, so that however one approached the hall, the vista was impressive.

William Huntington, whose title of honor as heir to the peerage was Baron Beaumont, came home by boat. In the flat plain below the rise on which Beaumont Hall stood, generations of peat diggers had made waterways. William loved the expanse of water and knew it well from 'iis childhood waterfowling. He himself had supervised the last repair work on the pier at the foot of the rise during one of his holidays from his regiment.

He tossed his travel kit onto the pier while the boatmen held the craft steady, distributed coins to the oarsmen, and then, alone, stood to let his eyes feast on the beauty of what would one day be his. He was in no hurry to be called Viscount Beaumont, for he was decidedly fond of his rotund, always cheerful father.

William Huntington was a sturdy Englishman. His years in the regiment had broadened his shoulders and made his carriage proud and erect. He was tall, almost six feet, and handsome in a rough-hewn way.

He heard her horse before he saw it, the hoofbeats pounding a madcap gallop. He smiled widely when a splendid black stallion burst around the end of the ruined Roman wall and slowed only slightly on the last slope to the waterside. William had his arms open and he was shouting a pleased greeting when his arms were filled with a flying girl—she, too, tall, slim, and shapely. Her flame-red hair, hanging loose past her shoulders, brushed his face as she kissed him repeatedly on the cheek.

"William, William, William," she was chanting, "how beautiful you look."

William laughed. In his mind, all the beauty in the family was owned by his ebullient sister. He pushed her to arm's length.

"Beth," he said, shaking his head at her outfit, a man's riding habit. "You've forgotten that you're a girl."

She made a moue. "You're not going to start that again." She smoothed the jacket of her costume. "One of these days I'm going to have *you* put on a stone's weight of skirts and flounces and try to ride decently."

An early hint of fall was in the air. In the open fields inside and around the ancient Roman walls, Beaumont Hall's tenants were busy harvesting the forage crop that would feed the cattle through the coming winter. William always looked forward to coming home, and he longed for the day when he would spend all of his days and hours at Beaumont.

With a rattle of wheels on outcrops of flint, a surrey came down the slope from the manor. Far off, across the expanse of river, a rain shower darkened the sky, moving slowly toward them.

"So tell me, Sister," William said, "why it was so vital that I come home."

A cloud seemed to cross Beth's face. "First let's go speak with Father. He'll be so pleased to see you."

"Father is not ill?" William asked worriedly.

"He's aging," Beth said. "So much." She brightened. "Would you like to ride Nelson? I'll bring your things in the surrey."

William laughed. He had not spent much time with his beautiful sister, having gone as a ten-year-old to a public military school. He did not know as much about her as he would have liked, but he did know that she had an uncanny knack with horses and that some of her chosen mounts could be called tame only by a long stretch of the meaning of the word.

"I'll take the surrey," he said as the vehicle drew up and an old man in the driver's seat nodded respectfully to William and Beth. William tossed his kit into the vehicle and boarded. Beth threw herself into the saddle as strongly and as agilely as a boy, and the horse confirmed William's assessment by pawing the air and snorting. Beth clung easily to the saddle and spoke gently to the stallion. Then, as the surrey began to move, she danced the horse around and around the moving vehicle, calling out questions all the way up the rise.

In the courtyard a footman took William's kit. Inside, there was a pleasant patina of age to the suits of armor in the entrance hall and a welcoming smell that was unique to the house. Cedric, Lord Beaumont, was waiting for them in the library, his favorite room, amid darkened oak paneling that went back to the time of Charles II. Leather-bound volumes mounted to the high ceiling, behind balconies and ladders for access. He was surrounded by heavy, deucedly uncomfortable Elizabethan furniture.

Lord Beaumont's chubby face did not give away his age. It was his body that stamped him at first glance as an old man. It was heavy and sagging, atop spindly legs seemingly too weak to hold his weight. He struggled up from a chair, a glad smile on his face.

"My boy!" he shouted. "We didn't know exactly when you'd arrive—"

"Father," William said, sincerely wanting to embrace the old man but preserving proper English decorum by settling for a handshake.

"A pleasure, my boy," Lord Beaumont said. He fell into a spasm of coughing that prompted William to cast a concerned look toward Beth. "And I see you've had that promotion. Captain, eh? Good. Good."

"Sit down, Father," Beth urged softly. "I'll pour some of that excellent sherry."

"Splendid idea," Lord Beaumont agreed, wiping his mouth with a dainty handkerchief and settling heavily into the sagging chair he favored.

"Father," Beth said, "it wasn't convenient for William to come home just now, and he can only stay a little while. Would you like to discuss business with him directly, or shall we wait until dinner?"

Cedric Huntington cleared his throat and looked, William thought, somewhat ill at ease. "Ah, my little gadfly." He sighed. "Must we discuss sordid things so soon after William's arrival?"

"No," Beth said, handing delicate glasses of sherry to her father and brother. "We can wait until after dinner." She was looking at her father with a mixture of fondness and gentle insistence. "But we must talk then, Father."

"Fine, fine," Lord Beaumont said. "Now, William, seat yourself and tell me how things are out in the great world away from this backwater of Norfolk."

Beth smiled and, deciding to change for dinner into her best and prettiest gown, made her way quietly out of the room.

William found his sister in the dining room, where, having overseen the preparation of the evening meal, she was arranging the flowers.

"The old boy fell asleep," he remarked sadly. "He has aged so much in the short time since I last saw him."

"God willing, we'll have him for many more years," Beth said, "but I felt that it was time you became aware of the state of affairs at Beaumont."

"You make it sound rather grim," William said.

"It is," Beth answered. "Our father has not been the best of money managers, and Beaumont has never been a rich manor."

William nodded. He knew that full well. His allowance had always kept him very alert, for it took alertness to maintain himself in horses, weapons, uniforms, lodgings, and food on the tiny allowance that his father sent him.

"And it's Father's health that convinces you that I should become aware of Beaumont's financial situation?"

"That and other things," Beth said. "Such as Father's last outing to the races at Trevelyan in Suffolk."

William scowled. "The old boy's at it again?"

"Perhaps it would be best if you heard it from him."

The meal showed no indication of financial problems. The table groaned under its load, and the servants would feast well on the leftovers. At last Lord Beaumont heaved his weight to his spindly legs and led the way to the library, accepted brandy from Beth, sighed heavily, and closed his eyes.

"Father . . ." Beth warned sharply.

"Eh? Oh," Lord Beaumont grunted, forcing his eyes open. "Yes, well. Uh, William, our beautiful gadfly here has suggested, since you will be the viscount of Beaumont at the Lord's bidding, that we have a chat."

"Whatever you say, sir," William said.

"As you well know, my boy, no one has ever accused the Beaumonts of being among the realm's richest men." He looked at Beth. "However, things are not quite so black as indicated by some."

"William, I have the books here," Beth said, hoisting a heavy leather-bound journal. "I've been helping old Parker with them, so I'm fairly familiar with the accounts. Now here, at the beginning of 1786—"

"Hold everything," Lord Beaumont interrupted in a loud voice. "Don't waste our time with numbers and figures."

"It is numbers and figures that tell the story," Beth said. "And the long and the short of it is that our creditors could, at any time, take Beaumont and all its lands and leave us a short breath away from debtors' prison."

Lord Beaumont's face went red, but he said nothing. He finished his brandy in a gulp and waved one plump arthritic hand. "Nonsense. Gentlemen do not have their assets seized. William, my boy, it is merely a temporary situation. I have admittedly been a bit too reckless." He coughed. "Damned Trevelyan."

"He lost a wager of five thousand pounds to Lord Trevelyan," Beth explained.

William's face went pale. Five thousand pounds! A fortune!

"Trevelyan is a gentleman and a peer of the realm," Lord Beaumont said. "He will not push for his money. In a year—"

"Father, the net profits of Beaumont for five years would not pay the debt to Trevelyan," Beth said. "It is not Lord Trevelyan who concerns me. It is these—" She pointed to a column of figures in the journal. "Simple tradesmen: the butcher, the tailor, the greengrocer, the fishmonger, the carpenters, the man who built the last boat Father bought, and all these others. They have been more than patient, William. But some of them are in danger of ruin because of our debts to them. They'll be asking us to settle soon." She turned a page. "These are other gambling debts, debts of honor. And this"—she held up a legal document—"is the most worrisome of all. It is a note for ten thousand pounds, past due now by some two years, to the moneylenders of Yarmouth. They, above all others, must be feared if something isn't done quickly."

"I should have married off this fussbudget a year ago," Beaumont grumbled.

William was stunned. In a few minutes he had seen his future darken to the point where it all seemed hopeless. He took the journal from Beth and let his eyes run down the columns of figures. He had a good head for figures. "So much . . ." he breathed. Without having the total, he had added up the indebtedness to a figure representing more than the worth of Beaumont Hall and all its lands. It seemed to William that he faced that most shameful of all fates, seeing the ancestral home and lands sold to strangers.

William looked at Beth, his face dark. He could not find words. For a moment he felt quick anger toward his father, but that soon faded. Cedric Huntington had always enjoyed life as William had seen few men enjoy it. It was difficult to fault that, even when the cost of his father's enjoyment might mean pauperism for his son and daughter.

"William, I have written down some suggestions," Beth said. "Perhaps you can add to them."

"Wants to let go all the servants," Cedric snorted.

"And sell off some of the horses," Beth added. "We'll turn the fields that have been used to grow forage for the horses into corn crops. We'll use the immediate revenue from the sale of the stables to pay small amounts to all our debtors—"

"Wants to go begging to tradesmen," Beaumont complained. " 'Please, sir,' " he said in a falsetto, " 'don't be angry with me. I'll pay you sixpence now and sixpence next month.' " He pulled himself up. "Sensible thing is for you to marry young Joseph Hingman, girl. Solve all our temporary problems."

Again William looked at Beth.

"*Young* Joseph Hingman," she said, "will never see fifty again, has rotten teeth and bad breath."

"And money," Beaumont said.

"And money," Beth conceded. She added, her eyes flashing, "of which he's offered quite a sum to our dear father—a reverse dowry, if you please."

Lord Beaumont grunted and closed his eyes.

"He's tired," William said.

"Yes. Father, perhaps you'd better go to bed," Beth urged.

"Yes, yes," Lord Beaumont mumbled, pulling himself up. William took his arm and walked with him to the stairs.

"Don't need help getting up the stairs yet," Lord Beaumont said. "Good night, Son. It's splendid to have you home again."

For a long time William stood at the foot of the stairs watching his father pull his bulk upward; then he went back into the library. He seemed moody, and Beth held her silence until he spoke.

"I'll not have you saving my financial hide by a hasty marriage," he vowed.

"Thank you," Beth said simply.

"But there is this," he continued, not looking at her. "With Beaumont as a foundation, you could make a good marriage. If, as you fear, the worst happens, you'll be penniless, and even those of good family who now might accept you without dowry will think twice before marrying off their son to the daughter of a bankrupt."

"William, I would like to think that I will have some say in whom I will marry."

"Of course, of course."

"Would you care to go over the books now?" she asked.

He shrugged and sat down. She sat beside him and

pulled the heavy ledger in front of them. William's gloom deepened as she showed him that his father had been not only careless of money matters but also wildly extravagant. When it seemed that all was lost, he rose, kicked a heavy chair, snorted, and with a quick good night went off to his bed. He awoke to the sound of his door opening. It was dark, and he sat up, alert, until he recognized the heavy, feeble form of his father, holding a candlestick, entering the room.

Lord Beaumont sat on the side of the bed and panted for a moment, catching his breath, before he spoke. "Seems a dark picture, eh, lad?"

"Bad enough," William admitted.

"We Beaumonts seem to feel that the good life will go on forever." The old man sighed. "Always win back a bad wager, that sort of thing, eh?" He cleared his throat. William, thinking that his father had come to him to win his forgiveness, waited.

"Reminds me of when I was a young man, just your age," Lord Beaumont said. "Full of juice and vinegar, I was. Went off a-privateering, you know?"

William chuckled. As a boy his favorite stories had been those told by his father about adventures enjoyed as a would-be pirate.

"Saw fat, gold-heavy Spanish galleons in my dreams," Lord Beaumont went on. "Saw bloody few of them in real life, and not a one gold heavy."

"We could use a gold-heavy galleon now," William said.

Lord Beaumont coughed, reached into the folds of his robe, and pulled out a discolored, much-folded parchment. "Captured one ship, we did," he said. "One ship, and she, be-damn her, was outbound, after off-loading her gold in Spain. But I got this."

William put his hand on the parchment, but Lord Beaumont did not release it.

"Been fat and happy too long, my boy, we Beaumonts. Living off the achievements of our ancestors. Still

11

living off land earned by the original Huntington. Mostly flint and peat bogs, but it's served us well. It's time one of us got up off his fat bottom and did something a little better. I had my shot at it, boy, and missed. We picked a ship that had nothing on her but horses, men, and food. We had to fight like the devil against all those bloody Spanish soldiers and lost a lot of men. It took the wind out of those who lived, and all I got was this—and some information."

Once again William tried to take the parchment from his father's hand.

"We've got an old name, and a title," Lord Beaumont said. "And one hope left."

"I think I'd better see this hope," William said, opening his father's hand and pulling out the parchment. He unfolded it carefully. The inked lines were faded, the writing was Spanish.

"It's real," Lord Beaumont assured his heir. "The ship carried an expedition to follow that map. Drawn by some priest—it has his name on it somewhere. The Spaniards we captured said if we'd throw in with them, they'd split with us. Most of us had already lost enough blood and taken enough risk winning that ship full of young Spanish soldiers. I managed to keep the map."

The map showed a portion of New Spain. William knew a little bit of the geography of North America. The area shown was to the northeast of Mexico. In the midst of that great and largely unexplored land was a crude drawing of a mountain. An X was labeled "El Oro del Diablo."

"A buried treasure?" he asked, feeling his hope fly out the open window into the mild Norfolk night.

"A mine," Lord Beaumont said. "The Spaniards attested to much gold taken away, but more left behind. In ingots. Mined and smelted. Impure, but gold. Enough to make Beaumont Hall the showplace of England. Enough to buy Beth a husband from the royal family."

"Well, Father, you're tired," William said, not willing to tell his father how he felt about the treasure map.

"Yes, yes. And I'm sure you're tired after your journey." He rose, left the map. William looked at it for a long time, then let it drop to the floor beside his bed.

When William awoke again it was to his sister's cheerful voice. She was calling to him from the door. He pulled the feather comforter up to his eyes and moaned.

"You're missing the most beautiful part of the morning," Beth chided, coming in. "Dress yourself quickly. I'll get you a spot of hot tea, and I'll saddle one of the more gentle horses."

"I won't be at all disappointed if you go without me," William said.

"Oh, get up, sleepyhead," she teased, coming to the side of the bed to tickle his forehead with her fingers. She stepped on the map. "What's this?"

"The salvation of the Beaumont name," he groaned with irony as she picked it up. "A golden treasure there for the taking."

"How exciting," she said. "Where?"

"Oh, just across a few thousand miles of stormy ocean and more thousands of miles of unexplored wilderness."

"But, William, a mountain of gold!"

"Beth, it's the dream of an old man who, I fear, has gone a bit spare."

"Look, here's a name. Father Luis. And a date, 22 December 1610. And what are these figures down here on the far-left corner of the map?"

William looked and read. " 'On this date, 22 December, the year of our Lord 1610, we leave this devil's mountain with thirty pack mules laden with gold.' " He shrugged. "Well, that shouldn't have left much. Thirty mules."

"What else does it say? I must learn to speak Spanish."

"No need. You already speak French very well."

"What does it say?"

" 'We leave more behind in the care of our blessed Jesus Christ—may his grace guide us.' "

"There, you see? They couldn't carry it all. You can teach me Spanish on the ship."

"What ship?" William asked, sitting up in bed.

" 'El Oro del Diablo,' " Beth read, but with a French accent. " 'The gold of the devil'?"

" 'Devil's gold,' " William said.

"*Our* gold," Beth said, her blue eyes gleaming.

"Beth, do you have any idea how large the American continent is?"

"No, but I know how large our debts are. I know that you won't even be able to stay in a regiment without money to live on. I know that I'll have to marry someone like, ugh, *young* Joseph Hingman with rotten teeth."

William looked at her earnestly. "Now suppose, just suppose, that this map shows a real mine. Suppose, and this is a corker, that I had the money to travel to the New World. This is all totally ridiculous, but suppose that there is gold and by some means I travel all those thousands of miles, escape the wild savages inhabiting those lands, manage not to run afoul of the Spanish who hold that territory, and make it home. Our father would not, in all probability, be alive when I returned."

A quick tear came out of the corner of Beth's left eye. "I would still be willing to take that chance."

"What do you mean?" William asked. "There would be no question of *your* going into such a wilderness."

"I don't see why not. I can ride better than you."

"You're a girl." He grabbed her flame-colored hair and tugged. "Savage Indian want red hair for to decorate wigwam. Swish. No scalp."

"Will you at least discuss this further with Father?"

"Talk means nothing. Talk does not pay debts."

"But you'll talk?"

"I'm sure *he* will."

Lord Beaumont did. He came down to breakfast in a bulky, thick, warm robe, his face all smiles, carrying a leather box with a rounded top. "I say, I've been mucking about in the attic. I found your great-grandfather's papers.

Thought there'd be something of interest for you, my boy. The more you know about where you're going, the better your chances, what?"

"Absolutely," William said.

He did not, however, open the box until after he had ridden Beaumont's acres with Beth, had lunch, and was in his room for the luxury of an early-afternoon nap. What he found in the box caught his interest to the point that he forgot about sleep and, instead, called his sister to come into his room.

When Beth saw the contents of the old trunk spread over William's desk, her eyes sparkled with interest.

"Our great-grandfather was quite a student of the American colonies, and he carried on quite an extensive correspondence with several men there," William said.

"Is there anything about New Spain?"

"No. His friends were mostly in the North," William explained. "The interesting part is that Great-Grandfather acted as sort of a sponsor, or host, for a visitor from the colonies, a Seneca Indian. Well, he wasn't really an Indian, being white—"

"Oh?" Beth asked, no longer so interested.

"This white Indian's name was Renno. He had an audience with Queen Mary and put on a fascinating weaponry display at William and Mary's court. Listen to this. At King William's request, a duke took a beaver cloak from one of the court ladies and hung it over the back of a chair. I'll read you the rest:

> " *The savage stood within arm's reach of the monarch and could assassinate him with a single slash of his knife. Suddenly he whirled and, without appearing to take aim, threw the knife. The point of the blade cut through the center of the cloak and pinned it to the chair.'* "

"I don't see—" Beth began.

"The king then examined the Indian's tomahawk. When

Renno took the weapon back, he threw it all the way across the audience chamber and severed the plume from the earl of Lincoln's hat. And that wasn't the last of the earl's embarrassment. This American Indian then proceeded to take the earl's hat right off his head and skewer it to the wall with an arrow."

"William, I still don't see what this has to do with—"

"Here's the point," William said. "Great-Grandfather is quoting this Renno: *'In the land of the Seneca are nearly two thousand warriors. In the land of the Iroquois there are more than three thousand warriors. All use knives and tomahawks and bows and arrows.'* " William looked up. "And that's not even mentioning how many weapon-wielding savages might be down in the Southwest, where this gold mine is supposedly located."

Beth opened her mouth to speak, but the voice of their father came from the hallway, and then Cedric appeared in the door. "Find anything interesting?"

"Yes, stories of infallible Indian warriors who make me quite reluctant to pit myself against unknown thousands of them," William said.

"Pooh," Cedric scoffed. "A Beaumont is a match for a few thousand savages."

"Father," Beth said, "is it really there, this gold?"

"The Spaniards believed it was," Lord Beaumont replied. "Enough to equip a whole expedition to go after it. In fact, there was a priest aboard the Spanish ship, who unfortunately was killed in the early fighting. He was of the order of the very friar who had helped carry away a packtrain of the gold. Or so I was told." He resisted a cough. "I imagine, William, that you are hesitating because of the state of my health. You're afraid to leave me. If you'll remember, dear boy, your grandfather lived to be over eighty years old, coughing for the last fifty years of his life. I assure you that I will hang on to life with tooth and toenails until you get back. I will defy Death himself just to see the faces of those Yarmouth moneylenders when you pay them off in gold."

"Well, that's not the only consideration," William said.

"Ah." Lord Beaumont's hand went into his heavy robe, pulled out a small leather pouch, and tossed it onto the bed. It clanked. It was heavy when William picked it up, and when he poured out the contents, they were good, solid, golden guineas. "Does that alleviate another of your objections?"

Beth dived onto the bed, gathered up a handful of the gold coins. "Father!" she cried. "Where?"

Lord Beaumont laughed. "Ah, I wouldn't have told you about them, my lovely maiden. You'd have parceled them out one by one to tradesmen. This is called a stake. A gambler always has a stake, and we Beaumonts have always been gamblers. I warrant there's bloody enough there to meet the needs of an expedition to the New World."

"I should think so," Beth said, counting rapidly, liking the heavy, almost warm feel of the coins, and imagining a mountain of that magical, beautiful metal.

"I'm sure you are aware that I, like my father and grandfather before me, have an interest in the American colonies." He snorted. "That is to say, the former colonies. I have kept up a correspondence with certain of the good men who won that unfortunate, ill-fought war and can send you on your way with letters of introduction."

"William," Beth said, eyes gleaming, "your concern about the Indians is justified. But what if we had just one or two like this Renno to act as our protector and guide?"

"Think, Beth. The man is long dead," William said. He moved near his father and put a gentle hand on Cedric's shoulder. "You believe in this, Father, don't you?" he asked quietly.

"A man must have something in which to believe, yes. But I do. I do. Always fancied it would be me going after it. Somehow I never got around to it. Having too much enjoyment out of life, I suppose. Almost went when your mother died, but what with Beth just a baby—"

"All right, Father," William said. "Let's pursue it. I'll go to Yarmouth, to the library, and begin to learn something about this land across the sea—"

"I can do that for you," Beth offered.

"Yes, good idea," William said. "Then I'll contact my regiment—"

"There are volumes about America in the library," Beth continued. "I've read almost all of them, you know." She turned to face their father. "I'll *have* to go with him. I know more about the country than he does, and—"

"Beth . . ." William started.

"—and I can ride better than he, and after all, that gold on the bed represents the last of *my* wealth, too. Not being nasty, William, but you've always had a tendency to give up when things don't go smoothly, and I can nag you into going on."

"You will not go," William stated flatly.

"I *will*. I won't be a burden."

William smiled without humor. "I'm going into a wilderness where no Englishman has ever gone, traveling through country peopled by red savages who are skilled with knife, tomahawk, and bow. The money I'll have is limited. I can't afford a regiment of mounted cavalry and a couple of fieldpieces, so the money must be used to hire men skilled with weapons and their fists if fighting becomes necessary. It would be dangerous and wasteful of our meager resources to take you."

"I can fight as well as you," Beth retorted, sounding much younger than her nineteen years.

William laughed heartily, and in throwing his head back, he missed the sly look that passed from father to daughter.

"If I can prove to you that I am your better with musket, pistol, and even the longbow, will you still object to my going?" Beth asked.

"Don't be ridiculous," William said.

"That sounds quite fair to me," Lord Beaumont interjected.

"All right," William said disgustedly, "let's get this over with so we can move on to more important matters."

Lord Beaumont, who would not have missed the show for anything, joined his children in the garden and watched William set up four bottles as pistol targets at a distance of twenty paces. Beth had carried down her father's dueling pistols and was hefting them, one in each hand.

"If the target is too far away," William said condescendingly, "we can move it closer."

"I think," Beth replied, lifting her weapons, "that the distance makes it too easy." Both pistols spoke at once, and two bottles smashed at the same instant.

William did not try to hide his surprise. True, he had not spent a lot of time at Beaumont Hall since his tenth birthday, but he did not quite understand how Beth could have developed such skill without his knowing.

"If you think that was an accident," Beth said, "watch this." She had been loading the pistols and now stood poised to shoot. She fired the pistols one at a time, and the bottles were blasted asunder.

"By George, I think she's got you, my boy," Lord Beaumont exploded through his laughter.

Beth was equally impressive with the long muskets. This time the target bottles were farther away. She fired as she had been taught by her father, easily lifting the musket in one smooth movement and firing the instant the stock touched her shoulder. The competition continued until one missed, and the one who missed was a disgruntled William.

"You are not going," he insisted.

"There is one more test," Beth said, running to a gazebo, where she had placed the longbow that had been made especially for her. It did not have the pull of a man's bow, but it was bow enough to send a barbed arrow winging straight and true to the bull's-eye of a target set up a full ninety paces away against the garden fence. William matched her shot for shot, using a bow of the same type used by English archers at Agincourt and Crécy, where the archers put an end to the long supremacy of the cavalry charge.

Cedric had taught Beth how to draw the bow, not with the strength of her arms, but the strength of her body. He had, as she grew, ordered her bows made to match her increasing age and strength. Now her bow was only slightly smaller and slightly less thick than the traditional bow drawn by William, and her aim was fully equal to his.

"I will admit," William said, "that I am impressed, but you're still not going."

Lord Beaumont coughed and cleared his throat. "It seems to me," he said with a chuckle, "that only an hour past I heard the word of a Beaumont given."

"Father, she is a girl, and a young girl at that, and—"

Cedric stood firm. "She is a Beaumont too, and she outshot you with both pistol and musket and matched you shot for shot with the longbow." He sniffled, and there were tears in his eyes. "My heart will go with you both."

Beth followed William into the house. "Please don't be obstinate, William."

"Why the bloody hell are you so determined to go?"

"If I stay here and our father, heaven forbid, is called to his reward, what then? I'll be forced to marry *young* Joseph Hingman, with his rotten teeth and putrid breath. Please, please, William. I won't be a burden. I can even disguise myself as a boy. I'll wear boy's clothing. I'll spit and curse and wink at buxom lasses and—"

He was laughing. He turned and put his arms on her shoulders. "It will not be necessary to go that far." His face sobered. "It will be very dangerous."

"Should things go badly, we'll be together. Rather that than becoming the wife of a man more than twice my age. Rather that than hearing the derision if Beaumont is taken from us. And I can be helpful, really."

"Yes," William allowed, "I'm sure you can."

Chapter II

Only the lures of high profit and high adventure could induce men to venture into the late-winter storms of the North Atlantic. One nineteen-year-old girl found herself on a ship that seemed to shrink in size as soon as it cleared Portsmouth harbor and then dwindle to insignificance when the first of the Atlantic storms struck only a day after the ship passed Land's End. Cold unlike anything she had ever felt penetrated to her bones and kept her shivering even as she gave way to the very unladylike spasms of her tortured stomach.

That she had been warned about the Atlantic in winter was no consolation as she shivered in her misery and often prayed for a peaceful death to relieve her of her sufferings. At such times, William, a good sailor, offered solicitude and, when that did not work, laughing scorn.

"This is the easy part of the journey," he taunted. "There are no wild beasts or savages here."

Beth would have gladly faced a horde of savages and a menagerie of wild animals if only the encounter took place on solid ground. But William's laughter served one purpose: it made her angry, and with the wild winds sending sheets of frigid water over the ship's bow, she forced herself to join William on deck, where, after a giddy, weak time of almost giving in to her nausea, she began to feel the rhythm of the mighty seas and began, after a while, to glory in this evidence of God's might. The storm took on a beauty that brought tears to her eyes, and she spent the balance of the voyage tending to unfortunates who did not fully gain their sea legs until the ship reached the calm waters of Chesapeake Bay.

William had insisted on traveling light because English clothing would not be suitable for the American wilderness, and food and other supplies would be purchased in America. As a result, only two large trunks had to be transported on the journey north to meet the man to whom Lord Beaumont had addressed his primary letter of introduction. The overland trip was, when compared to the Atlantic winter crossing, a thing of little consequence, even though the majority of it was made in a snowstorm and into the face of an icy north wind, which drifted the snow so high across the road in some places that William and Beth had to join the driver in digging a way through walls of snow.

They reached their destination as the storm ended, but the fields before the impressive country house were gleaming with two feet of virgin fall, and the sun was reflecting blindingly. A black footman accepted William's card and escorted them into a waiting room, while other black men saw to the comfort of the hired driver and the horses.

Soon a tall man with a grim, tired-looking mouth, a

bedraggled powdered wig, keen, piercing eyes, and a grip that belied his age when he shook William's hand was greeting them. George Washington was fifty-four years old. His strenuous frontier and military life had aged him beyond his years. His smile was genuine. He escorted them into a snug but untidy library, and servants were soon offering mugs with the welcome warmth of a steaming hot toddy.

"I know your father, Lord Beaumont, by correspondence," Washington said, "and he is a man of goodwill and common sense. I welcome you and your sister to my home and to my country."

Washington had many things on his mind. The chaotic political conditions in the thirteen states often made him pessimistic. He had, in fact, just penned some notes in which, among other things, he had said, "Something must be done, or the fabric must fall, for it is certainly tottering."

He was exhausted, yet he was being pushed to take part in a federal convention. He had fought his war against what most thought were insurmountable odds, and now the men he had made free were squabbling over such issues as control of navigation of the Potomac River. There were moments when he almost despaired. At such times he welcomed the diversion of guests at Mount Vernon, and he was genuinely interested in this handsome young man and woman who had made the difficult winter crossing. As a patriot and a visionary, he knew that the United States would have to have many new settlers—and he hoped they would be people like William and Beth—if the country were to fulfill the destiny he envisioned for it. The thirteen states sat perched on the very edge of a vast continent that still harbored many enemies: the English to the north, the Spanish to the south and southwest, and remnants of the French, who might side with any enemy against the states.

Lord Beaumont had sent a gift, a set of fine silver drinking cups. While Beth and William were making their final arrangements, Cedric had had the cups engraved with a likeness of the flag under which Washington had fought, the first national flag of the United States, with its thirteen stripes and thirteen stars in a circle.

"The cups are quite old, sir," William pointed out as Washington admired the set.

"Here, where everything is of a newness, we value the old," Washington responded. "It is a most generous gift. Now, sir, what may I do for you?"

"We ask only for the benefit of your experience in the form of advice," William said. Then he quickly outlined his plans to travel far into the southwestern interior, into Spanish possessions.

"I admire your ambition," Washington said, shaking his head in amazement. "But are you aware of the enormity of the difficulties of this expedition you plan? In England, no point is more than seventy miles from the sea. You think to undertake a journey of well over two thousand miles, sir. There are no roads or white men where you're going—only hostile Indian tribes and perhaps the Spanish, whose chief desire is to dominate."

"But such a trip is possible, isn't it?" Beth asked, her eyes wide.

"It is possible, but I would hesitate to undertake such a trip with fewer than six thousand men, most of them mounted cavalry," Washington replied.

William laughed. "Our finances could not support an army. It is my intention to travel light and fast, with the aid of five or six frontiersmen who know the wilderness."

"No one knows the wilderness beyond the Mississippi, except some few Spanish explorers," Washington said.

There was a silence while the men drained the last of the toddies from their mugs. Beth saw discouragement creep into William's face, so she spoke up. "And yet there are men who travel as they please in the wilderness," she said. "Our great-grandfather befriended one such man a long time ago, when he visited England. He was a white man who had been reared as a Seneca Indian."

"Ah," Washington said, nodding. "You speak of Renno, the white Indian, a truly extraordinary man. I knew his grandson—Ghonkaba—well and fought with him in the last war. After the war, he brought a portion of his tribe down to settle in the lands of the Cherokee." Washington was silent for a moment, musing. "I also know Ghonkaba's son, named Renno after his great-grandfather. He's the leader of his people now, since his father's untimely death. He and the Cherokee have just won a sizable war against the Chickasaw, who were urged by the Spanish to invade both Cherokee lands and the lands of white settlers."

"If he's half the warrior that his great-grandfather was described to be by my great-grandfather's accounts, I'd like to meet with him," William said.

"Even that is a long and difficult journey," Washington warned. "And there is no guarantee, of course, that Renno would choose to leave his lands to travel into the Southwest."

"Well, sir, we must try," William said. "Tell me, would this Renno and his tribe have use for gold?"

Washington's eyebrows went up. "Renno is an enlightened leader. He realizes that the future of his people lies with the United States. He knows that sooner or later the Indian must adapt to our ways or perish. Yes. He could use gold, to buy weapons to protect his lands, to buy the products of civilization for his tribe."

"If there is gold in that mine," Beth said, "we will divide it with our guides and protectors."

"My advice to you is this," Washington said. "There is great opportunity here for men and women of courage and ambition. It is not necessary to travel to the frontiers. Great fortunes, great families, and great landholdings are going to be built right here in Virginia in the coming decades. There is opportunity for a young man such as you, William, to build a place for himself. I suggest that you give up this idea of yours and become a citizen of Virginia. I will help you to become established."

Beth started to speak, but William silenced her with a look. "I fear, sir, that our course is set to the southwest."

Washington knew that Lord Beaumont was not a rich man and most probably did not have the funds to outfit and equip a large expedition of armed men. "You both are determined?"

"Yes, sir," William and Beth answered together.

"Well, then, you will be my guests until the weather moderates, and then we'll see about finding you a guide to take you to Renno. You will have a letter of introduction from me to Renno, who is my friend. The rest will be up to Renno and you."

"How may we repay you, sir?" William asked.

"By being our friends when you have gained your fortune and gone back to England. By remembering that we Americans are men and women of English blood and that we stand here alone against the world's mightiest countries. We need friends in England, sir, and as we grow, England will find it advantageous to have friends here."

"You have our friendship, and gladly," William promised.

The social life at Mount Vernon was simplicity itself. Martha Washington set a good table, and the dining guests ranged from powdered and tight-breeched gentlemen to rugged frontiersmen. It was the latter who excited both Beth and William's interest, and at each opportunity they listened to the men who had journeyed past the bounds of civilization, and were transfixed by tales of savage fighting, huge bears, and vast, empty, endless stretches of virgin forest.

William, impatient to get under way, asked Washington politely if he had found a guide. The initial leg of the journey, leading through Virginia and North Carolina and then across the Great Smoky Mountains into the would-be state of Franklin, would not, he felt, be difficult. If that portion of the trip were completed during the last part of the winter, the expedition could then set out toward the southwest in early spring.

So it was that William and Beth met Blue Feather. Having been informed by Washington that a guide had been found, they waited eagerly in Washington's library. When the door opened, William's face went blank and Beth had to suppress a laugh.

Standing in the door was a thin, bent, wrinkled old man. He wore a beaded vest, well-made buckskin shirt, trousers, and moccasins, and in his jet-black hair were two blue feathers from the jaybird.

"This is insupportable," William whispered to Beth as the old man gazed at them with eyes that seemed to be the only living part of him in his motionlessness.

"You are very young," Blue Feather noted in a crackling, harsh voice.

"Thank God some of us are," William whispered.

He rose and offered his hand. Blue Feather took it solemnly, gave it one shake, and dropped it. Then the old man turned to face Beth, and his eyes twinkled, and his old, wrinkled face took on a new life in a smile that showed perfect white teeth. "With him," he said, inclining his head toward William, "I would not undertake such a journey in wintertime, for my bones are cold. But *your* beauty, young lady, will warm them."

Blue Feather turned, strode purposefully toward a bookcase, removed three volumes, and with a sigh of pleasure withdrew a hidden bottle of brandy. "Good," he grunted. "You drink?"

"No, thank you," William answered as Blue Feather poured one of the handsome silver cups from Beaumont Hall's pantry full to the brim and half emptied it in a gulp.

"You will be cold," he told William. He turned to Beth. "You will be very tired."

"We are not worried about that so much as—" William began.

"You give me money. I buy what we need," Blue

Feather said, finishing the rest of the cup of brandy with a smack of his lips.

"Yes, we'll talk about that later," William said, raising an eyebrow at Beth. "First I'll just speak with General Washington."

"Don't let that old devil's looks fool you," Washington told William.

"But, sir, he drinks," William protested.

Washington laughed. "That's what keeps the old devil alive. Trust me. You asked about men like the white Indian, who travel the wilderness at will. That is what I have found for you. That old man has seen more of this country than most. He speaks a dozen Indian dialects and can quickly pick up others. He once led one of my patrols through an entire redcoat division without discovery. He will get you to Renno."

So, with great doubt, William turned over good gold guineas to Blue Feather, who used the money to buy horses and food for the trail, plus quantities of glass beads, fabric, and cooking utensils for use or for trading or gifts, and, to William's chagrin, two full cases of a potent rum that required one horse to carry it.

Blue Feather carried a tomahawk, a knife in a buckskin sheath, and an unusually fine bow and a quiver of strong, handworked arrows. A small medicine bag on a thin thong was tied around his neck. Under one arm was a deerskin pouch containing a pipe, tobacco, a pair of spare moccasins, finely worked and beaded, a supply of pemmican and jerky, and containers of paint that, William would find, would change the old man's looks almost daily.

Blue Feather insisted on being present when William and Beth bought clothing for the trip, and he concurred with Beth's insistence that she not be burdened by skirts and petticoats.

"Look good in buckskin," Blue Feather told her as he selected shirts and trousers. "Need to stay warm," he said, tossing two pairs of heavy long underwear into her hands.

When Blue Feather appeared in Washington's library

two evenings later, it was sleeting outside, and a very cold north wind whipped the pellets of ice painfully into the face of anyone unwise enough to be outside.

"Tomorrow we go," Blue Feather announced.

"In this weather?" William asked, but the old man had turned and was out the door without answering.

"Tomorrow we go," William said, spreading his hands in helplessness.

The morning was cold, windless, and clear. Sleet and ice coated the roads, trees, and rolling hills. To William's surprise, Blue Feather had not purchased himself a horse.

"Here we go," he said, setting off at a trot.

It was William's job to lead the packhorses laden with their supplies, their trade goods, and the contents of the two trunks brought from England. It took him a while to overcome the animals' initial rebelliousness, and he had to push them hard to catch up with Beth and Blue Feather, who trotted tirelessly, his feet sometimes skipping on the icy coating of the road. Soon the pack animals were adjusted to their task and followed along docilely on their lead ropes. Beth's face was flushed from the cold air and her excitement. At last they were under way, and even though the roads led through heavily populated areas of Virginia, she was swept up in the spirit of adventure.

The old Indian proved to be a hard trail master. When the sun was obviously past the meridian and Mount Vernon had been left far behind, William called out, "I say, Blue Feather, isn't it time to stop for lunch?"

The old Indian slowed to run beside William's horse. He was chewing a piece of jerky. "It's a long way to go," he said. "You eat in the saddle."

"I'm not sure this is really necessary," William grumbled as he gnawed the very hard-to-chew jerky.

"Long way to go, Brother," Beth said, grinning and breaking off a bite of the almost frozen dried meat.

It was a half-hour before sunset when Blue Feather announced, "We make camp."

"But there are any number of comfortable inns on this road," William protested.

"Inns make you soft," Blue Feather objected. "Camp here. It's good training. Will build character."

Within an hour Blue Feather had a fire roaring, had raised a tent, covered the cold ground inside with branches cut from pine trees, had hot food steaming in a pot over the fire, and had consumed a full three inches of potent rum from a fresh bottle.

"Do you need some help with the food?" Beth asked.

"Don't need help," Blue Feather said, showing his surprisingly sound teeth in a wrinkled smile. "But it's nice to have you around." He reached over and playfully pinched Beth on the rump through her buckskin trousers.

Beth, a sweet girl who had had no experience with men, was shocked at first; then she reached out, seized a portion of flesh on Blue Feather's rump, and twisted it as hard as she could between her thumb and fingers. Blue Feather leapt and yelped in pain and surprise. Beth gave him a devilish grin.

"I get the message," Blue Feather said with a wry smile. "Won't do that again."

"Thank you," Beth responded sweetly. "Now, do you need help with the food?"

"Only to eat."

At first the roads were well traveled, and the trio was frequently meeting other riders, coaches, wagons, carts, or countrymen on foot. Beth had tucked her flame-red hair under a very warm fur cap, so people they met did not always realize that they were speaking to a girl. She came to enjoy their surprise when they did realize that the boy wrapped up warmly in buckskins, furs, and a blanket was, indeed, a quite attractive female.

The first leg of the journey was not an inconsiderable venture. It required traveling almost the entire length of the state of Virginia, north to south, skirting the mountains, and then traveling southwest through northern North Carolina. As he studied his maps, William quite soon began to realize why Blue Feather insisted on long days of nonstop travel. Several times they had to exchange horses with farmers along the way, and the money William had to put up to equalize the trades further eroded his diminishing store of gold.

No strangers to inclement weather, the Huntingtons were still surprised at the changeability and the fierceness of winter in this new world. But they were young and sturdy, full of hope and health. The long, cold miles slipped underneath the horses' hooves with a pleasing consistency. There were always new things to see, new people with whom to chat briefly. They talked to black slaves on woodcutting detail, small farmers who owned no slaves and spoke of the hardships of this land, gentlemen planters so English in accent and manner that, had it not been for the wild, endless expanses of the country, the Huntingtons would have felt as if they were at home.

It had not taken William long to realize that Washington had done him and Beth a great service by obtaining Blue Feather as their guide. In the late afternoon, having selected a camping spot, Blue Feather would disappear into the forest and come back, sometimes within minutes, with a fat turkey or a rabbit. He was a splendid trail cook. He could take a freshly speared trout and a green branch and work wonders. He could make a passenger pigeon taste as good as the finest meal in a fancy London club. Passenger pigeons became Beth's favorite breakfast. Every evening Blue Feather would cover the birds with wet clay, bury them close to the embers of the campfire, and in the morning all one had to do was crack away the hardened clay to find perfectly cooked fowl.

That February was a hard month. Almost every morning Beth had to crack ice from a stream to freshen herself, and as they neared the foothills of the North Carolinian mountains, winter seemed to take its best shot at them with a series of fiercely cold northwesters, with sleet and snow and freezing rain. But Beth and William were hardened now, and coming closer and closer to their first goal. Warm and snug in the clothing Blue Feather had bought, they seemed actually to thrive on the elements and the hardships. William's muscles were fit, and he had long since lost the small amount of extra weight he had put on in the relatively luxurious regiment life back home in England. Beth's girlish softness had hardened, and on those days when it was not necessary to bundle up, William saw that her body had become even more feminine, even more shapely, with a delicately thin waist, proud, firm breasts pushing against the buckskin shirt, and shapely, strong legs.

As February ended, March brought more clement weather, with the sun so warm at times that Beth would remove her hat and revel in the soft heat of it on her forehead. The trail wound upward, upward, through mountains that closed in on all sides, through a virgin forest from which, at night, came the scream of a deer under the claws and fangs of a mountain lion, or the gruff challenge of a black bear. They encountered the first real Indians they had seen—Blue Feather excepted: in the mountains they met their first Cherokee.

"We camp here," Blue Feather announced very early one afternoon.

"There are hours more of daylight," William pointed out.

"Wait," Blue Feather said, even as he stepped into the woods from the clearing he had indicated as a campsite. It was left to William and Beth to set up camp, water and feed the horses, make a fire, and cook. With darkness imminent, there was still no sign of Blue Feather.

The campsite he had chosen was beside a beautiful mountain stream. Ice rimmed still pools, and the water was deliciously cold and tasted of mountain freshness.

"Well, I don't suppose he's lost," William said as they ate the evening meal, cooked by Beth, who had been taking lessons from Blue Feather.

"Listen," Beth said.

From downstream came the distant sound of human voices, a song, a chant, the boom of far-off drums.

"Indians, William," Beth whispered in a soft, frightened voice.

"There are no hostile Indians here," William assured her.

"Cherokee," Blue Feather said, materializing as if by magic into the firelight. "Come."

"They are friendly?" Beth asked.

A young, slim Indian woman stepped into the firelight and put her arm around Blue Feather.

"Very friendly," Blue Feather said, looking very pleased.

Beth looked at William, her eyes wide. The girl, she saw, was quite pretty, with long braided black hair, dancing eyes, and a lush young body.

"Need fuel," Blue Feather said, diving into the rum carrier to lift a bottle and take long, deep swigs. The Indian girl put out her hand, but Blue Feather pulled the bottle away and spoke harshly to her. He winked at William. "Rum makes Indians crazy," he explained, then killed another full inch of the bottle in one gulp before replacing it.

William had grown accustomed to Blue Feather's drinking habits. No matter how much rum the old man put away, he never seemed intoxicated. What William had not become accustomed to was another of Blue Feather's seemingly inexplicable gifts—his attraction to and for beautiful women. As William and Beth followed Blue Feather down the stream to the Cherokee village, the young Cherokee maiden clung to the old man and looked up at him with adoring eyes.

The village was not at all as Beth would have imagined. These Cherokee were far east of Cherokee lands, and they lived in well-built log cabins, spoke English, and served a fine meal of turkey and dried vegetables. The travelers were guests in the cabin of Wounded Bear, a man of regal bearing, patriarch of the small group of

Cherokee, called Chief. A cheery fire roared in a natural stone fireplace. Beth was given a place of honor at a table made of rough-hewn planks, where she ate until she was stuffed. Blue Feather chose to sit on the floor, his skinny legs stuck out in front of him, a plate of food on his legs being constantly replenished by, now, two handsome Cherokee women, one older than the girl who had come to the camp with him.

"Widows," Wounded Bear explained, chuckling, when he saw Beth watching Blue Feather with an amused smile.

William, too, was amazed at the care being given the old man, and he winked at Beth and whispered, "The old boy's doing all right for himself, isn't he?"

"But they won't be able to convince him to settle down," Wounded Bear said with a deep chuckle.

The wife of Wounded Bear, not introduced, hovered around the table, eager to refill plates or to pour another serving of a hot, spicy herb tea with a peculiar taste that seemed to grow on Beth.

"Oh, no, thank you," she said, leaning back and rubbing her stomach when the wife offered more turkey. "It's delicious."

"Old family recipe," Wounded Bear explained. "I would like to share another old favorite with you."

"That's very kind," Beth said.

"It's for dog-head feast, for fifteen Indians and fifteen whites," Wounded Bear said. Then, without waiting for comment but noting Beth's stricken expression, he continued, his face quite serious. "First take out teeth from dog's head and put aside for use. Then boil dog's head with wild onions, cattail tubers, and a little salt. When meat is cooked off dog's head, use a ceremonial spear to lift skull and examine. Lift dog's eyeballs in spoon and test with fork to see if soft."

Beth was looking down at her hands, her stomach feeling just a little queasy.

"Show dog's head and eyeballs to all fifteen whites,"

Wounded Bear said, "then wait fifteen minutes for the last white to make his excuses and leave."

William began to chuckle.

"Then bring out turkey and vegetables, and you have plenty for all fifteen Indians," Wounded Bear finished with no hint of a smile.

William roared with laughter, and Beth began to giggle, and at last a great, sly smile touched Wounded Bear's lips.

During the two days they spent with Wounded Bear's people, neither saw much of Blue Feather. When they said good-bye at the end of the final evening and headed back toward their camp, Blue Feather was nowhere to be seen. He was in the camp at daybreak, however, as Beth was warming the meat given to them by Wounded Bear. He looked pale and even more fragile than usual.

"Ride today," he announced, and when they got under way, he slumped forward on a spare horse's neck and seemed to sleep for the first few hours as the animals followed the switchbacks in the trail, which climbed into a pass at the end of the little valley formed by the stream.

Although both Beth and William had taken successful turns at bagging game, they usually left the taking of food to Blue Feather. It was easier traveling to have the muskets on a pack animal, and William usually rode with nothing more than a pistol in his belt. That did not change until a full week after the pleasant visit with Wounded Bear. They had encountered two settlements of Cherokee, and both times Beth and William were amused and amazed at Blue Feather's ability to find, almost immediately, at least one beautiful Indian woman to spoil and pamper him.

"I don't know what that old man has," William said after the second time he had witnessed two Indian women waiting on Blue Feather hand and foot, "but if we could bottle it and sell it, we wouldn't need to travel thousands of miles for gold."

Blue Feather, well-dined, then well-lubricated from

his private stock of rum, would return from his romantic interludes with a peaceful look on his face.

Now the way was downward, with occasional uphill stretches over diminishing mountains. William's maps and information from the scattered Cherokee told them that they were now out of North Carolina. Knoxville was, they were told, about ten days' ride.

"We camp here," Blue Feather said one afternoon when the March sun was still hours high.

William knew better than to protest. He had seen the signs of cultivated garden plots showing last year's dried stalks, and he knew that an Indian settlement was near. He rather enjoyed the visits and had become, he felt, an old wilderness hand. At that moment, with the weather warming and the first wildflowers beginning to show, he would have been content to spend the rest of his life in such beautiful surroundings, where a man could live well off the land and where the people were friendly and of a charming simplicity.

The evening with yet another small clan of Cherokee was pleasant, the food good, and the next day was a glorious advance sampling of spring.

"Carry musket today," Blue Feather said as they broke camp. "You too, missy."

He had seen Beth shoot and had allowed her to use his own bow. She could draw it as well as he, and once she had adjusted to the slight irregularities of flight of the handcrafted arrows, she had been able to match him shot for shot, even bringing down passenger pigeons on the wing.

"Why the muskets?" William asked as he mounted and got the string of pack animals under way.

"Maybe nothing, maybe something," Blue Feather said. "If I say shoot, shoot to kill."

Beth's face paled, and she gripped her musket more tightly.

"The Cherokee are friendly," she said as she drew her horse up alongside the jogging Blue Feather.

"Bad Cherokee, bad whites," the guide explained. "Fall back twenty paces behind me, missy, and keep your eyes open."

The trail followed the white-water course of a mountain stream. The morning was a duplicate of many other mornings, with more pleasant weather. They ate in the saddle, a habit that no longer seemed inconvenient. They were making good time along the valley at midafternoon when Beth saw Blue Feather halt and freeze, then turn to motion to her to stop. They relayed the signal to William, who was leading the animals. Blue Feather made a signal that told them to stay, and running more rapidly than either of them would have imagined, disappeared down the trail.

He was back in fifteen minutes. Without speaking he went to a certain pack, took out feeding bags for each horse, and put them in place around the horses' noses. "We go," he said. "Dismount. No noise."

Beth looked at William questioningly but obeyed orders. Blue Feather led the way, his moccasins seeming to make no mark on the trail. The horses' hooves were muffled by a sodden, rotting layer of pine needles. All moved silently around the bend, where the trail branched away from the river and into the piney woods.

At first William was sure that his ears were deceiving him. Then, as they continued down the trail, he identified voices raised in raucous song. The trail was now about fifty yards from the river, moving along the lower side of a steep hill. Blue Feather once again warned them to be silent, and the singing voices grew louder, in two languages and off-key—the sound of drunken men, and now and then the shrill giggle of a woman. It seemed, for a time, that Beth, William, and Blue Feather would pass within feet of the revelry, but then the voices began gradually to fade as the trail angled back toward the bank of the river. After several long minutes, they removed the feeding bags from the horses. Then Blue Feather began his mile-eating pace, so Beth and William kicked their horses to keep up. He held that pace for a full two hours before slowing.

"All right, now," he said, "no more noise than necessary."

"Who were they?" William asked.

"Didn't ask, don't want to know," Blue Feather replied.

The sun was already down behind the last line of blue mountains ahead of them. It was evident that there was to be no early camp, and the horses began to be restless—it was time for them to be watered and fed. But Blue Feather pushed on until darkness and then directed them into a small clearing as far from the trail and the stream as the encroaching ridge allowed.

"Fire?" William asked, having picked up Blue Feather's habit of using as few words as possible.

"Small. Just enough to warm tea."

"Do you think we were in danger from those men?" Beth asked William as Blue Feather built the fire.

"The old boy seems to think so," William said, shrugging his shoulders. His heart went out to Beth. She was so sheltered and naive, and the wilderness understandably held terrors for her. And yet she was uncomplaining through it all.

Beth was sitting on a rock, a musket at her side and her dueling pistols in the belt of her buckskins. The tea boiled quickly, putting out a heavenly smell. The food, however, was pemmican and jerky. No hot meal for the travelers. The horses had to be led, two by two, to the stream for water, then issued their small allowance of oats. Some of the animals were getting quite thin, but soon the new grasses of spring would be poking through the thin layer of snow to supplement their diet. In fact, the journey would soon be almost over, with Knoxville only days away.

Chores done, the small fire only a dim glow in the clearing, Beth prepared for sleep. She took down her hair, let it fall, and began to comb it. Blue Feather seemed already to be asleep, curled on his side near the fire.

William sat with his back against a tree, a musket across his knee.

Beth had succeeded in getting the tangles out of her flowing red hair. The dim firelight gleamed, reflecting off her hair, and she wondered if it would be warm enough tomorrow to wash her hair—and herself—in the icy stream.

William heard the noise first and jerked his head up.

"I wouldn't touch that musket, sonny," said a rough, deep voice from the shadows.

William's hand stopped its motion. In a circle around them, six men stepped into the dim glow of the fire, three white men, shaggy, bearded, and three Indians. Each held a musket. "Well, lookee here," said one of the white men, seeing Beth for the first time. "Ain't she a sight for sore eyes?"

Chapter III

In the first days of March, with the winds of spring
moderate, rainfall adequate, and the sun cheery and
warm, the adjoining villages of Rusog, who was chief of
the Cherokee since his father Wegowa's death several
weeks earlier, and Renno, sachem of the southern Seneca,
rang with the shouts of laughter of children at play. Dogs
gamboled among the children, chasing sticks and their
tails, for they too felt the renewal, the coming of spring.
All doors were open to the pleasant weather. The accumu-
lated staleness of winter was being aired from all lodges.

The boy who was destined to become a Seneca leader,
Os-sweh-ga-da-ga-ah Ne-wa-ah, Little Hawk, played in
the fond view of his father, Renno. Little Hawk was just
past his first birthday, but he moved with occasional hints

41

of physical grace that were beyond his age. He was trying to catch the tails of a new litter of black-and-white pups, and the pups were enjoying the game as much as Little Hawk. Time and again a pup would evade the baby's awkward hands, dashing in to plant a wet, warm tongue on the boy's face.

To Renno the boy was ho-ah-wuk, son, and an endless joy. The boy, not yet browned by the sun, was fair of skin, for he carried the blood of the white Indian and the white blood of his mother, the former Emily Johnson. By blood, then, he was one-quarter Indian. But by temperament and training he would be, as was his father, all Seneca, all Nun-da-wa-o-no.

Renno, who had gained much honor even though he was a young man, was sprawled on a buffalo robe, clad only in his loincloth. Emily, smiling as she watched her son play with the pups, sat by Renno's side, her legs folded under her, her long wheat-colored hair braided. She wore a clean, fresh doeskin dress and gaily decorated moccasins. She was happy, and almost at peace, her serenity clouded only by a certain restlessness that she sensed in her husband.

The great-grandson of the original white Indian was in his mid-twenties and a strongly built, powerful man. His light-brown hair was long and gathered at his neck by a leather thong secured by a silver clip fashioned by his friend the Cherokee Se-quo-i, a young man of talent and wisdom.

Renno's restlessness had deep roots. As he watched Little Hawk with bemused, fond eyes, his thoughts ranged far.

Although he was young, Renno had traveled vast reaches of the similarly young United States and the wilderness at its western frontier, and his excellent memory for landmarks, for the contour of hills and mountains, the shape of the flow of a river or a creek, formed a mental map in his mind. He had been having dreams, the dreams of sleep and not of vision, and in his night dreams he saw the deep, cool, virgin forests of the North, in the lands of his ancestors, in the lands of the Seneca and the League of the Iroquois.

Soon, he knew, he would have to seek solitude, would run far into the wilderness to be counseled by the manitous, for he was troubled without knowing why, had questions without answers, and felt heavily the responsibility that was his as the leader of those around him. Now, however, it was pleasant in the sun, sweet to see Little Hawk so happy, and good to sit by the side of the woman he loved. It was a time for thought, and he let his mind roam from the snowy lands of the North to the heavily forested mountains to the east and those lands west of them that were now his home. In his mind he reviewed history, thinking that it would somehow shed light on his doubt and questioning.

Although there were scattered groups of Cherokee Indians throughout the vast, rugged areas of the Great Smoky Mountains, survival in the high areas came hard, especially in winter. The majority of Cherokee hunted in the virgin forests on the western foothill slopes and the rolling, beautiful lands extending for over two hundred miles toward the Cherokee hunting grounds and the Father of Waters, the Mississippi. White settlements had pushed past the blue Smokies, with Knoxville having become the center of the southernmost grouping of settlers.

Knoxville had been established not far from the first white intrusion into the lands of the Cherokee, Fort Loudon, established on the Little Tennessee River by a party of Virginians in 1756 and destroyed, in a general massacre, by the Cherokee in 1760.

The land west of the blue mountains owed its settlement largely to a popular uprising against taxes in North Carolina in 1771. Called the Regulator Insurrection, its defeat at the hands of Loyalists sent hundreds of whites over the mountains, where land was purchased peacefully from the Cherokee.

Peace reigned in both Indian and white areas of the

Smoky Mountain frontier. The political status of the territory was still unsettled, for North Carolina, having agreed to the formation of the would-be state of Franklin after the War for Independence, had rescinded that agreement and once again claimed the area. John Sevier, elected governor of the would-be state, remained in office, however, and the residents of Knoxville still had hopes for statehood.

Sevier's right-hand man in Knoxville was Renno's father-by-marriage, Colonel Roy Johnson, a tall, spare man with graying hair. Johnson had fought side by side with the Cherokee and the self-exiled Seneca on several occasions, the most recent being a bloody little war against Spanish-incited Chickasaw.

There on the far frontier, with a rugged mountain range between them and the confused, weak, just barely united states, the white settlers had come to recognize that their only defense against the wild tribes of Indians to the west and north and south—and against the Spanish, who had shown a definite desire to move into the mid-Mississippi areas—was the strength of their own arms and an alliance with the Cherokee.

During the winter of 1786, Colonel Roy Johnson had stayed in Knoxville. The war against the war chief Oklawahpa and his Chickasaw had sapped much of his strength, and he was content to stay at home and spend long, cozy evenings by the fire with his wife, Nora. A well-informed man, Johnson knew that the next few years would be fateful for all the people of the Tennessee frontier. If Johnson had been given a special title, he might have been called the official Franklin agent to the Indians, for he had definite ties of friendship with the Cherokee and, because his daughter, Emily, was married to the sachem of the relatively small but powerful Seneca, both friendship and blood ties there.

As he thought of his father-in-law, Renno smiled. Knowing the man as he did, he knew that spring would be having an effect on Johnson, that he would be a bit restless too.

Renno was not surprised to learn that Emily was also thinking of Johnson. "I wouldn't be surprised to see my father turn up one of these days," she said.

"He'll be eager to see the boy," Renno agreed.

"And Mother," Emily added.

"If she's well," Renno said.

"I think she'll come even if she has to ride the entire distance on a litter," Emily replied.

Renno nodded, and his thoughts strayed again to his ancestors.

That portion of the ancient and once powerful Seneca tribe living in the Tennessee lands was there, far from the northern hunting grounds, because of a choice made by Ghonkaba, grandson of the original white Indian. He had gone against his own tribe, for the Seneca honored their treaty with the British when the American colonists rebelled against colonial rule, to fight on the side of the revolutionists. As a result, when the war was over, it was not possible for those Seneca who had followed Ghonkaba to return to their traditional home. Instead, Ghonkaba had led his people south and had been welcomed by the Cherokee as brothers of the same Algonquin stock, who spoke a language with common roots.

The Seneca had come to a fair land. Virgin forests of hardwood and conifers made game plentiful. In the small gardens tended by the women, the rich soil produced a succulent plenty of corn, peas, beans, potatoes, cabbage, pumpkins, and melons. The weather was far more moderate than that to which the Seneca were accustomed, and even in the depths of winter, warm air could move over the area from the south and produce days when only the lightest of clothing was adequate.

Young warriors could hone their hunting skills on woods buffalo and deer and could dress themselves and their women in the skins of panther, wolf, fox, raccoon, opossum, and bear. Trade with more southern Indians bought seashells from which combs and trinkets for the women were fashioned.

The Seneca had found a good life, but not without cost. To the west were the war-loving Chickasaw; to the south were the vast Choctaw and Creek nations. Even in peace—the peace that came after the defeat of the Spanish-inspired war with the Chickasaw—warriors kept their skills fresh, and young men were trained in the use of knife, tomahawk, bow, and musket. And the wilderness was the training ground and playground for young men aspiring to join the ranks of warriors.

The annual ceremony of the new beginning had come and gone. Once again the forces of good had overcome the forces of evil, and the first green was beginning to show. Soon the women and children would be roaming the forests and meadows, gathering the young green fruits of spring, and the diet of winter would be supplemented by this season's plenty. It was a good time, but still Renno was restless. Questions recurred, nagging at him. He did not, of course, question the wisdom of his father in having brought those Seneca who had fought with George Washington to the lands of the Cherokee, nor the solid and rewarding alliance with Rusog's people. He had faith in his ancestors, for they had been guided by the manitous. It was his own wisdom that he questioned. He had the uneasy feeling that change was coming, and he wanted to be the director of, not the passive victim of, change. What of his people? Should he relax, be happy with his good life, and content to stay in the mild climate and rich hunting grounds west of the Smoky Mountains? If so, why did he dream of the homelands, of the forests of the North?

He looked up at the flawless sky and took a deep breath. *Give me the wisdom of my fathers*, he prayed silently.

"Look," Emily said, putting a soft hand on his arm. Little Hawk had captured one of the pups, and the little animal was licking him on the face. The boy looked doubtful for a moment; then his mouth opened in a glad smile.

From down the slope toward the Cherokee village

came the fierce cries of a band of young boys playing at war. Overhead, a lone crow winged its way, high. In the trees around the village, jays, sparrows, mockingbirds, and others chattered their spring songs, staking out areas for nest building.

When the sound of rapidly approaching horses came from up the slope, Renno raised himself lazily on one elbow and shaded his startling blue eyes. The horses, neck and neck, burst from a trail leading into the forest and plunged down the hill recklessly. A shrilling, warbling war whoop came from one of the riders. The other, a slim girl, yelled encouragement to her mount and, for a moment, took the lead.

"Young love," Renno commented with a wry grin as he fell back to cushion his head on his hands and look into the flawless sky.

"A beautiful romance," Emily remarked. "If both survive it."

The thundering horses reached the cleared areas at the edge of the village, then skirted around, still galloping at top speed at the urgings of their riders. At last the horse ridden by a stalwart young warrior pulled into the lead. At the far end of the village the horses were reined in and came panting and prancing back toward the center compound to halt a few paces from where Renno lay.

"Emily," complained the young warrior, "Holani claims foul simply because my foot touched hers at the finish."

"It was deliberate," snapped the girl, her dark eyes flashing.

"What we need," Renno said under his breath, "is a small war to occupy the young bloods."

Emily raised one eyebrow at her husband, for he himself was only in his twenties.

El-i-chi, Renno's brother—for it was he who was disputing the foul claims of the beautiful young girl against whom he had raced—was looking at Emily pleadingly. Emily's heart went out to him, for his courtship of Holani the Chickasaw had been anything but smooth. El-i-chi had

47

brought the girl home from the Chickasaw war, and for months now she had resisted his offers of marriage.

In many ways, Holani reminded Emily of the eldest of Ghonkaba's offspring, Ena, sister to Renno and El-i-chi and wife of the Cherokee chief, Rusog. True, Ena was mellowing after years of marriage and no longer felt it necessary to compete with her husband and other men to prove her worth. But when Ena was younger, Emily knew, she had been very much like this slim, strong young Chickasaw girl who had not yet learned that it is better to be loved by a good, strong warrior than to compete with him.

"Make the racecourse longer," Renno suggested. "Say, to Knoxville and back."

El-i-chi looked at his brother in surprise.

"And take a few weeks to rest in Knoxville before you return," Renno said, "so that we can have some peace and quiet here."

"We are not wanted here," Holani said stiffly.

"Not at the expense of your horse trampling my son and my new pups," Renno agreed.

The horses were wheeled, then urged into a mad gallop as they cleared the village, taking the trail to the nearby stream.

El-i-chi reached the stream first, for it seemed that Holani had lost the urge to race. He was rubbing down his steaming horse when she arrived. After caring for the horses they allowed the animals to drink from the clear water and then left them to graze on the scattered sprouts of green along the banks. El-i-chi sat on the carpet of new moss, the ground still a bit cold through his buckskins. Holani stood indecisively and then at last sat down at a considerable distance from him.

"You deliberately bumped my horse," she said.

El-i-chi made a face. "It is no matter. You won. Does that content you?"

"No," she said, "for you were unfair."

El-i-chi was moodily silent. When he spoke his voice

was soft. "My sister Emily told me that to win you I must speak to you of your beauty."

Holani flushed and looked away.

"Your laugh is sweeter than the sound of water running over small stones," El-i-chi said. "Your hair blacker than the night. The sight of you fills me like well-roasted meat, and I think that it is time. You told me that we would be friends, and that friends do not try to kill each other. And yet you fight me. You shame me before my people by refusing me."

"I did not seek your attentions," she reminded him sharply. "I did not choose to leave my people."

"Throughout the long winter I have given you my attentions," El-i-chi continued gently. "You asked me to be patient, to give you time, and I did. Now it is the new beginning, and my bed is still empty."

"There are many among your own people and the Cherokee who would gladly share it," she said.

"But none is Holani but Holani."

After a long silence she turned to face him. There were tears in her eyes. "I do not mean to shame you."

"Then we will speak to my mother and my grandmother and make the arrangements."

She shook her head. Her hair had come unbraided during the wild riding and hung in inky beauty to below her shoulders. "First I would see my people," she said.

El-i-chi felt pain, for at the beginning of the Chickasaw war he had been a part of a Seneca war party that had decimated Holani's village.

"Perhaps some lived," she said, as if reading his thoughts.

"Have we not become your people?" he asked.

"They have been kind," she admitted. "Emily, and also your mother—"

El-i-chi mused for a long time. "And if I would take you to see your people, what then? What if they are all dead, as I believe?"

"I must know," she said. "Then—" She straightened her shoulders. "Then—" But she could not find the words.

He moved to sit by her side, put his hands on her shoulders, and turned her to face him. "I cannot believe you care nothing for me."

Her mouth seemed to soften, and he kissed her. At first she did not respond, and then, to the gladness of his heart, her lips parted and her arms came to cling to him.

"You see?" he asked, relieved and happy. "It is going to be joyful. I am El-i-chi. To be the wife of the brother of the sachem, a warrior, is not a fate to be despised. It will be my joy to provide for you, to dress you in the softest skins, to adorn you with combs of copper and shell."

She was weeping soundlessly. "I must know," she said. "Please, I must know if any of my people lived."

He kissed away one tear, then two, and held her close. "So be it," he decided. "I will speak to my brother, then I will take you to the lands of the Chickasaw. But whether your family be living or dead, you will then return here with me and become my wife. Is that agreed?"

She smiled through her tears and nodded her head and met his glad kiss with a kiss of her own and with a trembling and a strength in her arms that fired his blood. She did not resist but aided him as he loosened her lacings and began to reveal her smoothness.

"You are my wife," he whispered as he gloried in the beauty of her and as she responded to his caress. And there, on a mossy bank, with the warm spring sun on his back, he gave himself totally, and she returned his gift, at first with tightly held lips to keep from crying out in pain, and then with that fierce competition that was a mark of her character. Competitiveness became an asset to their union, which was at first fierce and hungry, with each seemingly intent on devouring the other, and then coming naturally into a shared joy that made them forget time and themselves as individuals, knowing only that greatest and most joyful gift of nature, love. The result so surprised her that she cried out, her voice full of joy.

When their desires were sated, they came to Renno's lodge, for it was the time of the evening meal. "Sit. Eat," Renno said, for he knew that there was plenty.

Emily immediately noticed a difference. El-i-chi's face no longer showed a wild yearning, and Holani's beautiful face seemed to have softened. Emily smiled knowingly at Renno, but he was intent on his food.

"I had thought to hunt soon," Renno said. "To the west."

It was, El-i-chi knew, an invitation, and ordinarily he would have been eager to tramp the wilderness with his brother. "With your permission, Brother, I will travel west, but not to hunt."

Renno looked up quickly and saw that Holani's hand was lying lightly on El-i-chi's thigh. "And the purpose of this journey?"

"Before we are married," El-i-chi said, "I will take Holani to visit her people."

Emily smiled, but Renno's handsome face was impassive. "There are those among her people who do not think kindly of us," he said. He knew that the peace agreed to by the Chickasaw war chief, Oklawahpa, was, like all Chickasaw agreements, good only as long as it served Oklawahpa's own purposes.

"Nevertheless," El-i-chi said, "I have promised. We are one."

Emily blushed in spite of herself, although she had been certain of a definite change in the relationship between El-i-chi and Holani. She did not often interfere in decisions that were the responsibility of the sachem, but as a woman, she was sensitive to the looks Holani had for El-i-chi and was happy that they had at last worked out their differences. "If a part of their compact is that Holani visits her people, is that trip so dangerous?" she asked.

Renno shrugged. "There is danger in living," he said. "Is this, then, a compact?"

El-i-chi nodded. "Do I have your permission?"

"I do not want another war with the Chickasaw,"

Renno said with a smile. "Can you two young mountain lions conduct yourselves with dignity?"

"We can try, Brother," El-i-chi said, filling his mouth with Emily's delicious venison stew.

"Make your preparations," Renno said. "But delay your departure until I return from my hunt."

Emily's eyes fell. She had seen his restlessness, and she never made any attempt to keep her husband from his periodic journeys into the wilderness. As much as she and Renno loved each other, there was something in him with which she could not compete, something that demanded the solitude of the wilderness. She had seen all the signs that he was yearning to be away, so she had delayed telling him that she was pregnant again, for she did not want to let that news influence him against doing what he had to do. There would be time when he returned, renewed as the earth itself was renewed each spring.

El-i-chi and Holani had much to do. Toshabe, El-i-chi's mother, was not surprised when she was told of the compact. She had known from the first time she had seen the Chickasaw girl that she was the woman for her youngest child. The only surprise she had known was Holani's reluctance, for the Chickasaw's position was not at all unique. Toshabe herself was not born a Seneca. Product of a white father and an Erie mother, Toshabe had gladly become the wife of Ghonkaba, and a Seneca, for she knew the value of love.

"Do we have your blessings, Mother?" El-i-chi asked shyly.

"You have them, and happily." Toshabe embraced them. "You will be gone how long?"

"A moon, no more," El-i-chi said, "with the help of the manitous."

"Then we will plan the wedding for the month of late plantings," Toshabe decided. "My heart goes with you on your journey."

*　　*　　*

Renno, traveling light, carrying only a bit of jerky and his weapons, was miles away by that time. Although more and more Cherokee and Seneca owned horses, he still preferred to travel by foot, as Seneca had always traveled. He liked to feel the earth under his moccasins, to see the miles pass under his feet as he moved in that tireless, almost effortless warrior's pace. He avoided villages, killed small game for his food, and then he was where he wanted to be, to the northwest, in land he had never seen.

In a dense stand of hardwood he found a sparkling stream, erected a shelter of boughs, killed a deer, and ate heartily, hanging the surplus meat high, out of the reach of small animals. Then he swam in the stream and turned his mind to a problem that had been troubling him for a long time. He was Seneca. His father had allied his people with the Americans and had left his homeland. Far to the north was the main body of Seneca, his blood brothers.

He knew that what Ghonkaba had done had been necessary. But was it the will of the manitous that his Seneca remain forever in the lands of the South? Was it the will of his ancestors to see more and more blending of Seneca and Cherokee? If so, soon the Seneca would cease to exist as a unified, separate entity, for the Cherokee were more numerous. They too were brothers, and if it was the will of the manitous that the two tribes become one, so be it. Often he fantasized about leading his people back to the snows of the northland, to be reunited with their blood brothers. The thought of such a journey appealed to him, but he was fully aware of the hardships involved and knew that such a decision would meet with resistance among those who had married Cherokee.

It was not that old, burning question alone that had brought him into the wilderness, for he often felt the need to fast, pray, and consult the spirits for wisdom.

The first sign came to him in the form of the hawk, one of the totems of the Bear Clan, of which he was a member. The hawk was young, a yearling, and not yet of the dark color of the adult. The bird soared over him for a long time and then lit in a cottonwood tree near the stream. There it preened itself, then flexed its powerful claws, causing bark to fall from the limb on which it perched. The hawk turned its feral eyes to stare directly at Renno, opened its cruel beak, and gave one fierce, wild cry before spreading its impressive wings and flying directly toward Renno's face before soaring up to disappear.

Renno watched the hawk until it was a tiny dot in the sky. He was content; he had eaten well and felt the strength of life flowing in his veins, the youthful power in his limbs. He got up and ran with no destination, no purpose except to feel alive, to feel his legs pump and his heart increase its beat. He ran in a great circle around his campsite and returned there at dusk to drink deeply, build up his banked fire, and seat himself within his shelter to await the darkness, when the sky was jeweled by stars and the moon came to give a silvery light. He still sat there when, after a day of goodness and deep meditation, the moon rose again. He did not feel hunger or thirst. His prayers went up to the lights in the sky, to the spirits, to his ancestors.

At the end of the third day the moon was full, and with it, as it rose in the east, early in the evening, there came a great burst of light. Renno chanted his prayers for wisdom and squinted his eyes at the light that seemed to float just above the ground. In that light was the most powerful totem, a great bear—muscular, massive, its white teeth exposed in an open mouth.

Renno waited patiently. Time stood still. The bear's shape seemed to come and go, and it was first manlike, then completely ursine. He knew that he was being favored by the spirits, just as generations of his ancestors had never been betrayed when they had sought such guidance. His father and his father's father and beyond had always enjoyed the favor of the manitous.

"Have you wisdom for me?" he whispered.

There was no answer. The great bear reared, clawed the air, and there seemed to be a warning in the gesture.

"My spirit reaches out to you," Renno whispered. "I sense danger. Will you share your wisdom, great one?"

And then the bear's face became a familiar, beloved face, the face of his father, Ghonkaba.

"I honor you, my father," Renno said. "May your life be pleasant in the lands where our ancestors roam."

"West," the spirit whispered, the eerie sound seeming to seep, rather than emerge, to sigh among the trees and to fade into the darkness.

Renno's heart leapt, for he feared, for a moment, that he was being told that his time was near, that he would soon be called to join his ancestors.

"I bow to you," he whispered.

The light seemed to glow brighter. His father's face became clearer. "The way is far. The mountains are dry. Trust the white one. Alert yourself for the sign of the cat, for there is a child who will become a great chief at risk."

The words seemed to engrave themselves on Renno's brain. The light began to fade, and Ghonkaba's image faded, then reappeared, each time weaker.

"Do not leave me feeling so puzzled, my father," Renno begged, willing his eyes to hold the vision.

"Your son," the voice said, very distant now.

"Yes?" Renno asked, straining forward.

"He will be a great chief, but you will know sorrow. The flame-haired one is the future."

"Wait, wait," Renno pleaded as the vision began to grow dim.

Now the voice was gruff, growling, the sound of the great bear that had taken the place of Ghonkaba's face. Suddenly a vision of Emily sprang into Renno's mind, her pale hair on a pillow, her face so beautiful, her smile so radiant, her love coming so strongly to him that he ached from it. And, as if in answer to that, the growling voice said, "No, you must go alone and you will feel alone, but the manitous will be with you."

The light faded, leaving only the pale light of the

moon. Renno rocked back and forth, chanting his prayers, asking for wisdom, for clarification of the vision, but there was only the hooting of an owl and the sigh of a rising wind in the new green leaves of the trees.

West. He would go to the west. And he would go without Emily, and he would feel alone, but not—and this was clear to him—without the company of others. He would be alone only as far as Emily was concerned, and this brought a vast ache into him, sent him running, eating as he ran, toward her. He felt great fear for her. What was the meaning? He would know sorrow. He had known sorrow before, at the time of the death of his father. But Emily? Would he lose her too?

After hours of running, he reached the Seneca village and burst into the lodge in the middle of the early morning, during that time when man's spirits are low and death comes to the sick and aged. Emily greeted him with a sleepy smile, with her soft arms and her warm body, and his fears were lessened.

Lying in his arms, with the fires of their love burning and their bodies united, Emily decided it was time to tell him her glad news. She spoke softly to him as he held her closely, passions spent, both of them savoring their closeness, their love.

"Will you ask the manitous for another son?" she whispered.

He laughed. With Emily in his arms it seemed that the prophecy of the spirits meant only that he would be taking a trip, marching toward the west. She would be here, in their home, when he returned. "Of that I am uncertain. Sometimes I ask for another son, sometimes for a daughter with your face and your hair."

"Perhaps you could ask for both at once," she whispered.

"Two like the one we have would strain even the generosity of the manitous," he said; then he raised himself on his elbow, and in the glow of the moon coming in the ceiling opening he saw that she was smiling. "I think I am being slow to understand," he said. "Are you telling me . . . ?"

"Yes," she whispered. "Are you pleased? Two moons now have passed, and I am sure."

He squeezed her until she felt that she was becoming a part of his body. "You have always filled my hours with the greatest joy," he said.

He was awakened early by El-i-chi, who shouted into the door. Emily was protesting that he had had little sleep, but Renno grunted, threw a robe around his shoulders, and came out into a beautiful morning of March sun.

"A day for traveling, Brother," El-i-chi said, smiling. "I thank the manitous for your return."

Renno considered long before he spoke. "I have given you my word that you could take Holani to the land of the Chickasaw," he said. "But now I must ask something of you."

"I am your warrior," El-i-chi said with an elegant nod of his head.

"I will need you, Brother," Renno told him. "It is not my pleasure, but it is as simple as that."

El-i-chi allowed one quick look of disappointment. "So it will be," he agreed. "Order me."

"The time is soon," Renno said. "I can say no more."

Holani, however, could say much more. "He is hateful," she hissed when El-i-chi told her that, contrary to what he and Renno had promised, he could not take her to visit her people at that time.

"He is the sachem," El-i-chi replied, hoping to console her. "He would not take back his word without reason."

"It is because I am Chickasaw," she countered.

"Waiting will be sadness for me," El-i-chi said, "but I have given you my word, and until I have fulfilled my promise, I will not ask you to be joined with me as my woman."

Holani felt a quick surge of loss. She opened her mouth to speak, to say that they were one and that this new development would not change it, but she was young, and she had just suffered a great disappointment. She closed her mouth and said nothing.

"We will go soon," El-i-chi promised, "when I have served our sachem."

But the days passed with a sameness. Holani, in spite of her urge to go into his arms, became more distant as she brooded on being treated unfairly. El-i-chi received Renno's permission to hunt, not more than two days' distance, and he made himself scarce, for, having been one with Holani, it was torture to be near her without her love.

A late storm swept down from the vast areas of the midcontinent to send a last message of winter in the form of light snow, and some of the green growth fell victim to the cold. But March was not yet old, and the cold was accepted with glowing fires in the dwellings and the children had one last chance to tramp in virgin whiteness.

Renno had plenty of time to muse over the vision he had been blessed with in the forest, and it was not difficult for him to convince himself that any sense of foreboding was out of place. He had always been susceptible to the call of far places and welcomed the opportunity that had been promised him by the spirits. *The mountains are dry,* the spirit of his father had said. He dreamed of rugged, arid mountains, and because he had never seen anything of the kind, they seemed odd and fanciful.

He took his son into the snow and delighted in the baby's joy but was chided mildly by Emily for it, for there had been a few cases of the winter fever in the two villages, and Emily knew and feared the power of that sickness. Even though Little Hawk had been initiated into Seneca tradition by being dunked, while still a babe in arms, in a river from which the ice had been broken, he was the picture of health, and as soon as he was warm, he wanted to go back into the snow with his father.

Renno's sister, Ena, and her husband, Rusog, came to take an evening meal. Renno sensed in Rusog the same spring restlessness he knew himself, and they smoked the pipe and spoke of distant places, the war with the Chickasaw, and the welfare of their allied peoples, while Ena tried both to carry on a conversation with Emily and to listen to the men talk at the same time. Little Hawk also tried to demand his aunt's attentions, so that, frustrated, Ena said, "Stop!"

Renno and Rusog looked at her in puzzlement.

"If you will talk of interesting things you will include us," Ena demanded.

Rusog smiled mildly. He was accustomed to, and indeed admired, his wife's spirit. "You have only to listen," he said.

"You two are like young bears in the spring," Emily teased. "Wanting to leave the den, to begin to wander. Why don't you both go hunting?"

"And I will go with you," Ena said.

Emily laughed. "And a young she-bear, too," she said.

"I will not sit in the lodge chewing skins," Ena vowed.

"My sister, too, has winter fever," Renno said with a laugh. "Perhaps she would take El-i-chi's place and accompany Holani to see her people."

Ena turned away with a flounce. "I will not be a guardian for your willful, wild young girl," she said, and this brought even more laughter from Rusog and Renno, for no one had been wilder and more willful than Ena.

"There are those among us," Rusog commented, his face showing no expression, "who are not content with their lot. Perhaps they should pray to the spirits to be taken and to be reborn as men."

"I don't need a man's body," Ena retorted. "I am the match of most men as I am."

"True, true," Renno conceded. "But you still have to squat, Sister, to relieve yourself."

Rusog roared with laughter. Emily blushed. There were times when the humor of her chosen people could be a bit crude. Most of the time her Renno was a perfect gentleman in his conduct. He had spent much of the winter working with her to improve his knowledge of the white man's wisdom, reading many books with her. He had been fascinated with two separate accounts of the late War for Independence, reading them aloud and breaking in now and then to say, "But that was not the way it happened." Or, "But what of the Seneca, for we were there." He had talked with her about the omission of the contribution of Indian tribes who fought on the side of the Revolutionists, and she had agreed that the writers and the accounts had shamefully wronged the Seneca and others who had helped win freedom for the United States.

There had been evenings shared with the gifted young Cherokee Se-quo-i, who also came regularly to have Emily teach him the white man's reading and writing. But now it was as if those lovely winter afternoons and nights were a part of the distant past, for Renno was Seneca and very much the Indian, smoking a clay pipe with Rusog and talking of war.

That night, hearing the men talk, Emily felt a pang of sadness, for she knew that something was on Renno's mind. She did not know what, but she felt within her that it would soon take him away from her again.

Chapter IV

The events that would have great impact on Renno's life reached one crisis point on the very night Renno was seeking the wisdom of the manitous. In the early darkness of night, six men—three bearded white men and three renegade Cherokee—stepped into the flickering light of a small campfire, muskets at the ready.

William Huntington had heard a small noise and was reaching for his musket. The old Indian, Blue Feather, was curled into his blankets. Beth was combing her flame-red hair into cascades of glinting color reflecting the light of the fire.

The largest of the white men, a mountain of a man, had eyes only for the slim figure that, from the woods, he had taken to be a boy. The flow of hair, the shape of her, now that he was near, sent desire throbbing through him. "Well, lookee here," he said, "ain't that a sight for sore eyes?" He would hold his fire and would have his musket and his pistol to take care of any of his fellows who contested him for the woman. There was more than enough firepower from the other five to take care of the old bag of bones who was sleeping and the dandyish white man. Unfortunately for his hopes, he was the first to die, as, with a blur of motion, Blue Feather rolled free of his blankets and let fly a heavy-hafted knife that entered neatly between two of the large man's ribs and penetrated his heart. And even as the man fell, Blue Feather was yelling, "Shoot!"

Beth's reaction was swift. "When I say shoot, shoot," Blue Feather had said, and the words seemed to echo in her mind even as her hands dropped the comb and reached for her father's dueling pistols. She cocked, then fired without any obvious aiming, and the two balls took an Indian and a white man square in the chest, sending them crashing backward. Two of the intruders' muskets blasted, and the balls passed close by William's head as he flung himself to one side, his hand snatching up his own musket.

Blue Feather tackled one of the Indians low, and the pair of them went sprawling, and there was a flash of metal as Blue Feather's tomahawk rose and fell. In the first seconds four men were dead, and the remaining Indian whooped, having fired his musket, and leapt toward William with his tomahawk raised, only to be met with the ball from William's weapon, the shot taking him on the forehead and producing a splatter of blood that rained droplets on Beth. Blue Feather's flying tomahawk turned once in the air and buried itself between the shoulder blades of the last white man as he turned to flee, and then there was an almost eerie silence.

Blue Feather groaned as he lifted himself from the ground. "Twisted my back," he said as he walked, bent, to examine each of the fallen men.

Beth's hands began to shake uncontrollably. She wanted

to weep, and she wanted to shout out her anger. It was the anger that won. "How dare they?" she yelled. "How dare they force us to do such a thing?"

"Easy for such men," Blue Feather explained calmly, standing with one hand low on his back and trying to straighten up. "Missy, you walk on me."

"What?" Beth asked, astonished.

"Help me to ground first, William," Blue Feather requested.

William looked at Beth. His own hands were beginning to shake a bit, but at the old Indian's insistence he took Blue Feather's arm and lowered him to the ground, where the old man lay face-downward, not three feet from one of the dead.

"Walk, missy," Blue Feather said. "Start at ass and walk to shoulder with feet on either side of spine."

"What on earth?" Beth asked, still angry. She had just killed two men. Their blood still oozed from their wounds.

"Do as he says," William told her, taking her arm and helping her to balance as she stepped onto Blue Feather's withered rump. The buttocks under her moccasins were surprisingly firm. She moved her feet minutely, walking slowly up, placing her weight carefully, her feet on either side of Blue Feather's bony spine. When she had her weight fully on his shoulders she heard a loud crack and a sigh of relief from Blue Feather.

"Enough," he said.

She stepped off, and the old Indian leapt lightly to his feet and ran to jerk his knife from the chest of the big man and with one deft swipe took the man's scalp. Beth gasped and almost fainted. William caught her and she watched, horrified, as Blue Feather quickly took the other scalps and strung them onto a forked stick to dry.

"We move camp," Blue Feather ordered. "Can't sleep with this stink."

"We'll have to bury these fellows," William said, just beginning to be able to control his voice.

"We move," Blue Feather ordered. "More men back there on stream."

"Shame," William said as he led his horse out of the clearing, Beth ahead of him. "Even they deserve a decent burial."

"They feed foxes," Blue Feather said. "Feed crows and buzzards, too. You want to stay and dig holes, fine. Be ready to entertain their friends if you do."

It was rough going in the dark. Now and then a horseshoe would strike fire from a rock. Horses stumbled. Beth fell more than once. The events that had taken place in the clearing happened again and again in her mind, and she began to weep. She thought she was making no sound, but Blue Feather was alerted, for he came to her side and said, "Those men are not worth your tears." At times he spoke like a white man, belying his usual abbreviated use of the English language. "They would have used you, and then they would have added your scalp to ours. Your hair, missy, would be the prize of any Indian's lodgepole." He chuckled. "As for me, missy, I prefer it right where it is, on your lovely head." And he reached behind her to give her a playful tweak on her rump before moving swiftly away. In spite of herself Beth giggled through her tears.

There was no stopping. Bruised and weary, they met a bleak, wet dawn and marched in the rain all day. Then the worst of the trip was behind them. The days passed swiftly, and before them was the town of Knoxville in the would-be state of Franklin.

It was a market day in the town, and the dirt streets were filled with movement. Painted Cherokee walked in twos and threes. Occasionally a Cherokee would prance past on a fine horse. White and Indian street urchins dashed back and forth. An Indian woman called out, displaying a basket of fine pecans.

"Get directions," Blue Feather said, detaching himself to head toward a group of Cherokee men.

"At least there aren't any widows with them," William said with a grin, just as a chubby, smiling Cherokee woman joined the group of men. But in spite of William's roll of eyes, the woman paid only the normal attention prompted by curiosity to Blue Feather, and he was back soon.

"We go," he said, pointing ahead.

Roy and Nora Johnson were at home, preparing for their trip to Renno's village. Roy quickly invited the three travelers in, smiled as Blue Feather accepted the offer of a drink of pure white homemade whiskey and downed three fingers from a glass at a gulp, and was full of curiosity about the pretty girl and her brother. He was told the details of their quest over dinner and after a significant glance at his wife admitted that, yes, he knew Renno, that the English visitors had been directed to the right place for information. He did not give any information, however, until he heard from William that Renno had been recommended by George Washington as a guide in a venture, had looked at George Washington's letter of introduction, and had asked countless questions about the Beaumont connection with the original white Indian. Only then did he tell them that he and his wife were going to Renno's village the very next day and would be happy to have company.

That night Beth and William slept in beds for the first time in months. Blue Feather thanked Johnson for his invitation but declined and went off. The next morning he was found sitting on a boardwalk, his feet crossed under him, smoking his pipe with that familiar contemplative and smug look on his face. A pretty Cherokee woman—William guessed that she was probably a widow—was waving to him as she walked away with a sad look on her pleasant face.

The three-day journey to Renno's village was a good one for Roy and Nora Johnson. They found William to be a fine conversationalist and Beth to be a lively, interesting person, in addition to being a pleasure to look at. Blue Feather, happy to have been able to replenish his drinking supply with jars full of the Johnsons' potent frontier corn liquor, quite often burst into song. He was carrying the six fresh scalps on the forked stick stuck into the pommel of his saddle, for he rode now that he had a guide in Roy Johnson.

Beth saw the joined Cherokee-Seneca villages from the top of a ridge and felt a surge of joy at the beauty of the setting. As they rode down the trail they were spotted by a group of young boys, who surrounded them with great whoops and carried out a mock attack. When one fired an imaginary arrow at Blue Feather, the old Indian screamed in agony and pitched forward over his horse's neck, to the delight of the young would-be warriors.

The village did not as a rule have many white visitors. As the four riders and the pack animals entered, the villagers began to line the route toward the center compound. Many called out greetings to Roy and Nora Johnson, which they returned. Black-haired Indian women smiled and pointed admiringly toward Beth's red hair. Blue Feather had dismounted and was now leading the way. As it happened, Ena was visiting Emily as the visitors arrived. She followed Renno and Emily out of the lodge to see what the commotion was about and smiled a great smile when she saw the bony, thin old man who was leading the way. She pushed past Renno and ran to throw her arms around Blue Feather as Nora went quickly to Emily's lodge to see her daughter and grandson.

"You old goat!" she said. "You have not traveled to the resting place of our ancestors yet?"

William grinned at Beth with a raised eyebrow. "Here too," he said, amazed. "That old lech gets around."

Beth had eyes only for the man and woman who stood in upright dignity before the door of a large, well-built lodge, where Nora had gone inside. The woman was obviously white, the man only slightly darker. And he was by far the most charismatic man she had ever seen, proud and tall and sturdy, with blue eyes that had, as he drew near, the look of eagles.

"We come with a letter from George Washington,"

Blue Feather announced, having disengaged himself from Ena's arms.

"You are welcome to my country, to my village, and to my home," Renno said ceremoniously after glancing at the letter.

Blue Feather made flowery introductions in Cherokee. Renno stood patiently, for he, too, knew the old man from the War for Independence, when Blue Feather had been one of Washington's finest scouts. He felt that Blue Feather deserved his moment, for he had traveled far and had brought his charges safely. But as the old man talked on and on, Renno smiled, put his hand on Blue Feather's shoulder, and said, "Thank you, my old friend, but now you need rest." He leaned close and whispered, "I'm afraid there's nothing to drink but barley beer."

"I come prepared," Blue Feather responded, thinking of the jars of corn liquor on a pack animal. He looked around. He had heard of the Chickasaw war and knew that the village would have many widows. His responsibility was finished, and he was content.

"Please come in," Emily said, walking to take Beth's hand. "You must be weary. My mother tells me you've come all the way from Virginia."

Renno was reading the letter from George Washington. Finished, he handed the letter back to William and said, "General Washington requests that I give ear to your plan. It is my pleasure. First, however, you will want to refresh yourselves and rest. You will be my guests for the evening meal."

He watched the flame-haired one—*the flame-haired one is the future*—enter his lodge with Emily. First he directed William to a guest lodge and detailed two young widows to serve his needs. Then he walked swiftly out of the village and sought the nearby forest. *Trust the white one*. It had come. Whatever was to be would be.

Beth was surprised by the quality of the food. She could not understand how Emily could turn out such delicious dishes with nothing more than a few basic utensils and a cookfire. During the journey from Knoxville, Nora had told her about Emily, but Beth was nonetheless enchanted by the pretty, fair-haired woman, and so full of curiosity that she could scarcely contain herself. But she had little chance to talk with Emily—the men dominated the talk, for Renno had invited the important men of his tribe and of the Cherokee.

Rusog was there, and El-i-chi, and Casno, the medicine man of the Seneca, and the old Cherokee chief Loramas, who had married Renno's grandmother. The men could not get enough of William's tales of England and the crossing and the long trek from northern Virginia. They had questions about everything, about the big waters, the state of affairs in that part of the United States traveled by William and Beth, the differences between English weapons and their own. And they were silent, grunting only in appreciation as William told once more the tale of the original Renno's exploits of arms at the court of William and Mary.

The evening ended too soon. And the morning found the men gathered in the council house, with all the beloved men—the elders of both tribes—present, the place jammed with them and with senior warriors. There was much ceremony and many speeches, with all of the elders expecting their turn to express their pleasure at the visit of an illustrious baron from far England. William was biding his time, for he had no intention of blurting out his plan to so many. When the oratory was at last over and the pipe had been passed it was finally time to hand out his gifts.

"My father, the viscount of Beaumont, has sent tribute to the great sachem of the Seneca," he said. "May they now be presented?"

Renno nodded. Young warriors were drafted to carry four large packs into the council house. From the packs William took two matched muskets, both with stocks of engraved silver. He laid them ceremoniously at Renno's feet. Renno examined the weapons with great admiration, then passed them around the circle of men, to admiring grunts and comments. Two pistols, equally fine, were next. Renno could not have been more pleased. He hefted the pistols, smiling his appreciation as he examined the powder bag and priming rod that came with them.

"I have gifts for the lady, as well," William said, "and one final gift for the sachem that I will save for the last."

Emily wept with gladness as her gifts were presented outside, so that all the village might see. First there was a set of twelve fine crystal goblets, they having made the long trip miraculously unbroken, packed in containers filled with straw. Then there was a set of silver flatware, and cooking utensils. And for the villagers, William and Beth brought out small bolts of fine cloth, sparkling beads, scarves, and pocketknives. It was a gala time, and William had made certain that everyone present received some small gift.

The ceremony took most of the day. At last William was alone with Renno, in Renno's lodge, the women having gone to the nearby stream to take advantage of the warming weather for a bath.

"You have brought me much," Renno said as he seated himself facing the Englishman. "The weapons are the finest I've seen, and you have brought great pleasure to all with your generosity. I am in your debt, and I have been asked by General Washington to listen to you. Are you ready to speak?"

William began tentatively but gained confidence as he showed Renno the map marking the hiding place of the gold. He spoke confidently, and he was pleased when he saw a gleam of interest in Renno's blue eyes. Renno listened patiently to the end, then asked a few questions. He leaned back, closed his eyes, and was silent for a moment. *Trust the white one.* Gold would indeed be of use to his tribe. There was a need for weapons. But above all, Renno knew that gold was security and power, which might be needed in the future to ensure the independence and prosperity of his people.

"We would travel far," he said after a long silence, "into lands known by no man here." And, saying it, he felt a small thrill.

"It is far," William conceded.

"I cannot take a large number of men, for we lost many warriors when we fought the Chickasaw."

"I had thought, Sachem, that a small group, moving swiftly, would be best."

"Perhaps," Renno agreed.

"You will go, then?" William asked, then held his breath.

Renno's first thought was that he would consult the manitous, but then he realized that he had already received their advice. "I will go," he said.

"Excellent!" William exclaimed, leaping to his feet. "If you have the patience, Sachem, there is that one more gift I mentioned."

"Please call me Renno." He rose, motioned William ahead of him into the late-afternoon sun. William soon had a leather case from a pack and looked around.

"I think, Sach . . . Renno, that up there would be a fine place to demonstrate your gift."

They walked together into the woods, where William removed an English longbow and several finely made arrows from the leather case. "My father insisted that I bring you this," he said, handing the bow to Renno.

Renno strung the bow, his muscles bulging. William nodded in approval; not every man was strong enough to string a longbow. Then Renno fingered an arrow, admired its weight—much heavier than one of his own arrows— and put a testing finger on the honed metal tip.

"I saw your own bow hanging on the wall in your lodge," William said.

"It is not like this," Renno mused, testing the pull of the bow.

"Long ago the wars in Europe were fought by men in heavy metal armor," William said. "They fought as armored cavalry. War was a simple thing. The army with the largest number of armored cavalry won, for no one could stand against an armored cavalry charge. But England was a poor country, and so we had to develop a weapon to substitute for large numbers of knights in armor. Thus was the longbow developed. The art of the longbow is a difficult one and was never learned by our enemies. The knack of sending an arrow through armor was an English monopoly for a century, and saved us our nation."

"*Ummm*," Renno murmured, placing an arrow, lifting the thick, strong longbow, and with one swift motion drawing and firing an arrow straight and true to pierce all the way through a three-inch sapling a hundred feet away.

William's eyes went wide. "I say!" he said.

"I shot too high," Renno mused, reaching for another arrow. "I expected more of a drop in the arrow's flight.

"Two hands' span below the arrow," Renno said as he drew, aimed, and fired in the same motion. The arrow *thunked* through the sapling about a foot below the other arrow. "A fine gift," he said, smiling genuinely. "The finest of all, for it has the power to kill at a distance and in silence." He offered the bow to William.

William strung an arrow. "Between the two," he said, pulling and firing to see his arrow pierce the three-inch sapling equidistant from Renno's arrows. Renno clapped him on the shoulder. "Now I know I am right to say that I will go with you," he said.

Both had been intent on the shooting, but Renno had noticed the movement among the trees toward the village. He was watching out of the corner of his eye when Beth emerged from the trees, carrying a bow much like the one William had presented to him.

"Ah," she said, "I saw you two gentlemen leave the village with the case, and it is as I suspected." She stepped to Renno's side and nocked an arrow. "To the left of the middle arrow," she said, drawing and letting fly. The arrow's tip grazed the feathers of the arrow already in place and sent its barbed tip to emerge on the other side

71

of the sapling. "That's just in case, Brother, you have forgotten our agreement and are thinking of leaving me here with Chief Renno's wife, charming and dear though she is." And with those words she turned and walked proudly away.

"Sorry about that," William muttered.

Renno laughed. "It is a small world, and people are much alike," he said.

"What do you mean?"

"Even the English have their warrior maidens," he said.

William expected to see preparations begin immediately for their expedition. Instead, nothing seemed to happen. Indians, he was to find, were a patient, contemplative people. First there was a ceremonial meal in the lodge of Loramas, where an old woman of great beauty and dignity drew Beth toward her immediately. When Beth realized that Ah-wen-ga was Renno's grandmother, she encouraged the conversation around to talk of Renno's grandfather and great-grandfather, for she had been fascinated by the accounts of the original white Indian's feats of arms in England and wanted to hear more about him.

The next day Beth went along on an afternoon outing with some of the younger women, bathed in the still-icy stream, to emerge shivering and feeling very much alive. And so another day passed, and another evening attended by both Seneca and Cherokee with ceremonial dancing and singing in the village compound.

William was awakened early by the white Indian, before the sun on the next morning. He expected Renno to speak of the journey, but instead Renno said, "We hunt."

William was flattered to see that Renno carried the English longbow and a quiver of arrows and one of the fine muskets. Breakfast was a bowl of moistened, roasted corn, and then they were walked toward the outskirts of the village under the first light of the sun. Renno turned when he heard running steps behind them. It was the flame-haired one, graceful but looking somewhat bedraggled in her travel-worn doeskins.

"Please, may I go?" Beth asked, not looking at William but at Renno. She was carrying her own longbow.

"I saw you shoot," Renno said, turning and starting to walk again.

"Is that yes or no?" Beth called after them.

"Come," Renno said, and Beth ran to catch up.

By midday she was not sure coming along on the hunting trip had been a good idea. Although he walked, Renno set a fast pace, and the day was warming. A winter of hunting had made deer scarce near the Cherokee and Seneca villages, and it was midafternoon before Renno slowed the pace.

"It is necessary to be silent," he said. To his ears the progress of his two guests through the forest was a continuous thunder of small sounds. "Look first to choose placement of the feet. Later, you will find that the feet themselves have eyes. Stay poised on the balls of your feet. The normal heel-to-toe movement of walking is too noisy." He demonstrated. Both Beth and William found this to be quite an unnatural way of walking, and soon Beth's ankles were aching. Their progress was, however, less noisy.

It was impossible to say what alerted Renno to the presence of a deer. Suddenly he froze and, being a few paces in front, seemed to disappear, blending in with the flora that was just beginning to show spring buds. He turned and put his finger to his lips, then motioned to Beth to come forward. When she was looking over his shoulder, she saw nothing. He again put his finger to his lips and moved silently through the underbrush, Beth following. When he paused again he pointed to Beth's bow, made a motion to show her that she should nock an arrow.

In England, Beth had killed deer. They were not plentiful at Beaumont Hall, but she had been allowed to accompany her father on hunts, where the animals were more available. She had done her stag shooting, however, from comfortable stands, and with a musket. It was very different in the American forest, where the slightest careless movement might cause the crackling of a dead branch or the swish of the barren underbrush.

Renno pointed. Beth could barely see through the limbs and branches, but there, drinking from a small stream, were a buck and a doe. Renno moved aside. Realizing that she was expected to kill the buck, she took a deep breath, drew her bow, waited until the buck had raised his head to look around, and let the arrow sing through a small opening in the brush. The buck bounded only once, across the stream, landed with its legs weak and powerless, and was dead.

"Good shot!" William shouted, crashing forward through the brush, much to Renno's disgust.

Renno took out his elaborately decorated Spanish stiletto and slashed the buck's throat, hoisted the heavy animal upward to hang it by thongs from the tree limb so that it would bleed. He dipped two fingers into the gushing blood and smeared streaks of blood on Beth's forehead and cheeks. Her every impulse was to wipe it away, but she restrained herself.

When the buck was dressed but not skinned, Renno set off again. It took longer to bag a second buck. This time it was William who made the kill, with a musket, for Renno had directed him to circle the edge of a large meadow while he and Beth continued through the trees, causing three deer to go bounding ahead of them across a neck of the clearing to give William his shot. Then William too was blooded, and carrying a very sizable and surprisingly heavy dressed animal across his shoulders, with the blood of the animal running down his back, across the miles to the Cherokee-Seneca village.

Renno had had two reasons for taking William on the hunt, and his decision to allow Beth to accompany them had not been based merely on politeness. He had wanted to see how they conducted themselves in the wilderness and to test William's stamina. He had also wanted to lay in a supply of fresh venison for his family. Emily would, of course, be cared for during his absence, but it would be good to leave her with a fresh supply of meat.

Renno, carrying the larger of the slain deer, moved as swiftly as he had walked without a burden. The sun fell behind the western horizon, but there was still some distance to go before they would reach the village. By that time William was thinking that it would be impossible to take another step. Beth, walking behind or beside him, saw that he was very tired, but she knew that he was being tested and that it would be ill-advised to call a halt. By the time they saw the fires of the villages, every bone in William's body felt like jelly and his muscles were liquid fire, but he staggered on, panting from the effort. Renno seemed not to notice.

At last they reached the compound in front of Renno's lodge. People gathered to make admiring comments on the kill, and El-i-chi took the buck from William's shoulders—much to William's relief—but still he would not obey his body's command to collapse, for Renno and El-i-chi were hanging the deer and skinning them. It was Emily who saved William's life by pulling both him and his sister away, saying, "Come. Wash. We will eat soon."

Left alone with Renno, El-i-chi finished skinning the smaller deer before Renno, who was working slowly and deliberately. The skins would replace those that were being used to make new clothing for William and Beth.

El-i-chi had not yet been informed of the plan to travel farther to the west than any Seneca or Cherokee, or, perhaps, any man east of the Mississippi. He knew that the coming of the whites had something to do with Renno's request that he delay his trip with Holani to the land of the Chickasaw, and he was full of curiosity.

"The flame-haired one shoots well with the longbow," Renno remarked after working for a long time in silence.

"This one," El-i-chi said admiringly, "the arrow was directly in the heart."

"You will shoot with my longbow," Renno said.

"It will please me."

"It is more powerful than our bows."

"But the musket reaches out farther to kill."

"The longbow, or our bow, fires several arrows while one reloads a musket," Renno said.

"The English are here only to hunt?" El-i-chi asked, unwilling to avoid the main question longer.

"To hunt, but not for food," Renno confirmed.

"Rusog buys horses," El-i-chi commented. "Many horses. Strong."

"Yes," Renno said, "it is time. My thinking is done." He cleaned his knife by thrusting it into the ground, then wiping away the dirt with his hand. "I had thought to order you to accompany me far to the west, my brother. In thinking, I know that I am not being fair. You have your compact with the girl. You are free to keep it."

"The English go west with you?"

"They, and only a few. Myself and three warriors."

"To the big river?"

"Far beyond. Into the lands of the Spanish."

"I will go," El-i-chi said.

"I give you the choice . . ." Renno told him.

"And it is made."

"Good," Renno said, clasping El-i-chi's hand and forearm, both their hands still bloody.

El-i-chi needed to ask no more questions. His chief, and his brother, had spoken, and in time he would speak further of the destination and the purpose. El-i-chi's heart beat hard as he thought of the coming adventure. Beyond the big river? Unable to contain his excitement, El-i-chi suddenly vented a great whoop. Renno smiled, the smile unseen in the darkness. Emily stuck her head out the door and called, "What's going on out there? The food is ready. El-i-chi, you'd better eat with us."

Roy and Nora Johnson had been spending their time playing with their grandson and visiting with Emily while Renno, Beth, and William had been hunting. The lodge was crowded for the meal, but it was a congenial group and the talk pleasant, even if Renno seemed at times a bit preoccupied.

Rusog brought the horses the next morning. It was then that William first realized that Renno had attended to preparations for the expedition, for the animals were strongly built and chosen for endurance, not for speed. Beth examined the teeth of a couple of the animals, handling the half-wild beasts with skill and a confidence that soon had them docile under her hands. Rusog was all curiosity too. He found a way to get Renno alone while the Seneca widows who had been detailed by Renno to make new clothing were doing the final fittings on Beth and William.

"My brother is silent as to his plans for these animals," Rusog said, raising an eyebrow.

"I will be gone long," Renno replied. "I have not spoken to my brother about coming with me because our people must not be left leaderless in my absence."

"There is peace," Rusog said. "My grandfather, Loramas, is well. The Seneca have Casno, and there are the beloved men to help with any decision. My feet itch with the urge to travel, Brother. It is my thought that you might need the strong arm of your brother."

"There is no other I would rather have at my side," Renno said.

"Then it is settled."

"What is settled?" Ena asked, having come up to hear just the last.

Renno grinned. "It is a matter among men."

Ena made a face. "It is obvious, Brother, that you are going on a journey with the English people. Don't think for one minute that you're going to take my husband without taking me."

"I would not even consider such a possibility," Renno said. He valued the wilderness and warlike skills of his fiery sister only slightly less than those of El-i-chi and Rusog.

The number of those who would accompany him was

growing: he, El-i-chi, William, Beth, Rusog, and Ena. His agreement to allow Ena to go along was not without consideration, for Rusog had been among his very first choices from the beginning, and having Ena along would give Beth the company of another woman. Moreover, having women in the group would be a clear sign to any tribes encountered along the way that he was not leading a war party.

Renno needed only one more warrior to make up the group of seven he had in mind. He walked through the Cherokee village, where he found Blue Feather seated on a pile of soft skins in front of a lodge, one pretty young widow offering him something from a dish, another holding a gourd cup, most probably filled with rum. Blue Feather waved at Renno with a contented smile as he approached.

"I am glad you have made friends in our village," Renno commented wryly.

Blue Feather made shooing motions, and the two young widows vanished into the lodge. "Why did Rusog buy horses?"

"For the English people's journey," Renno explained.

"So soon back east?"

"West," the white Indian said.

"They are going back home?"

"No," he said.

"Then my job is not done." He rose, and Renno actually thought he heard a creaking of bone. "When do we leave?" Blue Feather asked, to Renno's smile.

There was to be one further addition to the travel party. El-i-chi, with a mixture of anticipation for the journey and sadness because of Holani, asked Renno if the Chickasaw girl might travel with them only as far as the land of her people. There she would remain until the travelers returned.

Chapter V

Now the preparations were made. On his last night at home Renno sat beside the fire, Little Hawk trying to pluck the Spanish stiletto from its sheath. Emily was sewing a new doeskin shirt for the boy. She could see her own sadness mirrored in her husband's eyes.

"Don't be concerned about me," she said. "What you're going to do frightens me, but it's a worthy cause, Renno. Lord knows we ourselves could use some gold, and it will do the people much good."

"I will not be here when our daughter is born," Renno said, for they had come to agreement that having a little girl would be a great gift.

"Ah-wen-ga and Toshabe will take good care of me,"

she assured him. "And my father and mother are going to stay on for a few weeks."

"That is good for you to have them here," he agreed.

Emily mused. "If I weren't pregnant, would you take me with you?"

Renno laughed and put his hand on her arm. "You are a good wife, and strong."

· "That's not an answer," she said. "Oh, I know that Ena can fight better than most men and can run all day and has eyes like an eagle and that the English girl can use a longbow and that she killed two men back in the mountains. But I've become a pretty good Indian wife, haven't I?"

"The best wife," Renno assured her. "Yes, I would take you with me, for we go not to fight. With women along, we tell those we meet that we come in peace, not in war."

"She's very pretty," Emily said.

"Ena?"

"No, you goose. You know who I mean."

"She *is* pretty. She will go back to England with her gold and marry a rich man of great property."

Emily smiled. "I'll tell Ena to watch you very closely."

He laughed. "The old man will do the romancing, if there is any."

"I'm teasing, you know," Emily said.

Renno looked down. Little Hawk had tired of playing with the exposed hilt of the stiletto and had fallen asleep with his head on Renno's knee. He picked the boy up and put him in his bed and then sat beside Emily.

"I will think of you often, and each night, when the darkness has come and I am in my blankets, I will picture you here, and you will think of me, and in that way we will be together."

Emily wept silently, and when they were in bed she clung to him long after he was asleep.

*　　*　　*

There was a general turnout, for the word had spread that the chiefs of the two tribes were leaving on an ambitious journey with the white foreigners. The leave-taking was without ceremony or overt emotion. Renno had said his good-byes the night before. Now he gave Emily and his son one final salute and turned his face to the west.

With the exception of Holani, who would be traveling with them only for a few days, each member of the group had two horses. William, who had thought that he and Beth had traveled light on the trip from Virginia, was still musing about the sparsity of items selected by Renno for each of them. Renno, Rusog, and El-i-chi carried their weaponry upon their persons, with balls and powder in the light packs carried by the spare horses. The packs also contained pemmican, jerky, and the chewy Cherokee concoction made mostly of ground nuts. Beth's pack had spare items of clothing, and atop each pack were spread warm skins in case the weather turned cold. Each rider carried his bedroll on the horse he was riding, the blankets and skins rolled neatly, and in the case of William and Beth, lashed behind their saddles. The Indians had no saddles, only blankets. It was evident that Renno planned to live off the land. Leather flasks for holding water were not even filled as they departed.

William had long since wrapped the precious map, their only clue to their far destination, in a piece of oilskin as protection from the elements. He carried the map on his person, and he had a small compass on a leather thong around his neck.

As the troop reached the outskirts of the village, Renno swiveled on his horse to look back one last time. Around him small boys were waving good-bye. Behind him those who had been in the compound to watch their departure were already going about their business, with the exception of Emily, who stood with Little Hawk in her arms. She faced him from the center of the village square, her head high, her light hair gleaming in the early-morning sun. She lifted one of Little Hawk's hands to wave at his father, and Renno lifted his own hand. And at that moment one of the more mournful sounds of the wilderness came to him, from quite near, surprisingly near. It was the long, drawn-out, eerie howl of a lonely wolf. It was very unusual for a wolf to be so near the village. A sense of foreboding came to Renno, but he waved to his son, told himself that it was only a wolf, and smiled as he saw a group of adolescent boys, bows in hand, dash from the village in the direction of the lonely howling.

Somehow the word of their journey had already spread throughout the Cherokee nation, and as they passed Cherokee villages the group was greeted by the local chiefs and elders. William felt too much time was wasted in ceremonial dining and oratory. But Renno soon eased William's mind about their slow progress by saying, as he pointed to the mountains, "The snows are melting. Rivers are in flood."

Because of the visits to various villages, it was several nights before the group made a camp in the wilderness. They were still well within the peaceful area of Cherokee control, and their successful war against the Chickasaw had worked to keep that warlike tribe at bay. So far Oklawahpa, the Chickasaw war chief, was keeping his end of the peace treaty, and there had been no Chickasaw raiding parties active in Cherokee lands. The Choctaw to the south, much impressed by the Cherokee victory over one of the most warlike and skillful tribes in the United States, also refrained from sending their inexperienced young warriors into Cherokee territory to be blooded.

Wildlife was becoming plentiful. When Beth saw her first opossum, she had to laugh at the ungainly, stupid-looking animal.

"Very fat," Blue Feather said about the opossum. "If you eat it in cold weather, it gives much energy." But their fresh meat consisted of rabbits, turkey, and once they were beyond the villages of the Cherokee, venison.

Spring was beginning to be serious about its annual work now, and the farther they traveled, the greener the hardwoods became. The new growth was jewellike, sparkling in the sun. A profusion of wildflowers grew in open areas. Various migrating songbirds had begun to move back toward the north, plus vast flocks of robins, passenger pigeons, and many small, twittering birds.

Now Renno became the guide, and he set a steady, mile-covering pace designed not to overtire the horses. It had been months since he had last traveled west, but his memory for landmarks and the lay of the land led him unerringly toward the first scattered outposts of the Chickasaw.

Each morning the Indian men, including Renno, spent a few minutes in applying their paint. Questioning Ena about this custom, Beth learned that there was a pattern of paint for every purpose. El-i-chi, Rusog, and Blue Feather applied paint that identified their tribal affiliation, while Renno's face was also decorated with the distinctive pattern of a medicine man. As sachem of the Seneca, he was automatically a member of the False Face Society and an honorary medicine man, so he was well within his rights. His paint, and the paint of the other three, was another sign to any Indian encountered that their mission was a peaceful one.

Holani, who had ridden beside or behind El-i-chi, began to recognize distant ridges as landmarks, and her emotions, which had not been quiet since she had given herself to El-i-chi, made her moodier and even more silent than she had been during the entire early part of the journey. While it was true that she needed to know the exact fate of her family, somehow she knew and accepted that those who had been closest to her had indeed died in the Seneca raid on her village. It all had happened, it seemed to her, a long time ago, and her hatred for those who had burst upon the village in the dark of night had cooled. Death, raiding, and war—all were a part of life. She could never remember a time when someone in the village was not mourning the death of a warrior.

She told herself that it was not the fault of the strong,

handsome young warrior who rode before or beside her that things were the way they were. Chickasaw—mostly small groups of young, ambitious warriors—were always ready to make war, raiding tribes to the west, north, and south. And she herself had heard the talk of the bearded Spaniard who had promised the Chickasaw all of the Cherokee lands, so she had come to agree with El-i-chi that it had been the Chickasaw, urged on by the Spaniard, who had started the war that resulted in the destruction of her village.

Yet she was Chickasaw. That was her blood, and she should have hated the man who had captured her. But he had been so kind, even though it was within his rights to take her anytime he wanted her, for she was a captive. She could have become a slave, doing the work for the old women of the Seneca village. Instead he had treated her with every consideration, sometimes to the tune of laughter, as other warriors said behind his back—never to his face, for he *was* El-i-chi—that he was soft, that the Chickasaw girl had bewitched him into making a courtship like that of the white man, who let his woman lead him around by the nose.

There were times when she wanted to tell El-i-chi that she had reconsidered, that she would ride back alone to the village to await his return, but she was proud, and she harbored the hope that some of her kin had escaped on that night. It would be sweet, for example, to see her mother's sister, her nearest kin, the woman who had raised her.

When she questioned El-i-chi regarding the length of time he would be gone, he could only shrug. "We go where the mountains are dry and rainless," he said, and she could not imagine a place so distant. He would be gone many moons, and she would be among the Chickasaw, people who had, in the time she had spent in the Seneca camp, become like strangers.

This was her mood when Renno led them to the location of her village. He remembered it well. He had scouted the entire area himself, and he had planned and led the attack. The stream was there, and there were mounds of debris under dead grass, and the beginnings of new grass where the lodges had stood. The village had not been rebuilt, for the deaths there had made it a place of evil spirits.

At the next Chickasaw village they were greeted with surly suspicion. Holani spoke to the village chief, who, learning that she was Chickasaw, became more open. She quickly learned that her mother's sister had indeed survived the raid, for Renno had not made war on women and children, but the woman had died three moons before, of the winter fever. The woman's warrior sons had died during the raid, and Holani's father's brother and his one son had been killed during the war.

There was no offer of hospitality from the Chickasaw, only a grudging consent to let them pass protected under the treaty with Oklawahpa, and as peaceful travelers with women in the group.

Holani was faced with a problem that touched both El-i-chi and Renno. The people of her former village were dead or scattered. She was a stranger in her own land, and the more she thought about being alone in the village of strangers for many moons, the less attractive the prospect became.

When they made camp that night, after she had learned the fate of those she knew, she could not eat. She eased out of the light of the campfire and sought solitude a few yards away from the fire, among large, sheltering trees, and there she spread her blankets and skins. She had no hope of going to sleep, but she needed to be alone to think out her situation. When she heard someone approaching, deliberately making noise so that she would not be surprised, she sat up to see the familiar and suddenly very dear form of El-i-chi. He squatted beside her, a chunk of roasted venison in his hand.

"You did not eat," he remarked.

"No."

"You will be hungry later," he said, and she took the meat and stuck the stick on which it was impaled into the ground beside her.

El-i-chi rose and turned to go. She took a deep breath, let it out without speaking her desires, and saw him fade into the darkness before she called his name. He came to squat beside her again, and she did a very hard thing. "I have been wrong," she whispered. El-i-chi's heart leapt. "All day, as I rode behind you, I looked at you," she said. "And I see you."

Now, he thought bitterly, it was too late, for he would have to leave her in some Chickasaw village, perhaps at Chickasaw Bluffs, on the Mississippi.

"You have always been in my eyes," he said.

Beth enjoyed the evening meal beside the campfire. Blue Feather, their self-appointed cook, worked magic, as usual. Ena, who had a special fondness for the old man, liked to recall the times of war, when both she and Blue Feather had acted as scouts against the British. Rusog liked to hear both William and Beth speak of England. The talk was good, and when it turned to abstract ideas, both the English people were surprised by the depth of Renno's knowledge of men, politics, war, and the human condition. It was almost as if he himself had traveled the world. When he confessed that he had, but only through the books brought into his home by his wife, that seemed to be even more impressive.

"It's quite admirable," William commended, "that you and the Cherokee have come to work so closely with the people of Franklin."

"It is in the best interests of both peoples," Renno answered. "We have much to learn from each other."

"There are times when I wonder," Rusog said.

William had noted, in early conversations, that Rusog was not a total admirer of the white settlers and their ways.

"What are your reservations?" William asked.

Rusog had only been learning to speak English in recent months from Emily and Renno, so his command of the language was not as polished as that of his wife and companions. "I recall a Cherokee fable," Rusog said. "A warrior come back from hunt with quail. See small, pretty snake beside trail, see that snake brother is hungry, give quail. Few days later warrior come back from hunt with rabbits, see pretty little snake, bigger, still hungry, give rabbit. Few days later come back from hunt with turkey, see pretty little snake, still bigger, give turkey. Few days later come back from hunt with two deer, see pretty little snake no longer little, give whole deer to snake brother because he is hungry. Few days later pretty little snake so big it coils around whole village and is still hungry."

"I think I see," Beth said. "You're comparing the pretty little snake with the white man."

"I am Mohawk," Blue Feather interjected. "And I ask, where are my people who once were as many as the leaves of the trees? I ask, where are the Pequot? Where are the Narraganset? Where are the Mohican and the Pokanoket?"

William looked puzzled until Renno said, "All are tribes that have more or less vanished before the white settlement."

"As the snow under a summer sun," Rusog added. "Pretty little snake eats land. Does not know that the land belongs to no man. All land belonged to the Indian, all the children of the same parents, and they were put on the land to travel over it, to live on its game and its fruits, or to fill it with happy people, all with an equal right to the land. The land belongs to all for the use of each. No man has the right to sell the land, not to another Indian, not to strangers."

"That is the talk of an old one," Renno said gently. "Things change. We will change with the times."

"Isn't that why you're going with us?" Beth asked. "For the gold?"

"I have wondered about that myself," Ena admitted.

"What use have we for gold? We grow or hunt for everything we need."

There was to be no answer to that question, for at that time there came a soft, low cry that had different effects on those seated around the fire. Beth leapt to her feet. "What's that?" she asked, thinking that something had happened to one of those missing from the fire, El-i-chi or Holani. Blue Feather chuckled, and William's face turned red, for all had recognized the nature of the cry except the innocent Beth.

"It is nothing," Renno said.

"But I heard—"

"Oh, Beth, do sit down," William insisted, his face still red.

Renno began talking again to cover the moment of embarrassment. He would, he concluded quickly, have to warn El-i-chi and Holani to pitch their blankets at a greater distance from the main group, for it was evident that the two young ones had once again discovered the joys of being one. And there was a new problem for him to consider: he had noted Holani's reactions when she discovered that she was the last of her family alive, and he knew that El-i-chi would be coming to him soon to ask permission to take Holani with them on their quest for gold.

El-i-chi did not prove Renno's guess wrong. He waited until they had stopped beside a stream to refresh themselves, water the horses, and take a midday meal. "She knows no one here," El-i-chi said, having come to Renno when he was standing alone.

"A sensible one would have guessed that," Renno replied.

"She cannot travel alone back to our village."

"No."

"We are one, at last," El-i-chi said. "I would take her with us."

"We will need an extra horse," Renno said simply.

The journey to the Father of Waters, the Mississippi

River, was made through familiar territory, land Renno had scouted, land on which he had fought the previous year. At the tribal settlement called Chickasaw Bluffs they found Oklawahpa living in a lodge made from the timbers of the Spanish fort that had been under construction on the Mississippi during the Chickasaw war, and Renno was both surprised and pleased by the cordiality of the war chief's welcome. There were, of course, a ceremonial feast and much oratory. Chickasaw were like Cherokee and Seneca in their love for talk, giving the lie to William's notion of American Indians as a stoic, impassive, and silent breed.

There were those in Chickasaw Bluffs who had journeyed west across the Mississippi. In the flatlands just across the river were the Quapaw, old enemies of the Chickasaw, and beyond the Quapaw tribe, the Natchitoches. Chickasaw warriors had raided into the lands of both tribes, so some solid information was available, but the areas beyond the land of the Natchitoches were a fabled land of great, grassy expanses. There antelope ran swifter than the flight of the eagle, and odd sheeplike animals with huge curved horns could climb sheer rock faces.

"The dry mountains?" Renno asked each man who spoke of the land beyond the river, and in each case he received blank looks and a negative shake of the head.

As usual, Blue Feather disappeared soon after they had been welcomed to the Chickasaw town. He was located late the next day by William, lounging in the warm spring sun in front of a collapsing lodge. The woman who was passing food to him was short, squat, chubby, and not nearly as pretty as the women the old man usually found.

"Was going to come to you," Blue Feather said, "with this one."

William looked more closely at the woman, and she simpered coyly. He had been picking up phrases and words in the Indian language and he spoke cordially to the woman. She looked at him blankly.

"She does not speak Cherokee," Blue Feather explained. "Nor Chickasaw."

"What does she speak?" William asked.

Blue Feather shrugged. "Only one language important between man and woman anyhow."

The woman said in Spanish, "I have food for you."

"Thank you," William answered in Spanish. "I have eaten. You're not Spanish."

The woman spat into the dirt at the word. "Hairy-faced ones took me from my tribe to bring me here to work for them."

"And what is your tribe?" William asked.

"I am of the free people," the woman answered. "Across the big river and far to the south and west, where the grass grows to here." She indicated a height at her waist. "Where the buffalo number more than the drops of a summer rain."

William dug out his map, and the woman looked at it blankly. "Here we are," he said, "at Chickasaw Bluffs. Here is the big river. Here are the unknown areas to the southwest. Where are the free people?"

"I know nothing of your white man's scribblings," the woman said contemptuously. "My people far away."

"Blue Feather," William said, "could you possibly bring this woman to talk with Renno?"

"She will do as I say," the old man said, rising, speaking harshly in some Indian language, but speaking more emphatically with the flat of his hand on the woman's rump. She followed docilely as they walked to the lodge where Renno was resting.

Renno's interest was aroused immediately. Through William he asked questions of the woman. She could not be more definite about the location of the land of the free people, but through careful questioning they did learn that she had been captured by a Spanish slaving party in an area of open plains and taken south to a place where there were many of the white ones with hairy faces, then to the big river and to the north. She had been a slave to the Spanish, who had come with horses, long sticks with pointed heads, and thunder guns, the fieldpieces that El-i-chi had turned on the Spaniards and the Chickasaw in the climactic battle of the Chickasaw war.

"Ask her," Renno said, "about the dry mountains."

The woman listened, then spat. "In dry mountains, Apache." She spat again, as if to clean her mouth of a hated word.

"Are the Apache great warriors?" William asked.

"Fight well, but not as great as free people," the woman replied. "We drive them into the dry mountains from the grasslands, where buffalo are plentiful."

"Are the free people great warriors?" William asked.

"Ride like the wind, kill all," she said proudly. "Kill hairy faces, too, but they are many."

"Would they be friendly to travelers who come in peace?" Renno had William ask.

The woman shrugged. She looked at William's white face, touched it with a plump finger. "The free people do not like whites," she said. "You, Indian, come in peace, perhaps go in peace. But this one?" She shrugged.

"Perhaps," William said facetiously, "I can dye my face red."

"Don't rule out the idea," Renno said. "Ask her how far from her home to the dry mountains."

"Many moons," was the only answer the woman could give.

William had one more question. "You speak Spanish. Do the free people speak it as well, perhaps in order to trade with the Spanish?"

"Some," she answered. "Most Apache speak Spanish." She spat again.

Alone with Renno, William laughed. "At least there are no tales of dragons out there. Only the world's fiercest warriors, who kill every white man. Luckily, I'll be able to talk to them. Funny, I thought I'd never have a chance to use my Spanish, thought I'd wasted time studying it, since we don't seem to be able to strike up a nice little war against them these days."

"I will learn this Spanish as well," Renno said.

"Good idea, old man," William said, giving Renno a friendly slap on the shoulder. "Let us begin now. The word for 'to eat' is *comer*,' and that I am ready to do."

The Mississippi had passed its highest spring flood stage, but far across the river one could see that the flatlands were still half-covered with water and that the mud left by the floods would be a problem to all travelers. A few miles downstream, however, the Chickasaw had established a canoe crossing to an area of higher ground with trails leading past the riverside flatlands.

A few items from William's bag of trade goods had acquired an extra horse as a spare for Holani. A few more trade items secured the aid of Chickasaw boatmen. The crossing was not without its dangers, for the horses had to be forced to swim a great distance against strong current. First the women were taken across in canoes. Then the horses were tied by ropes to large two-man canoes and forced, whinnying and protesting, into the muddy water along the eastern bank. Eight trips were required to get the horses across, and that operation used up most of a day, with the only incident taking place as the last pair of horses was being transferred: Renno was riding in the canoe with the two Chickasaw boatmen when a carelessly tied knot came loose and one horse was freed. It immediately took the course of least resistance and began to swim with the strong current. Renno, without hesitation, dived into the water and, swimming strongly, caught the horse's tail. He reached forward to prod it in the side and push its head toward the western bank, urging the horse slowly in the right direction.

He was, however, swept far downstream before the horse's hooves began to touch the soft mud near the shore, and it took him a full hour to find a way through the riverside swamps back to high land, where he was being awaited anxiously by the rest of his party.

Meanwhile, the last of the weapons and supplies had been ferried across, and since it was late, they made camp beside the river, although Renno would have preferred to have put some distance between them and the Chickasaw boatmen, who were a surly, almost hostile lot. He and El-i-chi alternated watch during the night and kept a fire going. Their vigil prevented any incident.

The rains of April were late in that mid-Mississippi country, but they caught up with the travelers a half-day's journey from the river to keep them wet, off and on, for days.

Throughout the journey, Renno had taken every opportunity, without being too obvious about it, to teach wilderness skills to Beth and William. He had found both to be eager, receptive students and was pleased with their progress. Now it was time for him to be the student. He asked William to teach him Spanish so that he might be able to speak with the peoples of the Southwest.

William sighed. "I never was much of an instructor, old boy," he said, "but Beth is a paragon of patience, and she's quite good at languages."

Beth was only too happy to help. She wished she had books and writing materials, but that could not be helped, so she set about teaching Renno a basic vocabulary and was pleased to find that he had an excellent memory and a knack for mimicry. By the time the late-April rains ceased to be an almost daily event and they were well away from the river, Renno was conversing in rudimentary Spanish, taking every opportunity to learn more. Thus it was that he was often riding at Beth's side during the day, with either El-i-chi or Rusog scouting, and at night, instead of joining in the nightly conversations, he and Beth would be aside, sometimes with their own fire, discussing the peculiar conjugation of Spanish verbs. This made for a definite splintering of the group, for El-i-chi and Holani, still so new at oneness, disappeared at first dark, to be seen not at all until the next morning.

Emily, of course, had not followed through on her teasing threat to ask her sister-in-law to keep an eye on Renno and the flame-haired Englishwoman. Nevertheless, Ena could not fail to note Renno's constant companionship with Beth. She thought that Beth's laughter, ringing out throatily in the evening as the two of them studied Spanish, was not consistent with learning a new language. In her mind, two people who spoke the language were enough, and she did not understand why Renno had to learn the language as well.

"Keep your peace," Rusog told her roughly one night when she commented, with obvious displeasure, on the time Renno was spending with Beth.

"Renno is a man alone, without his wife. The young lovers"—she said it with amused contempt—"steam the very air with their passions. I do not blame Renno."

"Renno is a man of honor," Rusog reminded her.

"My brother is a handsome man," Ena said, "and the flame-haired one is much woman."

The next day an interruption in routine took Ena's mind off the matter, for the trails showed signs of being well-traveled. There were patches of cultivated land now, and soon they would have their first encounter with the Quapaw. There seemed to be no avoiding it, for the signs of population increased, and in any event, a meeting would occur sooner or later. Blue Feather, who was still complaining about having sore buttocks from having to ride a horse when he would have preferred to walk, was halted around a curve in the trail when Renno came, leading the others.

"We have company," Blue Feather mentioned, and Renno quickly picked out several men half-hidden in a thicket along a creek that crossed the trail ahead.

"Tell the others to be ready," Renno said, "but not to show any weapons unless I give the order." He waited while Blue Feather rode back to pass the word along, and then rejoined him. They rode forward slowly, their right hands raised in friendship. From the thicket stepped a tall young warrior. Renno and Blue Feather halted their horses at a respectful distance.

"I am thankful that you are well," Renno said, the words a traditional Seneca greeting, the language Cherokee.

The tall warrior spoke in a language Renno did not understand, except for the word "Chickasaw."

"He says that we are not Chickasaw," Blue Feather said.

"You understand his language?"

Blue Feather nodded slowly. "Enough to know that if he had said we were Chickasaw, the arrows would be flying from a dozen bows."

Blue Feather dismounted, walked a few steps forward, and began to experiment with several Indian dialects. He found a combination of Chickasaw and sign language that allowed communication. After a while, a smile appeared on the Quapaw's face, and he seemed to relax. Blue Feather turned to Renno. "You are a great medicine man who travels seeking the secret of life."

"A secret worthy of the seeking," Renno said.

"You are welcome, you and your friends, as long as there are no Chickasaw," Blue Feather said.

"There is a girl who has just become Cherokee," Renno said with a smile. "Please inform her of that fact and its importance."

Renno motioned to El-i-chi to bring up the rest of the party. Beth had just washed her hair the night before in a clean, sweet stream, and she had not braided it, leaving it to hang in glory to her shoulders. Nor was she wearing anything over it on a sunny, warm day. When she appeared there was a gasp from the group of Quapaw warriors who had emerged from the thickets.

"What are they saying?" Renno asked Blue Feather.

"I don't quite understand," the old man responded.

The Quapaw formed an honor guard around the group. The trail led across the stream and through a hardwood grove to a village seemingly filled with barking dogs and running children and people of all ages who stopped what they were doing to stare at the newcomers. The village was laid out much like the villages of the Cherokee, with the large council house and the chief's house fronting a central area. The Quapaw chief was a dignified white-haired oldster who stood ramrod straight and extended an openhanded greeting to the visitors. His orders brought women running to tend Ena and Holani, who had been warned to speak only Cherokee and to answer, if asked, that Holani was Cherokee. Two women immediately attached themselves to Blue Feather, but Renno, needing the old man to help him understand the talk of the Quapaw, motioned to him to stay. Blue Feather smiled and made sign to the two women that obviously meant "later."

"I will stay with the horses," El-i-chi said, as Quapaw women started to lead the animals away.

"I too," said Rusog.

That left Renno to enter the council house with William, and Beth, and Blue Feather, who strutted in his importance as translator.

There were food and water, and Renno expressed his gratitude through Blue Feather. The council house began to fill slowly. There seemed to be no hurry about eating, for the feasting continued for a long time. Afterward the pipe was passed. Beth took a draw and coughed, then smiled and said, "Good," in a strangled voice as she passed the pipe along.

The old chief then rose and began the usual oratory. Blue Feather could manage to gather only a few words, but he began to look more and more puzzled as the chief repeated the same words time and again, as he motioned to and looked at Beth.

"He says," Blue Feather told them, "that the flame-haired one has come."

After all the oratory and the ceremonial drinking of a fermented horror made from fruit, the mystery was solved when a grizzled warrior approached the seated visitors and addressed Renno in the language of the Chickasaw.

"We extend you welcome and honor, Medicine Man," the Quapaw said, "for your coming has been foretold."

"It is so," Renno replied, thinking quickly, willing to take advantage of any opportunity to travel peacefully.

"You are blessed by the spirits," the Quapaw said.

"So we are," Renno said, knowing that he was telling the truth, for he had always been blessed by the manitous and the spirits of his ancestors.

"So it was foretold by the great shaman of the hot springs," the Quapaw said. "And for many moons we have looked for you. Your blessings can be our blessings, shaman, with your goodwill, for it is foretold that the flame-haired one who heralds your presence is a favored sign."

"Ah," Renno said. And he, too, remembered a prophecy. *The flame-haired one is the future.* He could not understand all events, but he had faith in his manitous. "I share the favor of the spirits with all who allow me to pass in peace," he said, spreading his hands in blessing for all those present, rather liking the part he was playing.

Chapter VI

Never had the signs from the spirits been more confusing for Renno. In addition to his own vision, in which his father, in the form of a great bear, had told him of the coming of the flame-haired girl, there was now another prophecy. This one came to an honored shaman of the Natchitoches and had spread eastward from the place of peace near the Mountain of the Hot Springs, an area still to the west of them. It was puzzling. In some way not fully explained, the coming of the flame-haired one was to be an omen of peace and plenty for all.

Renno never doubted the spirits, for he had always received wisdom and inspiration when he fasted and prayed. Indeed, most of the important decisions of his young life had been influenced by a vision message from a spirit in the form of one of his Bear Clan totems or the form of one of his great ancestors. He realized that to look upon the prophecy of the shaman of the hot springs as being designed by the spirits merely to help him and his friends was self-serving, but he could not imagine a deeper meaning for the mere passage of Beth Huntington of the fiery hair. Perhaps, Renno thought, Beth's almost mystical effect on the Quapaw had to do with the novelty of her fair skin, which she protected as much as possible from the sun, and the unexpected fire of her hair. He did not question his good fortune, however. He accepted it as being another sign of favor from the manitous of the Seneca, who apparently had more widespread influence than he had guessed.

In a land where life had a sameness from day to day and year to year, the passage of the strangers made ripples that began with the first Quapaw encountered to the area where low, rolling, hardwood-covered hills began, and beyond. The coming of the great medicine man from the East and his flame-haired omen of good things was carried ahead of Renno's steadily moving group by runners, and their welcome was assured in first Quapaw, then Natchitoches, villages.

Renno and Blue Feather were constantly improving upon their ability to communicate with the Indians of those areas, for they were all of a common racial stock, and although their language was different, it had many things in common with the language of the Southwestern tribes.

Fortunately, growing conditions that spring were perfect in the areas through which they were traveling, and as the slow, steady miles passed under the hooves of their horses, they rode through a land blooming in goodness. William counted almost two hundred different types of trees—over forty varieties of oak alone—and he was sure that he had missed some.

Some days they traveled as many as thirty miles while the country was still relatively flat. Information about well-traveled trails was always available from the local Indians, and William and Renno did their best to adhere to a straight-line course extending from Chickasaw Bluffs on the Mississippi to that area called New Mexico by the Spanish, where the Rio Grande turned northward.

Soon, however, the hills became more rolling and the going slower. William, the man from a country where no point was more than seventy miles from the sea, had indeed underestimated the vastness of this American continent. It would be, he began to realize, speaking in the Indian's time reference, many moons before they reached their destination.

The valley of the hot springs, home of the great shaman who had predicted their coming, was surrounded by rounded, low, hardwood-covered mountains. Their greeting there was warm, both from the people who lived there and from Indians who came on long marches from all points of the compass to partake of the healing powers of the mineral springs flowing from the Mountain of the Hot Springs.

The medicine man whose fame had spread far from his home on the side of the Mountain of the Hot Springs honored Renno. People of several tribes, all gathered in peace in the valley of the healing waters, danced their individualized dances and chanted in a generally proclaimed day of feasting and oratory. Gifts were exchanged.

Renno gained great respect for the shaman of the springs when the old man presented him with a beautifully cured complete bearskin—the head still intact, the dead eyes replaced by shining, rounded bits of clear, sparkling stone—for the old man had no way of knowing that Renno was a member of the Bear Clan and that the bear had sacred implications for him.

At first Renno felt sorrow, for to kill the bear, a sacred totem, was shameful. As if to reassure him, the old shaman said, "In another sign of your coming, Sachem from the east, a great storm toppled a huge oak tree atop this animal. The skin of your sacred animal will warm you in the snows of winter and will keep the spirit of your totem ever with you, serving you well in other ways."

So saying, the shaman helped Renno don the bearskin. The legs of the skin had been sewed back together with small leather thongs, so that when Renno slid his legs and his arms inside the leg skins of the bear and the shaman had laced the slit belly skin closed, it was as if a great bear had come to life. Thus, as the travelers left the valley of the hot springs, word preceded them about the sachem Renno, Man-Who-Becomes-Bear.

All along the way, as the heat of early summer caused the Indians, including Blue Feather, to strip to loincloths and made the doeskin clothing of the women uncomfortably hot, Renno talked with any man who had traveled to the west. More and more he began to gather information about what lay ahead of them, and after several crossings and detours around low mountains, the reports became more grim.

One grizzled Natchitoches warrior who had known the wanderlust as a youth spoke. "Plenty buffalo," he said. "Move north in summer, come south in winter away from snows. Many Indians follow buffalo. Osage, Kansas, Crow, Wichita, Pawnee, Kiowa."

"If they follow the buffalo," Renno said, "they will be in the north now, is that not true?"

The old Indian shrugged.

"If we encounter any of these buffalo people," Renno asked, "will they allow us to pass as peaceful travelers?"

The old Natchitoches spat, then bared his arms. Renno saw great welts of burn scars. "I wore no war paint when I was taken by the Crow."

Renno pointed toward the southwest. "We go there, far. We go where the Spanish are."

The old man quickly raised a hand in blessing. "Comanche," he said, and although he did not, of course, show overt fear, there was awe in the word. "The free people."

"Tell me of the Comanche," Renno said.

"Bad, bad," the Natchitoches said, shaking his head. "And then burning sands, no water, and Apache."

"You have seen the burning sands and the dry mountains?"

The old man nodded. "Far. Many moons." He counted on his fingers. "Seasons change. No water. There are the cities of the dead, many evil spirits."

William, who had been listening carefully, knit his brow when the old man had gone. "I would not call that an auspicious forecast, Renno. These Comanche sound quite warlike and very unreasonable."

Renno had his trust in the spirits, who had been with him so far, but he let his hand drop to the handle of one of the fine dueling pistols that William had given him, to show that he was willing to aid the spirits with his own strong arm. "The Comanche are Indian," he said forcefully.

William nodded and placed his full confidence in Renno's ability to weather any storm. He estimated that they had traveled almost a thousand miles without mishap since leaving Renno's village. That movement, of course, was not always in a straight line, the nature of the varied country forcing them away from their course. He guessed their straight-line progress at no more than ten miles a day, and already the trail was long, the early spring fading, and from the indications, a hot summer awaited them. He could make only a wild estimate of the distance yet to be traveled, for maps of the interior of North America were based on scanty information brought back by early Spanish or French explorers. The treasure map he had was quite detailed in the areas of New Spain and north into the area past the Rio Grande, where the Spanish had established missions not far north of that river. Farther to the north, where their route would take them, the map was blank.

Three weeks after leaving the valley of the hot springs, there were more low mountains ahead. Blue Feather, who had lived like a king, tended by friendly widows at almost every stop in the lands of the Quapaw and Natchitoches, had once again taken his place on rotation as scout, and as the country began to change, he became more alert, more tense. The mountains were much like those of home, covered with fir and pine, with beautiful valleys and streams. Unlike the usually soft and humid air of the Smoky Mountains, however, here the air was dry, and there was a certain sense of sereneness. They traveled for days without seeing people, but watching the countryside alter, flatten into rolling scrub-oak hills. A few buffalo were seen, and the meat of one calf added some variety to their diet.

Day meant movement. They were under way by sunup. Beth had taken to reading in the saddle, for she found the books William had collected back in England and brought with him on this trip to be fascinating. She had read them before, of course, but now she studied them, for they were the accounts of the Spanish conquistadores: Álvar Núñez Cabeza de Vaca, who turned a shipwreck into an opportunity to search for fabled jewels and gold in the plains of the vast land ahead; Francisco Vásquez de Coronado, the dashing Spanish cavalryman who sought the Seven Cities of Cíbola, where there was gold; and Hernando de Soto, who penetrated the central lands farther than any man—who had, in fact, tramped the very plains toward which, if their map was right, they were headed.

In all of the books were accounts of warlike Indians. All spoke of the hardships. Beth found the reading to be grim, and she shared the books with Renno, talking with him about the information the books contained, although they had been written long ago.

"Are we, too, chasing treasures that don't exist?" she asked him as they rode through sparsely wooded rolling country under a hot June sun.

"Only time will tell," he answered.

"The conquistadores found no gold," Beth said.

"But this map was drawn by a priest," Renno reminded her. "Tell me what is in the book about the priests who founded the missions and did their own exploration."

Beth found brief references to Friar Marcos de Niza, who, like Coronado, sought the land of Cíbola. "The priests," she told Renno, "apparently went where not even the armored conquistadores dared to go. They went under the protection of the cross. Perhaps they *did* find gold."

One thousand miles of travel now lay behind them without serious incident. It was, to Beth, an incredible distance, which she had associated previously only with the expanses of oceans. They began to get an idea of what the buffalo plains were like, for now, between areas of woodlands, on slopes and ridges and along watercourses, were long, open stretches of rich land where the grass grew to the horses' knees. With water more scarce, an additional burden in the form of the waterskins had to be added to the loads carried by the spare horses. Nevertheless, they did not experience the awful hardships described by the Spanish explorers. Thanks to the hunting skills of Renno, Blue Feather, Rusog, and El-i-chi, they never went hungry. They felt cold, yes. Hot, yes. Dirty, sweaty, and tired, yes, but all in all, it was a grand adventure, seeing a greater variety of terrain—and more miles of it—than almost anyone else alive. The country seemed to be so thinly populated that Renno was coming to believe that nearly all Indians had followed the buffalo to the north. It was not difficult to avoid encounters when any signs of habitation were noticed in the form of a freshly used trail, the remains of a larger animal obviously killed and dressed by man, or, infrequently, the smoke of a campfire.

Nonetheless, Blue Feather's hackles were up. He sensed a strangeness to the land, and occasionally his sensitive nose would pick up the smoky essence of those campfires or a hint of the odor of people who had a scent unlike any he had ever smelled. He did not have to caution Renno. Now that Holani's and El-i-chi's initial ardor had been moderated by familiarity, they offered no objection when Renno told them to make a more compact camp, and on nights after seeing signs of human habitation, the warriors alternated watches throughout the night.

Aside from Ena's suspicion of Beth in her close relationship to Renno, it was a compatible group. The accounts of the Spanish conquistadores were new fodder for the daily talks over the cookfire. Beth and William agreed that Renno's command of Spanish was now equal to their own. They were all fit and lean and, although tired at the end of the day, in such good health that it was no chore at all to rise with first light, break camp after a filling breakfast, and face another day of their slow traverse of a major portion of the continent.

Renno had taken to selecting the campsite not for comfort and convenience but for defensibility, and as a result there were dry camps. On such occasions, the women, especially Beth, regretted not being able to bathe and rinse the perspiration from their clothing, but no one complained, for they could see the nervous alertness of Blue Feather and the constant watchfulness of Rusog, El-i-chi, and Renno.

It was in one such camp, made atop a slight rise among exposed sandstone boulders, that Renno was to first meet the free people, the Comanche. He had taken the last watch of the night. He had posted himself behind a rock, his musket across his legs, and made himself at ease on a cushion of grass. He had seen nothing out of the ordinary during the previous day. Now the white Indian watched the nearly full moon disappear, saw the stars fade and then glow most brightly after the false dawn. The pleasant coolness of early morning was a joy to him, for the days had been hot.

He was first alerted by the call of a quail. When that call was answered from another quarter, he knew that the calls were not from birds. He waited until the darkness began to fade, then, still seeing nothing, crawled, hardly moving the tall grass, to rouse El-i-chi and Rusog with a soft touch on their shoulders. Then, having explained the situation to the warriors, he woke the others. There was no need to waken Blue Feather; the old man had been brought from his deep sleep by Renno's stealthy movements.

The attack came with first light. They came from all sides of the camp, racing from scant cover at the signal of a howled war cry. Lean, impressive-looking warriors in loincloth and leather decorations, they were armed not with muskets but with bow, tomahawk, and knife. Their brilliantly painted faces spoke of war.

Rusog's first concern was for the horses, which had been hobbled with leather thongs. He glanced quickly up the slope to see that they were still more or less in a group.

Renno was also concerned about the animals. Had he been leading the attack, he would have taken the horses first, for they had grazed during the night to a point some one hundred yards away. That the horses had not been taken was a grim omen, for it meant that the attackers were so sure of themselves that they thought to take the horses at their leisure after dealing with their owners.

As the painted warriors raced toward them, Renno counted them quickly. Over thirty men. Their plan was simple: to brave the defenders' arrows and then close quickly for hand-to-hand fighting. Perhaps, he thought, they had not encountered musket fire before. He had arranged his people in a circle among the exposed sandstone boulders, so each was well shielded. Everyone had muskets except Holani, since she had not been intended, at first, to be a part of the expedition. She was near El-i-chi, and she stood ready to reload for him after he had fired.

Renno gave the order to fire at long range, and the resulting marksmanship pleased him, for as seven muskets rattled, five of the attackers jerked, sprawled, and fell. The firing from that point was sporadic, depending upon how quickly the person was able to reload the musket.

This time there was not a miss, and seven men fell. Renno accounted for two more and Beth and William one each with their pistols before the remaining invaders—so close now that individual features could be distinguished—turned, giving vent to frustrated, piercing yells, and raced away.

"They'll go for the horses now," Blue Feather predicted as he crawled toward Renno's position. Rusog had already anticipated that, and motioning to El-i-chi to follow, he raced up the slope, after having reloaded his weapon to drop a painted Comanche, who was, indeed, moving toward the horses. Soon the hobbled animals were hopping down the slope to be gathered into the center of the defensive circle, where they milled, whinnying in fright at the memory of the gunfire, and created heat with their bodies.

Renno was satisfied with the results of the resistance to the first attack. Two of the fallen enemy were trying to crawl away, obviously no longer able to fight. The attackers who had not been killed or put out of action would think twice before making another attack. Renno did not welcome the idea of fighting a running battle with the Comanche, who could ride ahead on their own horses and, being familiar with the land, could lie in wait. He would give the free people time to consider the deadliness of the gunfire and make up their minds. If they had not made a second attack so that he could deplete their number even more by midday, he would move out.

Blue Feather calmly set about warming strips of buffalo meat that he had cooked the night before, and breakfast was served. The sun began to hint of the coming heat of the day. Renno noted that almost everyone had come through the skirmish in good spirits. William seemed especially keyed up, most probably with the lingering stimulation of a battle to the death, and Beth seemed sad, a natural enough reaction to killing.

When the sun's position indicated that it was mid-morning, Renno was considering packing up and leaving. That possibility was short-lived, terminated by the arrival

of more than a dozen Comanche. They came riding fast
and disappeared behind a rise where the survivors of the
first ambush had retreated. Soon there came the sound of
chanted war hymns, and then another attack was mounted,
the swift plains ponies circling the defended area with
their riders hiding themselves from the musket fire by
bending low over their horses' necks or by clinging with
one leg to the horses' backs, bodies behind the bulk of the
animals, sitting upright only long enough to send arrows
toward the defenders.

An arrow zipped past Renno's ear to pierce the thin
stomach wall of a horse behind him. The animal reared in
pain and screamed, and Rusog rose quickly to fell it with a
musket ball to the brain before it went berserk and did
damage to or panicked the other animals.

Much against his wishes, Renno called out, "Shoot for
their horses," for he and his group were not getting clear
shots at the Comanche. The next volley felled horses and
sent the riders sprawling, so the attack broke up.

"They learn fast," Rusog remarked.

Renno did not like the situation. New warriors were
already arriving. His fears that there would be more were
not groundless, for with a thunder of hooves and shrill war
cries, at least fifty mounted warriors came galloping from
the distance. He knew that his force would be able to kill
many from their protected position, but in the end, the
sheer numbers of the Comanche would take the advantage. He had only two courses of action to prevent a long
and deadly siege: his small group could run for it, or he
could try to talk their way out. He preferred fighting to
talking, but he had the fate of the others to consider.

The white flag was a universal sign of truce, and his
white flag, one of Beth's camisoles tied onto a stick, was
honored when he walked down the slope and stopped at
the bottom, looking up the next slight grassy rise. Two
befeathered Comanche appeared on the crest of the hill
and began to walk toward him. He met them halfway up

the hill. They halted five paces away and stared at him impassively.

"You see that my face is not painted for war," he said in Spanish, and was pleased when he was answered in the same language.

"Since I know not that paint, I cannot say if your face is painted for war."

"I am the sachem Renno. I have come from far into the rising sun on a mission of exploration and peace. We did not ask for this fight. We ask only that our brothers, sons of the same ancient parents, allow us to travel on in peace."

The Comanche snorted. "The sachem from the east has killed on the hunting grounds of the Kotsoteka. I, Buffalo Shadow, chief of the Kotsoteka, promise only an honorable death in battle to those who trespass on our hunting grounds."

"That we are not a war party should be evident, for we have women among us," Renno said.

"Women who killed my warriors skillfully with the magic fire sticks," Buffalo Shadow replied, "but we do not make war on women. Send your women to us, and they will be treated as they deserve, as prisoners of war."

"That is not to my liking," Renno said, his blue eyes icy. "Is battle, then, your only offer?"

Buffalo Shadow nodded.

"So be it," Renno said. "But before you take one scalp from us, count your dead and consider if it would not be better to offer friendship." He turned and, his back stiff, walked back to his position.

"They're chanting again," Beth said nervously to Ena, who was behind a rock to her right.

"You have fought well," Ena said grudgingly. "Let us make every shot count, so that we may send many free people to the land of their ancestors before we ourselves are killed."

Beth swallowed quickly, fighting back the urge to weep. Until Ena had spoken, she had not known true fear.

She had built such confidence in the men of the party, especially in Renno, that the idea of dying on that rocky, grassy hill had not occurred to her, in spite of their being quite obviously greatly outnumbered. Her first thoughts turned to England, her father, and how beautiful the flowers were at home in the summer.

The governor of those Spanish areas in New Spain north of Mexico and east of New Mexico, Baron de Carondelet, was not always grateful for the wet, watery distances that separated his mansion in New Orleans from Spain. There were times when he wished that there was a solid pathway leading back to his home in Castile. Had there been, he would have started walking. Most of the time he was a happy man, in spite of the recent failure to establish Spanish strongholds in the mid-Mississippi area with the aid of the Chickasaw. He had his pleasures— good wine from the sunny vineyards of home, a lovely French widow who had managed to hang on to her considerable fortune in spite of the changing times, and not too much interference from the government in his country.

When interference did come, it usually came in the form of a gowned cleric. De Carondelet could always handle the perfumed dandies sent out from the royal court, but the clergy—they were cats of a different breed. The Church had built a power equal to, or in some cases greater than, that of the king himself, and when a priest had the official blessings of the king, *there* was power not to be disputed.

Such power had the bald, spare, hard-faced friar named Sebastián, who had arrived months earlier in New Orleans unannounced but with impressive credentials. One look at Sebastián's cruel face told de Carondelet that it was time to speak softly. A look at his letters had merely reaffirmed his initial impression, for Father Sebastián was of the most powerful Spanish order, the Dominicans. Moreover, he was a member of the supreme council of the Inquisition. Although the fearful excesses of the Inquisition had reached a peak earlier, in the fifteenth and sixteenth centuries, there was still power there. The Inquisition was to be not only respected but also feared, especially by a man who found life in the far provinces to be gay, free of preaching for the most part, and liberal to the point of excess. A single report about one of the governor's French mistress's parties to this Father Sebastián would be fodder for recall to Spain and a questioning by the Inquisition that could lead to no less than loss of position and months of endless confessions.

Friar Sebastián was, in addition to his other credentials, the official envoy of Manuel de Godoy, an ambitious and influential man who was, in effect, acting king during the ill health of King Charles III. Father Sebastián and the governor had first met shortly after the regretful Chickasaw war, when the good friar had accused the baron of being too lenient with the Indians. Now it seemed that reports had been exchanged across the ocean and the friar had been given farther-reaching responsibilities.

"My patron," Father Sebastián told the governor, "is highly distressed that the flow of treasures in the form of gold and silver has all but dried up."

"Not everyone was as fortunate as Cortez and Pizarro," de Carondelet explained. "The gold, Father, seems to be in the Far South."

"My patron and I think that is not wholly true," Sebastián said. "Gold did come from New Mexico long ago."

"A little," the governor admitted. "True. But the mines were quickly played out. The native Indians had not the stamina for the work, but that is no matter. The important thing is that those few deposits of gold that were found were isolated pockets."

"You would not, of course, disagree with my patron and with the king himself," the friar said. Sebastián seemed never to smile, even when trying to speak lightly. It was as if all humor had long since been squeezed from his lean, thin frame by the weight of his woolen robes and the heavy cross he wore on a large chain around his neck.

"Of course not," the governor said. "What are the wishes of the king?"

"That you give me men. I will mount an expedition of exploration into New Mexico."

The governor spread his hands, thinking about the relief he would feel from watching the friar leave New Orleans on such a long journey. "Ah, Father," he said, "I will be most happy to arrange such an expedition for you. How many men do you need, and when will the march begin?"

"We will not march from here," Father Sebastián said coldly. "We will take a ship for Corpus Christi and follow the course of the Rio Grande, thus never being far from water. I will require at least two hundred mounted men."

De Carondelet's heart began to beat faster. He had not reported the loss of a large number of cavalry and his best fieldpieces in the Chickasaw war. Manning such an expedition would be a severe drain on his manpower, but he dared not object.

"I have brought with me the latest in firearms," the friar continued, "so two hundred will suffice."

De Carondelet swallowed hard. Two hundred fit fighting men would strip his garrison to dregs. He tried to measure the priest, to see if he could get by with palming off the drunkards and others of little worth, but seeing the glint of Sebastián's gray eyes, he quickly decided against it.

"We will use the ship on which I suffered the crossing," the priest said. "I will want your best officer as my aide and troop commander."

For a moment the governor wished that Guy de Rojas were alive, for if two men had ever deserved each other, it was the priest and the opportunistic but unfortunately dead de Rojas. He quickly ran down his small roster of officers. He would not send the best, for that man was his friend and a companion in his revels. Ah, but there was

Barca, a commoner, a boor. Lope Barca. Yes, he would do nicely. He presented a good enough appearance until one got to know him and recognized the soul of a greedy peasant under the fancy uniform. If ever a man had less honor than Guy de Rojas, Barca was the man. How he had gotten a commission as an officer was beyond de Carondelet's comprehension. Some said it was because he had served in the *pudridero*, the rotting room where dead kings and princes lay for five years before entombment. There were times, although he knew it was his imagination, that de Carondelet could almost smell the ripe odor of decaying flesh clinging to Barca.

"There is one thing," the governor said. "My men are soldiers, not miners."

"Have no fear," Sebastián assured him. "That problem was solved long ago."

De Carondelet felt an inner shudder. He knew what the priest meant. It was the same old story: when the Spanish had first settled in the New World, they had exterminated entire tribes by enslaving people who had lived their lives out-of-doors without knowledge of hard labor. Well, that was the affair of the priest and the Church. The governor told Friar Sebastián to get some rest while he looked to the details.

The governor did not know it, but Captain Lope Barca was as eager to be away from the governor's influence as the governor was to get rid of him, so everyone was happy except the soldiers who boarded the small, stinking ship. The decks were crowded with horses, pack mules, and gear, but most of the soldiers chose to risk a hoof in the ribs rather than venture into the putrid depths of the vessel.

De Carondelet would much rather have been sending the soldiers up the Mississippi to teach a lesson to those pesky Cherokee who had foiled his plans for a new empire in the mid-Mississippi valley, but he had his orders. He waved a gaily colored kerchief from the pier as the ship, already smelling of manure from the horses, put out on the falling tide.

Father Sebastián had interviewed his troop commander previously and had found him to be satisfactory. He was pleased by Barca's peasant background—such men were more tractable, more in awe of the power of the Church than men born to riches and nobility. Yes, he and Lope Barca would get along well. And his own right-hand man, Carlos Montenegro, would serve as a buffer most of the time. He established the relationship quite early, as the ship left the mouth of the Mississippi and entered the calm Gulf of Mexico, by calling Barca to his cabin.

"I want it understood from the beginning that we are not on a quest for glory," the priest stated. "We have a definite mission, and that mission comes first. There will be no attack on Indians unless we are attacked—at least not until we have reached our goal. Is that understood?"

Barca, the youngest and therefore the least well-fed of his family of twelve, had not come to the New World for glory. He had come as thousands of others had come, lured by the gleam of the gold that had been sent back from Mexico and Peru. He had come, as had many others, noble and otherwise, to seek his fortune, and all he had found thus far was the steamy, debilitating, mildewing heat of Louisiana. He nodded. "I am sure, Father," he replied, "that you will inform me of this mission in your own time."

"At the moment you need to know nothing," Sebastian said. "See to your men. When we land at Corpus Christi we will take time only for provisioning. There will be no drinking or brawling, or your men will suffer severe punishment. My intentions are to be marching west from Corpus Christi not more than two days after landing. I want you to locate breastplate armor in the garrison, as much as you're able to find, as added protection on our journey."

"I will see to it," Barca said, although armor had not been used for over a hundred years. He had been studying the priest closely and recognized raw power when he encountered it. Although Barca was still a young man, he had lived by his wits in a city where to be poor was to be in a constant fight for survival. He had seen many men like Sebastián come and go after he had luckily found favor with a nobleman and been given various positions at court. He had never killed a priest, but that prospect did not make him weak in the knees. A priest was a man. It had yet to be proven to Barca, who had never had God speak to him, that God spoke to any man, including a priest who was on the supreme council of the Inquisition. One thing Barca knew: He was out from under the thumb of the aristocratic de Carondelet, America was the land of opportunity, and he was not the one to let a mere priest stand between him and any opportunity that arose.

"If I am to buy the provisions," Barca said, "I will need to know the approximate distance to our destination."

"I will handle that myself," Father Sebastián responded. "I suggest that you use our time in Corpus Christi in drilling the men. I have always hated to see a ragged column on the march."

Barca groaned inwardly. He was familiar, too, with frustrated men who had never had the ability to command troops but who thought they could.

"You may join your men," Father Sebastián concluded, dismissing Barca from his mind even before the man had left.

Barca knew most of the men. Some, however, had arrived while he was on a journey to Pensacola. The governor was always dreaming up semiuseless errands for him, seemingly just to get him out of the garrison. He would make it a point to know each of them by name, to memorize the names of the members of their families back in Spain, to learn their hopes and fears and dreams. A commander who knew his troops had control. Moreover, a commander who knew his troops, who was a friend to them without letting go of the reins of responsibility, would be in a fine position should he need their help for his own plans at some time in the future.

Like most Spaniards in the New World, Barca dreamed of golden idols of the type taken by Cortez and Pizarro. He dreamed of returning to Spain with a trunk full of freshly minted gold coins.

For five years he had tended the body of a prince rotting in the *pudridero*. He had not been required to go into the stinking chamber often, but even once was too much. Spain owed him for this. It was not likely that Spain would pay her debt voluntarily. So Lope Barca, if given half the chance, would collect the debt himself.

In his cabin, Friar Sebastián had taken out a folded piece of parchment and spread it on his Spartan bunk. He had spent much time studying that document and the records of the friar who had drawn it. He was risking his reputation and some years of his life to prove that the friar had not lied. Since he had discovered the copy of the map in an ancient Dominican monastery, it had obsessed him. He had faith in the truthfulness of members of his order, even the word of long-dead ones such as the beloved father Friar Luis. If a Dominican brother said that there was gold in New Mexico, then indeed there were several tons of mined and smelted gold hidden in a shaft in a mountain with a disconcerting name.

And Friar Sebastián, with God's help, would recover the gold, the devil's own gold, *El Oro del Diablo*, from the devil's own mountain. That he had promised to himself and to his God.

Chapter VII

The devastating hail of magic pellets that brought instant death had impressed the Kotsoteka Comanche, the buffalo eaters. The large group of newcomers was eager to attack and have their chance at coup, so they were secretly pleased that the trespassers had not already been scalped. The survivors of the previous attacks tried to explain how the strangers had magic power to reach and kill at a distance. The awe affected the reinforcements, and thus the next attack was a tentative one, made on horseback, the object being to ride within arrow range and loose a missile and then dash back beyond the reach of the fire sticks.

Renno's force fell into a rhythm of loading and firing, and even though the range was sometimes extreme, their marksmanship paid off in dead or fallen horses and Comanche. At the height of the battle a group of young Comanche, emboldened by their chanting and wild war cries and infuriated by watching their fellows fall without doing damage to the trespassers, mounted a charge along a common line. Two dozen warriors joined in to dash directly up the slight slope toward the rocks. The muskets, at closer range, took a terrible toll, while the pistols in the hands of Renno, William, and Beth dropped all but one Comanche. The last one fell to an arrow from the bow of Rusog.

In a period of quiet, Renno's party could hear the chants from behind the hills. He had noted that the attackers were beginning to understand the rhythm of musket fire, for he had seen several warriors dash forward to loose an arrow after a musket had been fired and while it was being reloaded. When the chanting ceased, Renno searched for a solution. He felt certain that the Comanche had suffered enough casualties to madden them with anger and to cause them to eliminate all caution. There were perhaps fewer than fifty of them left, but that number, Renno knew, was more than enough. He backhanded the perspiration from his eyes and glanced up at the midday sun, then looked around at the others in the group. Their muskets and pistols could drop some Comanche, and arrows still others, but a determined, straightforward charge that did not turn back would see the enemy swarming over the protective rocks—and not even the expedition's backbone of three men who were, perhaps, the greatest warriors of the Cherokee and Seneca would be able to prevail over seven-to-one odds.

But Renno was not one to accept fate passively. His faith was not shaken. The manitous, he felt, favored those who acted, but there were few options open to him now.

Except . . . With the manitous, everything had a purpose. His thoughts turned to the heavy bearskin given to him by the medicine man of the hot springs. He had debated the wisdom of transporting that heavy skin, but for some reason he had. The bear was a powerful sign. The bear was, even among those who did not hold him sacred as a brother, a symbol of strength and courage. The old medicine man of the hot springs had said that the totem of the skin would serve him well, and now was the time.

"What on earth is he about?" William asked his sister as Renno took the great bearskin from its lashing atop a pack and began to crawl into it.

"Help me," Renno told Ena, who, without question, laced the belly flaps of the skin together. "When the attack comes, hold your fire until I give the word," Renno ordered them.

It took only a few minutes for the heat of the day and the weight of the skin to make Renno feel as if he were inside a sweat house. He concealed himself behind the largest of the rocks and waited. He did not have long to wait. A chorus of war cries came from behind the hill, and a long line of mounted Comanche appeared in good formation, chiefs at the center. The chief with the most elaborate headdress raised his hand and, after a long, suspenseful silence, let it drop. With shrill whoops the line of warriors kicked their mounts into a gallop, and the line, wavering only slightly, came charging down the slope, into the slight depression, and then upward toward the rocks.

"All of you gather around me," Renno called out, and even though they were puzzled by the order, all obeyed, grouping themselves in front of the rock behind which Renno was concealed, allowing him to crawl forward unseen by the charging Comanche.

To the attackers, the action of the defenders was surprising, grouping themselves tightly to make a single target for arrows.

"El-i-chi," Renno said, his voice muffled as it came from the bearskin, "stand directly in front of me."

El-i-chi did as he was ordered. Soon the horsemen would be within arrow range, and he was ready, musket cocked and primed, bow hanging over his shoulder.

The leading attacker let fly an arrow, but he was not near enough, and the arrow fell to the ground well in front of the bunched group. "When I give the word, El-i-chi, drop flat to the ground," Renno said. And then, almost immediately, he shouted, "Now!"

To the Comanche it seemed that El-i-chi had, quite suddenly, lost his human form and had been transformed into a great black bear who reared on his hind legs and sent forth a bellowing, spine-chilling battle challenge. The leading riders gave startled cries and reined in their horses so suddenly that riders behind them crashed into them, and for a few moments there was chaos among the ranks of the Comanche. Renno once more gave the challenge of the great bear and said to El-i-chi, who was hidden in the deep grass, "When I say 'Now,' spring up suddenly, Brother."

The charge had halted, and the Comanche milled around, confused.

"William and Beth, time for your longbows next," Renno said. "Nock arrows and shoot for the breasts of the horses of the chiefs when I tell you, after El-i-chi takes my place.

"Now!" he shouted to El-i-chi, falling as his brother sprang up, then slithering, with some difficulty, on his belly behind the concealing stone. "Spread out into defensive positions," he said as the Comanche once again cried out in surprise at the miraculous transformation of bear into man. They obeyed quickly.

"William and Beth—now!" Renno shouted as he broke lacings and came out of the bearskin in time to see two long, straight English arrows take a flight almost without trajectory to bury their barbed heads deeply into the breasts of the horses of the two most befeathered chiefs. One of the chiefs was Buffalo Shadow, who had promised death to Renno. His horse fell instantly, the other reared and fell sideways, banging against yet another horse. The arrows had found their deadly marks many yards beyond the range of the strongest Comanche bowman, and there was a murmuring from the attackers.

"Hold your fire," Renno called. He stood, climbed atop a rock, and stood there, his arms crossed. One of the horseless chiefs stood and shouted something to the milling, muttering warriors. The mass of Comanche turned their horses and rode to halt halfway up the opposite rise. The two chiefs who remained, their headdresses damaged by their fall from the dead horses, stood gazing at Renno for a long time; then, as one, they bowed, extending their arms in a sign of honor and peace. Renno returned the gesture, crossed his arms again, and waited. The two Comanche walked slowly and proudly up the hill. They halted ten paces away.

"Truly the spirits are with you, Man-Who-Becomes-Bear," Buffalo Shadow said.

"We have come in peace," Renno replied, "and our brothers force us to use the power of the spirits against them, a matter not to our liking."

"What do you want with us, great medicine man?" asked the other, elder chief.

"Only to give you the blessing of brotherhood, gifts for you and your women, and stories of faraway lands," Renno said. "Shall we be brothers in peace?"

"It shall be as you wish," Buffalo Shadow agreed as the others nodded fervently. "Come, we will feast and smoke the pipe."

"Your warriors have slain one of our horses," Renno said, pointing to the dead animal.

"I will make you a gift of a finer animal," the elder chief offered.

"Your gift will be accepted in honor," Renno replied. "We will gather our belongings." He nodded to the others, who, looking incredulous at the turn of events, began to load the gear and supplies onto the horses.

William sidled over to Renno. "I say, can we trust these fellows?" he whispered to the white Indian while the two chiefs stood with crossed arms and watched closely as the party prepared to move.

"Do we have any other choice?" Renno asked with a chuckle. "Go occupy our new friends so that I can hide the bearskin."

William, a bit nervously, walked to extend open hands to the two Comanche, who returned the gesture. "The land of the Comanche is a fair land," William noted.

"It is good," said the elder chief.

"And are the lands of the Comanche great in extent?"

That question, appealing to the pride of the chiefs, accomplished the purpose. The two Comanche turned, and one spread his arms to the western horizon. "Many days' ride," he said, "and still the lands are those of the Kotsoteka."

"The Kotsoteka?" William asked.

"Kotsoteka are Comanche," explained Buffalo Shadow. "The valley of the river is our home. Many buffalo."

Out of the corner of his eye William had seen Renno carry a large blanket-covered bundle to put it in place on a horse. The bearskin.

"Your skin is white," noted Buffalo Shadow. "And yet you are not like the hair-faces from the south, the Spanish."

"I am a subject of the great white chief who lives beyond the great seas to the east, in the land of England," William said. And then, seeing that the party was nearly ready to move, he decided to do some constructive lying. "Even there, in England, where there are riches beyond imagination, the fame of the Comanche warrior is known."

Buffalo Shadow grunted.

"And the great king of the English sends his regards to the Comanche and desires to live with the Comanche in honor and friendship."

Again Buffalo Shadow grunted. The elder chief said, "Great white chief will show friendship with gifts of the magic fire stick."

Whoops, William thought. Aloud he said, "We will talk of such things."

The importance of the plains buffalo to the life of the Comanche was quickly evident to William as the group, surrounded by Comanche, rode into the Comanche camp in the late afternoon. The dwellings were conical tents made from buffalo hides. The meat cooking over open fires was buffalo meat. He had learned during the ride that the word "Kotsoteka" meant "buffalo eaters." And although the Comanche were not overly liberal in giving answers to his questions, he was informed that many warriors were hunting to the north, even though enough buffalo remained in the river valley and on the surrounding plains to have delayed the northern migration of the main segment of the Kotsoteka tribe.

The nomadic life and culture of the Kotsoteka were built around the horse, an animal not native to the Americans, and the buffalo, which was. A few weeks later, William thought, there would have been no encounter with the Kotsoteka, for they would have been, by then, far to the north in pursuit of the masses of buffalo.

As it happened, he came to believe that it had been luck or perhaps the influence of Renno's manitous that had led them into battle with the Kotsoteka. For Renno's astounding medicine had convinced the Kotsoteka that the white Indian was a great man with powerful magic, and it would be an asset to them to aid and befriend him. The formal presentation of a horse to replace the one killed in the battle took time, as did the giving of gifts to the chiefs and their women, and a distribution of smaller gifts to other warriors and their women. The feast that followed was of buffalo meat and maize. Drums made of buffalo skin began to sound, and warriors danced in honor of the chief from the east who had such awe-inspiring medicine.

Renno, silent and patient during the festivities, bided his time before questioning Buffalo Shadow about the country ahead of them. It was quite late when he finally broached the subject.

"For a moon of marching you will be in the lands of

the Comanche," Buffalo Shadow told him, "where you will travel as a friend."

"I will speak of the wisdom of Buffalo Shadow to all who hear me," Renno said. "We travel far. Beyond the land of the Comanche."

Buffalo Shadow grunted. "There are dry mountains, seas of sand, and a scarcity of water. And Apache. There you will need great medicine."

Although the hospitality of the Kotsoteka seemed genuine, there were no voiced objections when Renno started his little band toward the west shortly after sunrise. The leave-taking was swift and simple, delayed only as a Comanche medicine man, on the orders of Buffalo Shadow, wiped the Seneca paint from Renno's face and applied orange and ocher shades in a pattern peculiar to the Comanche.

"Learn this pattern well, shaman," the medicine man advised, "for it is the paint of the Comanche medicine man, and it will stay the arrows of the Comanche and enable you to show the sign of friendship of the Kotsoteka."

The Kotsoteka token of friendship was a buffalo horn, intricately carved. "This is the mark of Buffalo Shadow," the chief said as he presented the horn to Renno. "It will be honored by all Comanche."

The horn was cumbersome to wear. Pierced at the large end, it was hung by a thong of buffalo leather around Renno's neck and tended to bang against his chest as he rode. But the trouble, he soon found, was worth it, for the paint on his face first caused the Comanche they encountered during the coming weeks to hold their fire, and the carved buffalo horn caused them to listen and then to honor the pledge of the Kotsoteka chief for friendship from all Comanche. Once again Renno thanked the manitous, for although the Comanche were thinly settled in those vast plains that began to open up before Renno's expedition, the Comanche were skilled warriors and seemed to have a sixth sense enabling them to detect intruders into their lands.

In campfire talks with the Comanche, Renno learned more about the Spanish settlements along the Rio Grande to the south and, as the hot summer days passed and the distances passed under the hooves of the horses, about the Apache and the arid lands that they called their own.

The character of the land was changing slowly. Soon they found themselves riding across sun-browned, semi-barren, waterless plains. Odd forms of vegetation were seen—dead-looking, low-growing bushes and spiked, meaty plants that William identified as members of the cactus family, plants he had seen only in books about Africa and the Caribbean islands. Water became more and more important, for the heat of the summer had dried many water holes, and the small streams that crisscrossed the flat, semiarid plain were dry, although green vegetation along their banks told them that there was running water there at some times of the year.

The month was July. The sun baked them, and the heat tired the horses quickly. And yet, as far as the eye could see, there was only the flat, barren earth and the vault of sky that seemed to overpower all. Their encounters with Comanche became less and less frequent. The hunting was sporadic. There were no buffalo. There was a swift, graceful, deerlike animal that was so leery and cautious that it took all of Renno's skill to bag one. And there were plentiful rabbits of a type Renno had never seen, large, long-eared, swift, and tough on the teeth.

With July over half-gone, they had not crossed a stream of any consequence for weeks. The sameness of the landscape made for a certain restlessness, a boredom. Still there was no view of dry mountains, no burning sands to tell them that they were nearing their destination.

"It is easy to understand why the Spanish have not moved to the north," William remarked to Beth as they rode side by side, the horses walking slowly, with Blue Feather, clad only in his loincloth, slumped, half-asleep, just ahead of them. "First, in the parts of this country that are fit for human habitation, there are the Comanche, and then this—" He spread his hand to indicate the landscape. "It's not fit for man or beast."

But there were some animals. Now and then during the days Renno would catch sight of animals similar to wolves but smaller, animals that were shy, swift, and man-wise. At night the expedition would hear the animals howling—sharp, staccato yip-yips followed by a mournful wail. The Comanche-Spanish word for the animal was "coyote."

Toward the end of the long, hot day, Renno saw a line of trees in the distance and set that as his goal, for the trees denoted water. It was almost dark when the stream was reached. It ran low, but the water was pure and clear, not deep enough for bathing, but delicious and cooling to human and horse. The stream had a white sandy bottom under a mere trickle of water. Beth, who thought that a bath would be the most divine thing she could imagine, began to scoop out the sand to create a hole, a natural bathtub. She and Ena and Holani had walked downstream from the camp, where Blue Feather was roasting antelope meat. The Indian women, understanding Beth's intention, began to help, all three of them on their knees, digging out the white sand with their hands, kneeling in the water, heedless of getting their worn clothing wet. In that arid climate, doeskin would dry quickly, and the clothes were ripe for washing.

The water was deliciously cool, as if it had come from a spring. Holani playfully threw a cupped handful of water into Ena's face and laughed as Ena sputtered. Ena said, "Ah!" and began to splash water on Holani. Beth, being splattered, began to splash water on both, so that soon all three of them were drenched to the skin, giggling, and feeling cool and refreshed for the first time in days.

When all had tired of the water fight, Ena sat down in the hole, and the water came to her waist. "Good." She sighed deeply.

Holani, with the casualness of the Indian to nudity, removed her clothing and began to rub her skin with the white sand to cleanse it. Soon both Holani and Ena were nude, sitting side by side in the deeper water, laughing, occasionally splashing each other, and leaning back to let their hair lie in the more shallow water to be rinsed.

Beth, from a different culture, could not be as casual about nudity as the others. At last she removed her clothing and soaked herself. When they heard Blue Feather's whistle, meaning that the evening meal was ready, all three dressed quickly and ran back to the campfire that was burning cheerily. Nights cooled off quickly there in that land, and Beth was longing to return alone to the stream, to bathe in the natural bathtub they had excavated and to use the last of her carefully hoarded soap to wash her hair. But she was hungry. Living in the open, she had found, was the finest of appetite stimulants, but although she ate almost as much as the men, she did not gain weight. She was trimmed down to basic woman—curved, slim, and firm.

"We will rest here tomorrow," Renno announced. "The horses need it. There is good water. We will hunt from this place, for the antelope must come to the stream to drink."

"I second that heartily," William enthused. "I could use a day without that blasted saddle."

Since there were no objections, it was settled. Blue Feather crawled into his blankets as soon as he finished eating. There had been a very pretty little Comanche widow at the last Indian camp, a woman of considerable passion, and he was still a bit tired. El-i-chi had been giving William knife-throwing lessons. They picked a tree outlined in the glow of the fire, which was blazing merrily as it consumed large quantities of the dry, fallen limbs that had been lying along the creek, and began their almost nightly practice.

"Renno, do you think it will be all right if I go just downstream and bathe?" Beth asked. It had become standard procedure for each of the women to be certain that at least one man knew where she was at all times, even when she withdrew from the camp for reasons of personal privacy.

Renno nodded. Beth took her last bit of precious soap and disappeared into the darkness. Rusog and Ena, although they rarely left the others at night, picked up their blankets and walked together upstream. Holani was seated by the fire, occasionally feeding sticks into it from the pile gathered by the men. Renno sat, his legs crossed, staring at the fire, deep in his own thoughts. It was the time of night that he concentrated on thinking of Emily. Her time would be nearer now. She expected that the birth of their child would come in the early autumn.

He concentrated his thoughts on one of the more pleasant moments of the day and pictured his wife. She would be in their lodge, perhaps playing with Little Hawk. Her belly would be big with their daughter. Perhaps she had taken her pale hair down, so it would be hanging to her waist. Maybe she was using one of her white-man's brushes. When she brushed her hair in the wintertime, it gave off little cracks and sparkles of life. It was the color of wheat and was always clean and fragrant to his nose as he held her in their bed.

I see you, he thought, with an intensity that surely would send his love winging backward over the moons of travel, the endless miles. *I see you, my wife*.

Beth, in the privacy of the night, with only the early and brilliant field of stars to give light, sat in the hole in the clear creek and dipped her hair, soaped it, rinsed it, then lost the last tiny scrap of soap to the stream and could not find it. Oh, well, she thought, it had been just a tiny scrap. She would now use clean sand to scour herself, as the Indians did, and she would just have to rinse her hair longer with no soap to clean it.

The sky was so filled with stars that she lost herself in admiration, lying back, her nude body covered to the waist, her back in shallow, inches-deep running water. She thought of home. It seemed so distant. She thought of the wonders she had seen, the long leagues she had traveled. She remembered the childlike delight of the water fight with Ena and Holani and smiled. People were the same the world over and, given the chance, could be friends. In this savage land, where men fought for sport, coup, honor, glory, or just to steal a horse, friendship could be a powerful and moving force. Holani was always warm and friendly to her, if a bit preoccupied with the very handsome El-i-chi. If Ena sometimes seemed cold and distant, well, Beth assumed that that was her nature. She hoped Ena would warm to her over the coming weeks, although she did not expect to fall into long, womanly conversations as quickly and naturally with Ena as with Holani.

She should have been shocked, she told herself, to know that Holani and El-i-chi had gone through no official ceremony. Here things were more simple. Here, apparently, a man and a woman had only to say, "We are one," and it was so, for she considered Holani and El-i-chi to be just as much married as Ena and Rusog, or Renno and his lovely white wife, Emily.

How would it feel to be married to a man like Renno? Handsome, he was. Strong, brave, considerate, kind to his friends and yet so deadly in battle, so much the Seneca. Had he and his Emily said, "We are one," and made it so? She thought not. Emily, after all, was white, and during her brief stay in the Seneca village, Beth had come to know her as a God-fearing woman. Could she ask Renno if he and his wife had had a Christian marriage? No. As open as he was, Renno was a private man about his family life, often withdrawing to live in his own thoughts.

But how would it be—and this thought made her blush—to be the wife of a man like Renno, to live in his lodge and be in his bed?

She sat up, disconcerted by the heat that that thought had generated, splashed, and directed her thoughts elsewhere. She was not ready to go back to the camp, for the water was deliciously cool. She sat very still, and her thoughts went, not back to Renno, but to a man like him, and she wondered: How *would* it be to kiss him, to be taken into his arms, to be his?

She was far away, somewhere in a dream world, when a sizable segment of the local coyote population decided that it was serenade time. The animals, having come down to the stream to drink, had congregated on a small hill not over a hundred feet upwind from where Beth, thinking some rather daring thoughts, lolled in the cool stream. They burst into song as if on a signal from a band director.

Yip-yip-yip-ooooooooooooooow.

Beth screamed and leapt from the hole, fell, caught herself with her hands, and heedless of her nudity, raced up the shallow creek toward the fire. A coyote's song heard close at hand and unexpectedly is an eerie thing that, like the sudden rise of a covey of quail underfoot, can spook even an old wilderness hand.

The scream tore Renno away from a dream world of his own, and even as it vanished he was moving, musket in hand, leaping to his feet and disappearing into the darkness before El-i-chi and William could move. He heard Beth running rapidly in the shallow water and met her fifty feet outside the circle of firelight. But Beth's scream had apparently been taken by the coyotes as approval, or perhaps participation, and the serenade was now in full voice. He saw that nothing was pursuing her, halted, and was almost bowled over as a hundred and ten pounds of naked female threw herself into his arms.

"All around me," she gasped. She was shivering. She was naked and wet, and she had tried to make herself a part of Renno for protection, and he was a man with a shivering, warm, nude woman in his arms.

A questioning owl hoot came from behind Renno, and he heard two people coming fast.

"It's all right," Renno called out. "The song of the coyote startled her. Go back."

El-i-chi had come near enough to see two people making one profile as they stood in the shallow waters of the creek—his brother and Beth in close embrace. El-i-chi analyzed the situation correctly and thought nothing of it. In fact, it seemed funny to him.

"Yip-yip-yooooowwwoo," he howled, then roared with laughter.

"It isn't funny!" Beth called out, indignant. She was still shivering. Suddenly it dawned on her that she was naked and in Renno's arms. "Oh!" she cried, pushing away.

Renno let her go. In the dim light of the stars he saw her pale beauty and had the memory of her warmth and softness against his chest, in his arms, pushing in fear against his loins. "Go and get your clothing," he suggested softly.

"Yes," she said, taking a few steps before a new chorus of the coyote serenade burst the silence.

"Renno," she whispered in a little girl's voice.

He walked to her and took her arm and once again she became aware of her nudity. "No, go back," she said. "I'm—"

"In the dark I see only that you have a very white rump," Renno said with a chuckle.

In the dark he did not see that another had arrived nearby, a silent, grim-faced Ena, who hid in the shadows, watching, listening.

Beth was glad that Renno could not see the redness of her face. She stepped on a stone in the bed of the stream and her weight went against him, soft flank to his. She jerked away.

"Here we are," she said, seeing the dark shadow of her clothing on the bank. "I'll be just a moment."

Renno watched as she pulled the doeskin dress over her head, and now he saw a darkness instead of the white of her nude body. "Our furry friends are in good voice," he commented casually. "Look, you can see some of them. There, their outlines show against the sky."

He stepped forward, and his foot went into the hole the women had dug and he sat down with a great splash.

"Are you all right?" Beth asked anxiously, running to him. "I should have warned you."

"I'm all right," Renno answered.

"Are you sure?" she asked, squatting beside him.

She smelled wet and clean and womanly, and Renno got to his feet hurriedly, took her hand, and helped her up. "Come," he said. "I have already had my bath." But he soon released her hand, for there was a soft touch there that disturbed him, that made him seek the image of Emily and hold it very close.

"Yip-yip—" William called as they walked back into the light of the fire.

"Oh, button up your big mouth," Beth said.

"Yip, yip, ooooooooo," William howled.

The day's rest was good for all of them, not just for the horses. In the heat of the afternoon the women enlarged the excavated natural bathtub in the streambed. Being warned of male invasion, the women put on their clothing and were joined by Rusog, William, and El-i-chi, who built a sand dam across the shallow creek high enough to create a pool of clear, cool water large enough and deep enough for all to wallow in playfully and to give water for a series of water fights.

During the enjoyable afternoon, Beth had no idea that Ena had seen her with Renno, nude and shivering in his arms. When Ena took her arm and pulled her upstream, away from the others, she went with a smile on her face.

"What it is, Ena?" Beth asked after they were out of earshot.

Ena turned Beth to face her, her hand firm on Beth's arms. "Englishwoman," Ena said, her voice low and intense, "I tell you this once, and only once. The others may not have seen through that charming little scene you played last night, but I did."

"What do you mean?" Beth gasped.

"No more," Ena said flatly. "No more flirting, no

more flaunting of yourself to my brother, do you understand?"

"Ena, it wasn't like that—"

"For he has a wife, and a son, and yet he is a man, with a man's natural wants. And I will not see you tempt him."

Ena turned and left an astounded Beth standing alone. It was some time before she recovered enough to walk back to the camp, where she found Holani and Ena preparing the meal.

The morning hunt had been quite successful. There were fresh antelope meat and parched corn and all the fresh water one could want. But the next morning, they were headed west again.

The water from the creek fortunately lasted both humans and horses for two days, for it was that long before they found a water hole in the bed of a dry stream—a hole much used, judging from the tracks, by animals ranging from small to large. And then the lack of water intensified. After days of riding, low, barren hills appeared on the horizon, and days later, the group, dry, thirsty, caked with blowing dust, began to make its way through rugged badlands that often required the retracing of their trail and another try to get past some dry, deep, impassable canyons.

It was there, in the dry hills, not yet worthy to be called mountains, that Beth, still somewhat in shock from Ena's unjustified and surprising accusations, saw another aspect of Renno's character and his remarkable and inexplicable gifts. Amid a desolate landscape, their lips cracking with thirst, their throats parched, and their horses lathered by the dry heat, Renno halted and held up his hand until the others halted. He cocked his head and listened for a moment, then told them to stay while he dismounted. Showing no hint of thirst or tiredness, he began to scale a rocky slope. Some one hundred feet above those who watched, he reached a ledge and extended his hand, and for the first time Beth saw the object of Renno's climb—a hawk.

Renno had heard the bird's cry, and it was as if the cry had been uttered for his ears alone. He had long been a keen observer of hawks of all species, and he had recognized something different in the cry, something he could not have explained until he reached the ledge and saw the hawk, a half-grown bird with the dark markings of the fledgling. He thought at first that the bird simply was not old enough to fly, until it cried out to him again plaintively, making a sound he had never heard from a hawk. He saw then that one wing drooped, as if broken. He took out a piece of pemmican and extended it in his hand. The bird hopped forward and took the bit of food.

"You are hurt, Brother," Renno said soothingly, extending his hand slowly. The hawk made only one defensive stab at Renno's hand, and when Renno did not jerk his hand back, the bird relaxed and let Renno touch the injured wing. Slowly, slowly, he moved to the bird and examined the injury with both hands.

"It is not broken, my brother," Renno said, "and that is fortunate." He picked the bird up carefully, positioned it so that it perched on his bare forearm, the talons clamping just tightly enough to hold but not pierce the skin. He made his way down the rocky slope carefully. The wing of the hawk had looked as if it had been chewed. Perhaps the young bird had tried to eat something that bit back. Some feathers were missing or broken, but they would grow back, and the lacerations would heal in time. The chief dangers to the bird were starvation and dehydration during the healing process.

Beth moved her horse close as Renno cupped his hand and poured water from a skin into it. The hawk drank, dipping its fierce beak and then lifting its head skyward.

"That is enough for now, Brother," Renno said. He took a piece of doeskin from spare material in a pack, wrapped it around his left forearm, and the hawk had a perch on Renno's arm as they rode.

That night the hawk perched on the limb of a dry

mesquite bush and tore at the fresh meat that Renno fed it. The next morning, after a dry camp, Renno wore a buckskin shirt in spite of the heat and placed the bird on his shoulder, for it was tiring to hold out his wrist and arm for the hawk's perch. They found water in the afternoon, its presence foretold from a distance by greenery, and there, in a narrow canyon, was a beautiful clear stream cascading down a thirty-foot waterfall. The pool below the falls was the center of an oasis of greenery, and they made an early camp to allow the horses to partake of the thick green grass. At the evening meal the hawk sat on Renno's left wrist, tearing at a chunk of fresh meat held in one talon. The bird made a contented sound very much like that made by a purring cat.

The traveling now was very slow and sometimes dangerous. Squalling, frightened horses had to be led along trails on the sheer mountainside, with a drop of two hundred feet below them. Once Renno caught just a quick glimpse of an animal, high above them, a sheeplike animal he had thought to be a fable. The animal seemed to find purchase with its hooves on a sheer face and, just as Renno sighted movement, made three or four tremendous bounds, once finding a landing place on a sharp point of rock. Then it was gone around a ridge. Once Renno had seen the huge, curled, magnificent horns, he promised himself the honor of taking one of those animals. He knew that it would be impossible to follow that mountain sheep along those sheer cliffs, so he did not know exactly how he would take the animal, but he knew that he would be successful.

In that dry, superheated area, game was very scarce. When next they found water in a mountain pool, water that did not taste nearly as good as that of the waterfall, Renno told the others to make camp, for it was necessary to find game. He hunted alone. The others would hunt in different directions, with Blue Feather staying in camp ostensibly to guard the women. Everyone knew that Ena was capable of protecting Holani and Beth from danger, but the old Indian was beginning to show signs of his age, and the long, arduous trip was taking its toll on him. "Guarding the women" was a way to let the old man rest and keep his pride.

Renno hunted on foot, for he could move faster without a horse in that rocky, mountainous badlands area. He sought the sandy floors of the canyons, always alert for sign of the desert antelope. He was far from his camp when the sky began to darken. For weeks they had not seen rain. If it came, he would welcome it for its coolness and for its life-giving water.

Chapter VIII

In the Smoky Mountains of Tennessee, spring had brought the usual things to eat to the Cherokee and Seneca tribes, and the weather had been beautiful—so much so that Nora Johnson, usually not fond of outdoor living, was enjoying herself hugely during her stay with her daughter and her grandson in the Seneca village. Roy Johnson had had some fine hunting trips with the warriors and was in no hurry to get back to Knoxville. Nora participated in the outings of the women and children to gather the new, edible greenery. Emily, who always enjoyed the outings, went along on the first one but seemed to tire rapidly.

One reason for the Johnsons' extended stay with their daughter was Nora's concern for her daughter's health in the fourth month of her pregnancy. Usually pregnancy seemed to bring out a glowing health in a young woman but in rare cases the growth of new life seemed to sap a woman's strength, as if the developing child in her womb were demanding too much. Thus it was with Emily's second pregnancy. Instead of filling out and being more round in the face, she began to grow gaunt. While pregnant with Little Hawk, Emily had not been troubled with morning sickness and had only one or two bouts with it early in her second pregnancy. But in the fourth month it seemed that her stomach could not accept any food.

"I'm fine," Emily would assure her mother when Nora tended to fuss over her and to try to do things for her. "It's just that it's so hot."

Since the weather was still cool and pleasant, that comment only created more concern in Nora. "Emily, you're going back to Knoxville with us," Nora said firmly. "Renno won't be back for months. You can have the child in civilized comfort, and Renno can come for you when he returns."

"This is my home, Mother," Emily said. "I'm all right. You and Father go on home when you're ready. Ah-wen-ga and Toshabe will take care of me."

Nora and Ah-wen-ga had become good friends. Because Ah-wen-ga enjoyed the taste of the English tea Nora had brought with her, the two women had developed an afternoon ritual of having a cup in Ah-wen-ga's lodge, sometimes sharing it with a few others. When Emily showed signs of problems with her pregnancy, Nora brought up the subject one afternoon.

"She is strong," Ah-wen-ga said, "but she was not born and bred to our life."

Nora considered the meaning of those words for a moment. "I've asked her to come home with me and have the baby in Knoxville."

Ah-wen-ga nodded. "So she told me."

"Do you favor that course?" Nora asked.

"I would offer no objections," Ah-wen-ga replied.

"Do you think that riding would be dangerous to her or the baby?" Nora asked.

Ah-wen-ga spread her hands. "If it is the will of the manitous that the child be taken, it will be taken."

"It would also give me a chance to spoil my grandson," Nora added with a smile, trying to lighten the concern both women were feeling for Emily.

Ah-wen-ga laughed. "Yes, that is the joy of being a grandparent. It will be good for the boy to learn the ways of his mother and her people, as well as ours."

Ever so gently, Nora began to put more pressure on Emily to go home with her. Emily resisted. Even though her heart told her that Renno might return any day, her reason told her that he had gone so far away that it would still be months before she saw him. If he found the gold—and she was sure he would—then the return trip would be even slower, and she had only a vague idea of the great distances involved.

Nature made the decision for Emily one day when she was alone in the lodge with Little Hawk. He had fought taking his afternoon nap, but she had rocked him to sleep in her lap. When she rose to place him on his bed, the blood drained from her brain, all became blackness, and she awakened to see Little Hawk pawing at her, crying. She had fainted and dropped him, but, thank God, he was not hurt.

Of course she could have asked Ah-wen-ga or Toshabe to tend to her, or she could bring one of the young unmarried girls of the tribe into the lodge on a semipermanent basis. But in the end, it was the welfare of the unborn child that caused her to begin packing and to inform her mother that she would go to Knoxville. Yes, Ah-wen-ga was an experienced midwife, and there were other women in the tribe who had aided in the birth of many, many Seneca and Cherokee babies. But Renno had so wanted a daughter, and to think of disappointing him . . . The chance of anything happening to the baby colored Emily's thinking more than her own welfare. For

Renno she would give this child, who seemed to be having problems, the best care she could provide, with a white doctor in attendance at the birth.

She felt quite well during the early stage of the trip and rode without discomfort and with no apparent discomfort for the baby. The last day, however, was very tiring, and when they reached the Johnson house in Knoxville she gladly left the care of Little Hawk to her mother and went to bed immediately. She fell asleep quickly but awoke with a scream. She had dreamed that Renno was in deadly peril. The nature of the danger was not clear. She knew only that in her dream the danger was real and that she had felt, for a moment, an emptiness of such magnitude that she was weeping.

After a short but thoroughly uncomfortable voyage, the Spanish ship carrying Father Sebastián and the Spanish force of cavalry landed at the small settlement of Corpus Christi. The men were only too happy to get off the ship and onto dry land and did not protest too much when Lope Barca ordered them into camp outside the city.

For Barca, the short voyage had served a purpose: he had made the acquaintance of Friar Sebastián's right-hand man, one Carlos Montenegro, who dressed in finery as if he were still back at court in Spain and, after the initial establishment of Sebastián's authority, relayed the friar's orders and requests to Barca. At first Barca had disliked the man for his arrogance. As time passed, however, he began to understand Montenegro.

The initial clues to Montenegro's character came when he questioned Barca, rather casually, about the prospects for riches of the Incan and Aztec sort in the dry and distant lands of New Mexico. Instead of laughing at the man's ignorance, Barca fanned the fires of greed and ambition with trite tales of the Seven Cities of Gold.

Furthermore, Barca learned that Montenegro liked his drink, while the good friar, not against a bit of wine for the digestion, was strongly opposed to more potent beverages. Barca had brought aboard his own supply of good island rum, and when he began to share it with Montenegro, something as close to a friendship as possible between two such men began to form. Barca's main interest was to worm out of Montenegro the purpose and destination of their journey, and for days Montenegro played it coy, pretending that he himself did not know.

"Perhaps it is to convert the heathen Indians," Montenegro suggested.

"There is little profit in that," Barca said.

The two men tended to ride together once the expedition got under way from Corpus Christi. Barca's marching orders were simple: after striking the Rio Grande by marching overland from the coast, they would follow the river to the northwest. The store of supplies and ammunition being transported by a great number of pack animals told Barca that the journey would be a long one.

"Surely," he said as he rode side by side with Montenegro, who, even in the heat, insisted on wearing the outdated chest armor Barca had found in the garrison, "the good father is not mad enough to attempt to march all the way to the Pacific Ocean."

"No," Montenegro replied.

"Ah, but I thought you didn't know our destination. . . ." Barca said.

"In confidence," Montenegro said, "the distance is not more than seven hundred miles."

That was more than enough. "Does your master realize that we will be entering the lands of the most hostile Indians in this country, the Apache?"

"I'm sure that Father Sebastián has planned well," Montenegro assured him. "After all, we have two hundred men-at-arms. What can the Apache do against armored cavalry and gunfire?"

"Ask those who have tried to settle in Apache country," Barca suggested sarcastically. "I can only pray that that which we seek is worth the deaths that will result."

"You can be assured of that," Montenegro said.

Barca mused silently for a while. He had discovered some few things about Montenegro. In spite of his sometimes foppish appearance, the man was worldly-wise and had a certain native cunning. It was surprising, in a way, to find him as the servant and lieutenant of a man of God, for reliable sources had told Barca that Montenegro had been exiled from Spain after seducing a distant relative of the monarch at the Spanish court. That he had not been turned over to the Inquisition or summarily put to death was a puzzle answered, perhaps, by the fact that the powerful Friar Sebastián valued him and his services.

"If there is gold in New Mexico," Barca asked, "it could serve no better purpose than to further enrich the Church, is that not right?"

For a moment something approaching disgust showed on Montenegro's face, and Barca smiled inwardly. He had the man pegged now.

"I have always held the position that those who risk their lives by fighting or just riding in the desolate and arid stretches of the country deserve a fair share of any profit," Barca said. "Although, of course, I bow to the authority of Mother Church."

"I, too," Montenegro said, "bow to the authority of Mother Church." He turned in his saddle and looked into Barca's eyes. "But like you, I have an eye for personal advancement, Captain Barca."

"That is a subject worthy of some talk, is it not?" Barca asked.

"A subject that is indeed dear to my heart," Montenegro answered. "I understand that you spent some years at court?"

"I did," Barca confirmed.

"And how many did you encounter who were desirous of *your* welfare and advancement?"

Barca laughed. "Señor Montenegro," he said, "I do think that we are beginning to understand each other. It is true that one's own welfare and personal riches are seldom considered by others—unless there is common cause, and the promise of mutual benefit."

The two men spent several more days skirting the issue, and by then the Rio Grande was reached. Friar Sebastián, who had eaten well all his life, was having some difficulty adjusting to the hardships of the march and had a habit of falling into his bedroll quickly after having been served his evening meal. It was left to Montenegro to care for the father's personal equipment and to see to it that his tent was pitched in a quiet, dry spot. Montenegro took advantage of having free run among the friar's possessions on the first night in camp on the river. He sought out Barca, surreptitiously motioned him away from a gathering of men around a large campfire, and took him outside the camp.

"Light a small fire," Montenegro said. "You will need the light to see."

In a few minutes Barca had twigs blazing brightly. He accepted a piece of folded parchment from Montenegro and opened it carefully. He saw a crude map of that portion of New Spain extending northward from Mexico City and west of the gulf. The map showed the large curve of the Rio Grande. Two routes led to an area in New Mexico west of the Rio Grande—one from the south, one from Corpus Christi. It took him a moment to find the end of both routes, a common point near a mountain called Mount Diablo. It was in the heart of Apache country. But his blood began to race faster when he saw, on the side of the mountain, the representation of a cross and the words "El Oro del Diablo." He tried to memorize the map quickly before handing it back to Montenegro.

"I take it, my friend," Barca said as he stomped out the fire with his boots, "that you agree with me in thinking that the Church should be more generous to those who do its dangerous work."

"If that skinny, big-beaked hypocrite knew how little I think of the Church and all those associated with it," Montenegro said in a voice that expressed more than contempt, "I would have died on the rack long ago." He had his hand on the butt of his pistol, awaiting Barca's reaction.

"Are you sure that we were not fathered by the same man?" Barca asked, reaching out to clasp Montenegro's hand.

Montenegro laughed. "There is that possibility, although my father was an uncle to a king and neglected to share his name with me."

Now it was Barca's turn to laugh. "Then perhaps we have the same mother," he said, "for mine was sometimes careless about whom she let into her bed. It seems that we are one of a kind, my friend. I expect no help from those in power, and I think you are in the same position."

"I have watched you closely, Captain," Montenegro confessed. "I see you making yourself a friend of the men in your command. I see you sharing your rum with selected ones among them. I think that most of those men would obey your orders, regardless of the content, without question and with loyalty."

"You are very astute."

"And this is a large and lonely land. One man could so easily meet with ill fortune, and no one could be blamed."

"The dangers are many. The strenuous effort of the march, the sting of a viper, the arrows and weapons of hostile Indians," Barca said, his voice low.

"As it happens," Montenegro commented, "I spent much time with Baron de Carondelet in New Orleans. Although he is a nobleman, I found much in common with him, as I have with you. I know the de Carondelets. Their holdings in Spain are wastelands, unfruitful. The good baron has nothing in Spain to make him wish to return. But I have good reason to know that should it be possible for him to return to Spain with a sizable fortune—"

"I have underestimated you," Barca said.

"I have not made that same mistake with you," Montenegro responded.

146

"Let me involve myself in fancy for a moment," Barca said. "Let us imagine that the tales of the Seven Cities of Gold have basis. We find one or more of those cities. There is gold enough for you, me, all of us—enough to content my good and loyal men, and even enough to make Baron de Carondelet happy. Would it be presumptuous to imagine that the gold could be transported out of this country without the government and the Church taking big bites from it?"

Montenegro laughed. "Not presumptuous at all, with careful planning."

"I, for one, would not have returning to Spain as a top priority," Barca told him. "There are islands of surpassing beauty, where the local authorities do not pry too deeply into the affairs of a gentleman of quality who wishes to settle among them and establish himself."

"I would like to hear all about those islands," Montenegro said. "But now I must return the map to its place. The good father often awakens to relieve himself during the night. I would hate for him to notice the map is missing or to catch me trying to replace it."

The rare desert rainstorm came upon Renno with a swiftness that was awesome. He had been following antelope tracks toward the sandy entrance to a steep-sided canyon. It seemed that only minutes had passed between his noticing a darkness in the western sky and the arrival of thunder and lightning overhead. Lightning arced down from the suddenly dark sky and smashed a boulder atop the ridge to his left with a sound like a cannon shot. The dark line of clouds raced across the sky, covering the sun, and he heard a far-off sound like rushing waters. He looked toward the west and saw a wall of darkness moving swiftly toward him and realized that the sound was wind and the dark wall was windblown sand. He would not have sought shelter from the rain, but as the wind hit him like a giant fist—the velocity changing from a slight breeze to a force so strong that he could almost lean on it—he ran toward the canyon entrance and a cave he had spotted. Sand and small particles of rock lashed his skin until he found the shelter of the western wall of the canyon and, in a moment, ducked into the cavelike depression under overhanging rock.

Now came the rain. At first it was a reddish-brown rain, and then, the air having been cleansed of the wind-blown dust, and the incredible wall of wind having passed, the rain came thundering down. He stepped out into it and turned his face upward so that the rain could wash away perspiration and dust. There was a definite chill in the rain.

The storm ended as suddenly as it had begun. The torrent of rain tapered off and then ceased, and there was only the sound of water dripping off the rocky walls of the canyon. Any trace of the antelope tracks he had been following had been obliterated. The powder-dry soil of that arid place was unable to absorb the rain quickly. It puddled and ran, and within minutes the dry wash in the canyon's floor became a muddy torrent. Fascinated by the capriciousness of nature in that strange land, Renno watched the flow of water reach a peak, carrying with it trash and floating twigs, then fall.

He would now start back toward camp. There had been a promising-looking area for antelope off to the south, which he would explore on the way. He positioned his weapons for the march, looked up to see the sun, huge, hot, glaring, back in its place, and then jerked his head toward the sound of a shriek of deadly pain. He recognized the sound as the scream of a badly wounded horse. Had one of the others somehow ridden into the canyon ahead of him? He ran to find out. The canyon narrowed so that the sandy bottom was only a few feet wide, and then it began to open out into a bowl surrounded by high, dry, rocky cliffs. Ahead of him, at the center of the bowl of the box canyon, there was greenery amid huge tumbled boulders.

There were, of course, other possibilities to explain a

horse being in the canyon ahead of him, and none of them was particularly conducive to the personal safety of a wandering stranger. He was forced to temper his speed with caution. He ran lightly, keeping to the cover of the large, randomly scattered boulders, and then the ground began to slope slightly downward. He heard, quite near now, the challenging cough of a feeding cat, and even as that sound came, his eyes caught the tracks of a large mountain lion in the freshly dampened earth.

He remembered the message he had been given in a vision from the manitous: *Alert yourself for the sign of the cat, for there is a child who will become a great chief at risk.*

He bent to make himself less conspicuous and ran in that crouched position. The earth dropped away before him, and below was a hole of clear, pure water, green grass, boulders, two stunted trees, and a sight that chilled him: Beside the water hole lay a horse, and tearing at its freshly exposed, steaming entrails was the largest cat Renno had ever seen—a great, powerful, tawny cat. So no one from his group was in danger. A stray or wild horse had provided a dinner for the king of the dry hills. He considered whether or not to kill the lion. It was not especially good for eating, being gamy, rank, and tough. His group was not yet that desperate for food. The hide would make a good trophy, but it would take time to skin the cat and then to cure the hide.

Those deliberations, made as he watched with great interest as the cat ate, became academic when he heard a small sound, a sound of pain and distress that was, beyond doubt, human. It took him a couple of seconds to spot the source of the sound, for it came from the upper side of the natural bowl, up near where the fallen rocks from the far wall made a sloping mound to the cliffs. Renno saw just a flash of brown skin and the tawny movements of another lion.

The way to the second lion led directly past the feeding cat. He dropped down the steep little incline to the ground, ran as swiftly as he could along one side of the bowl, and approached the jumbled rocks with the English longbow in his hand, an arrow ready. There was a large and dangerous animal at his back, and he did not want to alert it with the sound of a musket shot.

Up ahead, at the base of the cliff, he saw a small, dark opening. Then he saw the mountain lion. The animal was dragging a small body toward the cave. The cat's teeth were clamped to the boy's shoulder, and the lion had to sidle backward, exposing just the angle Renno needed for a killing shot. He drew the longbow to its most powerful potential. The arrow flew forward to sing and hit with an audible thud, slide between ribs to pierce the cat's heart, and still have enough force left to break a rib and emerge out the other side. The cat dropped instantly and twitched only a few times. The boy was surely dead, but Renno did not have a chance to find out, for he heard a wild, snarled scream and turned just in time to see the other cat launch itself from atop a rock directly at him. He had, by habit, nocked a second arrow as soon as he had released the first, and that habit saved his life, for he was able to pull and release so that the arrow traveled only a few feet, caught the cat in midair, and pierced the tough muscles that protected the area of the heart from the direct front. Then Renno was trying to launch himself out of the path of the falling cat, but he had taken too much time getting off his shot. The mountain lion landed across his lower body, the weight bearing him to the ground with a jar that dazed him. He had trouble getting his breath, and even as he fought for breath he was reaching for his tomahawk, which flashed and descended as the dying cat sought, even in death, to reach Renno's face with its powerful teeth. The great force of Renno's arm pushed the blade into the skull, obliterating an eye and crushing the bone, and then all was still except his laboring lungs as he tried to regain his breath.

When at last he had air back in his lungs, he pulled out from under the feral-smelling body of the cat, gingerly

tested his limbs, and found himself to be all in one piece.
He was bruised but not blooded. He turned his thoughts
to the victim of the lion, and he was surprised to find the
boy alive. There were great tooth puncture wounds in the
boy's shoulder and another area of abrasions on his left
thigh. Renno poured water from his water skin and gently
used his hands to wash away blood and dirt and saw, to his
surprise, that although the teeth holes were deep and
jagged, they were not in themselves fatal. The leg seemed
to be more scratched than bitten. He was cleaning the leg
wounds when the boy spoke.

"I don't know you," the boy said.

"Nor I you," Renno answered. "The lion seemed to
know you well, however."

The boy turned his head, saw the dead lion, and took
a deep breath. "There is another one. It killed my horse."

"A pair," Renno said. "Male and female. I did not
consider it polite to send one to the West without the
other."

"I am Sky Dancer, son of Gerachise."

"You have lost much blood," Renno said. "I will carry
you to the water, where I can clean the wounds better."

"One does not touch the son of Gerachise without
permission," the boy replied regally, although his voice
was still weak.

"I beg your pardon," Renno said formally. The boy
was not over ten, he thought, for he was short and small.
"This traveler asks permission to touch the body of the son
of Gerachise."

"Be very careful," the boy warned.

"Of course," Renno said, gathering the small body in
his arms. He walked slowly, stepping over the fallen cat,
placed the boy on soft grass beside the clear pool, and got
more water. The boy winced but did not cry out when
Renno washed the wounds thoroughly, knowing that the
festering rot was most dangerous in puncture wounds,
especially bite wounds.

"I don't think it's necessary to bathe me all over," Sky Dancer said.

"Forgive me," Renno responded, still humoring the boy, who was showing great bravery. He knew that Sky Dancer was in considerable pain, for his lips were white and his face beaded with the perspiration of suffering. A boy that brave needed some humoring. Renno hoped that his own son, if he should ever be as badly hurt, would show as much stoic courage.

He took two fingers on each hand and held together the edges of two of the deeper wounds that were still welling blood. The pressure caused the bleeding to stop. Once the boy fainted, but he was soon awake, watching Renno from large black eyes in a flat, swarthy face.

"The bleeding has stopped," Renno said. "When you are stronger, I will carry you to my friends. It may be necessary to stitch some of the wounds."

"I will use my own two feet," Sky Dancer announced, "and I will not go to your friends, but to my home."

"Your home is near?"

He saw a look of suspicion come over the boy's face. "I am grateful for your help, but it is no longer needed," Sky Dancer said.

"Good," Renno answered, "for I have my own business, and since you are such a great and strong warrior who no longer needs help, I will be about it." He rose.

"Perhaps I will need your help just a little longer," Sky Dancer said.

Renno sat down and held his water skin to the boy's lips. The boy drank thirstily.

"I will tell my father not to kill you," Sky Dancer informed the white Indian.

"That is kind of you," Renno said with a raised eyebrow.

"I will make you my slave, and I will beat you only when you are arrogant, as you are now."

"Your kindness overwhelms me," Renno replied.

"You have the sly tongue of a Comanche," Sky Dancer continued. He seemed to be growing stronger, but when he tried to sit up, one of the wounds opened and Renno had to press it together again to stop the bleeding.

"I am Seneca. I have come through a march of five moons, from beyond the buffalo plains, from beyond the lands of the Comanche and the land of the hot springs and the mountains, from beyond the great river."

"You lie," Sky Dancer said. He flinched when Renno's blue eyes lashed him coldly.

"In my own lands I would punish such impudence with the back of my hand. Here, in yours, I will credit such words of a fool as being induced by the pain of your wounds."

Sky Dancer said nothing, but his eyes suddenly widened, and a smug look came over his face. Renno, seeing the expression, leapt for his musket and turned, in a crouch, to freeze in that position. He had fought with and against many tribes. Never had any other man surprised him so totally. Never had white or Indian come within striking distance of him undetected. Now, standing atop and beside the scattered, huge boulders, were perhaps twenty squat, dark, loin-clothed warriors. Their broad faces expressed nothing, giving him no hint of their intentions.

Renno straightened slowly but was careful not to raise the muzzle of his musket. One man, a bit taller than the rest, stepped forward, nudged the body of the dead lion with his toe, then walked slowly around the water hole.

"I am not badly hurt, Father," Sky Dancer said.

The warrior seemed not to hear. He halted, staring at Renno, and the moment seemed to be suspended in time. Renno kept his blue eyes glued to the dark ones of the strange warrior. Suddenly, out of the corner of his eye, he saw motion. Even as he raised his musket, one arrow, then another and another, zinged through the air to lodge in the carcass of the dead lion. Renno raised his musket to aim at the heart of the warrior facing him.

"If your young men want the coup of killing already dead lions, there is another near the cliff face," Renno said in Spanish.

The warrior raised one hand and barked an order in an odd, guttural language. Then he said in Spanish, "I read the signs. What say you, Sky Dancer?"

"The strange one killed two lions," the boy confirmed. "He pulled me from the jaws of the second. He is brave and should not die. I will keep him, Father."

"This is true?" the warrior asked Renno.

"It is as he said."

"Then I owe you for the life of my son, who, as you suggested within my hearing just now, will receive the back of my hand and more when his wounds no longer pain him."

Renno let the musket fall slowly. "I have come in peace to travel through the dry mountains, with the permission of the great chiefs of the Apache, on a mission of great medicine."

"You will go in peace, warrior."

"You are this one's father, Gerachise?"

"This is so."

"I am Renno of the Seneca, from far to the east, near the great sea of bitter water. Your women will use the skins of the lions?"

"They are yours," Gerachise said.

"Mine, and my gift to you," Renno offered.

"Come," Gerachise said. "We have killed antelope, and there will be fresh meat. You will be our honored guest."

"I have friends camped not far away," Renno told him.

"The friends of Two-Lion-Killer are my friends," Gerachise said. Only then did he take the time to look at his son's wounds, grunted, nodded, rose, and issued orders in his own language. Young warriors picked Sky Dancer up carefully and set him on a horse. Another warrior led a horse to Renno and handed him the reins. "I will go with you to fetch your friends," Gerachise said.

El-i-chi had also made his kill, a young antelope, whose meat would be tender. He was doing the final dressing on the beast in camp when he heard the call of an owl and returned it, watched until two horsemen, one of them instantly recognizable as Renno, came out of the badlands.

"*Españoles*," Gerachise said, the word filled with hatred, when he saw William and Beth.

"*No españoles*," Renno said quickly. "*Ingleses*. Many times they have fought the Spanish."

Gerachise was not convinced until he had accepted the hospitality of the camp, water and freshly cooked antelope, the meat hot, juicy, and red in the center. He was fascinated by William's tales of his home country and of England's various wars with Spain. He made no attempt to leave or to encourage the others to join him in leaving, and then it was dark. The talk went on far into the night.

"Beyond the river," Gerachise said after having had his fill of strange tales of far lands, "is the mountain of the devil. It is bad medicine. And there are the spirit cities of the old ones, the dirt eaters. Evil spirits. No Apache goes there."

"Would the Apache object if we did?" Renno asked.

"I do not speak for all Apache," Gerachise said. "This Chiricahua would not stop you. This Chiricahua would warn you that you are being a fool to go into the places of the evil spirits, but he would not stop such foolishness."

It was only a half-day's ride to the village where Gerachise was chief. His band of Chiricahua was small. The Apache tended to divide themselves into units, continuing down to the clan level, and there were no more than thirty families in Gerachise's village.

Once again Beth was a sensation. Although her exposed skin had long since become sun-browned, she was still the fairest skinned human being the Apache had ever seen, and never had they seen fiery red hair. She was the center of all eyes as Gerachise led Renno's party into the village.

Sky Dancer was lying on a pile of skins, being tended by a short, fat woman. He called out a greeting to his father, and then said loudly in Spanish, "The big one, the Indian with the pale skin, is mine, for I was the one who found him."

Still on horseback, Gerachise spoke, first in his own language and then in Spanish to Renno. "I have told my people," he said, "that you are my brother, and that insult or harm to you or your friends is insult or harm to Gerachise. Now the food and drink of my house are yours. Now we will call fiesta, and sing and dance in your honor, for you have saved that which is most precious to me, the life of my son, impudent and ungrateful though he may be."

"Look," William whispered to Beth as they sat on their horses side by side during Gerachise's speech. "Already!"

Two short, plump, broad-faced Chiricahua women had edged out from the shadow of their lodges and were eyeing Blue Feather, who sat ramrod straight in his saddle, his eyes straight ahead, on the back of Gerachise's head.

"What is it about him, Beth?" William asked, truly puzzled. "I can detect nothing. Is it some sort of scent that he puts out?"

Beth laughed softly. "He puts off just about the same scent we all put out after days in the saddle without bathing."

The food in Gerachise's house—a rude structure of sticks, hides, and thatch—was good, and there was an antelope stew filled with living fire that had a delicious taste and a horrid aftermath.

Renno, after taking a bite of the stew and experiencing a taste unlike any he had ever known, a taste that begged him to eat more but that left his mouth on fire, said, "Now I know the Chiricahua is brave."

Apparently Gerachise had been waiting for just such a comment. He roared with laughter and held up a large green pepper. "The only good thing to come out of Mexico," he said, "*chile*, the pepper of living fire."

"Good," Renno said, meaning it, but wondering how much water it would take to quench the fire in his mouth.

Chapter IX

The box canyon where Renno had saved Sky Dancer's life had been a beautiful place, but the canyon where Gerachise's group of Chiricahua Apache lived was even more beautiful. It was a wonder of sweet water and greenery amid a chaos of sun-bleached badlands. Since Gerachise was sincere in his hospitality and insisted that the group spend some time with him, Renno took advantage of the opportunity to allow the horses to rest.

There was also the opportunity to learn more about the land ahead of them, for it seemed that their journey was not yet over. As closely as William could convert the Apache methods of measuring distance, in days and moons, the mountain of their destination was two to three hundred miles farther to the west. And they would be traveling across semiarid plains into an area of true desert in the heat of the summer, in August.

The Apache were an interesting people. They did not farm and had a contempt for anyone who did—"dirt eaters," the Apache called them. The Apache were true nomads, and according to their descriptions, the range of their hunting grounds covered a wilderness so unlike the virgin forests of the homelands of the visitors that it was difficult to comprehend the emptiness. Everyone in Renno's group came to admire the Apache for his ability to eke an existence from those wide, arid stretches of land where a man either had to know the location of the scattered sources of water or perish.

Sky Dancer developed a fever as a result of his wounds and was very ill for two days, and then, with the resiliency of youth, he sprang back and was eager to get out of his bed to participate in the entertainment of the guests. Gerachise, genuinely grateful to Renno, seemed unable to do enough for him.

Rusog, William, and El-i-chi requested to be allowed to hunt with the Chiricahua warriors and returned with game and, at least on Rusog and El-i-chi's part, half-grudging praise for the skills of the Apache.

"Would Two-Lion-Killer like to hunt?" Gerachise asked Renno.

"Yes, an animal I saw in the dry mountains," Renno said. "A sheeplike animal that moved as if by magic along the sheer face of a cliff."

"Ah," Gerachise said, smiling, "the warrior sets himself a difficult task."

Renno did not again mention his half-formed desire to take one of those strange animals with the huge horns, but when he awoke with first light the next morning Gerachise was waiting for him, dressed for hunting with skin leggings to protect against the prickly brush and the rocks.

"We will be gone some days, perhaps," Gerachise remarked as they took a breakfast of rewarmed meat and tasty nuts from the piñon tree.

They rode far into the mountains and, in a spot of water and grass, hobbled their horses and began to make their way deeper into the rugged maze of canyons and hills. Renno, at the suggestion of Gerachise, had left his musket and pistols in camp. He carried only his longbow, the Spanish stiletto that never left him, and his tomahawk. Gerachise had seen the penetration of Renno's arrows into the dead lions, and he was much impressed by the oversized, thick bow.

In a hot, dry place of scattered rocks and mesquite, Renno heard a sound that he had heard only a few times during the trip out. He froze and his intent eyes located a large rattlesnake coiled in the partial shade of a mesquite bush. He was at a safe distance, so he merely stepped away and went around the snake.

"The scaled one has honor," Gerachise said approvingly as he, too, walked carefully around, out of striking range. "Unlike our enemies the Comanche, who fire their arrows from ambush, the snake gives warning. And he asks only for his own place in the sun. And unlike the Spanish, who believe that there is room only for them, the snake knows that there is room for all."

"It is a lesson we all should learn," Renno agreed. "I have not yet encountered a Spaniard."

Gerachise spat. "Once we moved freely from the green hills in the North, where there is snow, to far beyond the Rio Grande. We still ride where we want to ride, but to the south we ride as things hidden, for the hair-faced ones have claimed it as their own. To the west, where the dirt eaters built their cities of mud and stone, the Spaniard found an easier task than he found in his efforts to crowd both the Apache and the Comanche from their lands. There there is only death. Many dirt eaters died digging in the earth for the shiny metals so prized by the Spanish."

"These dirt eaters," Renno said, "do they still live near the evil mountain?"

"Perhaps a few. Only a few escaped the greed of the hair-faces. Of old they were great people and built their cities to tower to the sky. Now only the scorpion and the tarantula walk the streets, and there are ghosts."

They climbed in silence, for the going was rough. Renno noted that the short, squat Apache rarely drank from his water skin, and Renno steeled himself to drink only when Gerachise did. A rugged vista of rocky low mountains now stretched ahead of them, and at times they seemed to cling by toes and fingernails to the sides of the rocks. They made a dry camp high on a ridge.

"Tomorrow we will hunt," Gerachise said. "Even the mountain sheep must drink, and there is but one watering place near." And with that, having eaten jerky and taken a good drink from his water skin, he was asleep.

Gerachise had them in position, high on the side of a mountain, shortly after daybreak. "The mountain sheep has the eyes of an eagle and the nose of a wolf," he whispered. "If he comes, he will come there." He pointed across a drop of some three hundred feet to the sheer side of a rocky face. And then Gerachise was still, totally unmoving, and Renno emulated his immobility, the two of them fading into the rocks to be almost invisible.

Only once did they move, and that was when the sun was high and they drank sparingly. Once, from behind the opposite mountain, Renno heard an odd sound, a dull, hollow banging repeated at irregular intervals. "Two rams," Gerachise whispered, "fighting, perhaps, for the favor of a female."

Renno tried to picture what was happening and imagined the two mountain sheep leaping at each other to bang their large curled horns together.

When the mountain sheep finally appeared, it came with a suddenness that caught Renno off guard. He had been thinking of Emily, picturing her at home in his village with Little Hawk, so the swift blur of movement coming from up the mountain across the chasm was almost missed. Then he saw the animal taking incredible downward leaps, headed, just as Gerachise had predicted, for the water in the canyon below. The white Indian had his longbow in position so that all he had to do was aim, draw, and fire.

Gerachise, seeing the sudden tenseness in Renno's muscles, whispered, "He is too far, my friend. This one is not for us."

The sheep was still descending, leaping from one tiny foothold to another, and the distance was great, far too great for Gerachise's bow, but Renno saw that the next leap of the sheep would put it almost on the level with him and within range of the English longbow. He readied himself. The sheep leapt, falling as if it would never stop, came up short and surefooted on a projecting rock, and for a moment was still. The arrow made a hissing sound of power as it left the bow, and Gerachise was shaking his head in negation when it pierced the heart of the mountain sheep and the animal collapsed in place. For a moment the sheep's legs jerked out the last uncoordinated movements of its life.

"That was a shot to become legend," Gerachise commended, shaking his head in wonder. "But, my friend, by the time we get the sheep to the canyon floor, you will be wishing, I think, that you had missed."

It was necessary, first, to climb down into the canyon, where there was a spring of clean, fresh water with the tracks of mountain sheep and lion around it. Then the real work began. The way led upward through mesquite, which scratched and tried to hold them back, and then into the full blast of the afternoon sun on a rocky face that steepened as they came within one hundred feet of the dead mountain sheep. The cliff above them was too sheer to be climbed.

"We will look for a way," Gerachise said. He pointed to his left, and Renno began edging in that direction. Gerachise went the other way, and soon they could not see each other. Renno found a fractured chimney in the cliff face and, leaving his longbow behind because it interfered with his climbing, began to inch his way upward. Once, rock crumbled under his foot and he almost fell. Then a small rockslide thundered down into the canyon. A questioning call, the yip of a coyote, came from Gerachise, and Renno answered, then began to climb again.

He was very tired and dripping perspiration when he was able to reach up and touch the woolly animal. Managing to pull himself up, Renno stood on a precarious perch astride the fallen sheep and lifted his head to give vent to the howl of a wolf. He heard an answering howl and saw Gerachise, blocked by sheer rock and thus unable to climb higher, below him and to his right.

Getting the sheep down was harder than the climb had been. It kept getting stuck in the narrow rock chimney and then was a deadweight across Renno's shoulders for the balance of the descent. But he brought it down, and Gerachise was waiting. Working together, they dressed the sheep and made camp beside the water. By the end of the next day they entered the Apache camp with Gerachise giving out triumphant war whoops.

The meat of the sheep was gamy but good, and the feast was enlivened by Gerachise's description of the impossible shot Renno had made and of the power of the longbow.

A strong young Chiricahua warrior rose. The Apache were no different from other Indians in their love of oratory. "We are all grateful that the warrior from the East saved the life of our chief's son," the man said. "But I have not seen the work of this wondrous longbow. I am Socorro, and I would pit my bow against this wondrous weapon."

A chorus of approving comments came from the other warriors, who, being men, felt some jealousy, for never had their chief done such honor to a non-Apache.

Gerachise laughed. "Socorro is a brave warrior, and we value him for his strength and unmatched skill with the bow. Tomorrow we will see how Socorro shoots against Two-Lion-Killer."

The first test was for distance. Socorro shot first, drawing his bow until it came near cracking. His arrow soared up in a trajectory designed to carry it far. When Renno stepped up, he did not even use the full potential of the superior longbow, for he had no desire to humiliate the Apache warrior. The white Indian's shot carried fifty feet beyond Socorro's arrow, but he could have added many more feet to the distance.

The next competition was to test the warriors' accuracy. Buffalo- and antelope-skull targets were set up. At short range, Socorro matched Renno shot for shot, but as the distance increased, the greater accuracy and strength of the longbow told the tale, for Renno was able to send an arrow through dried, bleached bone time after time, while Socorro missed once out of three shots. Again, Renno did not demonstrate the full potential of the longbow, for he sensed that there was a growing resentment against him among the Chiricahua warriors.

"You have shot well," Renno told Socorro sincerely. "It is the English bow that is the difference."

Socorro grunted and glared at Renno. "There are other tests," he said.

Renno knew that he had to strike a delicate balance between losing face himself and humiliating his Apache opponent. He nodded. "I welcome tests in friendship, for it is good for warriors to develop skills by pitting themselves against each other."

"We will wrestle," Socorro said, and shouts went up from the Chiricahua. Renno looked at Gerachise, who nodded in the affirmative.

Socorro stripped himself to his loincloth. A circle formed around the two men. "This is a match between brothers," Gerachise announced. "There will be no blows, and the match will be over when one man's shoulders are held against the ground."

Socorro was shorter than Renno, but he was powerfully built, thick of chest, and strong of arm. His thighs

were very muscular, and he moved with the swiftness of a
striking rattlesnake. Renno guessed that the man would
want to be the aggressor, so he took position and waited.
He did not have to wait long for Socorro to come in with
his body swaying, his arms grappling. They closed, Renno
catching Socorro's arms, to find that he was indeed very
powerful. For a long time the bout was even. The comba-
tants would close and grapple, their hands sliding on
sweat-soaked bodies, and then one or the other would
break away and begin the cautious circling again. But
Renno had detected a weakness in Socorro's technique.
There was a way to turn a man's own strength against him,
and in that Renno was skilled. Socorro came pressing in
again, putting his full weight forward, trying to force Renno
backward. Renno, however, gave way suddenly, and Socorro
fell forward. Renno leapt astride Socorro's back and locked
his arms around the Apache's neck. The hold immobilized
Socorro for a moment, but there was still power there,
and the two of them went rolling across the sand.

In the end it was Renno's reaction time, his swiftness,
that were the deciding factors. He was sure that in a long
bout he could outlast the Apache, but he wanted to stop
the competition before ill will was built among the Apache
warriors. He moved with swiftness, giving Socorro an
advantage for a split second, their position face-to-face,
with Renno on the bottom. He used all his strength to flip
the Apache, who had not had time to set himself. In a
moment Socorro was on his back, with Renno's arms locked
around him, his legs wide, providing strong anchors to
hold the Apache to the ground. And still Socorro's great
upper body and abdominal strength held his shoulders off
the ground. Renno pushed hard and heard a yell from
El-i-chi and a groan from the Chiricahua.

"Enough!" Gerachise shouted. "It is over. Two-Lion-
Killer has won."

Renno sprang away from Socorro. The Apache came
to his feet, his face dark with anger. Renno gave him a
respectful bow.

"I will try this pale warrior with the knife," Socorro cried out, and a knife flew through the air, tossed by one of his fellow warriors. He caught it by the handle and fell into a knife-fighter's crouch. "Or does the thought of feeling a Chiricahua blade make the great Renno go even paler?"

Renno's blood sang. He sensed the thrill of combat and wanted to wipe the look of contempt from the Apache's face but felt the wholeness of honorable war in him. He stood stolidly. "The tests were in friendship. I will compete in other tests, but only in friendship. I have no wish to take my Apache brother's blood."

"Try," Socorro challenged. "Choose your knife, pale one."

"Gerachise," Renno said, turning away from the enraged Socorro. "May I speak?"

Gerachise nodded.

"When I am finished speaking, if there are any who doubt that I have taken my scalps, I will accept any honorable challenge."

He glanced at Socorro, who was still crouched, then noted that Rusog and El-i-chi were alert. He held out his open hand to them, cautioning them to keep calm.

"Many moons ago," he continued, "when I was at my home in the east with my wife and my son, the spirits came to me."

The Chiricahua warriors looked at Renno with more attention. The mention of a visit by the spirits caught their interest.

"I had never seen the lands of the Quapaw, the Comanche, or the Apache. In my lands the tall trees touch the sky in thick forests, the green grass covers the earth, and the deer are as many as the stars in the sky. And yet I knew that I would be coming to your land, to your land of dry mountains and scarce water, for this was the message of the manitous to me. I was told several things by the spirits of my ancestors, and it was good medicine, for much that was foretold has already come true. I was told of the coming of the white ones to my home and given a prophecy regarding the flame-haired woman who travels with us. She had been an omen of good for all those through whose lands we have passed."

The eyes of the Apache went to Beth, whose hair was now braided Indian fashion.

"I was told this by the spirits of my ancestors: '*Alert yourself for the sign of the cat, for there is a child who will become a great chief at risk.*' So I came to the land of the dry mountains and saw the track of the mountain lion. I killed the lions and saved Sky Dancer's life. For me to be in that particular place, at that particular time, after having traveled for many moons, was big medicine. I ask you, is this not so?"

"It is so," verified Gerachise, glaring at Socorro, who still held the knife in his hand.

"I ask you this," Renno went on. "Is the son of Gerachise the future great chief who was at risk?"

A few Apache women made sounds of approval.

"When next you capture a Comanche," Renno added, "ask him, before you kill him, about Man-Who-Becomes-Bear."

A warrior yelped in surprise and stepped forward. "It is so," he confirmed, eyes wide, nodding toward Gerachise. "For we heard this same name from the Comanche girl who was made a slave in the village of our brothers. She talked much of this Man-Who-Becomes-Bear, for the Comanche had given passage to a great medicine man from the east."

"I have fought," Renno said, "and this I prefer to talking. I talk now only because it is the will of the spirits, for my mission is not completed. I go to the land of the people you call the dirt eaters, for I have been directed there by the spirits on behalf of my people. I wish to go in peace. If, however, the brave warrior Socorro insists on proving his honor, so be it."

There was a silence. Socorro hurled the knife down,

to stick, quivering, in the hard ground, then stepped toward Renno with his right hand extended. "I will be the friend of this warrior turned medicine man," he offered.

Renno clasped Socorro's arm. "That is good," he said. "Perhaps Socorro will travel with me, to show me his great land and to guide this stranger in it."

"I will," Socorro declared.

A whoop went up, and some of the women began to sing and dance. The festive atmosphere continued into the evening. The men of Renno's group joined Gerachise and his leading warriors for a council, and there was much oratory. Although several more warriors expressed a desire to travel with Renno, none offered to go with him all the way to the mountain of the evil spirits.

"Long ago," explained the old, wrinkled medicine man of Gerachise's people, "the metal men came from the south on great beasts. None of the people had seen such beasts, which could run like the wind and carry a man on his back." He looked around. "We know now that the metal men were the Spaniards, and that they wore vests of steel to stop our arrows. We have made the horse our own, but at first the people were in awe. Many Indians died. The dirt eaters in their cities of mud and stone fought well, but their arrows would not pierce the steel vests, and the guns of the Spaniards killed them at a distance. Those who survived were forced to dig into the earth in search of the yellow dirt so prized by the Spaniards. No man came out of the holes in the earth alive."

The audience had fallen into a grim, respectful silence.

"The dead still lie there in the holes in the ground," the old medicine man warned. "And their spirits are angry, and they moan as they wander on that evil mountain, crying out for vengeance against the Spanish."

"Why did the Spanish go away?" Renno asked.

The old man shrugged. "Perhaps there was no more yellow dirt. Perhaps the spirits of the dead haunted them. Who knows?"

"Do you still fight the Spanish?" Rusog asked.

It was Gerachise who answered. "Our young warriors test their courage in raids to the south. There the hair-faces grow the white man's cow, with meat that is fat and bland. But the Spaniards come in the numbers of the stars, and when we kill one, many more come from their far country with guns and build themselves great fortresses around the place where their medicine men sacrifice and eat the blood and flesh of their three-headed God. In these places that they have made their own, they are too strong for us. Here—" He waved his hands to indicate the Apache's arid domain. "Here we make the land ours, and the hair-faces have given up trying to claim it. They have already taken the areas of good waters and growing things, which they eat like the dirt eaters."

"And there are no Spanish near the Devil's Mountain or near the old cities of the dirt eaters?" Renno inquired.

The old medicine man spoke. "Once, after they had killed the dirt eaters or worked and tortured them to death, they tried to enslave the Apache. They found that could not happen, for the Apache would die before becoming slaves. It is said so by our stories that are handed down, and it is said that our ancestors joined forces—all the Chiricahua, the Mescalero, the Jicarilla, the Lipan, and the Kiowa Apache—and drove the last of the hair-faces from the lands west of the river." He spread his hands. "There it is Apache land."

"It is time for me to go there, as I have been instructed by the manitous," Renno said. "Gerachise's hospitality has given us joy, and we ask that the Chiricahua think, as we do, that we are brothers, sons of the same parents in time long gone by."

"It is so," Gerachise agreed, and there was a grunt of approval from the other Chiricahua.

A young warrior leapt to his feet. "With the permission of the great medicine man from the east, I will accompany Socorro."

"Gladly," Renno said, and then, one by one and two by two, other warriors volunteered.

"Enough," Gerachise said at last, after twenty of his young warriors had committed themselves, "or there will be no man left to hunt and guard our women and children."

A day's ride west from the canyon of Gerachise's camp saw them entering wide, grassy expanses that the Spanish called the Llano Estacado. Deer and antelope became more plentiful as the miles were traveled, and there were wolves and, of course, coyote. The earth was pocked in large areas by the burrows of prairie dogs, and prairie-dog towns were avoided, lest a horse break its leg by stepping into one of the burrows. Renno's hawk, whose wing had completed healing during the stay with the Chiricahua, ate well on those plains, for it was but the work of a few minutes for him to claim an unwary prairie dog as his prey. The hawk spent most of the time soaring, sometimes flying far away, beyond Renno's vision, but he always came back to land carefully on the white Indian's shoulder, and found a perch at night on a bush or a piñon or juniper tree near where Renno lay sleeping.

Renno had taken to calling the bird after his own son, Little Hawk. The bird's attachment to him had been a continuing matter of awe to the Apache, still another proof that this man from far to the east had big medicine.

The next real landmark in the journey was the river named Rio Grande by the Spanish, and as the days passed, William and Beth became ever more eager to reach their destination. Only one thing marred Beth's total happiness, and that was Ena's coldness to her. She had become so fond of Ena and all the others. She had found that she loved the life she had been living for months now and had developed a quality she had noted in Renno, the burning desire to see what lay beyond the next rise, beyond the limit of vision when the country was a flatness under a bowl of the bluest sky she had ever seen. She experienced mixed emotions as the journey went into its last stage. She was, of course, eager to find out if the gold was really there in that mountain thought to be cursed by the Apache, but reaching the goal would be a turning point, for then there would be only the return journey, no more of that giddy feeling of pushing into the unknown. She would almost have welcomed a suggestion that they forget the gold and continue on, living off the land, to ride toward the setting sun and see what was there.

She wondered if that twinge of regret and discontentment were the result of Blue Feather's decision to stay in Gerachise's camp. On the morning of their departure, as the young Apache warriors made their good-byes, walked their horses up and down in impatience, called out taunts and good-natured insults to those who had not been selected for the adventure, she had noted that Blue Feather was not with them.

Already mounted, she rode to the far side of the camp, where Blue Feather had been lolling, smoking his pipe and drinking a potent Apache brew. He was sitting in the full glare of the morning sun, bare to the waist. One Apache woman was seated at his feet, massaging them. The other was nearby, with a container of food in her hand, preparing to feed him.

"It's time to get ready, Blue Feather," Beth urged as she dismounted. She nodded to the two women. Both were young, both attractive, for Apache. Neither of them would have matched the looks of the eager young widows Blue Feather had found among the other tribes during the journey.

"I will go no farther," Blue Feather announced.

"What? What do you mean?" she asked.

"Turn your face to the sun, missy," he said. "Never have I felt a warmer sun, and my bones have been often cold."

"So you're going to just sit here in the sun?" Beth asked.

Blue Feather nodded placidly. He reached out and patted the flank of the woman who was holding his food. "It is good here," he explained. "The heat of the sun keeps my blood flowing. I am old, missy. I have seen

170

much, and I have traveled far, but never have I found the likes of these." He indicated the two Apache women. "Now you have young Apache warriors from Gerachise's village to protect you. And when you return, you must tell me of your adventures and whether you have found gold, but I go no farther."

So it was that Beth was a bit sad as the journey got under way. She continued to miss Blue Feather over the passing days, for practical reasons when mealtime came, because she missed his excellent cooking, and for sentimental reasons, because she had grown quite fond of the womanizing old man. She and Blue Feather had ridden together much of the time because Holani and Ena kept together or with their men, and William and Renno spent much time together.

One morning El-i-chi, scouting with Socorro, killed a stray buffalo that had not gone to the north, and there was a feast in the camp that night. Well-fed, the group was already wending westward at sunrise, made good time, and was well on schedule to reach water by nightfall. Again Socorro and El-i-chi were in the lead. They rode hard, for Socorro wanted to be certain the small creek that was their destination for the day had not run dry in the heat of August.

Even though the Chiricahua was in his own lands where there was little danger of raids by other tribes and there had been no incursion by the Spanish within the memory of anyone living, he exercised a habitual caution. The next day, where a line of green appeared ahead of them to indicate a watercourse, buzzards circled, looking like small black dots in the sky. El-i-chi did not insult the Apache by calling his attention to the circling birds, knowing that Socorro would have seen them too. For the same reason, Socorro did not explain to El-i-chi why he rode into a grassy swale, dismounted, hobbled his horse, and set out, moving quickly and silently through the grass and brush toward the stream. El-i-chi followed.

They heard the harsh, angry voices while they were

still a hundred yards away. A man shouted out in Spanish, and there was a sound like that of a blow.

Socorro motioned that he would approach the source of the voices from the left. El-i-chi nodded and crawled to the right. He approached the scattered trees along the watercourse on his belly, moving as silently as a desert snake. He heard the angry voices, one predominant, and wished that he had taken the trouble to learn Spanish, as Renno had, instead of just picking up a few words.

When he reached the trees he crawled in among the dense brush and found a vantage point, from which he saw an Apache warrior tied to a juniper tree. Four Spanish soldiers sat nearby, while two stood on either side of the Apache. As El-i-chi watched, one of the Spanish soldiers yelled into the Apache's face. The Apache spat, and the Spaniard narrowly avoided taking the spit in his face. The Spaniard shouted, bent, and picked up a ramrod from the coals of a fire. The metal glowed red hot. The Spaniard traced a design on the Apache's chest, and El-i-chi caught the unpleasant smell of burning flesh. The Apache's face contorted and he bit his lower lip until the blood flowed, but he remained silent.

Then El-i-chi's eyes shifted. He saw why the vultures circled, for near the creek lay two dead warriors. One had been partially flayed, the skin removed from his cheeks, chest, and sides.

The Spaniard questioning the Apache tied to the tree shouted questions again, and before the red-hot metal could be applied, this time to the Apache's face, El-i-chi shot the tormentor between the shoulder blades, dropped his musket in the same motion, and had two arrows winging to take two more of the Spaniards before Socorro's arrows came from downstream. The surviving Spaniards shouted and leapt for weapons, but there had been only six men, and now four were dead and the remaining two went down quickly with an arrow from El-i-chi and another from Socorro.

After checking carefully to see if there were more

Spaniards with the horses across the almost dry stream, El-i-chi met Socorro on the run at the tree to which the Apache was tied. El-i-chi had his knife out and quickly severed the ropes. Socorro caught the warrior as his legs failed him and lowered him to the ground. The two Apache talked in their own language. And then, suddenly, the former captive took a deep breath, his chest made odd sounds, and he jerked in death.

The communication between Socorro and El-i-chi was limited, but El-i-chi got the idea quickly. "*Pronto*," he said, using one of his few words of Spanish, pointing back toward the main party. Socorro nodded and pointed to the ground to indicate that he would stay with the dead man while El-i-chi traveled quickly back to Renno and the others.

After hearing El-i-chi's report, Renno and Rusog joined him in galloping back to the creek. Only then did Renno, speaking Spanish with Socorro, learn the details.

"They were three young warriors from the village of Black Eagle," Socorro said. "He is also Chiricahua Apache and came to the great river to camp and hunt. These warriors were tired and slept here beside the stream. The hair-faces surprised them. They asked, 'Where is your main camp, how many in your tribe?' and the boys, being Apache, would not tell. So they were tortured, and then we came."

Socorro had collected the weapons of the dead soldiers. "The weapons and horses are yours," El-i-chi said, "to share with your brothers as you see fit." Socorro nodded in gratitude, for, by right of conquest, some of the plunder was El-i-chi's.

"I say," William said, having arrived on the gallop with the others, "Spanish? Here?"

Socorro nodded. "While I waited, I followed the trail of the hair-faces for some time. They came from there." He pointed toward the southeast.

"I am a visitor and a guest in your land . . ." Renno said to Socorro.

"Speak, great chief," Socorro urged, "and tell me what you want us to do."

"We must know how many Spanish have come," he said, "for six would not travel so far alone. We must have scouts to the southwest, Socorro."

"It will be done," Socorro said, already deciding how the Apache warriors who had volunteered to accompany Renno would be divided.

"And send the fastest rider to Gerachise to give warning," Renno told him.

Socorro singled out a young warrior and spoke rapidly. The warrior set out with a whoop along the back trail toward Gerachise's village. Others quickly left, heading southeast, their trails diverging slightly even as they remained in sight.

"I will see these Spanish for myself," Ena said, her green eyes blazing as she leapt onto her horse. Rusog reached up and seized her by the hand.

"The Apache know this country," he said.

For a moment it seemed that Ena would protest, but she shrugged and said, "That is true," and dismounted to examine the clothing and equipment of the dead Spaniards. "Do not warriors take the scalps of their fallen enemies?" she asked, noting that the dead still had their hair.

"Perhaps my sister would perform that for me," El-i-chi said, grinning.

"Scalp your own dead," Ena shot back.

"How far are we from the river?" Renno asked Socorro.

The Apache mused for a moment, looked at the sky, then to the west. "Two days' ride."

"And Black Eagle?" Renno asked, speaking of the chief known to be camping along the Rio Grande.

Socorro shrugged. "I will find Black Eagle and tell him of the coming of the medicine man and of the Spanish."

"Good," Renno responded. "We will join you in our own time."

Before nightfall one of the Apache scouts returned. "Great chief," he told Renno, "the trail of the hair-faces led to the southeast for some miles, and then circled there." He pointed toward the west, and the Rio Grande. "There their sign was joined to the passing of a great army, horses so many as to rival the prairie dogs in their towns."

"Headed west?" Renno asked.

"Toward the river," the scout confirmed, "and some four days ahead of us."

Chapter X

In Knoxville, Emily was determined not to become totally bedridden. In the mornings she forced herself to
join her mother and father at the breakfast table, and then
she spent some time with her mother as they worked to
prepare a layette for the new baby. As long as she sat in a
comfortable rocking chair Emily felt fairly well, but if she
moved around she became tired very quickly.

"I just don't know what's wrong," she complained.
"With Little Hawk I was full of energy. Now I'm so tired
all the time."

Nora Johnson, too, was concerned. But the baby was
alive and kicking, literally. And Nora had confidence in
Dr. Barlow, Knoxville's one representative of the healing
arts, even though he had wanted to bleed away the "evil

humors" from her daughter. Any damned fool who had seen anything of frontier life knew that bleeding weakened a person, Nora had told him, and Emily was already weak. She did allow Barlow to give Emily a tonic to "strengthen her blood," and the tonic seemed to do neither good nor harm. The important thing was that Barlow was experienced in delivering babies.

Emily was big with child in the heat of August, and she spent a lot of time in a rocking chair outside the cabin in the shade of a tree. Nora noted that her eyes were almost always focused on the trail leading to the west, toward the Indian lands, the direction from which Renno would come when he returned.

Chief Black Eagle had been much impressed by Socorro's account of the feats of the medicine man from far to the east, and he greeted Renno with Apache hospitality when the main group arrived. Soon, however, Black Eagle drew Socorro and the visiting warriors aside.

"If the reports did not come from the warriors of my brother Gerachise," Black Eagle said, "I would not believe that so great a Spanish force is traveling in our lands. I have sent scouts to the south. Soon we will know if the hair-faces have crossed the river, and in what direction they are traveling."

"Black Eagle is wise," Renno said.

"I have sent men to the north, to warn others," Black Eagle continued, "but they are far. We will not wait for them. When my brother Gerachise joins us, we will drive the Spaniards from our lands."

"Our scouts report that there are many of them," Renno said. "They will all be armed with muskets."

Black Eagle nodded. "You and your men have muskets."

"That is true," Renno agreed. He was not yet ready to commit himself to a battle against the Spanish. He was a long way from home, and his thoughts were often there, with his wife and son. He was definitely no friend of the Spanish, for he had fought against their greed before, but he had his purpose, and he had women with him. He had no desire to leave Ena, Beth, and Holani stranded in the lands of the Apache, and that was, of course, a possibility if he and the others went into battle against a large Spanish force.

The Rio Grande was not an impressive river at that point, but it had good clear water and a green belt along its banks. Beth, Ena, and Holani joined Apache women in privacy and had a much-welcomed bath. There was plentiful food and friendly curiosity from all the camp about the visitors.

After the council with Black Eagle, William took a walk alone. He, like Beth, had come to love the vast open spaces of this southwestern country, so different from little England. He stood on the banks of the river and was impressed by its beauty. He sat down on a rock, pulled off his boots, and let the cool water ease his feet. He was half-dozing when he heard someone approach and looked up to see a woman with water skins slung over her shoulders going down to the water's edge.

He watched idly. The woman seemed to be taller and slimmer than most Apache women, and her deerskin clothing was a bit the worse for wear. After she bent to fill the water skins, he noticed that she was quite shapely. When she had finished the job and turned, she walked toward him up the bank, and he sat up suddenly, for the face he saw was not the broad, flat face of an Apache. This one had sculptured, elegant features, a slim, beautiful nose, and full, expressive lips, but not lips like an Apache.

"You are not Apache," he said wonderingly when she was a few feet away and the beauty of her face quite evident.

The woman halted and looked around nervously. "I have been seeking an opportunity to speak with you, señor," she said in cultured Spanish. "I am a prisoner here."

"We can't have that!" William exploded, leaping from the stone.

"Be quiet, please," the girl implored, "or the women will beat me."

"We'll see about *that*," William said.

"I am Estrela Isabel de Mendoza. I was taken from my home in Mexico six months ago. Will you help me, please?"

"Of course," William said indignantly. "We'll go speak with Renno and Black Eagle about this immediately."

He reached out and tried to pull the water skins from Estrela's shoulders, but she resisted and shushed him. "You don't understand," she said.

"I say," William gasped, for a thought had come to him, a thought that made him blush. "They haven't . . . harmed you, have they?"

"I am a valuable property," Estrela said. "Black Eagle will trade me for many horses—when he has need of horses. He is in no hurry. You must not do anything rash, Englishman."

"My name is William."

"You must proceed carefully." She looked at him with her face tilted, and her dark, huge eyes seemed to play over his face as if they projected beams of light. He had never seen anything to match her dark beauty. "If you could buy me from Black Eagle—"

William was shocked.

"My father would repay you many times over," she finished. "But move slowly, Englis . . . William. Don't let Black Eagle know, or even think, that you want to help me. Be casual. Offer him, oh, ten horses in a way that shows him you don't really care whether he accepts or not."

"But I don't have ten horses," William said.

"Perhaps you have something else of value? Muskets?"

William mused. He could not take his eyes off the face of this Spanish woman. "I promise I will think of something."

"I must go now, before the women come to find out why I am slow with the water." She hurried up the bank.

William waited, then walked rapidly to find Beth, who was talking animatedly with a group of Apache women. He caught her attention, and she joined him out of earshot of the others.

"There's a Spanish girl here," William whispered. "She's been kidnaped. Black Eagle is holding her for ransom, and we must help her."

"What can we do?" Beth asked. "We can't jeopordize our friendship with these people, William."

"She says that Black Eagle will sell her at the right price. We must do something before—"

"Before what?" Beth asked.

"She is quite beautiful," William said. "So far they've not . . . not—"

"How could you possibly know that?" Beth asked.

"Well, I asked her, of course."

Beth giggled. "William, do I detect more than humanitarian interest in this Spanish girl?"

William blushed. "Of course not," he answered quickly.

"And what if this girl lied to you? Did you ask her straight out if Black Eagle had taken her into his bed?" After living with the Indians for so long, Beth had lost much of her English upper-class modesty. She could speak of such a thing without blushing.

"Well, in a way I did," William said, "but why should she lie?"

"I think *I* would," Beth said, "if I were in her position."

"Drat," William said; then his face calmed. "No matter. We will help her. We must help her get back to her people."

"We must be very careful," Beth warned. "We should talk with Renno before we do anything."

"Of course," William agreed.

"Yes," Renno said when William and Beth got him alone for a moment, "I have seen the Spanish girl. She is safe for the moment. The Apache think she is too thin and bony, so she holds little sexual appeal to them. Moreover, she is valuable. When Black Eagle gets a notion to go to the south, he will trade her for many horses."

"But—" William began.

"William, Black Eagle would not even listen to you in regard to this girl now," Renno said. "His concern is for the Spanish force that has invaded his lands. To speak with him about the girl would only cause irritation. Bide your time."

"But the women beat her," William protested.

"Only when she doesn't obey their orders," Renno told him. "You must not be seen in her presence. I'll have Ena tell her to be patient."

Friar Sebastián felt that he had made an excellent find in Lope Barca. Sebastián had told Barca that he wanted to move fast, and fast they had moved. At first they had traveled too swiftly for the friar's own comfort, but as the days became weeks and the trail long behind them, Sebastián, who was not yet forty, began to feel his muscles hardening and seemed to find a new source of energy.

The chain of command was functioning smoothly. Friar Sebastián had only to mention a thing to his right-hand man, Montenegro, the import of the friar's wishes was relayed to Barca, and the thing was done. Early in the journey the troop camped near Spanish missions, and at Sebastián's orders, the entire complement heard Mass and took the sacrament, then took themselves outside the settlements, for the friar would brook no fraternizing with the missions' women, who were, for the most part, local Indians who had been converted to Christianity.

Sebastián had studied the writings of the Franciscan Marcos de Niza, who had mistaken the Zuni pueblos of western New Mexico for the fabled golden cities but had found no gold himself. It had taken a Dominican, Friar Luis, to find the gold, but de Niza's descriptions of the countryside and of the Pueblo Indians gave Sebastián some idea of what was ahead. The chronicles of the Coronado expedition were also helpful. Sebastián thought that he might combine some of his spiritual work with his primary objective, which was to recover the gold that Friar Luis could not carry out. He pictured little communities of Pueblo Indians, whose ancestors had once been converted by the Franciscans who had traveled with Coronado. Perhaps some remnants of the true faith remained among the heathens and with a bit of effort could be rekindled, so that like the Franciscans who had come into this arid land before him, he could report to the Church and his monarch that the cross had been placed, once again, among the aborigines of New Mexico.

Although Friar Sebastián noted the growing friendship between Montenegro and Barca, it only pleased him and, he thought, made for a secure line of command. Because he knew the nature of man and knew man's natural greed, he had plans for keeping the common soldiers under control once the word got out that retrieval of gold was the purpose of the journey—which it must be once they reached Friar Luis's mountain. He talked with Montenegro about the particular problem:

"When the men see the quantities of gold that we are carrying, the temptation to them will be great. We must have a core group of dependable men who will stand with us against any attempt to rob Mother Church."

Montenegro, who knew that the problem had already been solved by Barca's courtship of key men in the troop and their loyalty cemented by promises of a greater share of the booty, agreed and suggested that the good friar depend on the loyalty of Captain Barca, who, with a solid cadre of dependable men, would keep the masses of the troop well within discipline.

Sebastián's first encounter with the Apache was, to him, a disillusioning experience. The army scouts encountered a small family group—a warrior, his wife, and their adolescent son—and had killed the warrior and wounded the boy in the shoulder. The woman and the boy were brought before Sebastián, and he tried to question them about their people, the land ahead, and their religious beliefs. He was answered with insults delivered in a bastardized Spanish, and all attempts to have the woman or the boy divulge information failed totally.

"They are loyal to their people," he told Barca, who was helping with the questioning. "They do not recognize me as ambassador for Christ on earth. Leave me alone with them for a few minutes."

He donned his priestly trappings over his dusty, worn robes, and for a full hour, with liberal quotes from the Bible, which he held as incontrovertible proof of his saintliness, he exhorted the unfortunate Indian mother and son in the true belief. "Now that you know," he said at last, "now that you have received the true word—for I have been given the task by our Savior to spread the true word to your far lands—you have no excuse for your obstinate behavior. You are aware of the heavy penalties for failure to respect the true word and the keeper of that word, Mother Church. Do you accept Jesus Christ as your master and your savior?"

The woman looked at him blankly. The boy was in considerable pain, although he tried hard to hide his discomfort. Sebastián repeated himself, and the woman nodded her head. "Yes, I do," she said.

"You do what, woman?" Sebastián thundered.

"I will accept your god," she said.

"Not *my* God," he said. "Your God as well."

"No, our gods are in the sky and the thunder and in the spirits," the woman countered. "But no matter, I can accept your god as well, if I do not have to eat of his flesh and drink of his blood, and if you will tell me which head of this god of three heads I am to honor."

"Blasphemy!" Sebastián thundered, and although he was eager to be traveling again, he gave them one last chance. He gave them a quick five-minute indoctrination and once again gave them their choice.

"This holy Mary," the woman asked, "whose child had no father—did her husband not beat her for sleeping with another man?"

This terrible blasphemy sent Friar Sebastián's blood pressure soaring, and he screamed out orders. It took the men half a day to find suitable trees, hew them down, notch them into two crosses, and only a half-hour to use the large spikes from Friar Sebastián's own personal possessions to nail the Apache woman and her wounded son to the crosses.

"Leave them," Sebastián commanded. "Let them be the message to the heathens, from God, that blasphemy is not to be tolerated." Offering up a few sincere prayers for their damned souls, Sebastián ordered the troop in motion, leaving the lonely crosses standing alone in the plain. The Pueblo Indians, Friar Sebastián also prayed, would be more receptive to the gifts of salvation.

Lope Barca knew that he was now in Apache lands. He hoped that most of the Apache had migrated farther to the north to escape the summer heat, but he was not a man to depend on chance. He kept parties of scouts in front and to the sides and rear in case the Apache tried to attack. It was one of the rearguard parties who captured the young Apache warriors sleeping beside a stream and then ran afoul of El-i-chi and Socorro. When, after several days, these scouts did not report in, Barca issued orders for double watches each night and intensified his scouting activities.

The crossing of the Rio Grande told Barca that the end of the journey was near. He had drunk and distributed the last of the rum, but he continued to talk with his selected men each night, to laugh with them, and to dream with them of their return to civilization with gold in their purses.

"We will be encountering the Pueblo Indians soon," Friar Sebastián told both Montenegro and Barca when a low line of dry mountains was in sight. "There are to be no hostilities. We will treat them as children of the Church, for we need them as workers."

"Father," Barca said, "I think that your expectations

of finding enough Pueblo Indians for a labor force are too optimistic."

Sebastián's face went red. "God has spoken to me!" he thundered. "He has shown me visions of teeming and peaceful communities. Do you dare disbelieve the word of God?"

Barca was effectively silenced. But later, when he was alone with Montenegro, Barca confided, "The crisis may come sooner than we expected. Your priest is living in the past. There are no peaceful and teeming communities ahead of us. There is only the dry and rocky desert. The Pueblo Indians have been gone for a hundred years. When he realizes this, he will try to force my men to dig in his mine if there is not enough gold left by Friar Luis. I can tell you this, my friend, they will not take kindly to that. We must be ready."

"We will be ready," Montenegro assured him.

"We are near now. I can feel it."

"The map shows that we are near."

"Then why are we keeping that pious windbag alive?" Barca asked angrily. "A rattlesnake in his blankets—"

"There will be time for that," Montenegro said. Secretly he was still trying to steel himself to the thought of killing a priest. He had not yet developed Barca's total contempt of the Church and its beliefs. He felt as if God Himself were looking over his shoulder, and although he was capable of committing heinous crimes, he had not yet developed the disbelief required for the killing of a man called by God.

Late one day Friar Sebastián, who had been studying the map, came to Barca. He pointed ahead. "There," he said. "That mountain with the sharp, jagged peak is our destination."

"That is good to hear," Barca said, although all day he had been watching the mountain and matching its profile against the drawings on Friar Luis's map, which he had committed to memory.

*　　*　　*

Another traveler saw the mountain. He rode alone, a man whose sun-bronzed skin was still paler than that of an Indian, a man who had left his companions behind on the Rio Grande with orders to wait until he saw the forbidden mountain for himself. Ahead of him flew a great hawk, leading the way as if guided by some supernatural power. Now and again the sunlight would reflect off the hawk's wings, flashing a signal back to Renno. He entered the dry hills, and the hawk led him to water—a poor water hole, shallow and muddy, but water. And then he rode slowly, picking his way, until he found what seemed to be a very old trail. Ahead and above the hills, the hawk circled, crying out its harsh call once, twice, three times. Renno rode on and mounted a rocky incline. Then he saw ahead a sight that lifted his heart for its beauty and its impressiveness.

Free-standing pillars of stone towered as high as three hundred feet into the air, and behind them was a sheer cliff surrounding a mesa. Atop the mesa was a city of towering buildings, golden and shimmering in the heat of late August. There was no grass, no trees, no greenery—only, as far as Renno could see, a patch or two of mesquite, browned by the sun.

To his right, two square towers, each showing the black holes of windows, extended above the level of the buildings. The profile of the city extended far to his left, and all around him was a silence that impressed him, making him forget the beauty of the scene, for there was the eerie feeling of being totally alone except for things long dead. He knew that the city was a dead city, and he knew that he had to see it from close up. He rode forward and began to circle the mesa, which towered three hundred and fifty feet over him. He soon came to feel that there was no way to reach the top of the mesa by horseback. He then began to look for a footpath or a way to climb the sheer cliff.

If only, he dreamed, it could be as easy for him as it was for Little Hawk, for the bird soared, glided out of sight over the dead city, then came back into Renno's view riding the warm thermals effortlessly.

The intense heat of midafternoon was upon him, and he had only the water in his water skin. The broiling sun heated the wastelands, causing heat waves to shimmer and dance, obscuring distant vision, and playing tricks on his eyes. Once he saw a huge blue sweet-water lake in the distance, with trees and grass along the shore, and he called on the spirits to undo this spell of the evil one, for he knew that he had crossed those dry and rocky spaces and there was no lake.

After riding halfway around the mesa, he was beginning to believe that one place was as good as any other to try to scale the rocks. He stopped to rest in the shadow of a stone pillar not directly connected to the cliff and had a swig of muddy water.

He heard a sound behind him and turned, a pistol in one hand and his tomahawk in the other. At first he thought that the evil one was playing tricks on him again, for what he saw was a man so old that he was nothing more than a stooped, drying, very small bag of bones with a face as full of crevasses as the landscape around him.

"You will not need your weapons, warrior," the old man assured him in Spanish, "for I am far too old to harm you."

"I greet you, old father," Renno said.

"Come," the old man said, turning with obvious effort and disappearing among the great pillars. Renno led his horse and followed, passing through a cleft in the rocks so narrow that the horse's sides brushed the stone, and saw a welling spring and patches of green.

"Drink," the old man invited. "And the horse too."

Renno did drink, and the water was sweet and pure. The horse guzzled for a long time, then fell to cropping the scattered tufts of green grass.

"My thanks, old father," Renno said.

"The sweet waters of the earth belong to all," the old man replied. "Have you come to see my city or are you, like all young ones, eager to be away from this dry and haunted place?"

"I have come to see your city."

"Come then," the old man said, starting off.

Renno hobbled his horse so the animal could continue to drink and eat. He caught up with the old man quickly, and they entered a pathway, the entrance to which was very well concealed, and began to climb. The old man's breath wheezed and the climbing was slow, but at last they reached the top, and Renno stood transfixed for a moment, taking in the vista of dry and arid badlands and hills around him. And there was the mountain, rising above the surrounding hills, dark in shadow, and totally dry, arid—and somehow evil.

He followed the hobbling steps of the old man through the dust of centuries and had to crouch low to pass through a doorway to one of the buildings, where he saw a few ragged blankets and the remains of a fire on the dirt floor. One half of a jackrabbit hung on a stick. Flies buzzed and crawled over the meat.

"Eat," the old man said.

"Thank you, old father," Renno replied, "but I have eaten. Now I would see your city."

"I have seen it," the old man said, seating himself carefully. "You will find me here."

Renno ducked his way outside. The sun was low in the west. The alleyways between the buildings were in deep shadows. A wind had come up, and the dust devils stirred by the wind gave illusions of motion, as if the long-dead inhabitants of the city were present in shadow form.

He entered some of the buildings to find dust, dirt, massive spiderwebs, and an all-pervading emptiness, a silence that seemed to seep into his bones. All signs of the people who had lived and loved and had borne their children had been dried up, blown away, taken by the ages. When he reentered the building where the old man had his poor camp, there was a mesquite fire glowing, and the old man was sleeping but awoke at Renno's light step.

"You do not fear the spirits?" the old man asked.

"They seem not to bother *you.*"

The old man cackled. "How do you know, young warrior, that I am not one of them?"

"A spirit does not stink," Renno answered with a laugh.

"Ah," the old man said. "If you are not afraid, you may sleep here, for the trail down is treacherous in the dark."

"How many summers have you seen, old father?" Renno asked, after allowing himself a deep drink from his water skin of the sweet water he had taken from the old man's spring.

"I know not the magic numbers of the Spanish," he replied. "Many summers. As a boy I saw the Spanish come to the place they called Albuquerque. I have seen the Indian—the Apache, the Comanche, and especially my people, the Navajo—fight him. My father fought in the revolt of the Pueblos, when the Spanish were driven out of our lands to El Paso, in the south. Many summers. Many summers."

"You call this your city. . . ."

"Does any other claim it? It is not the city of my birth, nor even of my people, and yet it is mine, for the spirits allow it, and here I have peace." He held out his hand. His fingers were gnarled and dirty. "Not that company is not welcome, young warrior."

"Where did the people of this city go?" Renno asked.

"Only the spirits know," the old man said. "The water failed. The crops withered. The Spanish came for the yellow dirt, and many died in their digging holes. But they are here." He looked around. The wind made a strange rattling noise outside. "Ah, you hear? Yes, they are here. Their city was old when the Spanish first came with their horses and their guns and their shells of metal like turtles. Those Indians who lived put a curse on this place, so the ghosts mutter in the streets in the dead of night. But they will not harm you if your heart is good."

"Then I pray to the manitous and the spirits of my ancestors that my heart is good," Renno said. "Tell me of the mountain, old father."

The old man glared at him with his squinted eyes, dark gleams emanating from behind folds of wrinkles. "The mountain. You will not go to the mountain?"

"That is my intent, old father."

"Then you must armor yourself with good, and bless the spirits, for there the curse is alive and active, and the evil ones hold sway."

There was a long silence. Outside the wind played through the dark openings of the buildings and swept through the spaces between the buildings. It was easy to believe that the spirits of the dead walked and cursed the Spanish and wailed for the days of the city's glory.

"You are not Apache. You are not Comanche. You are not even Indian. You are a white man dressed as an Indian, and you seek the gold," the old man whispered without condemnation.

"Almost you are right," Renno said. "But I have Indian blood, the blood of my fathers, the Seneca, from far to the east. You know of the gold?"

The old man cackled. "I have seen it."

Renno kept an expressionless face. "There is much gold?"

"Enough to laden many horses." He laughed again. "Take it . . . if you can."

"What is there to prevent me from taking it?"

"The dead. They guard it." The old man sighed. "I am tired." He was asleep almost immediately.

Renno sat for a long time with his back against a wall, then walked out into the moonless night. The glow of the stars lighted the mesa but did not penetrate the deep shadows, where the spirits walked and the wind made voices.

Renno raised his arms to the stars and began to chant.

He held that position, seeking his manitous, calling out to his ancestors, until his arms ached and the wind rose behind him and wailed around the long-deserted buildings. He turned to face the city, saluted it with his hands, and bowed to it. "Spirits of those who lived," he said, "I call to you in the name of my ancestors, and in the name of all Indians, who came from common parents in ages past. I come to rob you of nothing, but I wish you peace. I come for my people. If you inhabit the West, with my ancestors, speak with them, and they will tell you of Renno."

The wind began to abate. The wails of its passing faded, the swirling dust settled, and there was an eerie silence. Renno went back into the building with the old man and slept with his back against the wall.

He woke with the light of dawn and to a chill that penetrated to his bones. The old man woke, chewed on the flyblown piece of rabbit, and for a moment looked at Renno as if he did not recognize him.

At last he said, "Today you go to the mountain of the devils?"

"Yes, old father."

"The spirits will guide you."

"Thank you for your blessing. If I am favored with a kill as I return, I will bring you fresh meat."

"This old body requires little food, but fresh meat will be welcomed."

Renno left his horse hobbled by the old man's welling spring. The distance between the city and the mountain passed swiftly. Little Hawk appeared and led the way and was perched high on a rock when Renno saw traces of an ancient trail and followed it. When he lost the trail he climbed dry ridges, went down into canyons, paced lightly over sun-heated rocks and dry sand, and not knowing where to look for the entrance to the mine of the Spaniards, trusted to the manitous and their totem, the hawk, who soared, wings flashing in the sunlight, to lead him.

Moving ever to the west and southwest, around the

face of the mountain, Renno knew that without the help of the manitous, he would never have found the mine, for the entrance was half-covered by a rockfall, and mesquite grew around it to hide it further. But Little Hawk perched on a mesquite bush and called harshly, and then Renno saw, after pushing into the brush, the dark, half-buried opening. It was as if that dark opening emanated the very spirit of evil. The force coming from the darkness was so strong that he fell back a few paces and lifted his hands in supplication to the manitous. Little Hawk harshly cried out once and flew away.

Renno forced himself to approach the dark entrance. He knelt and peered within. Light failed to penetrate more than a few feet, but he could see that a shaft had been cut into the rock. He would need light. He could make a torch of mesquite brush. Reluctant to enter that dark pit, Renno found himself a level ledge, made a dry, hungry camp with nothing more than a bit of jerky for food, and began to meditate even as the sun fell and twilight was followed by the swift coming of night. He chanted and prayed throughout the night, then slept for a few hours before dawn. With the dawn he was ready, two mesquite torches formed and ready to be lit from the coals of his campfire.

He had received no sign from the spirits, but he felt cleansed by his prayers and was confident that the manitous were still with him. He crawled past the rockfall that partially blocked the entrance and then was able to walk, with his head and shoulders bent, under a rough rock ceiling. The shaft made a right-angle turn and widened, and he could see hints of sparkling quartz in the walls. Now and then there were branches from the main shaft that did not go far. He continued until his first torch had burned down to his hand and had to be dropped. He lit his second torch from the last flames of the first and hurried forward.

There was a smell of dust and dryness and something else in the dead, unmoving air of the mine. He knew that he would have to turn back soon and make more torches, and he had seen nothing except veins of quartz in the walls of the shaft to indicate gold. Then he seemed to burst into a vast black chamber where the light of his torch was absorbed, and he stepped on something dry that made a crunching sound. He looked down quickly.

The dry, dead air of the mine had preserved the corpse at his feet. He had stepped on a hand, and the dry bones had crumbled. "Forgive me, old father," he whispered, bending to see better. Dried skin stretched tautly over cheekbones. Fragments of clothing rotted on the well-preserved body. He stepped over and held his torch forward, and as far as the light extended he saw the dead. His heart heavy with their spirits, the white Indian prayed. They lay on the hard stone floor of the chamber or sat grinning against the wall that was visible in the light. He walked, saying, "Greetings, old fathers. Forgive me, old fathers. May your spirits rest, old fathers." In that large chamber, the vast circular excavation in the heart of the mountain, he saw the dead by the dozens, perhaps, without taking time to count, by the hundreds, and some of them had died violently, their skulls split, holes blown into their faces by gunfire.

He saw no gold—he was too fascinated, too shocked and repelled by the sheer numbers of the mummified dead, and his torch was growing short. He was a warrior and as brave as any man, but his very soul clamored to be gone from this place of ancient death, so he turned, half-ran back down the shaft, scrambled over the rockfall, and burst into the sunlight, with the torch beginning to burn his fingers.

Chapter XI

William had observed that the young Spanish woman always went to the river for water at a certain time in the late afternoon. He waited for her there, and she looked at him with obvious hope in her eyes. "You have made an offer to Gerachise?" she asked.

William felt that he had failed, and he took a while in answering, saw the woman's hopes fade. "I have talked with Renno. He advises me, and you, to be patient. He says that you are in no danger."

Estrela had put down her water skins. She stood, her shoulders slumped, a picture of dejection. "As I told the woman Ena, I am in no danger of being killed or raped. But I do not know when Black Eagle might change his mind and summon me for his use. I cannot live like this much longer." Her eyes filled with angry tears. "I am given gnawed bones to chew. Sometimes the women make me compete with the dogs for them. They toss them onto the ground, and I have to kick the dogs away to get them."

William's heart seemed ready to burst. He took two quick steps and put his hands on the young woman's shoulders. She wore the typical Apache clothing, which, in summer, was thin and clinging, showing her slim waist, her proud breasts, her flaring hips. "Great events are under way," he said, "and to try to bargain for you now would most probably meet with failure."

Estrela's shoulders shook, and she was sobbing quietly. William, shocked by his own actions, drew her into his arms and sent a soothing hand over her coal-black hair, saying, "There, there." Soon, however, he became so much aware of her softness, her woman's warmth, that he pushed her away. Her sobs had stopped, and she looked up at him, her long black lashes wet with tears.

"You will not leave me here, please?"

"Never," he said. "I promise you. When we have resolved this problem about the Spanish—"

"There are Spanish soldiers near here?" Estrela asked quickly, her eyes widening. "If so, you must tell me where and help me to run to them. They will take me home."

William cleared his throat. "Well, you see, that might not be the best thing to do, for it seems that we're destined to fight those Spanish soldiers."

Estrela's nostrils flared. "You, a civilized man, would take the part of these savages against Christians?"

"Perhaps you don't understand," William said. "The Spanish are invading Apache lands—"

Estrela turned away and picked up her water skins. She looked over her shoulder at him, her dark eyes flashing, her white teeth showing in an expression of scorn. "Renegade," she spat at him, and was gone.

* * *

Both El-i-chi and Rusog had wanted to accompany Renno on his exploration of the evil mountain, and with each passing day they watched the flats across the river for his return. Meantime, they saw to their weapons, honing knives to razor sharpness, testing the bindings on their tomahawks, and readying shot and powder for their fire-arms. The Apache scouts had reported that the Spanish force had crossed the Rio Grande and that the trail pointed arrow straight toward Devil's Mountain.

"Such a large force could not move as swiftly as one man," El-i-chi pointed out.

"No," Rusog agreed, "but if he has not returned in two more days"—that coincided with Apache estimates of the length of time it would take Renno to ride to the mountain, look around, and return—"we will go."

"Let us go now," Ena urged, "and see these Spanish soldiers for ourselves."

"Then we would miss Renno in the desert," El-i-chi said. "No, we will wait. Two days."

On the last day of waiting an Apache scout galloped hard into Black Eagle's camp. He had knowledge of what the Apache called the magic numbers of the Spanish, and he had counted over two hundred men, most of them fully armed, mounted cavalry, but some who walked and drove wagons pulled by mules. He had observed them, march-ing in good order, with scouts out to all sides, not more than two days' march from the evil mountain.

"Tomorrow we go," El-i-chi decided.

But all during the afternoon and early evening and then into the night, Gerachise's warriors began to arrive at the river, and the air was filled with the chants and war cries of eager men.

Rusog, El-i-chi, and William sat in on a council of war and listened to the typical oratory—promises from brave warriors about what they would do to this enemy who dared invade their lands. No time was set for an attack.

"They will dance and prepare themselves for at least

another day and night," Rusog said when he was alone with William and El-i-chi.

"Their numbers do not match those of the Spanish, if indeed the scout knew how to count," the Englishman said. "How will they do against disciplined soldiers armed with muskets and pistols?"

"They will fight bravely and die," El-i-chi said, shrugging, "for their plan of battle is simple: find the enemy and ride against him."

"Perhaps we should talk with Gerachise," William suggested.

"The man to talk to the Apache chiefs is Renno," Rusog replied. "He, more than any of us, has gained their respect." He shrugged. "Whether they would listen to him, I don't know."

"Why would the Spanish force be headed for our mountain?" William asked. He brooded for a moment in the silence, then added, "Unless . . ." He mused for a long time. "I just can't accept such a trick of fate. Surely *they* are not going for the gold. Surely not." But he was not sure in his heart. His map, after all, was a Spanish map. It would be a most coincidental happening to have another copy of the map in existence, and for some Spanish to lead an expedition to search for the gold just as they themselves were arriving at the mountain.

El-i-chi, feeling restless, went to the tepee where Holani was already asleep. He took her in his arms, and she muttered sleepily and clung to him. "I am going with you when you go to fight," she vowed, after he thought that she had gone back to sleep.

"No, no," he said, filled with love. "You will stay here with the Apache women."

Holani pushed him away, fully awake now. "Ena will go, for she is already preparing her weapons."

"Ena is Ena. You are my wife, and we have more to think of than just you and me." He reached for her, pulled her to him, and put his hand flat on her naked stomach. There was no overt evidence of the fact that she was carrying his child, but she had not received the signs of nature for two months now.

"I am Holani, Chickasaw, and the wife of a warrior," she said firmly. "I will not stay with the Apache women. If you force me to stay, I will steal a horse and follow you at the first opportunity."

El-i-chi was secretly proud of his wife's independent spirit. Her force of character kept him alert, made him feel more the man. But there were times when a man had to be forceful, and this was one of those times. He smacked Holani on her bare rump and said, "I have spoken."

There had been times in the past when such an action would have precipitated an all-out battle, but instead of fighting, Holani edged close and pressed herself against him. "And who will warm your bed during the chill desert nights?" she whispered, her lips fastened to his. "Will you go to your horse or to an Apache warrior for this?" She took his hand and placed it on a warm spot and smiled in the darkness when, as usual, just a bit of daring suggestion on her part fired her husband's blood so that the night was made light with their love.

Later, as she lay next to him, her arm across his chest, she said, "I will ride with you, and when the fighting begins, I will stay in the rear. I will be there to cook for you, to carry your scalps, and to tend the wounds of our friends."

"We will talk of this when the time comes," El-i-chi said. "With the light, I go into the desert to meet Renno, for he is overdue."

Renno fasted by necessity, for there was no game on Devil's Mountain. After seeing the chamber of the dead in the heart of the mountain, he spent the night in contemplation and prayer, and with the dawn he was making several mesquite torches. He had to force himself to reenter that black hole and make his way to the chamber of the old fathers. There he searched carefully and at last found a small, low tunnel that had been hidden by the mummified bodies of a woman and child. He had to crawl, but not far, for there at the end of the tunnel he found the gold. It was stored in rotting leather bags and was in three forms: there was a large stack of crudely formed ingots, gleaming with that reddish-yellow color, and bags of nuggets, and other bags, but fewer, of gold dust. The gold nuggets and dust would have to be repackaged, for the ancient leather burst almost at a touch. And he would need help removing the gold from the mine and carrying it down the mountain.

Outside in the blessed air, freed of the heaviness of sheer evil, he cried a hawk call back at Little Hawk, soaring overhead, and began to look for a better way to take the gold down the mountain. He soon discovered the remains of a wagon trail, which had been built up the mountain, cut into sheer stone in places. Although it had been destroyed in spots by rockslides and erosion, it would be possible to get horses up the mountain to a point near the mine. It was time for him to return to the river and inform the others of the good news.

He followed the old Spanish wagon track to the desert floor and was on the opposite side of the mountain from the old man's deserted city, and from his own horse. He ran lightly, pausing once an hour or so for one sip of water. When he heard the sound of horses from afar, he hid himself among the rocks and waited. Four Spanish soldiers rounded a rocky rise and rode directly toward him for a long time before turning toward the rough approach to the mountain.

Renno climbed atop a small hill and carefully looked over the top of a rock. He saw a large plume of dust in the distance, which he knew had to be made by the main column of the Spanish. He also saw two more patrols of mounted men. If they found his horse, they would surely steal it. He looked at the sun, midday high, and estimated how long it would take him to run back to the river. He had done enough traveling in the desert to know that it would be a severe test, but by stopping at the water hole by the old city he could refill his water skin. Maybe the old man could hide his horse from the patrols. He climbed carefully off the hill, having to detour once around a den of buzzing, angry rattlesnakes, and after checking carefully, he began to run toward the city, taking advantage of all the cover he could find.

He was dehydrated and his lungs were on fire when he reached the mesa and began to circle toward the old man's water hole. As he neared it, thinking of the cool, sweet water, he saw the tracks of shod horses, Spanish horses, either five or six riders, and he had to exercise caution, running from stone pillar to stone outcrop until he reached the entrance to the hidden nook that concealed the spring. All was silence, but there were boot and horse tracks all around. He crept into the narrow cleft, pistols at the ready.

The old man lay beside the spring, and the sweet, rich smell of blood was in the air. Renno ran forward. His horse was gone. The spring had been fouled by horse droppings and blood. The odor of death was everywhere. He looked down at the old man in sadness and saw one eye flicker, try to open.

He knelt. "Old father," he whispered.

"Ah, young warrior," the old man said, his voice very weak. How he lived with the severity of his wounds, Renno could not imagine.

"The spirits will accompany you on your journey to the West, old father," Renno said.

"Yes," the old man whispered. "Young warrior, you speak with the spirits."

Renno nodded. He had not told the old man of his protection by the manitous.

"The spirits have led you and your enemy here," the old man said. "Although the spirits are with you, your fate and the fate of many rest in the strength of your good right arm and in the cunning of your brain."

"So be it, old father," Renno said, seeing the last

spasms of death take the old man and knowing then that it was over.

He used his cupped hands to clean the rock basin that caught the slow drip of the spring, removed the horse droppings and the blood-reddened water, scoured the damp rock basin with sand and waited so that the sand, too, could be rinsed out. He had to have water to make the run across the arid wastes to the Rio Grande.

In the meantime, there was one thing he could do for the old man. He hoisted the small, frail body to his shoulder, finding it to be incredibly light, and made his way up the narrow, hidden trail to the top of the mesa and the old spirit-filled city. There he left the old man, in his own crude camp inside the empty dirt-floored room, and stood before him to offer one last tribute to the departed spirit.

The mesa afforded a panoramic view, and he took advantage of that, crawling to the edge of the cliff so as not to be silhouetted against the sky. He could see the main Spanish column now, and he counted carefully, totaling up almost two hundred mounted men, with others out scouting and patrolling. He knew that the Spanish would be well-drilled, trained fighting men, and that it would be impossible, even with the help of the Apache, to attack them head-on and win. He had seen the Spanish cavalry tactics during the war with the Chickasaw, and he had gained a healthy respect for cavalry, even if he had defeated them and killed them to a man.

There was enough clean water when he climbed back down to the spring to fill his water skin. He washed himself as best he could with the remaining water, adjusted his weapons, and set out. He knew that he would have to pace himself, that with the hot desert sun constantly drawing water from his body, he could not run as he would have run in the forests of his homelands. He would run for a while, then walk for a while, conserving his strength. First, however, he must put distance between himself and the Spanish, lest he encounter a patrol.

He was not averse to killing a few of them, but he did not want to alert them that an enemy was already near.

He welcomed the coming of night, for the sun was gone and there was the swift coolness. He regained strength and ran with a light wind in his face. He did not have to alternate walking with his running, and he could conserve his water. Once, however, as he sped through a mesquite thicket, dodging bushes skillfully, reveling in the good feel of movement, the workings of his legs and arms and body, he felt a thick, soft heat and a blow under his left foot. He cleared the thicket and paused to inspect his moccasin by the light of a rising moon and saw the fang marks of the snake he had stepped on.

The effects of that were a danger he would have to risk. He ran on. And the moon continued to climb and become smaller, and then it was high and the miles were gliding under lightly pounding feet, and he was Renno, Seneca, warrior of the running feet, and there was a fall of his spirit when his reason forced him to halt and rest, to catch a few hours of sleep before the heat of the rising sun brought him up from his slumber and sent him, after one drink of precious water, toward the east.

He began to alternate walking with his running as the heat of the sun began to build, and by midday he was walking without running, and still there were many miles ahead of him. In the heat of the afternoon he cut out the heart of a giant pulpy cactus and chewed the fiber for its moisture content, rested in its shade, and waited until the sun was low and he had slept rather fitfully for about two hours. Then he was moving with the setting sun at his back, and he knew that he would have to reach the river before the heat of another day caught him in those burning wastes. He drank what was left in his water skin and discarded it as the full moon gave a gentle, silvery light to the wastes of rock and sand. He could not bring himself to leave any of his weapons behind, for without them he was not a warrior but only a man.

As he ran he thought of Emily and his son and of the

wondrous flow of water in the Rio Grande. He seemed to see his wife on the far horizon, a small but recognizable figure beckoning to him, urging him to keep the pace, to keep his strong legs pumping, running, running, for without water, the heat of the day would cause his death.

Pain was his enemy now, the pain of an overstrained body, a body badly dehydrated and long without food. He ran in a sea of pain and forced his mind to ignore it by thinking of Emily and now and again of the river and its life-giving water. He did not see the dark line of trees and the bluffs on the far side of the river, for his vision was dimmed by his pain. He heard his own death chant first, and then realized that it was not the chanting of the spirits coming for him, but that of the Apache, and then, by squinting his eyes he could see the trees and the glow of campfires across the river, and he began to gasp out a chant of thanksgiving.

He paused on the bank of the river to give the Apache coyote cry of recognition and was answered from the far bank, and then he stumbled forward, falling once into the sand before he reached the water and threw himself face-down into it to take large swallows. Then he forced himself to wait, for to drink too much was dangerous.

Two Apache warriors came across the river, wading the shallow water. Renno allowed himself another small drink of the sweet water and then scorned the helping hands of the Apache to trot through the shallow water. It was almost daybreak. He asked one of the warriors to bring his brother to him, and El-i-chi came to Renno's tepee, accompanied by Holani, William, and Beth.

Beth impulsively ran to Renno and threw her arms around him. "We were so worried about you," she said before remembering herself and backing away, thankful that Ena had not been there to witness it.

Renno clasped arms with El-i-chi. "Get the others," he ordered. "I have news."

"You must be hungry," Beth said.

Without waiting for his answer, she went to her quarters and warmed a slab of the previous night's antelope meat, ran back to serve it, steaming on the forked stick on which she had suspended it over the fire, to Renno. She found that Rusog and Ena had joined the group.

As he ate, Renno told them of the gold and the chamber of the dead and estimated that it would require most of their horses to transport the heavy gold, which meant that they would either have to obtain more horses or walk.

"Renno," Beth breathed, her eyes gleaming with excitement, "it sounds as if there are piles and piles of it."

"Yes," he confirmed, "but there are problems. The Spanish are nearby, and it seemed that the main force was headed directly toward the mountain."

"At any rate," Rusog said, "the gold will have to wait. Black Eagle and Gerachise plan to leave to march on the Spanish today."

"With how many men?" Renno asked.

"Black Eagle will mount sixty warriors, Gerachise a few less," El-i-chi answered, "although a few more will come from the lands of Gerachise as the days pass."

"I must speak with the chiefs," Renno said, taking one last bite and handing the remaining meat back to Beth.

"And the gold?" William said as Renno stood.

"I am thinking of the gold," Renno told him.

El-i-chi and Rusog accompanied Renno. They found the two Apache chiefs seated in front of Black Eagle's tepee. Around them were grouped the more important war leaders.

"Welcome, Two-Lion-Killer," Gerachise said, rising to clasp Renno's arm. "We make plans to kill those who have invaded our hunting grounds."

"I have seen their force," Renno said, "and it is a powerful one. There are two hundred mounted soldiers armed with muskets, some with lances, and with pistols and sabers. Some wear the armor that turns back arrows."

"It is good that you have seen the enemy," Black Eagle replied. "You can guide us to him."

"He will be easily found, near the mountain of the evil one," Renno said.

An uneasy stir passed among the seated warriors.

"The great medicine man from the east will speak to the spirits," Gerachise said. "He will tell the souls of the dead that we come to avenge them, and the spirits will guide us."

"Indeed, I have been in the mountain of evil," Renno said, "and I spoke to the departed spirits of the old fathers who lie there dead but undead, their very flesh preserved on their bones."

A shiver of dread passed among the warriors, and more than one cast a quick glance over his shoulder.

"But the Spanish are many, and well trained. It is my advice to avoid open battle with them," Renno said.

"Are you asking us to allow them to pass at will through our lands?" one war leader asked hotly.

"No," Renno assured him. "But they are many and we are few, and they have muskets. We will nibble at them, as the attacking coyote pack nibbles at a wounded buffalo calf. We will kill their scouts and patrols one by one and two by two. We will strike, then vanish with the wind, and thus take our toll slowly, slowly, until their numbers are reduced and they sicken of this land of the Apache."

Black Eagle drew himself up, his chest thrust out, shoulders back. "To fight like a coyote is not the way of Black Eagle."

"What would Black Eagle do?" Renno asked mildly.

"We will fight with honor," the chief answered. "We will not vanish with the wind, but ride with the wind and hit the invader with suddenness. Once he has fired his muskets, we will give him no time to reload but will close with him, and there his lances and swords and pistols will be no match for the good Apache arrows and tomahawks."

"And how many will fall in the first musket fire?" Renno asked.

"Those who fall will have died the death of a warrior," Gerachise said, "and will be mourned with all honor."

"You have settled on this?" Renno asked.

"It is the way of the Apache," Black Eagle said flatly.

"Then I and mine will have no part of it," Renno said.

A tested warrior with the battle scars to prove his bravery rose and looked directly into Renno's eyes. "The great chief from the land of the rising sun has no stomach for honorable battle?"

Before Renno could speak, Socorro leapt to his feet. "In your ignorance, Hunting Owl, you know nothing. I speak for the bravery and the skill of this warrior, and he who insults this one also insults Socorro."

"I need no one to speak for me," Renno said with a warm look at Socorro. "I am a stranger in your lands, and I have only the right to make suggestions based on my past experience in fighting against armed, mounted Spanish soldiers. I and the ones who follow me have the right to choose the time and place of our own deaths, just as you have, and we choose not to die while making a hopeless charge against a wall of two hundred muskets."

Gerachise stood and extended his arms in friendship toward Renno. "Like Socorro, I know this warrior's courage. We would welcome you as a brother should you choose to join us, but as you say, you are a stranger in our land, and this is not your fight. The spirits go with you, Two-Lion-Killer."

"And with you," Renno said. "And know this, my brother—my mission in this land is not complete, and I will not leave these lands without leaving my mark on your enemies and mine."

Black Eagle leapt to his feet and gave a shrill yell. The cry was taken up by others, and soon the camp was a chaos of confusion as warriors mounted and raced out of the settlement, crying out their boasts of what they would do to the Spanish enemy. The sun was not an hour high when the last of the warriors splashed across the Rio Grande and made dust as they hastened to the west.

"Is all in readiness?" Renno asked El-i-chi.

"We are ready." He hesitated. "I have told Holani that she may come along and fall to the rear when there is fighting."

"Everyone must come," Renno said, "for we may not pass this way again." As soon as the horses were packed, Renno mounted. The Apache women and young ones watched in silence. William, riding next to the white Indian, felt agitated and kept looking over his shoulder as Renno led the way to the river. At the bank William halted and blew out a deep breath. "I will catch up with you," he said, and without waiting for acknowledgment, he spurred his horse back toward the village. Renno led the way, setting a course north of the route taken by the Apache war party. Only hours before, he had covered the same ground, and he knew it well. He set a pace to conserve the energy of the horses and did not look over his shoulder an hour later when he heard the sound of galloping hooves coming up from behind. He had known immediately why William had gone back to the Apache camp.

Estrela de Mendoza rode well, even without a saddle. She had been born on a ranch.

"So," Renno said to Rusog, riding at his side, "we have a new member."

"I would prefer a warrior," Rusog said with disgust, looking straight ahead.

Although Estrela's inclusion would surely complicate their mission, Renno had unswerving faith in the manitous and their ability to protect and help him. He was so near his goal, and he would not give up simply because a force of over two hundred cavalry stood between him and the mountain of gold. He now led the group at a ground-covering pace, made a dry camp after riding for several hours in the dark, and had them moving again at the first light. He was determined to reach the mine as quickly as possible, before the Apache and Spanish parties clashed. The swift pace put the ancient city atop the mesa in sight late on the second day. Renno scouted ahead himself, found the area clear of Spanish, and watered the horses and filled the water skins at the old man's spring. Before darkness he led his group around the mesa and to the western approach to Devil's Mountain. Just as he had done on his first exploration of Devil's Mountain, the Spanish had approached from the east, so although Renno's group now saw tracks left by scouts and patrols, they encountered no Spanish as Renno led them to the ancient wagon track leading to the Spanish mine. He soon saw by the tracks that a sizable force had climbed the old trail before them, and he sent El-i-chi ahead as he slowed the pace and continued to exercise all caution.

From a vantage point he saw an event below that saddened him: a dust cloud to the east told him that Black Eagle and Gerachise had arrived with their warriors, and as he waited for El-i-chi to return with a report, he saw the Spanish dismount, put their horses in cover, and prepare to fight from cover as dismounted cavalry. Their hillside defensive position had been chosen well, for the Spanish soldiers had a clear field of fire down a rock slope and would have plenty of time to load and fire repeatedly as the Apache struggled up the hill.

El-i-chi came back, panting after running hard. "There are thirty soldiers and a man in a black dress like a woman's," he said. "The man in the dress gives orders, and the others are carrying out new leather bags from a hole in the mountainside."

"Look well on folly," Renno told El-i-chi, pointing to the site of the coming battle.

They watched in grim silence. They could barely hear the war cries of the Apache as they charged en masse. Behind them, on the opposite hill, Black Eagle and Gerachise, who would direct the battle, sat on their horses. Even from this great distance, they made striking figures with their befeathered lances and headdresses.

"It begins," Rusog said sadly as the first of the Apache attackers began to fall, sprawling from their horses. Horses went down, and seconds after the riders and horses had fallen, the distant crack of muskets could be heard. Still the Apache charged up the hill, the hooves of their horses dislodging small stones to roll, creating confusion. The toll was heavy, for the Spanish were swift to reload and fire, and with almost a quarter of the attacking force decimated, the survivors, who had come within a hundred feet of the Spanish positions, turned and careened back down the hill, horses falling and men dying even in retreat.

"Now we must hurry," Renno said. "They will attack once more, perhaps. We must use this time to accomplish our mission."

He questioned El-i-chi carefully about the positions of the Spaniards at the mine. "Their attention is on the gold," El-i-chi reported. "There was one sentry, and he was watching the men carry the gold from the mine."

Renno turned to William. "We attack her people," he said, nodding toward Estrela de Mendoza. "Will she hold her peace?"

William could not answer.

"I will speak with her," Renno said.

Estrela had been trying to find a bit of shade beside a rock. She looked up expectantly as the man who led her rescuers came to her. "Now *we* fight," Renno said.

"You fight against the Spanish soldiers," Estrela said. "I am Mexican. If you and the others are killed, I would have to trust myself to the soldiers from the garrisons. But I will not interfere with you now or try to run away."

Renno nodded, satisfied. "You will stay with the horses."

"As you wish," she told him.

Renno's other doubt concerned the untested Holani, but he would leave her conduct to the control of his brother. She was armed with his spare musket and a pistol. He led the way carefully up the mountainside, found his position of observation, and saw that there was a growing pile of leather bags outside the cave's entrance. He had given his orders. Each person—including Beth and Ena, with Holani by El-i-chi's side—would find his or her position. As he waited, Renno could hear the voices of the Spanish soldiers. They talked of gold, gold, gold. And at any given time only a few of them were outside the mine, the others working to carry out the gold.

He gave everyone ample time to get into position and then gave the cry of a hawk three times. Overhead Little Hawk echoed him, and then seven muskets spoke almost as one and seven Spaniards went down. Without taking time to reload, Renno jerked the English longbow off his shoulder and sent two swift arrows. The arrows, at such close range, were more deadly than a musket, for they penetrated deep, going all the way through the chests of his victims. Arrows came from his right to finish off those Spanish outside the mine and then to catch three others who ran from the dark shaft to see what was happening.

Seventeen dead or severely wounded men lay on the hot, dry, rocky mountainside. Renno hooted like an owl and saw Rusog and El-i-chi close toward the mine entrance in time to use their tomahawks on two more soldiers. There was a long silence; then Renno signaled his friends to come from their cover and assemble.

William ran to look at the pile of gold brought out by the soldiers and hefted a few of the leather bags. "Do you think there is much more than this still inside?" he asked Renno.

Renno felt the bags. They contained rough ingots and the nuggets. "There is no gold dust here."

William considered, his eyes bright. "There must be at least ten men left in the mine."

"To go in and get them would be a great risk," Renno said. "The manitous have smiled on us so far, and we have much gold here at our feet. Is it not enough?"

William laughed happily. "Enough, old boy, to make us all rich."

"Good," Renno said. "El-i-chi and Rusog, guard the

mine entrance. William, take your woman and bring the horses up."

He heard the distant rattle of musket fire and knew that the Apache had made their last charge. He said a short prayer to the manitous to spare some of them. He had an urge to go watch, to see how many fell this time, but he had warned them, and they had not listened.

He heard the horses approaching. Rusog and El-i-chi, guarding the entrance, were alert, but no one appeared in that dark opening. Renno remembered how it had been inside the evil mountain, how the dead, shrunken eyes of the old fathers had seemed to stare at him in the flickering light of his torch. He did not envy those Spaniards who were inside.

"Don't overload the horses," he instructed, as William and the women, with Estrela helping, began to try to balance the heavy bags on leather straps thrown over the animals' backs. "We have far to go."

Chapter XII

Friar Sebastián had been pleased to find that the old map drawn by the Franciscan monk was accurate. Friar Luis had made all landmarks clear, so that there had been no wasted effort on the trip to Devil's Mountain, and when at last the distinctive profile of the mountain was in sight, he summoned both Montenegro and Barca to tell them that their destination was before them and that Barca was to choose thirty devout, pious men who could be trusted, men who would be pleased to serve the Church.

Sebastián's heart rose into his mouth when he saw the ancient city. He saw it first with the morning sun turning the mud and stone to gold, and for a few moments his plans soared up like fire. There would be his Indian converts and workers. He went on a patrol with Barca and was sore at heart when they found only a grazing horse and one old man who showed them his spring, gave them welcome, and steadfastly refused to listen to Friar Sebastián's preachings. Sebastián had not even bothered to climb the narrow, hidden trail to the mesa top, for he had no interest in a dead city. He made one last attempt to get the old man to listen to his message of divine grace, and when the old man had said quietly, "Perhaps we all worship the same great spirit," he was so incensed at that blasphemy that he gave orders and did not look back as two soldiers made the worshiper of false gods pay for his folly with his life.

They had little difficulty locating the mine's entrance at Devil's Mountain. A recent explorer, it seemed, had discarded his spent torches outside the mouth of the cavern. Sebastián's heart sank; had someone beaten them to the gold? It was, he decided, a mixed blessing. If the torches had not been found, the Spaniards could have searched in vain for days looking for the entrance. Barca, carrying a torch, had led the way into the mine, and his skin crawled for a few moments when he saw the mummified dead in the great chamber. Any feeling of fear and superstition was driven from his mind, however, when he discovered the small shaft and the huge store of gold at its end.

Sebastián sifted gold dust through his fingers and praised God. This hoard, delivered to Spain, would raise him to the highest councils of the Church, and there would be ways for him to divert enough of the gold to his private coffers to give him the other necessity of power, wealth.

Foreseeing the need of a means to carry the gold, Sebastián had brought strong leather bags with him from Corpus Christi, and now it was easy to package the gold and to form a work line of men to carry it outside the mine. He had sent one man back to the main body to bring up pack mules and horses. The gold made an impressive pile, which was growing steadily when Barca heard the sound of gunfire from outside. He was directly behind three of his men when they ran outside, to be felled almost instantly. He drew back into the shadows, waited, then peered out carefully to see dead soldiers lying all around the bags of gold.

He made his way back to the big chamber where Sebastián was supervising putting the remaining nuggets and gold dust into new bags. When he reported what had happened outside, the priest went pale and then shouted, "What are you waiting for? Take these men here outside and kill our enemies."

Barca spoke with a soft voice. "They have muskets. They dropped three men with three shots. Only two men can exit the shaft at one time. We would be picked off two by two."

"Are you disobeying my orders?" Sebastián screamed, frantic to think that the gold might slip from his hands.

"Father, when it comes to military strategy," Barca said, "I am in command."

"I will see you flayed," Sebastián shrieked. He turned and shouted at the men, who had stopped working with the gold. "Your commander is relieved. You will obey me now. I order you to go out and fight. There can be only a few of them, for we have seen no sign of large forces in this desert."

One by one the men moved to stand behind Barca. The priest's face flared red. He made a threatening move forward, but when he saw the cold expressions on the faces of the men, he halted.

"The gold," Sebastián gasped. "If you will save it, I'll give each of you enough to make you rich men."

"We will get the gold," Barca said, and the determination in his voice, the dangerous look in his eyes, gave Sebastián another fear, for there was a hint of possessiveness in Barca's tone.

"The gold belongs to the Church," the priest reminded him.

"Of course," Barca said, smiling. "We will wait until

the thieves have taken the gold. Where can they go? We have two hundred men. We can track them down and kill them all in the open."

Barca went back to the entrance and watched as a white man and woman and several Indians loaded the gold onto the backs of fourteen horses. He was pleased to see that only half the gold could be carried by the available pack animals. And he was more pleased to see only eight people—four men and four women. Perhaps there were more hidden in the rocks, he thought, but he would take no chances, for two of the Indians kept their eyes on the entrance to the mine at all times.

He waited for a good half-hour after the last of the horses disappeared down the trail and then went back to where the men had continued to bag the nuggets and dust. "We go now," he said.

"Someone must stay to guard the remaining gold," Friar Sebastián said.

"I will need all my men to recover the gold that has been stolen," Barca countered.

"Then I myself will stay until you can send a man to the main body and have soldiers join me here," Sebastián said.

"That is your decision," Barca told him.

Friar Sebastián was a well-organized man. He had anticipated that Friar Luis's mine would be deep and dark, so he had brought pitch torches and large candles with him on the wagons so that the large chamber was now well-lit. Many of the mummified dead had been kicked aside to clear a path to the gold. Barca and his men left Sebastián there, working to ease the rotting bags of gold dust into new pouches without spilling the precious yellow dirt. He worked diligently for a long time as the torches smoked and the candles burned slowly down. When he paused to wipe the perspiration from his forehead, he realized that he heard only the almost inaudible hissing of the burning torches. All else was an eerie silence.

He said a quick Hail Mary and looked around. The

dry, withered dead lay in untidy piles. Others were in their original positions against the walls of the chamber, and for a moment it seemed that their dead eyes were staring directly at him. He laughed. They were only dead heathens. The idea that this was the devil's mountain was a stupid superstition dreamed up by benighted Indians. He had his cross and his rosary to protect him, and yet there was a feeling of . . . something in the chamber. The cavernous eye sockets of the dead seemed to move in the flickering light.

"*Ave María,*" he began again, and then, angry with himself for nervousness, he paused and said, "Satan, get thee behind me. I rebuke you! I cast you out! You have no power here, for the grace of our Lord, Jesus Christ, is with me here in this place."

He felt better. He was, after all, a virtuous and holy man. He carried the true word. He tortured the unbelievers and punished the blasphemers. Had there been anyone who dared to tell Friar Sebastián—or any other of the friars who carried the word to the heathens of the New World—that it was not godly to crucify an Apache woman and her son, he would have been shocked that anyone would question his divine revelation. His Lord had given him the right to exorcise demons. He was a man of God. The gold he was recovering—well, most of it—would be used for God's work.

When he heard a dry, rustling sound, he froze, and his eyes went wide. Had something moved there in that chamber of the long dead? He muttered prayers and leapt to his feet. The rest of the gold dust could wait until Barca sent men. He had the need to breathe fresh air, for the torches had stolen the air from the chamber. He took one step and heard a low, moaning sound, and a sudden gust of moldy, foul-smelling wind rushed into his face. The guttering candles were extinguished first and then the torches as the wind increased suddenly. All was silence and total, abysmal darkness. Friar Sebastián screamed hoarsely.

"Oh, help me, God," he panted. Which way was the shaft? He moved, felt his foot crunch something dry and brittle, and heard low moans as if from many throats. He heard the soft rustling sound begin to build, and in the blackness he imagined *them* moving toward him, untangling themselves from the untidy piles into which they had been tossed, moving from their leaning positions against the walls of the chamber.

"*Ave María*," he began. "Hail Mary, full of grace, blessed art thou among women. Be with me now in the time of my testing—"

Something touched his leg, something cold and dry. He screamed and ran full-tilt into a solid rock wall, crushing dry and brittle bones with his feet and with the weight of his body as he fell back. A stench of dry decay assaulted him, and bony arms clung to him as he rolled and then crawled, brushing away the clinging arms and screaming like a rabbit caught in the jaws of a wolf. All his prayers were forgotten. He had only one thought—to find the shaft and to gain the blessed light. He felt a dry, sharp bone jab into his knee, and he leapt to his feet, feeling his way along the wall, hearing and feeling the dry, brittle dead being trampled under his feet, and then he found the opening and was running, feeling his way along with one hand on the wall of the shaft.

For terrified, desperate minutes he feared he had taken a wrong turn and had gone down one of the branching shafts, but then he saw the light of the entrance, fell heavily, and screamed again as the rough stones abraded his knees. He threw himself out of the entrance and scrambled, his nails digging into the hard, rocky dirt, then rolled down an incline to come to his feet running, running, with the fiends of hell on his heels and his mind in shock.

"El-i-chi, Rusog," Renno said, as they led the laden horses down the trail from the mine, "find the Spaniards' horses. We can use them."

Both El-i-chi and Rusog had been thinking the same thing. The horses had to be near, and there were only a few places of concealment anywhere near the mine. They found them together, hobbled in a dry wash two hundred yards from the mine entrance. Thirty horses. They could not handle so many. On a hooted signal Renno joined them.

"Good," he said. "We will take two each. Unsaddle the others and scare them away."

"There are enough to carry the rest of the gold," William pointed out. But before anyone could speak, he added, "It would not be worth the risk. We have more than enough already."

"We can make the decision later," Renno said. "Now we must guard against those Spaniards who were left in the mine. They will be following us, and quickly."

"I know of no better place to meet them than here," Rusog said, "for they will certainly come for their horses."

"Ena," Renno ordered, "you, Holani, and the Spanish girl lead our packhorses down the trail. Should you encounter any Spaniards, forget the gold and take to the hills. We will join you as quickly as we can."

For once Ena obeyed without question, although it was evident that she would have preferred to stay to kill Spaniards. Renno gave the men instructions: "The battle with the Apache is over. Large forces of soldiers could be on the move. We will use no firearms."

They nodded and took their positions. Not long after, they heard the Spaniards coming, making no effort, it seemed, to be quiet, apparently certain that they were alone on the side of the mountain.

Barca indeed felt that the small force that had stolen *his* gold would flee as fast as they could. He had ordered the men to get the horses while he kept a lookout. He had waited only a few minutes when he heard one hoarse scream, which was cut off quickly. He crawled through the rocks and looked down into the dry wash to see three

Indian warriors scalping his men. All ten of them had fallen quickly to a fast attack by arrows that ended when Renno, Rusog, and El-i-chi leapt from the rocks to close quarters with tomahawks.

Barca knew that he was in a serious situation. He could pick off one of the men below with his musket and perhaps get the other two with his pistols, but he was not sure now that there had been only eight of them.

He considered his alternatives. There was still a lot of gold back at the mine. Even if the thieves somehow escaped him, he would still profit. Furthermore, he was sure that once the thieves reached the open desert and tried to make their getaway, he could track them down and slaughter them with superior numbers of men. His first task was to stay alive. He waited until the grisly things being done to his dead men had been completed and the savages had gone, then set his course down the eastern side of the mountain to rejoin the main force, camped there in the open. He had not traveled far when he heard moans and cries and someone half sliding down a rocky incline. He concealed himself and saw the priest, his face and hands bloodied, with more blood soaking his soiled and torn robes at the knees. Barca's first thought was to show himself, but then he reconsidered. It was going to be necessary to rid himself of the priest sooner or later. Why not let the desert do the job for him? He waited until the sobbing, moaning man had passed his position, moving, he saw, at an angle that would not give him immediate contact with the main force on the flats below. He smiled.

"Well done, priest," he whispered. "Now, if you will turn just a bit more to the south, you will miss them completely."

Ena and the other women had made good progress down the old wagon trail with the gold-laden horses. When she heard horses overtaking them from the rear, she warned the others and turned to make a stand, just in case those who came were Spaniards. When she saw Renno in the lead on a fine black horse, she hooted a greeting and waved her tomahawk over her head. Now they had horses to ride again, and again there was mention of the gold that had been left behind, this time by Beth.

"Since it is the white man who is supposed to go crazy with greed when he finds gold," William said as Renno started to speak, "let me respond to my sister." He smiled. "We have eighteen horses, each laden with roughly one hundred pounds of gold. Even though some of it is only crudely refined and thus has impurities, and the other is in the form of crude nuggets, we have enough to make us among the richest families in England and to make Renno's and Rusog's people the best armed and richest Indians in America. I feel no greed, and I advise that we take what we have and go."

Everyone agreed, and El-i-chi, after patting Holani fondly on the arm, rode swiftly downward, to scout the way. The heavily laden animals had to move slower. The day had grown long, and Renno wanted to be off the mountain and in the open desert before dark. He pushed the pack animals as rapidly as possible. El-i-chi was using the Apache coyote signals to let them know at intervals that the trail was clear. Now the trail entered a long and twisting canyon with sheer walls and a sandy floor. The canyon cut through the last area of rocky foothills and emptied onto the desert. El-i-chi scouted ahead carefully, for there had been plenty of time for some of the men who had decimated the attacking Apache to reach the canyon's mouth.

As El-i-chi reached the last bend in the canyon, he exercised more care, for the canyon had widened and there was good cover on both sides of the sandy track down its center. He heard nothing, saw nothing. The heat was beginning to lessen a bit, and the canyon floor was in deep shadow. He peered into the shadows with his hawk-clear eyes and saw only sand, rocks, and brush.

The shot that killed El-i-chi's horse was a very lucky

one, fired against the orders of the Spanish lieutenant who had decided to make camp at the mouth of the canyon rather than try to ride the trail up the mountain in the dark. Shot through the heart, the horse dropped instantly and El-i-chi was tumbling to prevent a serious fall when his head hit an exposed stone and he fell into a thundering, then silent blackness.

"Rusog!" Renno beckoned when he heard the musket shot, and kicked his horse into a gallop. Rusog came behind him, and without permission Ena and Holani kicked their horses into a gallop to follow. Holani's heart was beating hard because it was her El-i-chi out there and she could envision him wounded badly or even dead. Renno shared Holani's concern. And their worst fears seemed to have materialized when they rounded the bend in the canyon and Renno jerked his horse to a halt, having seen El-i-chi's dead horse and El-i-chi himself sprawled a few feet away.

"Stay here," Renno ordered as Holani tried to ride past him. He moved his horse to block her.

"El-i-chi!" Holani cried out, and kicking her horse hard, she avoided Renno's horse and shot past him. Renno jerked his horse's head around and followed, yelling over his shoulder, "Stay here, all of you!"

After seeing the Indian fall, the Spanish lieutenant waited for a couple of minutes before telling two men to take a look to be sure the Indian was dead. The soldiers were walking swiftly forward when they heard the thundering hooves of horses approaching. They quickly took cover behind rocks and made ready to fire. From that position they saw that the fallen Indian was not dead, for he was moving, trying to sit up.

"Hold your fire," one of the soldiers said as two horses raced into view. "Take the two mounted ones first."

Holani saw El-i-chi struggling to sit up and knew great gladness. She jerked her horse to a halt, leapt off, and threw herself toward El-i-chi, to meet the ball from one of the Spanish muskets. Her forward movement carried her to him. She fell limply atop him as he, still dazed, rolled onto his back. Thus it was that his first fully conscious sight was Holani's face, blank of all expression, as she fell toward him. He managed to get his arms up to catch her, and his eyes were no more than inches from her blank ones, and from a hole in her forehead there suddenly welled up a gush of red, rich blood.

Renno felt the brush of death and heard the dull, cracking sound of a musket ball passing close by his ear. He flung himself off his horse and went to the ground. The soldiers, seeing him fall, stood, about to come forward to check on a total of three dead Indians. Renno could hear El-i-chi moaning in grief. He lay quite still until the two Spanish soldiers had come within fifty feet, and then he killed both with his pistols, one in each hand. He leapt to his feet even as they fell, to see, with great sadness, that Holani was dead. Her blood had reddened El-i-chi's face and chest.

A volley of musketry swept past him as he knelt, and that movement saved his life, as he saw the madness of grief in his brother's eyes.

"Are you wounded?" Renno asked.

El-i-chi seemed not to comprehend. He gently pushed Holani off him and placed her on her back, wailing a Seneca song of sorrow. Then he seized his musket and changed the song of sadness into a war cry and almost escaped Renno's frenzied grab at him. They tumbled to the sand together.

"El-i-chi," Renno hissed harshly, "at least a dozen muskets fired."

"Let me go!" El-i-chi demanded, trying to yank free.

Renno understood that his brother had lost the thing he loved most, and now he wanted only to die in the process of avenging Holani's death.

"You must avenge her," Renno agreed. "But you cannot do it by rushing into the barrels of a dozen muskets."

El-i-chi wailed something wild and fierce and incomprehensible.

"Together we will avenge her," Renno said, his face close to his brother's. "In the darkness, El-i-chi. We will kill them all, not just one or two."

"Yes," El-i-chi said as another volley of musket fire splattered dust around them. He picked up Holani and ran back down the canyon. Renno's horse, spooked by the gunfire, had already gone back, and Renno ran lightly behind El-i-chi, looking back to memorize the features of the canyon.

Ena and Beth ran forward to meet them. Beth was weeping. She put her hand on El-i-chi's arm and followed at his side until he placed Holani's body on the bearskin, spread by Ena. They would bury Holani in it.

"How many?" Rusog asked Renno.

"No more than a dozen," Renno answered.

"Good," Rusog said through clenched teeth. "We will kill them in the dark."

"My brother," Renno said, putting his hand on Rusog's shoulder. "This is now a blood matter, and it is the blood of my brother Ei-i-chi and myself. You will stay here with the women and William. If we should fail, you must abandon the gold and make your way to the open desert through the mountains."

Rusog understood. Had it been Ena lying dead, he would have been unable to control his passions, as El-i-chi seemed to be doing, but would have rushed to kill.

There was one weapon in Renno's pack that he had not used so far during the long journey. He had modeled it after the great medicine ax, a gift of the manitous, with which he had fought in the war against the Chickasaw. It had a stout, long handle, and the cutting edges were chipped flint. Only a strong warrior would have been able to wield it. He hefted the ax, then swung it so that the head whistled through the air. El-i-chi was sitting mutely beside his dead wife. The long shadows had become solid, and the sun was now down. There was nothing to do but wait. Beth and Ena tried to get the brothers to drink and eat, but both refused.

When Renno rose, El-i-chi leapt to his feet. Side by side they moved away from the group, and Beth could hardly hold her tongue, wanting to plead with Renno not to try to go it alone, to let the others join the fight, but she managed to keep her silence as William stood by her side and squeezed her hand reassuringly.

Renno motioned that El-i-chi would attack from the left. There was good cover there, all the way to the rocks that sheltered the Spaniards. Renno nodded grimly when he saw that the Spaniards were so confident that they had built two campfires.

"I will have an easier task than you," El-i-chi pointed out. "When you are in position, hoot once like the owl, and I will be among the men around the campfire on the left, even as you leap."

Renno grunted in agreement, and then they separated. At first Renno made good time. When he was less than fifty yards away he saw that the Spaniards had only two sentries posted just outside the glow of the fires. The man on his side sat on a large boulder, slumped, his musket across his knees. Renno moved with the silence of a snake, making himself a part of the ground, taking advantage of the slightest cover, for there was no room for him to skirt by the sentry. The canyon walls rose straight up to the right.

He was thinking: *Sleep on, Spaniard, and I will soon see that you have no more dreams.*

The last ten yards were barren. He inched forward on his stomach with the slowness of a tortoise, the great war club slung across his back, his knife in hand. Once the sentry coughed and shifted his weight, then let his head slump forward onto his chest again. Renno covered the last few feet scarcely breathing, moving slowly, slowly, careful not to make the slightest sound, and then he was moving past the base of the waist-high rock on which the sentry sat, and with one swift and deadly silent movement he was on his feet, his hand over the sentry's mouth, his knife slashing across the man's throat. There was a gurgling sound, and a sigh as of a low wind, and then Renno was lowering the body to drape over the rock.

He could see the campfires now. Eight men were seated around the larger fire; four were only about ten feet away. Renno inched closer. An officer at the smaller fire yawned and said it was about time to sleep.

Renno wondered if he should wait until all the Spanish were asleep, but he decided that El-i-chi was in no condition to be that patient.

Renno hooted once softly and launched himself at the group of eight men, his great flint ax hissing within range even as the more alert men began to turn their heads to face death. Out of the corner of his eye Renno saw a demon avenger land squarely in the midst of the four men at the other fire. Renno killed on the backswing and then, the ax held in both hands, muscles straining, he took purposeful, measured steps as a man would take who swings a scythe in a wheat field, but reaping death with grunts of effort. The ax whistled now, swinging inexorably as men yelled, and one screamed behind him and managed to fire a pistol just as Renno's club smashed his skull, so that the ball went into the blazing fire and sent sparks flying.

He heard El-i-chi's war cry and turned just in time to avoid a saber, ducking under the whispering slash of the sharp blade, and crushed the man's chest. El-i-chi was suddenly behind him, and he heard the sickening impact of a tomahawk in bone and flesh and whirled looking for another target but saw only El-i-chi standing, so he let his club down slowly.

One man tried to crawl away, but El-i-chi, with a cry, smashed his skull with his tomahawk and then checked all the fallen methodically, having to strike only one more blow to leave no Spaniard living.

"Come, Brother," Renno said gently as El-i-chi began to take scalps. "We have far to go, and we don't need that kind of evidence of our revenge."

But El-i-chi, moving with deft swiftness, scalped all of

the dead with grim determination and then tossed the scalps into the fire. Burning hair and flesh tainted the air. Renno heard an owl hoot and answered, and Rusog walked into the firelight.

"We must move now," Renno said. Rusog, after taking a look at the fallen, hooted three times, and Renno heard horses coming. They had wrapped Holani's body in a blanket and tied it to a horse. "We will bury her and mourn her in the desert," Renno told El-i-chi.

"I stay here to kill Spaniards," his brother replied.

"You will kill more by fighting at my side," Renno said. "We need you and your good right arm if any of us are to live."

"So be it," El-i-chi conceded. "I will fight with you until you are safe in the lands of the Comanche, and then I will come back, or go where I must, and kill Spaniards."

There was a moon, and the going was relatively easy. Renno set a route toward the ancient city of the dead, for they needed water. He saw a sea of campfires off to the east, near the base of the mountain. Soon the fires were lost to view behind the bulk of the mesa. With Renno leading, they were nearing the old man's hidden spring. Almost there, he heard a sound that stopped him in his tracks. He had left his horse with the others in order to move silently. The sound came from near the entrance to the spring. He recognized it as a horse in the process of one of nature's basic functions. He gave the cry of a coyote, the Apache recognition signal, and it was answered.

Renno moved forward slowly. "I am Renno," he said.

"Come, friend," a voice called back.

Two men moved to meet him, and there was enough moonlight for him to recognize Gerachise. He clasped arms with the Apache. He could see sleeping forms everywhere now, and the movements of horses in the shadows among the tall stone pillars.

"Tomorrow we will ride to avenge our dead brothers," Gerachise said.

"That is good," Renno said. "We, too, have our dead

to avenge. But now my friends need water." He ran back a few hundred yards, signaled with owl hoots, and soon all the travelers' water skins were filled with fresh water and the horses were being watered two at a time. Gerachise came to him, with Black Eagle at his side.

"Sleep now," Gerachise said. "We will talk at first light."

Renno was asleep instantly and woke refreshed in spite of having slept only three hours. He saw, with an aching heart, that only some fifty warriors had survived the assault on the Spanish to be present at the council. He sat next to Black Eagle and Gerachise.

"We will catch the Spanish on the march," Gerachise vowed. "We will attack from two sides and take many of them with us to the land of the spirits."

"The Apache are brave and great warriors," Renno said. "How many Spaniards did you send to the land of the spirits yesterday?"

Black Eagle glared, but Gerachise said, "Few. We could not get close because of the fierceness of their gunfire."

"Will it not be the same today?" Renno asked.

Gerachise shrugged. "We will choose the ground this time."

"At the mine and in the canyon, many Spanish feed the vultures because we chose our ground well," Renno said. "Hear me, my friends. They are many. We are few. To best them we must use our heads as well as our hearts."

"Why are we wasting time with this talk?" Black Eagle demanded angrily, and several warriors grunted in agreement.

"This warrior has great medicine," Gerachise said, keeping his voice calm. "I, for one, will listen."

"To gain revenge and to free your land of the enemy, we will do as I suggested once before," Renno said.

"Fight like the coyote," Black Eagle hissed in disdain.

"I would be a live coyote rather than a dead mountain

lion," Renno retorted. "Is there not more honor in killing the enemy and living than in dying?"

"The spirits are with this warrior," an Apache said.

Black Eagle stood. "Many times have I heard it claimed that the spirits are with this one or that one, and in the end, where war is concerned, I find that the spirits are with the strongest and the swiftest."

"Give us a sign, then, medicine man, to convince our chief," an Apache called to Renno.

"Yes," Black Eagle challenged. "Convince me of your medicine."

"The spirits are not children to be called when one wants them," Renno said. "I will pray. That is all I can do." He knew that by agreeing to do even that, he was taking a risk for the remaining Apache; he knew that another frontal attack would result in the deaths of most or all of the warriors left. He stood and extended his arms to the light in the east, where the sun would rise soon, and he chanted his prayer in the language of the Seneca. There was respectful silence from the Apache, and as Renno chanted and prayed for favor from the manitous, the light grew and the disk of the red morning sun poked up beyond the eastern horizon. Renno's heart leapt as Little Hawk flew overhead and cried out harshly.

There was a moan from behind him, but he continued his prayers. And then he heard a loud cracking sound, and he opened his eyes to see the Apache pointing and whispering in awe. He intensified his prayer, then turned to see the topmost part of one of the tall stone pillars begin to lean. Another sharp crack sounded as rock splintered, sending fine shards and broken particles ahead of the huge rock that was separating from the pillar.

He gave thanks then, and his voice was answered by the hunting shriek of the hawk. The rock overbalanced and plunged with a great crash that caused swift whinnies of panic among the horses. Then all was still.

Black Eagle made a ceremonial bow. "Now I will

follow you," he whispered, his eyes wide. "Order me, great one."

"I do not give orders to my friends," Renno replied as the awed Apache warriors began to speak excitedly among themselves. "It is my opinion that at least a part of the Spanish force will move early this morning toward the old wagon track leading up the mountain. The way leads through tortured and broken land, through washes, boulders, and hills. We will hide among those washes, boulders, and hills. We will sting the enemy, slay him quickly, and melt into the land, as shadows melt with the setting sun, only to ride ahead of him to sting him again."

"It is good," Gerachise said. "I would not go back to my people with a glad heart to report so many dead without the scalps of many of my enemies."

"Will the great medicine man fight with us?" Black Eagle asked. "And all of his warriors?"

"I fight," Renno confirmed, "and my brother, who has more Spanish blood to spill." He paused. "We carry the yellow dirt to the East, where it is valued."

Gerachise spat. "The yellow dirt is what brings the Spanish, but if you have a use for it, you are welcome to it."

"The women and my brother Rusog and William will stay with the yellow dirt and start toward the river," Renno finished.

"No," Rusog said. "I will stay with you and fight."

Renno bowed his head. He had feared that. "Then, William, you, Beth, and Estrela must go on alone with the gold, and we will join you at the river when our work is done."

"I'm afraid I feel as the others feel, old boy," William said.

"And I," Beth said quickly. "My bow will be of use in the kind of fighting you plan."

"Some of our warriors are wounded too badly to march," Gerachise said, "but they can guard your yellow dirt."

Renno nodded. "I had thought to hide our yellow dirt in the spirit city."

"Good," Gerachise said. "We will help you carry it, although it seems foolish to an Apache to waste sweat on such things."

"And I thought," Renno continued, "to leave something else there in the spirit city." He was looking at El-i-chi. "There Holani will be among the spirits of Indians, my brother, and not alone in the sands of the desert."

Her burial was quick and simple. There would be no mourning until more revenge had been taken. And the gold was hidden well, too, in the dusty floor of a building that once had known the smells of cookfires and the laughter of children.

Chapter XIII

It was almost noon before Renno had his force, now including some fifty Apache warriors, in position. He wanted to take best advantage of surprise. He knew that the Spanish leaders were not stupid and would learn swiftly, so the first ambush would be the most effective. He would have liked to have more time for planning, but that was not to be, for fifty mounted soldiers were moving at a purposeful pace around the lower slopes of the mountain and headed toward the canyon that gave access to the wagon trail. The leader of the force was a large able-looking man with a huge beard.

A full hour behind the force of cavalry came the rest of the Spanish force, under the command of Carlos Montenegro. With Montenegro were the wagons and pack animals to carry the gold remaining at the mine.

Lope Barca, leading the fifty men in the forefront, had discussed the situation with Montenegro, and decisions had been made: Barca would pick up the trail of the thieves at the canyon's mouth and recover the stolen gold while Montenegro went to the mine.

A chance happening saved Barca's life once again. As his force entered a broken, rocky, and arid stretch of badlands, he was called to the rear of the column to look at a man who had been bitten by a rattlesnake when he had stopped to relieve himself. The panicked man was thrashing and fighting against two others who tried to hold him down. His trousers were bunched around his feet, and his left buttock was beginning to redden and swell.

"Leave him," Barca ordered. He bent over the frightened man and said, "The others will be along in an hour, and they will care for you." But he knew that the man was as good as dead, for the reptile that had bitten him had been killed, and it was a huge, bloated thing with a body as thick as a man's forearm.

Renno struck while Barca was in the rear. Had Barca been in his usual position at the head of the column, he would have been the first target.

The trail led the Spanish between two rocky ridges that rose on either side in tumbled chaos. Renno, William, and Beth had taken concealed positions on the north side. Almost directly across from them were El-i-chi, Rusog, and Ena. Estrela guarded the horses in safety. They had let the two Spanish scouts pass by them. El-i-chi waited until almost half the column was past before he nodded, and three arrows flew unerringly to impale three riders in the middle of the column. There was confusion for a moment; then an officer began to bark orders, and about fifteen men spurred toward the source of the arrows. Three dropped from the arrows, and then, as the charge came closer to the rocks, three more fell in a blast of three muskets.

More men were sent to charge the positions of El-i-chi, Rusog, and Ena, and that was the time Renno chose to unleash the power of the three English longbows. He had instructed William and Beth to aim first at the soldiers who had not discarded their metal vests, for he knew the penetrating power of the longbows would have a decided effect on the morale of the soldiers when they realized that their armor was no protection. It would give the attackers a psychological advantage.

The sound of a metal-tipped arrow striking armor was a sharp clang. Three men toppled with arrows in their backs, for they were all facing north, the direction of the original attack. For a moment there was milling confusion, and then, according to plan, El-i-chi, Rusog, and Ena showed themselves for a moment up among the chaos of rocks on the ridge as a group of soldiers changed their direction and headed toward Renno's group.

"There are but three of them!" a Spanish officer screamed. "Ha *ha*!" He gave orders to a noncommissioned officer to take twenty men and kill the three, and then, as more metal-tipped English arrows dropped men around him, he himself led a charge forward to escape the ambush. He could see the trail opening up ahead of him as he rode as fast as his horse would carry him, his men thundering behind him. Once out of range of the ambush, he would re-form his troop and turn to face an unknown number of the enemy. He felt that there had to be a considerable number of them, for he had left almost twenty men dead back in the pass between those rocky ridges.

Twenty Apache warriors, led by Gerachise, fired their few muskets and arrows just as it seemed that the Spanish officer and his men would burst into the clear. More men fell.

Meanwhile, Lope Barca had galloped to the front to see one force fleeing and three other groups climbing into the rocks. One group seemed to be gaining on three Indians, who paused now and then to fire, ineffectively, at their pursuers.

"Get back down here, you fools!" Barca roared, but the men were too far away to hear. He saw most of them fall backward, wounded or dead, as they gained the rock-strewn crest of the ridge, for Black Eagle and more Apache lay in wait there, and the original three turned to join in the fight. Only three Spanish soldiers survived to make it back down the ridge.

Those who had chosen to chase Renno and the two English people met a similar fate, with the longbows joining in Apache musket and arrow fire.

Barca, once he had regrouped the few men left to him in the pass, knowing that there were more Indians ahead, put discretion above valor and rode back to join the main force, led by Montenegro. The men who had ridden through the last ambush were now in the open, and they formed into a defensive square in the harsh heat of the sun and waited there, thirsty and hot, until the main force arrived, having found no sign of Indians anywhere. It was as if the Apache had melted into the desert.

"This changes things," Montenegro told Barca when a final count totaled the number of men killed or so severely wounded that they would probably die. "There are more of them than we thought."

"I think it seems like more because our men panicked," Barca remarked.

"And these English arrows," Montenegro continued, holding up one he had taken from a dead man. "They puzzle me."

"Did you count the spent arrows at the main ambush?" Barca asked. "There are no more than perhaps a half-dozen English longbows in action. It was stupidity that cost us so many lives. Had the officers been alert and called for defensive positions at the flight of the first arrows, we would have cut our losses by more than half. We will keep our force intact in the future. We will march in defensive array, and we will be ready."

His methods were put to the test within hours as he

ordered the men to march from the canyon entrance to the wagon track. In a mostly flat stretch of land, arrows came from nowhere and two men fell. When men began to chase after two lone Apache warriors who showed themselves as they mounted their horses, he shouted orders for the soldiers to hold their positions.

Men fell twice more before his scouts went into the canyon to find it clear. Then three went down at one time, only one the next, and the attackers seemed to fade into the desert like shadows. The soldiers were understandably unnerved, for sometimes those at the forefront took the arrows, and at other times it was the men in the center of the column. Barca was gaining grudging admiration for whoever was coordinating the Indian attacks. The fighting was unlike anything the Apache had ever been known to do. He knew that there were hundreds of miles of empty desert and plains between him and any hope of reinforcements, and he could predict that the slow but steady attrition of his men from ambush would continue.

"We must give up the idea of recovering the stolen gold," he told Montenegro. "The gold left at the mine will meet our needs."

A bloody, dusty, ragged apparition stumbled into the camp that night. Barca cursed when he was called from his tent to see a half-dead friar gasping and sobbing as he sucked water from a skin. Montenegro was there before him.

"Thank God you're safe," Montenegro said.

"You deserted me," Friar Sebastián screamed hoarsely. "I will have you killed, all of you, for you left me to die." He seemed to gain control of himself and looked up to see Barca's stern face. "Forgive me, comrades, I am still half-mad from the sun of this devil-begotten place. What of the gold?"

"We will have to content ourselves with what is left at the mine," Barca said.

"Fool!" Sebastián screamed, leaping to his feet, to sway dizzily. "I order you to go after the thieves. I order you on the king's authority and on the authority of the Church."

"He needs rest," Barca said to Montenegro. "Feed him." He stood with his face near the sun-blistered, scratched, soiled face of the friar. "He has been deprived of his senses by the sun and his ordeal." He turned. Sebastián raised a hand, then subsided. He reached again for a water skin and drank deeply. Barca hoped the greed of the priest would finish the job that the desert had not done, or he would drink so much water that it would kill him in his dehydrated condition.

The slow and careful progress of the Spanish force to the area of the mine was without incident the next day. Renno had kept busy throughout the night preparing a surprise for the Spanish, however, with the help of a select group of Apache who, convinced that they would die while taking their vengeance on the Spanish, had overcome their fear and dread of the mountain.

Friar Sebastián, still weak but much recovered, was near the head of the column when the scouts came clattering back down the steep trail. "Hundreds of them," a wild-eyed scout gasped. "Everywhere. They're behind every rock."

"Excellent," Barca said with a grim smile. "They have lost patience with their cowardly ambushes and will face us like men." He rubbed his hands. "This will end it, my friends. There is one more battle to be fought, and then we will have our chance at recovering the stolen gold and will suffer no harassment as we journey home."

He rode back along the column, giving individual orders and words of encouragement to all of his men. He told them that if they would fight one more good fight that the worst would be over, that the relatively few Apache would be dead, or so decimated that those who survived would pose no threat.

"I will see these hundreds of warriors for myself," Friar Sebastián announced as Barca called the scouts to him and rode forward.

It was true. There was a warrior visible behind almost every rock surrounding the entrance to the mine. From a distance, they could not see more than a shape, a head, the outline of a bow. Barca saw that it would be a spirited little fight, but he had confidence that he could kill many of the Indians with musket fire delivered in volleys as he moved the men forward in a fighting square. He returned and gave his orders. It took a while to get the men formed, and then they marched to the inspiring sounds of a drum up the trail, expanding their square as they approached the slope leading to the mine entrance, and when they were in range Barca directed volleys of fire. He could see the still, patient warriors among the rocks taking hits, slumping, falling from sight. The soldiers loaded, advanced ten paces, fired in volleys again.

It was surprising to Barca that there was no return musket fire, and not even any arrows. He peered into the rocks, trying to catch movement, but the hidden warriors were silent, still. And then with great cries, as his front ranks advanced to within a few feet of the mine entrance, forms launched themselves from the rocks above. The war cries were bloodcurdling, and Barca's first thought was that the Apache above were leaping carelessly to their deaths, and then the first of perhaps a dozen forms landed atop and among the front ranks, shattering brittlely, dry bones snapping, a shriveled head rolling. The Spanish soldiers, attacked by the dead, screamed, threw down their muskets, and broke toward the rear.

Friar Sebastián saw the spectral forms leap from the rocks to attack, and in his mind he was transported back to the chamber of the dead, with the dry, rustling sounds and the clinging bony arms clutching at him, and his screams were added to those of the panicked soldiers.

The fear spread, and soon most of the Spanish army were rushing pell-mell down the track, to be met by steel-tipped arrows from three English longbows and a hail of Apache arrows. The panic became a wild rout as the dead continued to tumble from the trail, to roll heavily down the steep mountainside.

Barca met the retreat with the flat of his sword and managed by the sheer force of his determination to rally a few men. Montenegro followed his example, so that when silence fell again, almost fifty men climbed to the mine entrance behind their officers. There were no arrows or gunfire there, and below them the sounds of firing died out. Barca walked to the nearest of the concealed warriors—and saw one of the long-dead Indians from the chamber of the dead propped up by stones, a curved stick shaped like a bow in his fleshless fingers.

"You see the force that routed a hundred men," he said to those who had followed him nervously. "Now, let us forget our fears and take our gold."

The trail down the mountain was now clear, the ambushers having once again melted into the desolate landscape. Pack animals were brought up. The survivors of the wild rout down the mountain came back sheepishly. Another dozen men had died. But now the gold was secure, and by nightfall the Spanish force was camped in the mouth of the lower canyon, with enough sentries posted to assure against a night attack.

Before deciding to violate the peace of the dead, Renno had prayed and then discussed it with his friends and with the two Apache chiefs. It had been Beth who put forth the deciding argument.

"I can personally feel the spirits of this mountain," she said, and all agreed that there seemed to be an odd presence there. "But I do not feel evil. I feel good men and women crying out for vengeance. If the spirits could speak, I think, they would say, 'Use our bodies, for in that way we will speak to the Spaniards over the span of the centuries, and they will remember us.'"

The Apache had used up the bulk of their courage merely in coming to fight on that evil mountain, so it had been up to Renno and his friends to carry the surprisingly

240

light and frail bodies from the chamber of the dead into the starred night and position them. And, with the Spaniards camped far below, it was the same group who gathered both the scattered bones that had been flung down onto the Spanish soldiers and the bodies that had been placed among the rocks and returned them to the chamber of the dead.

Renno had noted that there was a rocky overhang high above the entrance to the mine. He had examined it, and with some careful, judicious work he loosened a huge boulder and sent it crashing down. The boulder created a rock slide from the overhang, and then it seemed that the manitous added their force, for the entire side of the mountain slid and fell with a thunderous roar, which was heard by the Spaniards far down the mountain. The entrance to the mine was now sealed forever.

"Rest in peace, old fathers," Renno whispered respectfully. "And now your spirits can go forever to the West."

Barca had his force moving at sunup, and their route gave Renno immediate concern, because the scouts were heading straight for the mesa of the dead city instead of moving east. William and Beth's and Renno's bags of ingots and nuggets were hidden in the dead city. The march was not made without cost. One or two Apache warriors sprang up at a time from concealment, took their toll, and melted into the desert.

Since the gold stolen from the Spanish was hidden in the dead city, Renno hoped that the soldiers' only intent in marching there was to obtain water. But a few Apache warriors were missing, their bodies unrecovered, and there was a chance that the Spanish had learned by torture of the hiding place of the gold, which many Apache had helped to carry to its place of concealment, and of the whereabouts of the concealed entrance to the pathway for the city.

The confidence of the Apache was growing. More and more individual warriors reported their kills, and the trail of Spanish dead was being extended all the time. Now the Spaniards were not even pausing to bury their dead. Whenever a man fell to ambush, his weapons and water skin were taken and his body left for the scavengers of the desert. Black Eagle stated openly that it was now time to mount the final, all-out attack, and Renno had to be both patient and persuasive to prevent many warriors from siding with Black Eagle.

When it was absolutely sure that the destination of the Spanish force was the ancient city, Renno called Gerachise aside and said, "I will not ask the Apache to fight to protect the yellow dirt that has no value for him, but I and mine will go ahead. We will take up our positions in the city of the departed spirits. It will be good if you continue to harry the enemy, protecting the lives of your remaining warriors carefully."

"I will cool the recklessness of my brother Black Eagle," Gerachise promised. "And should the Spanish try to send many men up the secret trail, we will give them something to think about."

Taking along a young Apache to remove their horses from the area of the spring, Renno and his group rode hard through the night to get to the mesa before the Spanish. As the new day dawned, Renno's friends were atop the mesa, able to see the vanguard of the approaching Spanish. When the Spaniards reached the spring, they camped, but no man tried to mount the trail to the top of the mesa. It began to appear that the only purpose of the Spanish commander was to store water, which, from the small spring, was a time-consuming process.

Carlos Montenegro was relieved when there were no attacks during the afternoon. The approaches to the mesa were quite open, and he agreed with Barca that attack was unlikely, at least during the daylight hours. Montenegro had been curious about the ancient city ever since he had first seen it, and he announced his intentions to visit the place. Most of the soldiers, weary after the fighting and riding of the past days, were content to lie in the shade of the mesa and rest, but there were several who shared Montenegro's desire to have a closer look at the city above them. Some few of them could not believe that a place appearing so impressive from a distance could be nothing more than empty shells of mud and stone buildings. The thought of hidden gold sent several of the men up the trail behind Montenegro, and there was a general disappointment when the city proved to be such a poor, deserted, arid place. Nevertheless, there were narrow alleys to explore and openings into the buildings to probe.

When Renno heard the men coming up the trail he passed the word to his well-concealed force to be ready. He was relieved when the group of about a dozen emerged atop the mesa without any digging tools and with only their light weapons. The actions of the Spanish soldiers soon convinced him that they were merely curious and that they would quickly tire of the sameness of the buildings and go back to join their comrades at the foot of the mesa. Had it been his decision alone—or had he chosen to exercise his authority in the matter—he would have kept his people in hiding and not risked bringing a larger force to the city where, in effect, he and his friends were trapped. He knew, however, that El-i-chi, still burning with his sorrow and his desire for vengeance, would be thirsting for Spanish blood, and he was not surprised to see his brother leap lightly from atop a single-story building and kill a Spanish straggler with ease and swiftness, then drag the body into a building.

"So be it," he said.

It was growing late and the shadows were long, the sun blood red in the west as it sank into a bank of distant cloud. Renno moved along the rooftops, a deadly hunter, saw two of the Spanish soldiers alone, walking slowly, talking about the city in hushed voices. It was a challenge to kill both silently, a challenge he accepted. He landed behind them, his tomahawk smashing down even before his feet touched, and then he dropped the tomahawk and shifted his stiletto to his right hand from his left and slashed the throat of the second man as he opened his mouth to yell in dismay.

He did not have time, however, to hide the bodies before three soldiers rounded the corner of a building and halted in surprise. An arrow from his longbow reduced the number to two, but then the other two fled out of sight, shouting an alarm.

Rusog and El-i-chi ended the shouts of those two, and Beth sent a steel-tipped arrow to end the life of still another. The remaining men shouted and ran to join forces. In panic they began to race for the entrance to the trail, and one by one they fell, to arrows or to a snarling, savage El-i-chi, who placed himself in the pathway of the last two men and met their swords with his flashing knife and deadly tomahawk.

Carlos Montenegro had taken cover in a building and watched the men die one by one. He noted the location of the bowmen atop the buildings and began to make his way toward the far edge of the city, hoping to find a way to the path without having to run that deadly gauntlet of silent killers. He was quite near the path when he saw a tall, solidly built man in loincloth, headband, and moccasins step directly into his path, tomahawk in hand. The man's skin was sun-browned, but lighter than that of the dead Apache he had seen, and he had startlingly blue eyes.

Montenegro's first impulse was to say a quick prayer for his soul, but when the blue-eyed man did not move but merely gazed at him from an expressionless face, he began to hope that somehow he could talk his way out of his peril.

"You and your men are brave when you kill from ambush," he taunted.

Renno had noted the officer's uniform worn by the man, and he postponed the Spaniard's death out of curiosity. He had seen many of them die, and he had seen the cruelty they could inflict. What manner of man was this?

"When you were men enough to come at us in honorable battle," Montenegro said, "we killed you."

"Why have you come to this land to kill men and women who have never threatened you?" the white Indian asked.

"I come on the orders of my king and my Church," Montenegro replied. "But I have seen enough killing. Let us agree to a truce, warrior, and we will leave these lands."

"To return with a larger force, with cannon?" Renno asked.

Montenegro had, with that comment, another indication that this was no Apache, no ordinary Indian. "A truce will benefit all. No more Apache will die. No more of my men will die."

"I have seen the result of Spanish promises in my own land, in the form of thousands of dead," Renno said. "I have seen it in Devil's Mountain in the form of dead women, men, and children." He shook his head sadly. "Had you wanted to live, you should not have begun this venture."

"So," Montenegro said, "will your man kill me with his bow from ambush?" He had seen movement above, and now Rusog stood on a rooftop, arrow nocked, bow drawn.

Renno had heard Rusog's approach. He looked up and held up his hand, and Rusog eased the pressure off his bow.

"It is natural for a man to want to live," Renno said.

"Yes," Montenegro agreed.

"The trail that leads to your comrades is just behind me," Renno observed coolly.

"Shall I walk to it in peace and truce?" Montenegro asked.

"You have merely to walk over me," Renno challenged, "and the trail is yours."

Montenegro's hand edged toward his pistol, but a sharp sound from Rusog, on the rooftop, stopped his hand. Rusog's bow was fully drawn, the arrow pointed at Montenegro's throat.

"Your sword and my tomahawk," Renno said, and Montenegro drew his heavy cavalry saber with surprising speed and leapt to the attack with such force that Renno had to give ground. The flashing blade reached time and time again for his life, and Renno either parried the stroke with his tomahawk or leapt out of its path, the strength of the Spaniard's attack pushing him back, back, toward the entrance to the trail and the sheer drop at the edge of the mesa.

It was there that they were observed by a sentry below, who called out. Soon most of the Spanish force was standing and looking up, watching the battling figures silhouetted against the setting sun.

Renno was adjusting to Montenegro's style of fighting now, and it was becoming easier to parry his strokes and lunges. The clash of sword on tomahawk could be heard by those who watched from below, and when the advantage seemed to be on the side of Montenegro, there were cheers and calls of encouragement. But Renno had seen a way to end it. He waited until Montenegro made one of his fierce and potentially deadly lunges, the point of his saber aimed at Renno's gut, and stepped aside, letting the blade whisper past his side, then grabbed Montenegro's arm, pulled the Spaniard close, and slashed with his tomahawk to open the Spaniard's throat. He held the arm, lest a dying slash injure him, until, eyes wide and lips trying to suck breath through a severed throat, Montenegro fell.

Quickly Renno bent and lifted the scalp with an adept stroke. He was now acting for the benefit of the Spanish soldiers below him. He held the scalp high. To add to the effect, Little Hawk, soaring above, dived and pulled out with a loud flutter of wings to land on the wrist holding the scalp and to tear at it with his beak.

"Men of Spain!" Renno called in his loudest voice. "This is not your land! Go back whence you came while you still live!" And with that he bent, lifted Montenegro's body above his head, and sent it, arms and legs flopping, to land with a dull crash among the awed soldiers.

"I am going to kill that arrogant son of a dog!" Lope Barca roared, charging for the trail, calling out the names of his more dependable men to accompany him, but at that moment, as dusk came to deepen the shadows of the mesa, Black Eagle struck from the west and Gerachise from the east, and Barca had to turn to rally his men against the swift attack that ended as quickly as it had begun, leaving four more dead men in the Spanish camp.

Sporadic attacks throughout the night kept Barca busy, and with the dawn he had his force on the move, bunched expertly around the precious wagons and pack animals that carried the gold, water, and provisions. From atop the mesa Renno counted the departing force. Of the original two hundred, just under a hundred marched.

Black Eagle and Gerachise awaited him at the spring. "They go," Gerachise said, "but with fewer men than they came."

"They will return," Black Eagle remarked gruffly. "They take their losses badly and have the fire of revenge in their blood."

"We must see to it that none survive to tell what the Apache has done to them," Gerachise said. "What of you, Medicine Man?" he asked, looking at Renno. "You have taught us well. We will not rush into the muzzles of the Spanish muskets anymore. You have your mission, the mission assigned to you by your spirits. Go with our friendship, Renno, and we will follow the Spanish through the barren lands and the great plains and leave his bones bleaching in the sun."

"I, for one, go with you," El-i-chi said.

Renno had hoped that El-i-chi had killed his fill of Spaniards, but he saw the hatred still in his brother's eye. He would not leave El-i-chi alone in this strange land.

"We will harry the Spanish together," he said.

A whoop of joy went up from the Apache, and Renno held up his arms for silence. "Go, then, my Apache brothers. Strike like the hidden rattlesnake. Nip like the coyote. Kill like the avenging spirits."

Renno had the gold dug up from its hiding place atop the mesa and brought down. When he had the packtrain organized, he gathered his group, with the exception of El-i-chi, who had joined the Apache for a quick ride on the trail of the retreating enemy. "Soon the madness of sorrow will be burned from the heart of my brother. Then he and I will angle toward the north and the lands of the Comanche. We have accomplished much and fought well, and I want no more risk to my blood, Rusog and Ena, or to my friends, William and Beth. Our duty now is to protect the gold and to return to our own peoples."

With the soldiers gone, Renno left the packtrain in the care of William, Beth, Rusog, and Ena, with Estrela riding along. The white Indian rode ahead to join El-i-chi and the Apache and saw a dead Spanish soldier on the trail. The long miles between the mountain of the devil and the Spanish lands in the far southeast would be bloody.

For a full day Barca's force marched without a single attack. Perhaps, he thought, the Apache were satisfied now that he was marching out of their lands. He prayed so, for the soldiers were in a bad way both physically and mentally. It would not take the loss of many more of their comrades to the sneak attacks to break their spirit and turn a well-trained unit into a mob that would be easy prey for the Apache. At the first water hole, a long march from the mountain, he called a halt in the middle of the afternoon and told his officers that they would rest there for at least another full day. That was a mistake that would cost him many men and would bring about events to alter Renno's plans as well.

The slow-moving packtrain moved into a dry Apache camp late in the evening. Renno met them and said, "The Spaniards camped early, at the water hole. They have pitched tents and show signs of resting there."

"Perhaps we can have some sport," Ena suggested.

"You will stay with the packtrain," Renno ordered,

and smiled inwardly as Ena tossed her dark head in protest.

The Spanish camp was in the open, and approach to it was not practical, so the Spaniards spent a peaceful night, losing only one sentry to a daring young Apache warrior who crawled a half-mile through open desert on his stomach.

The next morning word came to the Apache camp that Spanish patrols were being dispatched in groups of ten men in all directions from the camp. The patrols would make good targets. Assignments were made as war parties formed. Renno saw to it that El-i-chi was with him and then left Ena, Beth, William, and Estrela with a few lightly wounded Apache warriors to guard the camp and the gold. Thus the day's activity began.

In spite of the suspicions that Ena had strongly expressed regarding Beth's intentions toward Renno, Beth had come to admire Ena more than any woman she had ever known. When Ena came to her and suggested unsmilingly that they too participate in the day's sport, Beth nodded eagerly, even though she had a twinge of guilt at disobeying Renno's orders. Perhaps her decision was influenced by her desire to make Ena like her as much as she liked Ena. Being alone with Ena would give her a chance to bring up the touchy subject, to tell Renno's sister that although she admired Renno, she had no romantic designs on him.

They rode swiftly in the direction of the Spanish camp and entered a rugged area of gorges and rocky hills studded with tall, multiarmed cacti. Once they heard the clash of musket fire in the distance, but their area seemed to be inhabited only by lizards and a lazy rattlesnake coiled in the shade of a cactus. They rode down a sandy decline into a natural bowl, aiming toward the far rim, where a gentle slope would give them exit. The shot that killed Ena's horse came without warning. Beth, caught unaware when her horse bolted at the sound of the shot and the terrible scream of pain from the dying horse, was carried two hundred yards before she could control the mount. When she turned him, she saw Ena struggling with four Spanish soldiers, with more of them running down from the rocky side of the natural bowl. Beth jerked her longbow off her shoulder and rode hard to get within range, halted, then missed her first shot because of the nervousness of her horse. She leapt off the horse, set herself, halted a soldier in his tracks, and then began to fire as fast as she could whip arrows from her quiver and draw a bow. Three men were down, and Ena was free, running like the wind with men chasing her, coming directly toward Beth. Beth dropped another man and leapt to her horse, spurred it into a run, and then jerked him to a halt as Ena neared, the Spanish soldiers not ten yards behind her.

Ena caught Beth's arm, swung up behind her, and Beth yelled to the horse even as she sank heels into his flanks. The animal leapt forward, only to sprawl flatly as at least two musket balls ripped into its stomach. The women pitched forward, and then the Spanish soldiers were upon them. Beth saw Ena fighting, a snarl showing her fine white teeth, and then a fist connected with her own temple, and for a time she was dazed.

"I say we kill them now," a soldier was saying angrily. "This white bitch killed four men. And look at this arrow—I saw it driven all the way through the chest of my best friend."

"We must take them to Captain Barca," said another. "He will be able to obtain valuable information from them."

Beth opened her eyes. She was lying in the sand, her hands tied. Ena lay beside her, and she nodded her head when she saw Beth's eyes open.

"All right, we'll take them back to camp, but when the time comes to kill them, I will volunteer."

The women were thrown roughly onto horses, hands bound in front of them, legs bound with a rope running all the way under the horse's belly.

"Tell them nothing," Ena hissed to Beth as their

horses stood side by side. "They will try to use us against Renno."

"Silence!" bellowed the Spanish noncommissioned officer who had insisted on keeping them alive.

"May I have a little water?" Beth asked, for her head was aching fiercely and her lips and throat were dry.

"I hope you are as dry as the sand," said a soldier, his voice filled with hatred. "And I hope the good father burns you both for the witches you are."

Chapter XIV

It was early evening when Renno returned to the camp and found William angry and concerned. "I was seeing to the horses," he said, "and when I finished, Ena and Beth were gone."

When it became apparent that the women were not going to return, William wanted to ride out immediately and search for them. Renno, very much concerned himself, told him that nothing could be done at night. But with first light he and William were on the trail, having left Estrela behind with the slightly wounded warriors in the Apache camp. The question of Estrela's "ownership" had been settled by giving all captured weapons and horses to the Apache, so she was quite safe among the Apache wounded who guarded the camp. Rusog and El-i-chi had not returned to the main camp that night and were somewhere up ahead nearer the Spanish. Renno did not look forward to telling them that Ena and the Englishwoman were missing.

It was easy for Renno to see what had happened in the natural bowl, for there were two dead horses and four dead Spaniards with Beth's arrows in them. He saw two sets of moccasin tracks and tracks of the booted Spaniards.

"They are alive," he told William as he mounted and followed the trail toward the Spanish camp.

When Beth and Ena were brought before Lope Barca, he was puzzled to see a red-haired white woman in Indian dress. He told the men to give the women water, and then, as they stood, hands tied, he rubbed his beard and mused. A soldier showed him Beth's longbow.

"She killed four men with this," the soldier said. "And I saw an arrow like these"—he showed Barca Beth's almost empty quiver—"in the chest of my best friend."

"I don't suppose you'd like to explain why a white woman is here in the desert fighting with the Apache," Barca said.

Beth, thoroughly frightened but defiant, said nothing. During the ride to the Spanish camp she had been thinking how much her life had changed in so short a time. The flowers and the gentle life in England were but distant memories. It seemed that she had been living on horseback forever, and she suspected that her thought processes were similar to the Indians' now, for she hated this man who had led an invasion force and killed so many.

"I thought not," Barca said. "Would it be too much to ask for you to tell me how you know about the gold?"

"I don't think there's any harm in that," Beth answered. "My father, as a young man, captured a Spanish ship. A friar aboard the ship had a map among his possessions."

"A map drawn by one Friar Luis?" Barca asked.

Beth nodded.

"I didn't know the English bred women with your fire," Barca said frankly. He turned to Ena. "And you. You are not Apache either." He saw the defiance in Ena's green eyes and smiled. "Almost, I would believe the myth of the Amazons. A bit of water to clean you, a comb for your hair . . ." He shook his head. "It is astounding, and a tale to be told and retold, to find two such well-formed women here."

"You will not live to tell it," Ena predicted. From the moment of her capture she had considered herself dead, for she had seen the cruelty of the Spanish.

"Well," Barca said, "there is that possibility, but it will take more than the few who have been nibbling at us like wild dogs to do it."

"Hundreds are coming," Beth lied quickly. "The entire Apache nation has been summoned, and they are riding fast, with many warriors joining our forces each day. If you will talk to our leader, perhaps an end to this fighting can be arranged."

"I assume that you speak of the tall warrior who killed my friend Montenegro atop the mesa," Barca said. Beth nodded. "And how would I arrange a conversation with this man?"

"He will find you," Ena replied.

"In the meantime," Barca said, "I must ask you a few questions, ladies, and I pray that you will not be too stubborn. My men are nervous, and we, too, have a leader who is not noted for his patience." *Speak of the devil*, he thought as Friar Sebastián came riding up to see the captives.

Sebastián, too, was astounded to see two women, one fair and flame-haired, the other obviously not of full Indian blood. "Have you questioned them?" he demanded.

"This one says that the entire Apache nation is gathering against us," Barca replied, just to see Sebastián's face turn pale.

"Why is a white woman here?" Sebastián asked Beth.

"They had a copy of Friar Luis's map," Barca answered. "Her friends, led by the man who killed Monte-negro, have the gold."

"Torture them," Sebastián said, "and make them tell us where the gold is."

"Torture will not be required," Beth told him, with a confidence she did not feel. "The gold is on packhorses about five miles back along the trail."

"She's lying," Sebastián said.

Barca shook his head. "No, I don't think so, because there are quite a few Apache between us and a spot five miles back along the trail. I think it's there."

"Then go get it," Sebastián ordered.

"I'll tell you this, priest," Barca said, not hiding his contempt. "You are free to ask for volunteers and lead a force yourself to get the gold. I am going to concentrate my efforts on getting through some three or four hundred miles of Apache territory alive with the gold I have."

"I am going to have you hanged when we are back in civilization!" Sebastián screamed.

Barca's face caused the priest to back up a step. "That leaves me little incentive to keep you alive," Barca responded.

The priest swallowed and did some fast thinking. The man could kill him or have him killed at any time. "Forgive me, Captain," he said, hiding his pride and his rage. "I am distraught at the events that have overtaken us. I am a man of peace, and all this killing has confused me. You are right, and I leave all military strategy in your hands. Moreover, your service has earned you a greater reward. There will be enough gold for you to return to Spain a rich and powerful man. Let us see this thing through together."

Barca nodded grimly. That would do for now, but he still did not want the priest alive when they reached Corpus Christi, or even one of the Spanish missions en route. He felt he could bring a few of the men through alive, and the fewer men left, the fewer he had to pay off in gold.

"I will help you question these two witches," Sebastián offered. "I have had some experience in these matters."

"They have given us all the information we need from them," Barca said. "They are more valuable unharmed."

"What do you mean?" Sebastián asked.

"We know that we are fighting two Apache chiefs, Black Eagle and Gerachise. We know that a small force of outsiders, not more than, oh, a dozen, with muskets and a few English longbows, are fighting alongside the Apache. These outsiders, with some Englishmen among them, have come from the east, probably from the United States." He bowed to Beth. "I must express my admiration for your courage, all of you. It must have been a long and dangerous trek, and it isn't over, is it? Now you face the dangers of the return trip, with a heavy cargo of gold. "Am I not right?"

Without waiting for an answer, Barca said, "Our possession of two hostages will not stop the attacks by the Apache, for they have a blood debt to pay. On the other hand, I think that anyone riding near these two lovely ladies will be quite safe from ambush." He smiled at Sebastián. "I think, also, that these two ladies might just be worth much more than their weight in gold."

Sebastián's eyes gleamed at the thought, although he was a bit disappointed that he would not be able to use some of the things he had learned about pain on these two witches of Satan.

Renno knew that the Apache would not stop fighting to save Ena and Beth. Even as the Spanish column moved with the two women tied to their horses and surrounded by a guard of soldiers, the Apache continued their hit-and-run attacks. The loss to the Spanish was small, however, since they now rode in a tight column and were always alert, although men still died.

Renno had found Rusog and El-i-chi. El-i-chi advocated organizing all the Apache and making an all-out attack, but he was soon calmed under the influence of

Renno's cool reason. They rode ahead of the column and found a place of observation, lay there while the Spanish marched past, and saw that Beth and Ena were unharmed. Renno noted that the Spanish officer rode between the two women, making himself quite safe from attack.

At another point, Renno rode ahead and posted himself atop a hill, his horse hidden just below the crest, and stood with his arms crossed as the Spanish column approached. Men saw him and pointed, and one or two fired a musket at long range. As Barca and the two captives drew abreast of the hill, Beth saw Renno and felt hopeful. Barca wheeled his horse out of the formation and yelled, "Will you talk?"

Renno, just barely able to hear, pretended that he did not. However, the Spaniard's actions told him what he wanted to know. Beth and Ena were safe for the moment, because the Spaniard felt that they gave him bargaining power. He turned and left the hill.

That night, when the scattered Apache forces gathered, Renno called a council. "How far is it to the open plains?" he asked Gerachise.

"Five or six days' march," Gerachise replied.

"We must kill as many of them as we can while we are in the badlands," Renno said, "for when they reach the plains, attack will be more difficult. The time has come for more open challenges, for strong attacks by fast-hitting bands of warriors. Some will die, but if we choose our ground with care, and attack and fall back with swiftness, we will kill four or five to each one we lose."

"We are ready," Black Eagle said gravely.

The Apache, with Renno's men, struck the rear of the column at sunrise, just as it was moving out. They rode down from the hills in two forces, one on either side of the column, and the tired, sleepy Spanish soldiers responded slowly, with men dying before one return shot could be fired. The attack ended as suddenly as it had begun, leaving a dozen Spaniards lying in the sun and, miraculously, with only one Apache wounded in the arm. And just as the weary Spanish thought that would be the last of it for a while, the same force struck again, in the same place, at the rear, and this time the stragglers panicked and bolted forward to create so much confusion in the ranks ahead of them that the Spanish fire was sporadic and disorganized, and at least one Spaniard was killed by his own comrades in a hail of misdirected fire.

Barca reorganized the column, putting dependable men at the rear. But in an open area where he thought he was safe from attack, the Apache and Renno's force burst out of the rocks, sweeping backward along the length of the column so that the Spaniards either had to turn in their saddles or wheel their horses around to fire. The effect was deadly. At close range the Apache arrows took a toll that made Barca doubt for the first time that any would survive.

That same day, lone warriors harried the column, popping up in the most unexpected places, having found cover where even a coyote would have had difficulty. Barca decided to try once more to parley. He no longer was interested in trying to trade the women for the gold in the possession of his enemies. His sole objective now was survival. He put a white flag on a lance and rode away from the column, not at all sure that he would not meet a musket ball or an arrow but knowing that something had to be done. He rode to the top of a rocky hill and looked out over the wasteland. He saw nothing—no movement, not a single man. And then his horse shied, almost causing him to fall, and a rider was there, not fifty feet away. Barca saw a handsomely built man in buckskins, a man with pale hair and piercing blue eyes.

"It is you," Barca said.

"For the moment, I honor your flag of truce," Renno told him.

"Do you not value the two women we hold?" Barca asked. "My leader, the priest, and my men want me to kill them if there is another attack."

Renno felt cold, but he showed no emotions. He

could not stop the blood war of the Apache. He knew that an attempt to rescue Beth and Ena would most probably result in their deaths. He had only his courage and his faith in the manitous to sustain him. "From what I have seen, we value life more than you," he said. "But we value other things more. Our lands. Avenging our dead. It is true that I and others would mourn the death of the two women you hold."

"You have gold," Barca said. "We have gold. Let us both live to enjoy it."

Renno sat silently, waiting for the Spaniard to continue.

"You can kill more of my men," Barca said. "You have demonstrated your bravery and your ability, but we will be in the plains soon, and we will kill more of your men each time you attack. Let us call a halt to the killing now."

Barca could see his answer in the cold stare of the startlingly blue eyes of this strange man.

"Even if you sent the women to me now, I could not stop it," Renno said. "However, they represent your only safety. While they live and you ride by their side, you will live."

"The gold?" Barca asked. "Is it the gold that you want?"

"We have enough gold," Renno answered.

"So it goes on," Barca said. "But know this, and tell your Apache friends: even if we all die, more soldiers will come, in numbers like the grains of sand in the desert, for we do not die lightly, and our Spanish brothers will avenge us."

"That is your nature," Renno said, "just as it is the nature of the Apache to avenge their own dead. Guard the women well, Spaniard, and I will do my best to see that you live." And with that he wheeled his horse and rode swiftly, to disappear among the rocks.

Barca lost one of the gold wagons late that day. An attacking force of Apache cut the wagon away from the column as thoroughly demoralized soldiers deserted it. It was set afire, the gold fell into the sands of the desert, and even as night fell, a wind began to move the sand to cover it.

Barca sent out no more patrols. That, he found, was the surest way to lose men. He had to pull his advance scouts back to within sight of the head of the column, and even then he lost them, until it was difficult, even with stern orders, to get a man to lead the way. The men were exhausted, dirty, and thirsty, and they rode listlessly, as if they were resigned to their deaths. When a pack mule fell to an arrow, they refused to salvage the gold carried by the animal.

And thus it went, and slowly a trail of gold was left behind the column in the sands of the burning desert. The trail was marked by dead animals and dead men, men left to bloat and swell and be devoured by the desert scavengers. Only thirty-five Spaniards and two wagons of gold saw the beginnings of the plains.

Now it was more difficult to broach the still-deadly fire of thirty-five muskets, for there had been attrition in the forces of the Apache too. But each stealthy night raid took one or two Spaniards.

Now, after finding good water and grass for the animals, Barca was able to move his dwindling force faster. He was beginning to hope again, for the first of the Spanish missions was now within his reach.

Gerachise, who knew the country, called council. "In four days' time," he said, "the Spaniards will be safe, for there is a large garrison at the mission. It is time to finish them."

"That is the wish of the Apache?" Renno asked.

"We have vowed to kill all who brought death to our lands," Gerachise said. He shrugged. "Perhaps your women will die too. For that we are sorry, my friend, but we have vowed."

"I understand," Renno said. "I ask only this. The Spanish officer will stay close to our women, for he feels that guarantees his safety. If he flees, let him go. My brother El-i-chi and I will follow him when the battle is over, and we will follow him far enough to complete the vow of the Apache."

"It will be so," Gerachise said, and made that order clear to the Apache warriors.

The attack was made at the moment when the Spanish were more tired, in the evening, as they made camp. As Renno had known it would be, the attack was costly, for thirty-five muskets took a deadly toll of almost an equal number of Apache. Renno had told William and Rusog to hold back, to fire at the Spanish from cover. William was more than willing, and Rusog obeyed reluctantly.

El-i-chi was, of course, in the thick of the fight, charging in with Gerachise and his warriors, and Renno fought with Black Eagle.

The first assault was beaten off, with many dead on both sides, and then, without giving the Spanish time to rest, the final charge was made, and amid the smoke of muskets and the howls of war and pain and death, Renno saw a small group of horses break away and run for the south. He fell back from the battle and ran hard and caught a glimpse in the fading light of a group of four riders leading four gold-laden pack animals. The fading light of the dying sun gleamed on the flame-colored hair of Beth. It had happened as he had hoped: Barca and the priest were making a run for it, but in their never-dying greed, they were slowing themselves by taking some of the gold.

The last battle ended shortly before dark, with the Apache taking scalps and finishing off the Spanish wounded. El-i-chi, blooded but not by his own blood, panting and carrying many fresh scalps, found Renno with Gerachise.

"Is the fire cooled now?" Renno asked El-i-chi.

"It will cool when we have Ena and Beth with us," El-i-chi said.

"That will be for us to do—you and I," Renno said. "It is over now, except for that, and we must make plans to assure that our mission here has not been for nothing. Bring William and Rusog to me, and the Spanish woman."

The Apache were dancing and chanting a victory song that turned to a chant of mourning as Rusog, his left arm hanging at his side, a deep crease from a Spanish musket ball on the fleshy inside part of it, came and sat wearily. William and Estrela de Mendoza were not far behind.

"The Spanish commander and the priest are an hour ahead of us, heading toward the mission to the southeast," Renno said. "El-i-chi and I will go after them. We are far to the south of our planned line of travel, William. Can you use your compass and your maps to find your way back to the lands of the Comanche?"

"I can," William said, "but I want to go with you. My sister—"

"For you the gold means personal wealth," Renno said. "I did not come so far for my own gain. For the sake of my people I ask you to do as I say."

William nodded glumly.

"Rusog, you and Estrela will go with him. It will be a difficult task for two to handle so many pack animals. When you meet the Comanche, they will remember you. Tell them that I and the flame-haired one will be following you. Rest and wait for us at the hot springs in the mountains of the Arkansea. It may be that you will have to winter there. If so, you will wait until the new beginning, and if we have not come, you will go without us. Then, Rusog, it will be up to you to see that our share of the gold is used wisely by our people."

"I would go with you," Rusog said, "but I hear you, and I understand."

Estrela had been silent. She knew that they had been traveling southeast for days, and that they could not be too far from the nearest Spanish mission. "Renno," she said, "you must take me with you. From the mission I can contact my father, and he will come for me."

Renno had considered that, and he had sympathy for Estrela, but he was riding into the unknown, into the heart of Spanish strength. "No," he said, and when Estrela's face fell, he explained, "we will be Indians in the midst of the enemy. Spanish soldiers will fire on sight. You would be in danger, and your presence would slow us and thus endanger our chances of saving Ena and Beth. No, you will have to go with William and Rusog. It will be a long trip, taking months, but once you are in our country, we will arrange transportation for you to the coast of North Carolina, where you can take a ship for one of the Spanish islands and then a ship to Mexico."

William, who had been thinking that the logical thing to do would be to find a way to get Estrela to the mission, felt a considerable and somewhat surprising lightening of his heart. There had been no opportunity for him to spend time with the beautiful Spanish woman, but now he would have months in which to consolidate his confused thoughts about her. He was, in short, very pleased to know that he would not be separated from her.

During the long and exhausting retreat from the place of their capture, Ena and Beth at first had little opportunity to talk. As the Spanish soldiers became more and more harried, more tired, and more hopeless, however, no man had the energy to stop the women when they drew together and talked in English. At their first opportunity to talk, Ena seemed ill-at-ease until she extended her hand, put it on Beth's arm, and said, "I have wronged you."

"No, please," Beth responded. "I understand why you felt as you did."

"It is polite to accept an apology," Ena said, her face twisting with the effort to use a word that was so against her nature. She had done little apologizing in her life.

"Then I accept, and gladly," Beth said. "And it is forgotten."

Ena smiled.

"Is it because you feel we will be killed?" Beth asked, her voice breaking.

"They will come for us," Ena shot back fiercely.

Ena's courage gave Beth new hope. To ease her mind

away from thoughts of their danger, she encouraged Ena to tell her the history of Ena's family, from the time of Ena's great-grandfather, the original white Indian. And then, to help pass the long, weary hours, Beth talked of England, her father, and the things that would be accomplished with William's and her share of the gold once they had their riches back in England.

There was another matter about which Beth had curiosity, and she approached it with a blush that did not show through her sun-browned skin. She asked about Renno's wife and listened as Ena told of Emily's life, her bravery, how she had twice survived being captured by a deadly enemy. And Ena spoke of Little Hawk and how his destiny was to follow his father as sachem of the southern Seneca.

Ena had known all along that Beth's interest in Renno was more than casual, and the way the girl drank up any talk about her brother merely added to Ena's conviction that Beth felt a great attraction to Renno. Ena had hated her for it, but now that no longer seemed to matter. She knew Beth better now and knew that as a woman of honor, she would never take advantage of Renno's being a man long separated from his wife. In fact, she was pleased to know that such a beautiful and sophisticated English lady could find her brother attractive. She admired Beth's bravery in captivity and knew that Renno would never give up on them, that sooner or later he would make his move, and she knew that he would not do anything rash to endanger their lives. So she had no hope of rescue as long as the Spanish force remained intact.

When the Apache attacked in force, she knew that it was the final assault and that either the Spanish or the Indians would be killed to the last man. She pulled Beth down beside her when the firing began and tried to loosen Beth's bonds. It was painful, for the long captivity had left bleeding raw marks on the wrists of both of them, and she was just beginning to make some progress when Lope

Barca came, forced them to mount, and led their horses at a wild run out of the area of fighting.

They rode all night, and all four paid a price for that as stiff brush tore at their legs. "Renno will come now," Ena whispered to Beth. "Soon."

Renno and El-i-chi picked up the trail at first light. Behind them, Rusog, William, and Estrela were getting under way with the packtrain, heading northeast with the breadth of over half the continent between them and the lush hunting grounds of home. The Apache were caring for their dead and preparing to return to their own camps to the north.

Barca and Sebastián were traveling fast. Their trail was easy to follow at first because they were discarding all surplus weight. They were not discarding the remaining gold. Several months' travel to Corpus Christi lay before them, and Renno kept praying to the manitous that he would not see, in some desolate, arid spot, the bodies of two women.

Barca had a head start of several hours, and he pushed the horses unmercifully, always keeping a careful watch over his shoulder.

The fates intervened to allow Barca to keep his advantage. As Renno and El-i-chi traveled as swiftly as they could, sometimes at a gallop in areas where the tracks were easy to follow, Renno's horse stepped into a prairie-dog hole and fell heavily. Renno catapulted forward over the horse's head, landed rolling on his shoulders, and came to his feet shaken but unhurt. The animal had to be dispatched, silently, with an arrow from a longbow, and now it was necessary for Renno and El-i-chi to take turns riding or running. Renno took the first turn at running, and he set a pace that was just short of a sprint, so that in an hour he traded with El-i-chi. A full day's travel had carried them so far south toward the Rio Grande that the countryside was changing. They tracked by moonlight until they lost the trail, then slept. In the early light they were under way, and at noon they found the spot where

Barca had made camp. Renno estimated that they were about half a day behind now and could close that distance by the end of the following day.

The next day, however, Barca heard the lowing of cattle ahead, and upon topping a ridge, saw below a herd of cattle tended by Mexican vaqueros. He stopped his horse and waited for Father Sebastián to come alongside. He had his hand on his pistol.

"My saintly friend," he said, "we have reached a moment of decision."

"I have been expecting this," Sebastián replied, nodding.

"I will be brief and to the point," Barca said. "When there was much gold, I was willing to share with the Church. There is little gold now, probably just enough for two men to establish themselves comfortably on one of the islands of the Caribbean. There is certainly enough for one man to do so."

Sebastián had also been doing a lot of thinking. His plans for power and glory had dwindled with the attrition of the Spanish force and had suffered major blows each time a wagon or a pack mule had been left behind. The amount of gold on the surviving packhorses would not give him the leverage he would need to accomplish his ambitions back in Spain, but on one of the islands it would be a different story. There, half of the remaining gold would make him a powerful man.

"I think, Captain, that I could serve God's purpose well on a comfortable tropical island," Sebastián said. "And indeed the Church will not miss the relatively small amount of gold for which we have risked our lives."

"I had intended to kill you," Barca confessed.

"I know."

"Together—with your authority and my right arm—we can control the ship's company," Barca said, "and have ourselves and the gold put ashore on our chosen island. But should you try to cross me when we reach the mission or the ship, I will be at your side with my pistol ready, and even though I might die, you will be dead before me."

"Have no fear," Sebastián promised. "I have made my decision. I need you, as you need me." He made a sudden motion, and from the folds of his torn and dirty robes he showed a cocked pistol. "I was ready to kill you, my friend, had we been unable to work out an accommodation."

Barca lifted his head and roared with laughter. "We are two of a kind after all," he said. "Give me your hand on our partnership." Sebastián, putting the pistol away, extended his hand.

The vaqueros rode up and grouped around the two men so marked by their hardships. "My sons," Sebastián intoned, "we have been into the lands of the Apache to spread God's word, and the savages have killed all our force save us two. Even now we are probably being followed by savages intent on rescuing these two heathen witches we have captured."

The simple cowboys, awed by the priest's authority, had many questions about the flame-haired white woman but did not voice them.

"If you will protect our rear, my sons," Sebastián continued, "and allow us to reach safety at the mission, God will reward you."

Four of the vaqueros left their duties and instructed the others to move the herd toward pasture. They hid themselves and waited. In about three hours they saw one mounted man and one runner coming down the trail left by Barca and the priest and readied their muskets. They had chosen a rise covered with rocks and brush for their concealment. The tracks left by Barca passed through a sandy gap, with good hiding places on either side. The vaqueros did not pay any attention to a strong young hawk that soared in circles over them and, as the two Indians drew near, gave out three harsh cries.

Renno, running beside the mounted El-i-chi, said, "Our brother the hawk warns us."

"I see nothing," El-i-chi replied.

"There is good concealment atop that rise," Renno noted. "I will break to my left and circle in from that side."

Renno turned, ran as fast as he could run, and leapt down into an erosion gully, disappearing from the sight of the vaqueros. El-i-chi rode to the right, so he too was soon lost from sight.

The vaqueros could not imagine what had warned the savages, and this fact made them nervous. They were workingmen, not Indian fighters.

"Perhaps they are just being cautious," one vaquero guessed. "We will wait here. If they are merely circling around this place, we can catch them in the open when they start down the slope."

The vaqueros had a long wait. One decided to take a look around and left the other three in their concealment. The vaquero on the right side of the trail died alone and in silence as El-i-chi's knife sliced his throat. Renno, meanwhile, had positioned himself, and when he heard El-i-chi's quail call, he leapt from a rock and killed one man swiftly with his tomahawk, managed to knock aside the other's musket before it could be fired, and then sent his flashing tomahawk upward under the man's chin.

El-i-chi came forth on Renno's signal, saw the two dead men, and nodded grimly.

"The Spanish are far to the north," Renno said, "much farther than we expected. We will have to move with great caution now."

El-i-chi was cleaning his knife. He would not scalp these dead ones. He looked at the sun. "We must move."

And even as he lifted his head, the fourth vaquero, making his way back to join his friends, lifted his musket and took solid aim at El-i-chi's back. He was in a position not more than thirty feet away, with a sure shot.

Renno heard the harsh cry of the hawk and looked up to see Little Hawk, wings folded, diving at a point behind a large boulder. He saw the glint of metal there and started to shout a warning to El-i-chi just as the hawk landed, burying his talons in the neck of the vaquero. The man screamed with surprise and pain. His musket discharged, the ball going well over El-i-chi's head.

Once a hawk sinks its talons, the grip cannot be released easily. The vaquero began to beat at the thing that was hurting him so horribly, and the hawk's fierce beak tore meat from the man's hand. Before the hand closed around the hawk's neck, the beak jerked, tearing flesh from the man's shoulder. But the hawk was now loose, and the man wrung its neck like a chicken, yelling in pain, but his yells ceased abruptly as Renno threw his stiletto. The blade penetrated to the vaquero's heart.

The hawk was dead, its eyes filmed, feathers torn and ruffled. Renno stood over it sadly for a moment, then picked it up. "Thank you, Brother," he whispered. He smoothed the feathers and whispered a chant of mourning. "We will give our brother an honorable burial," he told El-i-chi, "for he has served us well."

He took only a few minutes for the ceremony, but he put his heart into it. He buried the hawk, then covered the spot with rocks so that scavengers would be unable to dig it up. He knelt, raised his arms, and gave one last blessing to the dead hawk, one of the powerful totems of his clan, and there in the glaring sun he had his first daytime vision. It was as if the face of Ghonka, foster father of the original Renno, great sachem of the Iroquois nations, appeared and filled a good portion of the blue sky.

Although El-i-chi saw nothing and heard nothing, he felt the presence of the spirits. An unnatural hush fell over the desert, and not even the wind stirred. He saw a look of awe and wonder come onto his brother's face, and he himself fell to his knees.

The vision of Ghonka spoke. The words were few: "The great canoe that travels on wings over the great waters is of wood and will burn."

Then a breeze sprang up, and the sun was harsh and

bright again, and Renno shook his head to clear it. He rose, looked into the kneeling El-i-chi's eyes. "We will travel far before we are united with Ena and Beth," he said. "We will be among the Spanish in their settlements. Strip the clothing from the Spaniard nearest your size, and we will become vaqueros."

"That was your message from the spirits?"

"You heard?"

"I felt, but saw nothing," El-i-chi said.

"Our way leads us to the great waters and the Spanish ship," Renno said.

The clothing of the vaqueros was dirty, and it stank. But the brothers had horses again, one for Renno to ride and three extra. They hid their bows in sleeping rolls, concealed their tomahawks under loose shirts and pistols in their belts, and rode south, once again following Barca's trail. When they began to encounter scattered Spanish ranches, they tried to avoid all contact, but once Renno passed the time of day in good Spanish with two vaqueros and thanked the manitous for Beth's excellent teaching.

They did not risk going into the town that was growing up around the Spanish mission, but they were able to get food and water from an isolated ranch house in exchange for the coins they had taken from the dead vaqueros. From their camp outside the town, they saw Barca and Sebastián—with a new escort of a dozen brightly uniformed soldiers—head east with Ena and Beth among them.

Chapter XV

While Rusog, William, and Estrela de Mendoza moved steadily northeastward into the buffalo plains hunted by the Comanche, Renno and El-i-chi were following the slow but steady progress of Lope Barca's new troop of soldiers through areas of scattered Spanish settlements. They had become accustomed to the rather uncomfortable clothing of the Spanish vaqueros and had washed them several times in the Rio Grande.

They had no difficulty in passing for Spanish cowboys, because both had just enough Indian blood to darken their skins to a soft, sun-bronzed tone, and not even the color of Renno's eyes was a hindrance, for over the centuries the Spanish had intermarried with many races, and there were blue-eyed Spaniards.

The month of September was well under way. Far to the north, Rusog's group saw the season begin to change, vegetation begin to brown, the leaves of the trees become dry. In the south, the heat of the sun was undiminished.

In Knoxville, Emily was almost totally bedridden. Now she was very big with child, and the dark shadows under her eyes told of the price she had paid. Now and again she would insist on getting up to walk slowly and with great effort to the porch to sit in a rocking chair and stare off to the west, in the direction from which Renno would come.

"He has accomplished his mission, Mother," she told Nora one evening as she enjoyed the softness of late September.

"I'm sure he has," Nora said to humor her.

"I can feel it. Somehow I just know."

"Then he's on his way back to you with the gold," Nora said, still humoring her daughter. "And when you're rich, perhaps you can have a real house and you won't have to sleep on skins and cook over an open fire."

"Oh, Mother," Emily groaned. "You've never understood, have you? Those things don't really matter."

"They matter to me," Nora retorted.

"I have never been warmer than in my bed of skins with the winter winds blowing," Emily said dreamily, remembering those winter nights with Renno at her side.

"I think you should move into town," Nora urged, warming to a subject that she had wanted to open for a long time. "Little Hawk should go to a good school. And this little girl—" Nora, like Emily, had concluded from the way the baby sat in Emily's womb that it was a girl. "Do you want her to grow up like Renno's sister?"

"I would be the proudest mother alive if she did," Emily responded defiantly.

Nora snorted. "How would you feel if your child, your girl-child, rode with Indian warriors and killed?"

"I pray that someday killing will no longer be necessary," Emily said. She was going to say more, but a sudden pain hit her like a giant fist squeezing her swollen stomach. She doubled over with a gasp, and Nora leapt to her feet.

"What is it?" Nora asked.

"I believe," Emily said, smiling through the pain, "that it is notice from my little girl that she is ready to meet her grandmother."

When Barca's party left the river and started directly east toward Corpus Christi, Renno began to anticipate the end. He and El-i-chi had been living well and eating well, for game was plentiful and there was never a shortage of water as they traveled along the river. It was easy to track Barca, for most of the time they could see the dust of the troop's passage ahead of them. They discussed, but only briefly, trying to rescue Ena and Beth, for by now Barca, they felt, must feel quite safe and would not be as alert as he had been. The risk was too great, however, and there was Renno's message from Ghonka. The time to save Ena and Beth was when they were taken aboard the ship.

But Renno was not at peace. For days now something he could not define had been darkening his spirits. There seemed to be a threat hanging over him, an almost terrible sadness, which seemed to taint the clear, hot air. At night he would often walk away from the camp to meditate and call upon the manitous for guidance, but there was no message until, one night, as he gazed at the stars and prayed to the manitous, his heart leapt and he knew a terrible loss. He knew it had to do with Emily. He needed to voice his sorrow, but he was in the heart of enemy lands, and all he could do was tilt his head back and open his mouth and give voice to the lonely howl of a coyote. From a half-dozen places around him the coyotes answered, and the night was filled with loneliness.

Lope Barca had been marching for long months now, and until they reached the first of the Spanish missions he had not taken a woman. He had remedied that with a *puta* of the town at his first opportunity. Now the missions were behind him, and each night he looked upon two of the most attractive women he had ever seen. He did not need the women as hostages any longer, for none of those he had fought—not even the blue-eyed white Indian— would dare to penetrate so deeply into Spanish lands. He had left his enemies far behind. It was time to get some return out of those two whom he had guarded for so many weary miles.

Although they were tied firmly together by their conspiracy, Barca and Sebastián had not developed a fondness for each other, and the priest always pitched his small tent on the opposite side of the camp from Barca's.

The more he thought about it, the more Barca knew that he had to have both of the "witches," as they were called by the priest and the soldiers. So it was that he was full of anticipation on the night he decided it was time. He walked to the tent where Ena and Beth lay, pushed aside the flap, and looked in. Ena jerked a blanket over her partial nakedness and glared at him. Beth was covered.

Barca's biggest decision was which to take to his bed first. He ached for the white skin of the Englishwoman, but he imagined a fiery response in the other. He had decided on Ena. "You," he said to her. "Get dressed and meet me in my tent." Then he was gone.

What the man did not know was that Ena and Beth, having anticipated such a problem, had already discussed their plan when Barca called for them. Ena had found a knife, dropped by one of the soldiers, and she had it concealed in her clothing, strapped high on her thigh under her tattered skirt. She had said to Beth, "When he comes for one of us, I will flirt with him, so that he will choose me first, and I will kill him in his bed."

"Then you will be killed," Beth said.

"Would you prefer to live and let him have you?" Ena asked, repulsed.

Beth had to think about that a bit. She had observed

her twentieth birthday—actually it had passed without her notice—somewhere in the deserts of New Mexico, and she had not yet even known the warm kisses of a man. Would being used by the Spaniard be worse than death? She wanted to live, surely. She hoped, with Ena, that somewhere in the darkness beyond the campfires Renno was waiting for his opportunity to come for them. That was their only hope, it seemed, for the priest seemed to take great pleasure in telling them that he was going to see to it that they were burned as witches.

"There may be another way," Beth said. "We must try to stay alive until Renno comes."

"What do you have in mind?" Ena asked.

Ena had never heard of the thing that Beth then described, and she had little faith that Beth's plan would work. After Barca had come for her, Ena put on her skirt and put the knife securely in place.

"What he finds under my skirt will not give him pleasure," she said grimly.

"No," Beth protested, pushing Ena back onto her blankets. "My idea will work, Ena. I know it will."

Ena knew that if she killed Barca, they were both dead. If the Englishwoman wanted to try her crazy scheme, then let her. As soon as Barca put Ena into his bed, they would both die, so what did it matter if the Spaniard had taken the Englishwoman? So she lay back and waited as Beth walked slowly to Barca's tent.

When Beth lifted the flap to Barca's tent, she had to bite her lip to keep from gasping, for he was ready, in all ways, as he sprawled naked on his blankets.

"You?" he asked with a slow smile. "I told the dark one to come."

"Please, señor," Beth said, "I have something to tell you."

"I will listen with interest," Barca said. "Come and lie beside me and we will talk . . . for a minute."

Beth sat on the blankets and looked into Barca's dark

eyes with as serious an expression as she could manage.
"Señor, I have lived among the Indians, as you know."

Barca raised an eyebrow. "Are you telling me that
you sampled the manhood of the savages?"

"Yes," Beth said, hanging her head.

Barca laughed. "No matter. The taking of a virgin is
vastly overrated." He reached for her and jerked her
down atop him, his mouth searching for hers.

"Wait, please," Beth gasped, beginning to be very
frightened. "Listen to me. The Apache—"

"I don't want to hear about the Apache," he said, his
hand roughly seizing one of her breasts.

"The Apache had a captive Spanish girl," Beth gasped,
fighting against his attempt to find her lips.

Barca was still for a moment, his hand still clutching
her breast. "Yes, some of my men reported that they had
seen a Spanish woman riding with the savages."

"She brought the Spanish disease into the Apache
camp," Beth lied quickly. "You have been kind to us,
señor, keeping us alive against the wishes of the priest—"

Barca did not give her time to finish. He flung her
away from him, and as she landed heavily, her skirt pulled
high to reveal her white thighs, Barca saw only obscenity,
for he had seen victims of the Spanish disease—men who
screamed with pain, men who were blind and paralyzed,
men who were drooling, hopeless idiots after the disease
had eaten their brains.

"I should kill you now!" he yelled at her, seizing his
sword.

Beth backed out of the tent on her hands and knees,
then leapt to her feet to run to her tent. Barca pulled on
his trousers and followed her, stuck his head into the tent,
where Beth was huddled in Ena's arms, both of them
looking up with wide eyes. Ena, however, had her knife in
her hand and was prepared to sell her life dearly.

"*Putas*," Barca spat. "When the priest burns you as
witches, I will light the fire myself."

Then he was gone and Beth's tears turned into a

hysterical giggle that she had to hold back with a hand tight over her mouth. "You should have seen his face," she gasped. "Renno with all his weapons could not have frightened him more."

"This Spanish disease must be a terrible thing," Ena said.

"Some have said that it is God's punishment to the Spanish for the things they did to the Indians of South America," Beth said.

The town of Corpus Christi was composed of a few government buildings, the docks, and a few adobe huts. Renno and El-i-chi scouted all around, laid out their route of retreat once they had Ena and Beth with them, and watched from concealment as Barca's group arrived. Both were relieved to see that Ena and Beth were still alive— thin and tired looking, but apparently unharmed. Renno left El-i-chi with the horses and walked into the town to see Barca and Sebastián board a ship at the docks. Soldiers pushed Ena and Beth aboard.

Renno noted that the women were pushed down a hatchway toward the rear of the ship. He lounged around the dock area, imitating the behavior of the few Mexican laborers, who seemed to be taking a prolonged rest. In a little while the troop of soldiers on the ship formed and marched smartly toward one of the government buildings, where they were greeted by a uniformed Spanish officer and then sent into the building, obviously the garrison barracks. In two hours of watching, Renno saw several alert-looking, well-disciplined soldiers come and go from the barracks. The rescue mission would have to be done in surprise and silence, Renno knew, for there were too many of the Spanish soldiers to fight.

When he was satisfied that he had all the details of both the town and the ship's deck firmly in his memory, he sauntered out of the town and rejoined El-i-chi.

"We will go to the ship tonight, while they sleep

soundly after their long journey," he said. "We will leave our muskets with the horses."

El-i-chi, in grim silence, tested the edge of his tomahawk with his thumb and nodded in satisfaction.

After dark they moved the horses to the north, where Renno had located a good hiding place amid shoreside growth. Then they began to make their way down the shore of the bay. It was growing late, and few lights burned in the buildings of the town. A dog barked idly. Soon they were near the docks, and Barca's ship—the only one in the bay at the time—was before them.

They approached the ship in the water, first wading, then swimming silently. The side of the ship facing the bay was deserted, but the glow of lanterns came from one or two of the ornate windows in the towering superstructures of the vessel. Renno had guessed that if there were a guard on duty, he would be near the gangplank from the ship to the dock. He motioned El-i-chi to climb the stern of the ship and waited until his brother had gained the top of the superstructure before swimming carefully around, between the ship and the dock. He waited there, heard a cough, and saw the guard leaning on the rail near the gangplank. He looked for a way to scale the side of the ship but saw none. He had anticipated that, however, and the signal to El-i-chi was the croak of a frog. At the sound the guard lifted his head but soon relaxed again. Renno saw a shadow move; then, with a swiftness that was deadly, the guard was seized and seconds later El-i-chi was easing the corpse down to the deck.

Quickly El-i-chi lowered a rope for Renno, who climbed up without a sound. That afternoon Renno had seen several barrels of pitch lashed to the deck of the ship. He had plans for them, but his first priority was to find Ena and Beth. He motioned to El-i-chi to stand guard, and made his way along the deck toward the lighted cabins. He slid back into the shadows as a hatch opened and Lope Barca came on deck, breathed deeply a couple of times, walked swiftly to one of the lighted cabins, knocked, and entered.

Renno moved to see into the glass, and Barca was seated by that time, reaching for a glass of wine offered by Father Sebastián. He could hear their voices clearly through the open window:

"We sail with the morning tide," Barca was saying, "and that's not a moment too soon for me."

Sebastián nodded.

"What are you writing?" Barca asked, indicating the papers and plume pen in front of the friar.

"I am informing my patron in the Spanish court that my health has been so ruined by the rigors of the unsuccessful search for Friar Luis's gold that I must take an extended rest on a tropical island," Sebastián answered.

Barca laughed.

The priest's face hardened. "I am also telling him, and the king, that I recommended a punitive expedition against the Apache. I am telling them that there were signs of gold to be mined and that the Apache would make good slaves to dig it."

"They wouldn't, you know," Barca said. "They would not live a month in captivity. They have a way of willing themselves to die."

"That is my intent," Sebastián said. "Those savages mocked God and me. They attacked a man of the cloth, an agent of the true God. For this they must be punished. The lure of gold will assure that the king will send an army there, and the savage will learn the true wrath of God."

"Just so I am not with the army," Barca laughed, taking a drink.

Renno vowed to himself that the friar's letter would not be sent to Spain and, more, that this evil man who spoke of God but did the devil's work would not see the morning's light. First, however, he had to find Ena and Beth.

He went to the hatchway down which he had seen them pushed, and found it to be secured with a belaying pin through a hasp. He opened the hatch, saw only darkness, and entered, knife and tomahawk ready. He caught rank odors and guessed that he was in a cargo hold. It was total darkness, and as he reached the bottom of the steps, moving silently, he felt something hot and frantic scurry across his foot. There was a sound of movement from the darkness, and he heard Beth's voice.

"It's back," she said softly, her voice quavering with so much fear that Renno's heart moved for her. "It's crawling on me."

Renno gave the coo of a dove very, very softly and heard soft thuds, as if a body were writhing and tossing on something hard.

Ena could not believe her ears. For a moment she could not think, knowing only vast relief and joy. "Renno," she whispered, and the thumping, writhing sound ceased.

Renno moved forward, feeling his way around barrels and bales. "Here," Ena whispered, and he could hear them breathing.

"Be very quiet," he whispered back, feeling for Ena's feet and finding them. He began to cut the ropes that bound her.

"Is it really you, Renno?" Beth asked. He put out his hand and it touched her thigh, and he squeezed softly. "Oh, thank God," she said. "The rats. The rats."

He had Ena free quickly, and she stood, rubbing her arms and legs, and then he was feeling the warm softness of Beth as he cut her bonds and lifted her to her feet. He led the way, with Beth holding on to his waist and Ena behind her, up the stairs and, after checking carefully, into the night air and starlight. El-i-chi was near the gangplank.

"Follow the shoreline toward the land end of the bay," Renno whispered to Ena. "You will come to a curve in the shore and a small indentation into the shoreline. The horses are there, hidden in the brush. We will be with you in a short time."

Together he and El-i-chi lowered Ena and Beth into the water and waited until they were well clear of the ship. Then the men began to work the bungs loose on the pitch barrels so that the sticky, highly flammable pitch began to flow slowly out onto the deck.

It seemed to take an age before the deck was well covered with the pitch. Then Renno motioned, and El-i-chi followed. The crew of the ship were, Renno thought, asleep. He prepared a torch, using a belaying pin and rags from the galley, went back to soak the cloth in pitch, and then left the torch lying beside the friar's door.

"We will take two lives," he told his brother. "The fire will do the rest."

Lope Barca did not even see his death as it came. He had been drinking steadily, dreaming of a palatial home on one of the Spanish islands, of beautiful women and good wine. Friar Sebastián saw the door open suddenly and caught a glimpse of a Spanish vaquero who, to his horror, turned into the blue-eyed demon of the desert, and then his death came so swiftly that he saw only Renno's leap and the flashing tomahawk, and heard El-i-chi's tomahawk split Barca's skull like a melon just before steel smashed into his bald forehead and he was given his chance to face his God.

Renno emptied his victims' pockets of money and gathered up the letter to Spain that the priest had been writing. Then he retrieved the torch from outside the door and thrust it into the priest's lantern. Out on the foredeck, he laid down the papers requesting a Spanish army to go against the Apache and set the blazing torch to the papers and the pitch.

The flames spread slowly, and the fire became a blazing hell of heat, lighting the night. The heat made the pitch more liquid, and it seeped down in blazing rivulets to the depths of the ship.

As Renno followed El-i-chi over the side to lower himself into the water, there was a giant explosion from below and fiery pieces of wreckage flew through the air. Renno and El-i-chi dived, swam underwater, and surfaced to see the ship a blazing wreck. Within it a man was screaming.

Men began to run down toward the dock from the town, so the two Seneca stayed well out in the bay until they had moved a distance away, and then they swam to shore and ran for the cove ahead. There Ena and Beth had the horses ready. There was no time for talk. Renno and El-i-chi leapt onto horses, and they headed west, toward the land end of the bay and the mouth of the Nueces River. By daybreak they had found a shallow ford of the river, and now they could cross and turn north. They rode steadily all day and made a dry camp. Then and only then was there time to compare notes, to talk about the events since Beth and Ena had been captured by Barca's men. Renno was relieved and amused when Beth told how Barca's plans to bed both of them were foiled. Ena nodded with grim satisfaction when El-i-chi told of Barca's end.

The next day Renno used his excellent Spanish and the money he had taken from the friar's and Lope Barca's pockets to buy provisions and goods to make their travel a bit easier, for they were not equipped for the long trek. The proprietor of a small store in a dusty, sleepy little village was glad to have the business. Beth and Ena had new clothing, Spanish wear for men, with huge leather chaps to protect their legs, and there were shot and powder for the muskets, new water skins, blankets, dried meat—the first Renno had ever purchased—and other items of food to hold them until they were away from the Spanish settlements and could hunt.

Renno set a course toward the north because they were far to the south of the route they had traveled on the way to New Mexico. He knew that winter would soon overtake them, and he was once again plagued by the feeling that something was very wrong. He knew that the chances of his finding the way to the hot springs in the Arkansea hills were slim, for there were hundreds of miles of unfamiliar country ahead, and he would not be able to identify any landmarks until, and if, he crossed the territory he had seen on the way west.

They had only one spare horse, and the animals had

been ridden hard, so the pace could not be as swift as Renno wanted it to be. He had an urge to leap from his horse, trust to his own feet and legs, and to run and run and run until he saw familiar hills of home, but he knew that was an impossible dream, that the distances were too great.

Now they had ridden for days without seeing any signs of Spanish settlement. Their diet was enriched by the kill of a buffalo, and then, one morning, in a scene reminiscent of their first encounter with the Comanche, they saw two groups of riders closing on them. Renno called a halt. The sign of favor, the buffalo horn given to him by the Comanche, had been left far behind, in the plains of New Mexico, and he could only sit on his horse, his hands outstretched in peace. However, the Comanche did not attack. Two of them detached themselves from a group and came forward warily; then one of them gave a whoop and pointed to Beth.

"Flame-hair!" the Comanche yelled. He urged his horse forward and pulled to a stop near Renno. "I greet you, Medicine Man."

"I greet you, Brother," Renno said.

The other Comanche came riding in, and many of them cried out in pleasure when they saw flame-haired Beth and the blue-eyed medicine man.

"The spirits have been with you, Medicine Man," said the Comanche war chief in charge of the roving party. "For we have seen your brothers, who had much yellow dirt, and we have heard of your battle against the Spanish with the Apache dogs. You were sent by the spirits, Medicine Man, for without you the Apache dogs could not have killed so many of the hair-faces."

Renno saw no need to dispute the man's opinion. The Apache were brave warriors, of course, but it was not up to him to convince their traditional enemies of that. He asked questions about Rusog and William's passage through Comanche land and was pleased to hear that they had traveled toward the northeast almost a moon past.

That night there was a feast in a Comanche camp, and over Renno's protestations—for he had nothing to trade or give as gifts in return—all four of them were outfitted in new clothing of deerskin, much more comfortable and familiar than the goods they had recently purchased.

"You will be riding into the winter cold," the Comanche chief warned, "and you will need warm clothing and sleeping skins."

"My brother shames me with his generosity," Renno said.

"He who kills Spaniards as if they were flies on the wall must not suffer cold," the Comanche said, and then, with the morning, there were fresh horses, with spares to carry the heavy buffalo robes and other items.

As if the Comanche had had a revelation from the spirits, a mass of cold air moved down the midcontinent, sweeping across the plains. After the heat of the desert and the south, the relatively mild cold seemed more severe than it was, and they rode bundled inside buffalo robes, with skins tied around their feet.

Apparently their exploits in the desert and the dry mountains had lost nothing in Rusog's telling, for word of their adventures had spread throughout the Comanche nation. Most of the Comanche had migrated back to the southern areas of their range in anticipation of the onslaught of winter, and at least twice a week Renno's group was regaled in some Comanche village—feasted, praised, and showered with gifts until Renno had to refuse, saying that the load was already too great for their horses.

He had been able to confirm that he was on course to reach the mountains of the Arkansea, and now they rode through the rolling scrub-oak hills and began to talk with great anticipation of rejoining Rusog, William, and the Spanish girl at the hot springs.

Ena had a new reason now to be concerned about Beth's obvious admiration for Renno. She had become quite fond of the Englishwoman during the trial of their captivity, and in addition to worrying about her brother and his wife, she now worried about Beth. She knew that Renno was a man of honor, a one-woman man, who would never betray his vows. There was nothing overt to cause Ena's concern, it was just that Beth always managed to ride at Renno's side, sit with him at the campfires, smile, talk, and ask endless questions about his life, the way of the Indian, and the wilderness.

Renno, although he recognized Beth's beauty and admired her courage, dreamed only of Emily, although he did not reveal to anyone his feeling that something was terribly wrong with his wife. He accepted Beth's friendship and used it to distract his mind, enjoying her laughter and tales about English life. She had a knack of finding the ludicrous in the customs and actions of people and did not spare her own.

"It must have been like this when the race was young," she mused one day, "when Moses led the people of Israel out of Egypt and into the wilderness. Perhaps we were intended to live this way, enjoying the bounty of God's earth instead of cooping ourselves up in structures of stone."

"This one should have been born Indian," Renno announced, laughing.

"Do you realize, Renno, that we've seen more of this great continent than most people alive or dead? How far we've traveled . . . and how fast! We've seen mountains and plains and rivers and deserts and many different tribes—and yet the people are all basically the same. They live by nature, and nature provides. We've ridden these miles and risked our lives for something that won't keep us warm, won't feed us, won't burn in the campfire. Somehow it all seems so futile."

"Your father will not think so," Renno remarked, "when you return to England with the gold."

"No. I do think of him, of course. And we must return there as quickly as possible, for it is his life, his very honor that is at stake, as well as William's inheritance." She was moodily silent for a while. "But I will miss all this so much. I will never look at the tailored meadows and copses of England without remembering the magnificence of the forests, the endless plains, or the desert and its wild beauty."

Winter joined them in the forested hills. Snow hissed down to melt in their campfires. Ice covered still waters and rimmed the margins of the streams. Beth and Ena slept in their clothing, under the same buffalo robes. Meat could be carried for days without spoiling as the temperatures hovered, even in the afternoon, around the freezing mark, so it was not necessary to hunt as often, and that contributed to the speed of their journey.

When Renno recognized the Mountain of the Hot Springs, he gave a whoop. It was distant, still at least two days' travel, but the miles went fast, and then they were encountering the local Indians and heard, to their relief, that the white man and the Cherokee who had journeyed to the land of the setting sun were camped near the springs. Then Rusog was riding toward them in the snow, whooping, and Ena kicked her horse into motion to throw herself from it into Rusog's arms.

William had been out hunting with some of the local Indians, and he too whooped when he returned, a deer lying across his horse behind him, and embraced Beth, clasped Renno's and El-i-chi's arms, and kissed Ena on the cheek.

Estrela had regained some of the weight she had lost as an Apache captive and, in warm doeskins, looked radiant. Beth soon noted that she was never far from William.

Renno paid his respects to the medicine man of the springs and then began to think about the advisability of continuing the journey, with the winter starting out so strongly and the coldest months still ahead. El-i-chi secluded himself, and there in that place of healing that was sacred to all tribes in the area, he fasted and mourned for Holani. Renno, too, took the opportunity for meditation.

Rusog and William had constructed a lodge of logs chinked with mud while they waited, not knowing whether or not they would winter at the hot springs. It was cozy and warm, and Beth was content just to rest, think, and help Ena and Estrela with the cooking.

When El-i-chi returned to the lodge, gaunt and silent but with the fierce light of hatred and loss gone from his eyes, Renno waited until they were all having their evening meal. "We are still far from home," he said, "and the winter is upon us. Traveling will be hard, and there is the big river to cross in the worst of winter." He fell silent and waited.

It was Rusog who spoke first. "We have seen much, and we have shared, talked, and fought with and against different peoples. But to me the sweetest sight of all would be the blue and smoky mountains in the distance, and the faces of my own people."

"If you're thinking that winter travel would be a hardship for me," Beth said, "we too are eager to see our home and our father."

"Renno, we know how badly you want to see Emily and the new child," Ena added. "Why wait?"

The changeable midcontinent weather gave them days of mildness and sun as they began the last leg of their journey. The horses were well rested, and their diet was supplemented by corn, a gift of the hot-springs Indians. Often they slept in the lodges of the Natchitoches and were welcomed for the stories they could tell about the dry and strange lands to the west. It was the same in the land of the Quapaw. There, however, the tribe was mourning, for the ever-restless and warlike Chickasaw had raided across the river before the onset of the winter and killed many.

William, who had been doing his best to keep track of the passing days on a calendar, announced one day at the end of the march, "If I haven't lost a few days here and there, tomorrow is Christmas Eve." The day was like all of those in the recent past, a day of forward movement, of working constantly to keep in line the packhorses laden with their precious gold. That night, in camp, Beth gave each of them a kiss as a Christmas gift, and to her great pleasure, Renno, who knew how the white man felt about his God, asked her to tell them the story of the birth of Jesus. They listened in silence and with great respect. Then Estrela, who had been deeply touched by Beth's retelling of the old and wonderful story, sang carols in Spanish. They were the guests that evening of a Quapaw subchief and his family, and the Indians asked Estrela to sing more, and so, with a new snow beginning to fall on a windless, quiet night, the voices rang out, and William and Beth added to the concert with English carols.

The next morning Renno rose early, went into the thickets and woods to bag two huge turkeys, and announced, on his return, that Christmas would be celebrated in the manner of the white man, with a day of rest and good eating. But his mind was on the big river and how they would cross it without letting the Chickasaw know the contents of the leather bags. The Chickasaw, who traded with the Spanish, would know the value of gold.

Chapter XVI

Although travel was cold and uncomfortable, spirits were high. There were only two major obstacles now between them and home: the Mississippi River and the Chickasaw nation. Ever unpredictable and always warlike, the Chickasaw were Renno's major concern. He would need their assistance in crossing the river, and he would have to have the forbearance of their chief, Oklawahpa, to travel safely from Chickasaw Bluffs to Cherokee lands. He was trying hard to think of something or some way to explain the heaviness of the leather bags carried by several horses.

When they reached the river just below Chickasaw Bluffs at the narrow point used by the Chickasaw as a boat crossing, they saw that the boatmen had already withdrawn to the east side of the river for the winter. The weather was fair and cold, and to the weather-wise Indians, there was the threat of storm in the air. The high clouds and the smell of the air indicated that the new year would start with the kind of storm that often brought snow or sleet and an extended period of cold.

Renno built a signal fire and waited. The fire caused some interest on the far bank, but there was no movement of canoes.

"They don't seem to be too interested in coming across to help us," William complained.

"Patience," Renno advised.

"We could build our own raft," William suggested.

"That would be a direct insult to the Chickasaw," Renno said, "even if it were possible." He himself had entertained the thought and had checked for suitable trees as they had approached the river. To build a raft large enough to transport horses, however, would be a lengthy task, sure to be interrupted by the Chickasaw, who were quite jealous of their control of the crossing.

With the morning a lone Chickasaw boatman started across the river. He approached the shore warily and landed only after he had recognized Renno. The white Indian told him that he and his party desired to cross the river.

"It is cold," the Chickasaw said. He indicated the lowering sky. "There is a great storm coming." He looked with contempt in his eyes at the animals, which obviously had traveled far. "Your animals would not survive an attempt to swim. The water is too cold. They would die." He mused for a moment. "We will take you across in exchange for the horses. We will not gain much by this, for we will have to keep these spent animals on this side of the river until the waters warm with the renewing."

Renno saw that he was not going to make any headway bargaining with the Chickasaw boatman. "You will take me to Oklawahpa, my brother-by-treaty, so that I may pay honor to him."

The Chickasaw started to speak, but Renno's stern look silenced him. Renno did not speak during the crossing, and he leapt from the canoe as it touched land, to walk swiftly to find Oklawahpa in his warm, cozy winter lodgings.

"So you have returned," the Chickasaw chief said.

"I have returned with a gift for the great chief of the Chickasaw," Renno said. "However, I am told that a river crossing is impossible at this time, and Oklawahpa's gift is on the far side of the river."

A gleam in Oklawahpa's eyes showed his interest. "What fool has told you that a river crossing is impossible?" He rose and began to shout orders. Soon a dozen canoes were moving toward the river's west bank. Oklawahpa rode in a canoe with Renno. As they neared the shore he eyed with curiosity the hard-used horses and the members of the party. Renno knew that Oklawahpa could not help but note the pile of leather pouches containing the gold.

"Where is my gift?" Oklawahpa demanded as he and Renno stepped ashore.

"In time," Renno said. "My surprise will be appreciated more in the comfort of your own lodge."

Oklawahpa glowered but made no objection.

"My friend," Renno added smoothly, "I would that I could give you the rich gift I have brought without conditions, but I am told that my horses cannot possibly make the crossing, that they would die of the cold and their weakness. But they are sound animals and will be valuable after rest and food. So it is that my gift comes with two conditions: I must cross the river, and I must have horses to continue my journey home."

"You state conditions when I don't even know the nature of this gift?" Oklawahpa sputtered.

"You have my word that you will not be displeased by the bargain."

Oklawahpa turned away, and for a moment Renno feared that he had lost his gamble. His hand was on his tomahawk when Oklawahpa turned and with a wave of his hand said, "Done." Renno had counted on the natural curiosity of the Indian and on Oklawahpa's greed. He had won—at least temporarily.

Renno called his small party together. "We won't be able to hide forever that we have something valuable in the leather pouches," he told them quietly. "Keep your weapons at the ready. Be alert. We will be separated as we cross the river. If it comes to trouble, sell your lives dearly."

Renno would not allow any Chickasaw to touch the leather bags as they were put aboard the canoes. After telling the Chickasaw boatmen that he was transporting spirit rocks of magical power from the land of the setting sun, he chanted mysterious things as each load of bags was moved. He was glad that Oklawahpa, tiring of the cold, had gone back across the river to his lodge, for such a ruse would not have fooled the chief. It served mainly to confuse the Chickasaw boatmen, and Renno had to suppress a smile when he heard a group of them questioning his sanity, wondering if he had been affected by the spirits in those far places where he had traveled.

Behind them, to the west, a great wall of cloud was moving swiftly, and the boatmen repeatedly urged haste, pointing to the advancing storm front. Finally all the gold was loaded and the last canoe was pushed away from the shore. Renno rode with the young Chickasaw man who paddled the canoe, four bags of gold at his feet. Now the sky had turned dark and the wind had begun to gust fitfully. They were just past midriver, and many of the canoes had already landed and Renno's party members were transferring the bags to fresh, waiting horses. The wind hit the canoe at an angle, blasting suddenly down from the northwest with a force that toppled the dugout craft instantly and threw Renno into the water, which was so cold it took his breath for a moment before he struck out with all his energy for the bank. Behind him he heard a coughing plea and turned to see the young Chickasaw boatman in trouble, perhaps in shock from the cold water. Renno's first impulse was to swim on, for he knew that his own strength would be rapidly sapped by the cold, but the look of pleading on the fellow's face touched him. He swam back.

"Turn onto your back and do not move," he ordered.

The young Chickasaw reached out toward Renno, and there was a danger that he would panic and pull both of them under. Renno pushed the man's head under the water for a moment, then pulled him up and yelled, "If you don't obey my orders, I will leave you to drown."

The young man calmed and rolled onto his back. Renno seized the neck of his buckskin shirt and began to swim. The current was sweeping them downstream, and the cold was seeping rapidly into his body. He could not feel his hands and feet and had to fight to restrain a convulsive shivering. He kept his feet kicking, his free hand digging into the icy water, watching as the far bank seemed to remain at the same distance for so long that he almost gave up hope. The wind was now lashing the water, and needles of sleet stung his face.

He called on the manitous. He willed his body to be warm, forced his limbs to keep pumping, and when he next looked up, the bank was closer, and with his lungs on fire and with vast shiverings interfering with his swimming, the bank came ever closer. He saw people running down the bank, keeping pace with the drift of the current, but no rescue canoes were launched into the storm-whipped water.

He would not have made it had Rusog not met him in waist-deep water. He would have given up there, so near land, for he was seeing blackness, and his body felt warm, and he was so drowsy that he would have slumped down to sleep right in the water. But Rusog was yelling and helping him, and then a Chickasaw was in the water to take the boatman, and they were on dry land. Renno's body was racked with tremors that caused his teeth to chatter. Someone threw a blanket around him, and he began to trot, staggering, toward the Chickasaw town upstream. Rusog stayed by his side.

The Chickasaw boatman had to be carried, so Renno and Rusog reached the town first and entered the first lodge they encountered, where a concerned woman helped Renno remove his wet clothing, wrapped him in dry blankets and skins, and sat him next to a blazing fire. He thought his shivering would never stop. He was just beginning to feel warm again when Oklawahpa entered the lodge.

"So once again you have shown your bravery," the chief said. "Few men would have tried to help another in that river at this time of year." Renno said nothing. "The boy you saved is my sister's son," Oklawahpa added. "I am in your debt."

"For what I did I ask nothing, for it was done freely," Renno said. He extended one hand. "Now it is time for us to discuss your gift."

Oklawahpa's face stiffened. "You speak of a gift when you have many horses carrying gold."

Renno accepted the accusation calmly. He had known that he would be unable to conceal the nature of his cargo from Oklawahpa indefinitely.

"Truly," Oklawahpa said, "the spirits are with you, Seneca, for I had planned to kill you and take your gold."

Renno nodded. "I doubt that you would have killed us, even had I not saved the son of your sister, for I had your pledged word, and Oklawahpa would not have put a black mark on his honor for mere gold."

"I advise you to leave quickly, Renno of the Seneca, and to travel far and fast, before my young men see through your lies about carrying rocks blessed by the spirits."

Renno was more than willing to comply with that advice. He gathered his group, loaded the gold onto Chickasaw horses, some of them not nearly of the quality of the good Spanish and Comanche ponies that had been left on the western bank of the river. Oklawahpa watched the loading glumly and did not move when Renno led two of the laden horses toward him.

"This is the gift I promised you," Renno said.

"You have much. This is all you would share with Oklawahpa?"

"We have lost much, and we have carried the remainder far. We will not see our reward dwindle further." He remembered the gold seized by Lope Barca and the priest during their retreat from the dry mountains. He would not lose any more, not without shedding blood. "To the hunter comes the reward of fresh game," he continued. "To those who sought, gold. Be content with my generosity, Oklawahpa, for the packs on these two horses represent good things for you and your people." He paused, and then added, knowing that it had to be said, "I wish only that you spend it well, for if the Chickasaw use this gold for weapons to be used against their neighbors, you must remember that they, too, will have new and powerful weapons."

The others were beginning to move out, the pack animals leaving deep tracks from their burdens. A group of Chickasaw warriors stood nearby, now and then whispering among themselves.

"From the actions of your warriors," Renno commented, "I would guess that they, too, are aware of the cargo carried by our horses."

Oklawahpa would not meet Renno's eyes. "Young men are sometimes difficult to control."

"Did you notice that the tall Seneca warrior, my brother, El-i-chi, was not among those who are with the packtrain?" Renno asked. Oklawahpa met his eyes for a moment, then looked away. "He left earlier," Renno said, "to ride fast, to carry the word that Oklawahpa had doubts about being able to make his own hospitality safe for his brothers-by-treaty because of his inability to control his young warriors. Should we not arrive in due course of time with our cargo, there will be another war."

Oklawahpa's eyes came up and bored into Renno's.

He knew a challenge when he heard one. "If that is the wish of the Cherokee and the Seneca, my warriors would be pleased to grant that wish."

Renno had anticipated such a reply. "I wonder," he mused, "if one more horse, with its cargo, would make it possible for Oklawahpa to control his wild young warriors?"

Oklawahpa smiled. "I knew that the sachem of the Seneca was a wise and generous man."

Renno whistled, and Ena appeared, leading a laden horse. Oklawahpa waited until the horse's reins were in his hands; then he shouted a summons, and the group of young warriors came quickly, anticipation in their eyes, an eagerness that faded when Oklawahpa said, "My friend and brother-by-treaty, Renno of the Seneca, will travel through our lands in safety and with all his possessions. Any who disobey this order will die."

The warriors looked away, faces blank. "Come," Oklawahpa said. "I will ride with you as you overtake the rest of your party."

Renno motioned Ena to ride ahead. He rode beside Oklawahpa. After a period of silence the Chickasaw spoke. "There will be no war."

"That is good," Renno replied.

"Our new weapons will be used for hunting and to protect ourselves," Oklawahpa promised.

"Oklawahpa speaks wisely."

"And now I leave you."

"May the spirits walk with you," Renno said.

Renno caught up with the others. They continued to move as swiftly as possible, with Renno and Rusog in the rear to guard against an attack from the Chickasaw, which was, in spite of Oklawahpa's word, still quite possible. The day passed without event, and in the evening, although he knew that he was very far from home, Renno could almost smell the mountains and knew that he would start the next day with a feeling that at any moment, any hour, the mountains could come into view.

The night's camp was without fire. A guard would be

posted at all times. Everyone seemed to share Renno's feeling that home was near, although there was little talk. When William came to sit beside Renno, he was silent for a time. "Will they be satisfied with that last bit, that additional tariff for safe passage?"

"The honor and word of a Chickasaw does not come cheaply," Renno said. He looked up at the night sky and heard the hooting of an owl. "He would have killed us instantly if he had thought he could get away with it. But he does not want war."

"Will he want war when he buys new muskets with the gold?" William asked.

Renno considered before answering. "A few young warriors might feel the need to try their new weapons. We will be watching and ready if they should."

"I didn't like the looks of those young Chickasaw warriors," William admitted. "We're not as rich as we were when we stood on Devil's Mountain and looked upon a miniature mountain of gold, but I guess the price we've paid, including that to Oklawahpa, was worth our scalps."

"We are not poor," Renno commented.

"My share will ransom my father's holdings," William said. "It won't establish us among the richest families in England, but it will suffice. I fear, my friend, that you've lost more than we, for your purposes are higher. Your diminished half won't do all the things you wanted to do for the Cherokee and the Seneca."

"There will be enough to arm every warrior," Renno responded. "When a man has good weapons, he can then make his own fate or fortune. Our needs are simple. We need the means to protect that which is ours against those who would try to take it. Our main concern is to protect our most valuable possession, the land itself, the hunting grounds that supply us with food and the necessities of life. I am content."

"And you're not worried that old Oklawahpa will use the gold to make war on you and your friends?"

Renno flipped a twig, spinning it away into the darkness. "When one lives his life in the wilderness, he comes to take a practical view of many things. There have been times in the past, when I was younger—"

William looked at him sharply, his smile hidden by the night, for in spite of Renno's manly body, fighting abilities, and sometimes surprising wisdom, he looked like a youth on the verge of manhood.

"—I would have fought Oklawahpa and all his tribe for that which was mine. For pride. For honor. But what honor would there have been in causing the death of my brother, my sister, and my friends on a matter of principle, on the chance that the gold I used to buy our way past Oklawahpa might be used against us later? There are too many miles on the trail behind us, my friend. Too many have died to get this gold this far. When all our warriors have new, accurate weapons, *then* if Oklawahpa's young bucks need exercise, we will give it to them."

"So," William said. "I too am content."

Renno looked toward the east and sniffed the air. Was there a touch of mountain mist in the night air, a hint of the Cherokee homelands? Content? Yes, he would have been totally content, had not, deep inside, a sense of foreboding, a thing of almost overwhelming sadness, kept growing.

The winter storm had passed, leaving new snow. Now, in the distance, there was the low line of the Smoky Mountains, and they had passed Cherokee settlements, dug in for the winter, warm and snug, some of them in log cabins patterned after those of the white man.

"Go," Rusog told Renno one morning as he saw Renno staring intently at the far mountains. "Travel fast and give my love to Emily and the new child."

The group was safe now. They were well within the protection of the Cherokee nation. Renno chose the strongest horse and set it, fast, up the trail toward home. He was reminded once again that the horse was not as much an asset in his forests as it was on the buffalo plains and deserts of the Comanche and Apache. Trails that he could have traveled at a run slowed him on horseback, and more than once his chest and face were whipped by low-hanging limbs. But in the snow he could make faster time on the horse. He pushed the animal, knowing sympathy for it, but also burning to ease that knot of fear and foreboding in his stomach.

He entered his village unannounced, trotted the tired animal among the lodges to the central compound, and jerked it to a halt when he saw the signs of mourning on the door of his lodge. He had ridden all night, and it was just after dawn on what would be a bright, chill January morning. He dismounted and, with his heart hurting, walked to the door and opened it. The fire was cold, only ashes. Emily's few cooking utensils were hanging in their accustomed place, but the sleep benches were empty, skins rolled and stacked neatly.

It is the new child, he thought. The new child, perhaps a daughter, had died. He turned and walked from the lodge and saw his mother standing in the door of her lodge across the compound. He walked slowly toward her, filled with a need to know but dreading the answer.

"Welcome, my son," Toshabe said. "My heart hurts that you must return to sadness."

"I thank thee that thou art well," Renno said, using a traditional Seneca phrase of honor for his mother. "The others are well too, with the exception of the Chickasaw girl Holani."

"So El-i-chi has told me," she said. "Come, I have warm food, and then you will want to go to Knoxville to see your son and your daughter."

A pain of sheer desolation almost bent Renno double, and in spite of himself, he loosed a moan of sadness. Toshabe nodded. He knew then that the spirits had been warning him all along that he would never see his wife again.

"She tried, Renno, and she was brave, but always

there was that reserve in her, an inability to conform totally to the ways of the Seneca." Then, having said the words, Toshabe wished that they had been left unsaid. She did not even know why she had made the statement.

Renno did not take time to eat. Nor did he take a horse. He needed to be alone, without even the animal to distract his mind from his mourning. He felt the urge to fight against his loss, to punish his body, perhaps, and he ran through the cold, ran until he was spent, numb, and still he pushed on, and always there was the knowledge that he had left her to bear the child alone, and that she had died while he was somewhere far to the west in the plains of the Comanche.

When at last he was forced to stop, he was not far from Knoxville, and he rested to compose himself to face Emily's parents and his two children. But he did not sleep. Sleep would not come as he huddled in his one thin blanket and watched the cold winter stars brighten and fade with dawn.

He had bristled a bit at Toshabe's statement indicating that Emily had not been the total Seneca wife, but in his sadness, in the cold of the early-morning hours, he remembered how Emily had protested the baptism into Seneca life of Little Hawk in a frozen stream, how she had worried Toshabe and Ah-wen-ga by removing the necklace of bear claws from the boy's bed, and other times when she tried to protect Little Hawk against the natural course of a Seneca boy-baby's life. And as if to confirm that Toshabe had been right, he felt a presence and began to meditate and chant. His most powerful clan totem, the great bear, showed itself, outlined against the pale light of dawn. The voice could not be identified. It was as if the bear totem were voicing the thoughts of all his ancestors when it said, "Mourn her. Yes, mourn her, for she was of us and yet not of us, else she would still be with us."

Renno spent an hour praying, searching for meaning in that message from the manitous. But he was never to know fully what was meant. However, the message would become a part of his family lore, repeated and considered by future generations.

Soon he was in the Johnsons' cabin, Little Hawk in his arms. Nora Johnson had the boy dressed in the clothing of the white man, and for a moment Renno was angered, but that emotion faded quickly as he heard the boy chattering at him, excitedly asking a million questions, and pointing with pride to his new baby sister in her crib.

She had Emily's hair and Renno's startling blue eyes. She was healthy and alert and made small baby sounds when Renno persuaded Little Hawk to leave his arms long enough for him to hold his daughter.

Roy Johnson was not at home. Nora told Little Hawk to be calm, to watch the baby, and she drew Renno into the sitting room, where a roaring blaze in the fireplace dispelled the winter chill.

"She called for you at the end, Renno," Nora said, tears in her eyes. "She did love you very much, so much that she never questioned the necessity of your being away."

"Yes, she understood," Renno said.

"She came through the birthing well, even though she was weak and sick. We feared that the baby would be unhealthy, but she was so beautiful, and absolutely perfect. Emily was very proud. She had named the baby Renna, after you."

"I am greatly honored," Renno whispered, unable to say more, lest he shame himself and add his tears to Nora's.

"I do pray that your trip was successful, that you have been able to help your people, for Emily talked about that constantly."

"It was successful," Renno said. "Her death was not in vain."

"Oh, don't feel that way, because had you been here, you would have been as helpless as we were. She didn't blame you in the slightest. She made me promise to say these, Renno, her last words: 'Remember me with fondness, and never, never blame yourself in any way for not being here, for you were doing what you had to do.'"

Renno leapt to his feet and turned his back to keep Nora from seeing his tears. After a while he asked, "She died in childbirth, then?"

Nora's voice was soft. "No. She came through the birthing so well, and it was quick and almost painless. She didn't even make a sound. It was afterward. Childbed fever."

"It brings me gladness that she saw the baby."

"Oh, yes, and then she—" Nora blew her nose. "It was peaceful in the end, Renno. She just went to sleep."

Sleep, love, Renno said to himself. *And soon, perhaps, I will join you on the other side of the River.*

"Renno, this may not be the best time to discuss it," Nora was saying, "but these two children have no mother now, and if you'll forgive me for saying so, an Indian camp is not the place for young children."

Renno turned to face her. "They are Seneca," he said flatly.

"They are Emily's children too," Nora countered bravely, in spite of Renno's stern look. "Renno, let me keep them. Let me raise them and send them to school, and you can visit them as often as you wish, and perhaps take Little Hawk in the summers when he is not in school."

"I know that your heart means to do the right thing," Renno said. "And I thank you. But my son will be sachem of the Seneca."

"And the girl?"

Renno walked to look down at the baby. She had fallen asleep. Little Hawk was playing with a carved wooden musket, pretending to kill armies of enemy.

"We will talk of the girl," he told Nora, who had come up beside him. "Perhaps it would be best if she knew the ways of her mother as well as the ways of the Seneca."

He visited Emily's grave. He could feel no trace of

her spirit—perhaps, he thought, because she had gone to the heaven of the white God. Was that a different place from the land of Seneca spirits, the West, the Place Across the River? He could not believe that even the mysterious God of the whites would separate them forever. But if the white God was jealous and allowed no Indians into his heaven unless they ate of his flesh and drank of his blood, what of his daughter if he allowed her to be taught as Emily had been taught?

He had, he decided, much to think about.

The word got out somehow that the packtrain that came into Knoxville several days later with Rusog, William, Ena, Beth, Estrela, and El-i-chi was laden with gold. Roy Johnson had organized armed men to guard it and volunteered to gather men to help Renno get the gold safely to Charlotte, where there was a refinery and a mint to press the gold into coins so that it would be more easily divided and handled. Renno agreed to leave Little Hawk and Renna temporarily with Nora Johnson, who was overjoyed.

Before leaving Knoxville for Charlotte, Beth Huntington had a strong effect on the social circle and totally won the heart of Renno's son. Nora, a bit jealous, said, "He doesn't take to too many folks, Miss Beth, but he does love you."

Little Hawk was talking, if not always in complete sentences, in two languages—the English of his mother and the Seneca of his father. He spoke to Beth in Seneca on the morning that the group was leaving, and Beth had to ask Renno to translate, although she knew a few Seneca words.

"He says that your red hair would make the world's most beautiful scalp," Renno casually informed her.

Beth laughed, picked up the boy, and hugged him, then looked into his face seriously. "Young man," she said sternly, "you're going to have to learn that my red hair serves a more practical purpose right where it is."

The trip to Charlotte was long but uneventful. Rusog

and Ena had returned to the Cherokee village, El-i-chi to his own lodge. In Charlotte, Roy took the chance to shop for some things that were difficult to obtain on the frontier, and Renno, a bit threadbare, bought a woolen suit, hose, shirt, shoes, and a handsome hat.

"I wouldn't have recognized you," Beth said admiringly when he joined them, dressed in his finery, in the hotel dining room. Except for his hair, which was a bit long, he looked very much like a sun-browned white gentleman.

There was a wait of several days while the gold was being processed. Beth discovered that Renno could dance quite respectably. William and Estrela seemed always to have their heads together, as if trying to decide some weighty problem.

Then the time was near for the final parting. The gold was in the hands of the North Carolina banking system, and William's share would be transported to the port of Charleston for shipment back to England. Roy advised Renno to make his purchases of weapons and other needed items in North Carolina and make payment upon delivery to Knoxville. The merchants were more than pleased because the number of new muskets ordered was astonishing to them.

William made his announcement—it was not totally unexpected—over dinner on the night before they were to part: "Estrela has consented to become my wife," he said. "It was a difficult decision for her, for it means going far away from her father in Mexico, but we have written to him, and once things are in hand in England, we hope to visit him."

Beth had been thinking of the excitement, not all of it positive, when the man who would be Lord Beaumont brought home a Spanish wife. But there was enough gold left to make the Beaumonts independent of public opinion, and she was pleased to know that the girl of whom she had become very fond was going to be part of her family.

Late in the evening Beth managed to get Renno alone. They had danced, and then she took his hand and pulled him off the dance floor and into the hallway.

"Thank you for dancing with me, Renno. I know that you were doing something that you didn't really feel in the mood to do. I know that you're still mourning your wife."

"I was doing something that did me no harm but pleased a friend," Renno said.

"I count myself fortunate to have such a friend," Beth said. She lowered her eyes. "You will always be welcome at Beaumont Hall, Renno." She looked up with a smile. "They still talk about the things your great-grandfather did in England. Why don't you visit us, and we'll astound them all over again?"

"It would be a pleasure," Renno said. "But who can see the future except through the eyes of the spirits?"

He had long been puzzled by one revelation from the manitous, and he thought about it often, now that he was about to see this flame-haired woman for the last time, perhaps. He had been told, "The flame-haired one is the future." For a long time he had assumed that the short-term future was meant, for Indians in the west had received spirit messages about Beth, making the journey safer. Now he wondered—even as he mourned for Emily, even as he made plans to do his formal fasting and mourning as soon as he was back home—if something more had not been meant. If so, then the manitous would intervene and the distance between them would not matter.

"I've been thinking too," Beth said, "about that beautiful little girl. When she is old enough, Renno, send her to me, and I'll help to complete her education in England. You yourself have talked about the rapidly changing times in your country. You say that the Indian must come into agreement, if not total conformity, with the whites. Wouldn't it be good to educate both your children in the ways of both people?"

"I have given that much thought," Renno said. "You speak wisely."

Then he was riding, with Roy, back toward the west. William, Beth, and Estrela were traveling in comfort in a closed carriage toward Charleston. The new year was well established, with winter putting on its last big show. When they reached Knoxville, Renno spent some time with Renna, then took his son back to the Seneca-Cherokee village, where he was greeted with much affection by his grandmother and great-grandmother. Little Hawk was happy, for it was time for the ceremony that cast out the forces of darkness and paved the way for the new beginning of spring.

Author's Note

It would be up to the descendants of the White Indian and historians of that period of American history to understand Toshabe's insight when she made her puzzling remark to Renno about Emily not totally being a Seneca wife.

The spirit message given to Renno was even more explicit: "She was of us and yet not of us, else she would still be with us."

In the light of modern knowledge, the death of Emily was the direct result of her not having become Indian in her heart.

In 1786, when Emily gave birth to the girl, Renna, only a few medical people fought against childbed fever by insisting upon cleanliness in the conduct of deliveries and drainage of the womb in a lying-in position after birth.

Emily gave birth to Renna so quickly that Nora Johnson herself acted as midwife. The baby was washed, her cord tied, and she was sleeping before the Knoxville doctor arrived. He had come from treating the infected arm of a hunter who had been mauled by a bear, and he came hurriedly, with a mere wipe of his hands on a towel.

The doctor handled the taking of the afterbirth. Emily began to show symptoms of septicemia shortly afterward, and Nora ceased giving the baby to her for nursing. The fever grew, Emily's pulse rate began to increase, and there was a malodorous discharge, and then spasms followed by a delirium. Emily rallied from that only long enough to give her mother the farewell message to Renno.

Renno was never to know that Emily's decision to go with her mother to Knoxville was most probably the cause of her death. It seems quite logical that had Emily stayed with Toshabe and Ah-wen-ga in the Seneca village, she would not have been exposed to the puerperal infection that killed her, for it was mainly a disease of civilization.

FIFTH ANNIVERSARY
SPECIAL EDITION

STAGECOACH

Stagecoach 31:

ROYAL COACH
by Hank Mitchum

In 1879 Austrian Count Wilhelm von Schiller and his sister, Cristiana, set out with two servants to cross America in a specially designed Concord stagecoach. Jake Dooley, Wells Fargo's top driver, and Scott Farnum, the country's best shotgun guard, have been hired to see them safely from Chicago to San Fransisco—but the trip is not the pleasant sightseeing venture that it seems.

The Austrian government, unhappy about the French canal to be built in Panama, has assigned Court Wilhelm to see America firsthand, then travel to Washington and attempt to persuade the U.S. government to join Austria in building a canal across Nicaragua, a site with more advantages than Panama. But someone is out to foil that attempt. . . .

The royal coach is accompanied by a regular stage, occupied by handsome businessman Tom Gunnison and reporter Roxanne Colway, who hopes to get exclusive coverage of the count's journey. These and other passengers of the two stages are besieged by thieves, threatened by sabotage, invited to a Comanche encampment, and endangered by the sinster plot to end the count's life. But romance flourishes even in these troubled circumstances, and the alliances that are formed surprise everyone involved.

Read ROYAL COACH, on sale September 1987 wherever Bantam paperbacks are sold.

**FROM THE PRODUCER OF WAGONS WEST
AND THE KENT FAMILY CHRONICLES—
A SWEEPING SAGA OF WAR AND HEROISM
AT THE BIRTH OF A NATION.**

THE WHITE INDIAN SERIES

Filled with the glory and adventure of the colonization of America, here is the thrilling saga of the new frontier's boldest hero and his family. Renno, born to white parents but raised by Seneca Indians, becomes a leader in both worlds. THE WHITE INDIAN SERIES chronicles the adventures of Renno, his son Ja-gonh, and his grandson Ghonkaba, from the colonies to Canada, from the South to the turbulent West. Through their struggles to tame a savage continent and their encounters with the powerful men and passionate women in the early battles for America, we witness the events that shaped our future and forged our great heritage.

☐	24650	White Indian #1	$3.95
☐	25020	The Renegade #2	$3.95
☐	24751	War Chief #3	$3.95
☐	24476	The Sachem #4	$3.95
☐	25154	Renno #5	$3.95
☐	25039	Tomahawk #6	$3.95
☐	25589	War Cry #7	$3.95
☐	25202	Ambush #8	$3.95
☐	23986	Seneca #9	$3.95
☐	24492	Cherokee #10	$3.95
☐	24950	Choctaw #11	$3.95
☐	25353	Seminole #12	$3.95
☐	25868	War Drums #13	$3.95

Prices and availability subject to change without notice.